Gathering the *Indigo* Maidens

Gathering the *Indigo* Maidens

A NOVEL

CECILIA VELÁSTEGUI

LIBROS
PUBLISHING

LIBRARY OF CONGRESS CONTROL NUMBER; 2011932906
Velástegui, Cecilia
Gathering the Indigo Maides: a novel/Cecilia Velástegui

Hardcover: ISBN: 978-0-9837458-0-8
Paperback: ISBN: 978-0-9837458-1-5

Published by Libros Publishing
24040 Camino Del Avion #A225
Monarch Beach, California 92629 U.S.A.

Printed in the United States of America
Set in Berkeley Book (see page 328)

Book Designed by Karrie Ross; www.KarrieRoss.com
Endpaper design by Karrie Ross

Endpaper credit: Virgin of the Immaculate Conception, oil on canvas, 18th century, Cusco, Peru, anonymous workshop. Connie Spenuzza.

*For Peter and Jay-Paul, my precious sons
And for Pete, my everything*

March 19, 2008
Laguna Beach, California

Maxime CCXXVII

Not to be a man of the first impression

*They who have bad intentions, hasten
to give their tincture to credulity.*

> Oráculo Manual y Arte de
> Prudencia
> By Baltasar Gracián
> 1647

I

We are all slightly delusional under the Southern California sun. Some of us even dare to believe we are in control of our lives. I certainly do. On this morning, like all my mornings, I sit under the hand-carved, travertine loggia, my body absorbing the warmth of a clear March day in Laguna Beach, but the ringing of my house phone destroys all hope of tranquility. I am not used to being called this time of day, and that phone shouldn't be ringing at all. It's my private line and the number is unlisted. My muscles tense under the white linen of my dress in anticipation of the next ring, but thankfully, the sound doesn't come. Maybe they have given up. It must be a wrong number, and I am certainly not getting out of my teak chair to get it.

The soft cacophony of beachgoers' distant voices and water slapping sand and rock is usually the loudest thing I can hear. Now although the phone is silent, I have that ringing in my head. It's like a stumbling in the ears.

Perhaps I have lived too long alone, but that phone call feels like trespassing. It *is* trespassing, and here of all places in my Mediterranean home on the bluff. This house and its contents are my sanctuary. I let my body relax. I know what is real, and what should be preserved. My delusions are choices—not fantasies, desperation, or boredom—and they order my life. I am more than safe here; I am happy. I turn the page of the rare book in my lap with gloved hand and breathe the sea air and know the phone will not ring again. It will not ring because I have decided it will not. Like I said, we are all slightly delusional under the Southern California sun.

But it is a fact that my time is not dictated by the needs, whims or timetables of others. I do not have any children and my late husband passed on over a decade ago. When I married a man twenty-nine years my senior I accepted that I would be a youngish widow. Perhaps youngish stretches the truth a bit far. I am fifty-four years old, but through the combination of shoulder-length hair maintained a glossy honey-gold and a petite dress size, I create a younger illusion. I have two closets of dresses that take me to openings, and parties, and museums, and galleries. All in the name of charity. All in the name of being in the right places with the right people. All to acquire and complete my life's work, the art collection I plan to donate to my *alma mater* for safekeeping.

My best friend Jen and I argued for weeks about the phone. I am not a technophobe. I have email and text and cell phones, different numbers for different things. I communicate electronically with the finest rare book dealers in the world in order to find tomes on my favorite subject, Spanish Colonial Art. I have a system, and it serves me, but I had no landline in the house, and Jen said it wasn't safe. As if a woman living alone is a particular problem. Most people seem to believe this. I don't know if it is their delusion or mine, but I have never felt alone or unsafe in this house.

My home above the bay is fortress, cloister, sanctuary, and garrison. I have studied art and history all my life along with languages and literatures. If there is one thing I have learned from history it is how to hold the land. The biggest tragedies in history, the most costly mistakes, come from an inability to keep or even understand what one is entitled to, which things have value, or that sky, land, river, wind and word can be owned in the first place.

I have a panoramic view from every side of my piece of Mother Earth. Ambush is not possible when you hold the high ground. The Pacific Ocean can be seen from every room, and in the distance on a clear day I can see the chalky cliffs of Santa Catalina Island. I imagine Spanish galleons sailing up the coast to edge the land with missions. I can see everything from here, the past, the present, the sea, and sky, and sun and the never ending flood of new comers who have been streaming to California for centuries. I think about them the most, because I know what they want. They want what I have. They want rose bushes and bougainvillea, the smell of the ocean, and linen clothes on quiet mornings. They want a rare book to read and a spent cup of tea on the ground next to a pot of white orchids. I close the book on my lap because it is fragile, and I don't want the wind to fold over or rumple the pages. Rare books are such a comfort to me.

The newcomers imagine that in America there is a golden social ladder they can climb. It's made of fool's gold, that ladder. I am luckier than most. I came north when I was five from Ecuador where the sun is an ancient force, not a piece of sporting equipment for surfers or a wrinkle and skin cancer machine to be avoided. The sun over Quito has more power and more secrets than can be seen from the Alta California coast. Once you know something's true nature, it is harder to be dazzled by it. There is enough of Ecuador left in me to know the sun is more

Pachamama than light, more protector than heat. These qualities come in handy when you are a woman and an art collector.

The living room phone rings again. And again.

"Stop it!" I yell over my shoulder into the house. "No one is home!"

I am not a person who shouts. But why doesn't the caller just give up? The ringing ceases. Thank God. I stick my legs out into the sun from the shady spot I have chosen for my reading chair. I concentrate on the hum of the beach, the sea, and birds. It's time for the swallows to return to Capistrano. This afternoon, I will know if they are home or not. It still may be too early.

The phone in the house rings again. I can't stand it. Against my best judgment I storm inside and answer that call.

The voice of a young woman sobs from my telephone. I move the receiver away from my ear and the sound of her fills the room. "Ñañita, ayudéme, le ruego, su merced, ayudéme." This woman has entered my sanctuary, breached my walls. The essence of her kneels here on the floor beside me. She weeps and begs. She tugs at me, and the cadence of her Andean-Castilian sings to me of my childhood in Quito. She uses words my nanny used. I don't want her closer to me despite what her words are stirring in me. I want her out of this room. I press the receiver with such force that I can feel the sharpness of my earring on my skin. She implores me to help her, addresses me in the archaic manner: your highness. On this morning, the waves arranged themselves into perfect sets for the anxious surfers below, the constant sun hides behind a cloud, and a voice from my childhood begs my mercy.

"Help me, I beg you. Estoy enjaulada! Me están violando!" I hear her supplications, but I can't believe. I can't make myself believe that this strange young woman is calling me. I can't believe what she says, that she is in a cage, and to my shock and horror, has been repeatedly raped. These are not words I want in my ears or in my mind or in my day. I do not want these words in the world. These words are sordid, dissonant, chaotic and frightening like the troops of black howler monkeys I ran from when we summered at my grandfather's banana plantation in Ecuador.

All the children in my extended family were glad to be out of their formal, private schools for the summer. They shed their woolen clothing for airy linen, and my cousins howled right back with equal ferocity at those horrid monkeys. They seemed like small monsters to me. I just wanted to sit under the shade and draw the immobile sloths drooping from their perches while I listened to the faraway sounds of a *zampoña* pan pipe as it entwined with the waterfall's splash.

I haven't thought of those howler monkeys or my grandfather's plantation for some time. It must have been the beginning of something for me, because I never wanted to join my cousins, and I never thought they were braver than me. I just thought they were doing it wrong. Why chase a noisy gang of monkeys when there is shade and peace and music to be had? Even to this day, I orchestrate my life so I only hear Vivaldi in the morning and select opera arias in the evening. Even my household help knows better than to chatter when I'm in the house.

The back of my earring has drawn blood. My platinum, French-clip, baguette diamond earring has broken my skin, and I feel dizzy. It's not from the small dot of blood I find with my finger. It's what she said next that makes the room go out of focus. The last sentence I hear between my caller's sobs before the line went dead is all wrong. Everything about it is wrong. "If you return the stolen painting of the *Immaculate Conception,* they will release me. The painting belongs to me. I am the rightful heir of its painter, Isabel Santiago." Is that pride I hear behind her hysteria? Is that even possible? The subtle shift in her voice makes me wonder if she is a woman of strength who has managed to hold on to an important piece of herself, or if she is a practiced liar and a con-artist. She could be a pawn, just a girl with the right accent. I don't know who or what she is, but I need to see my paintings. I need to see them now. The girl is gone from the phone line, but I don't hang up. I will not give that electronic monster the chance to ring again.

I walk into the foyer trying not to run, and being careful not to rub my blood-spotted fingertip on my clothes. I move from room to room efficiently, all business, looking at my cherished paintings like a headmistress counting precious heads during a school fire drill. There is cleaning going on in the house today, and I am not alone. I will not lose my composure in front of employees. I pass right under a ladder where a man is cleaning the massive, rock crystal chandelier I bought in Venice 15 years ago. The grimace on his face is distorted and magnified by the prisms of the crystal. "Who are you?" I demand of the man. He stares down at me and does not answer. I try again with a firmer voice. "*Como te llamas?*"

My housekeeper Lupe answers. "Sorry, Missus, I did not want to disturb you. He is Alfredo, the new window-cleaning man, he replace Carlos. He no hear very good, Missus. They shoot him close to ears in South America."

Instead of demanding to know what happened to Carlos, I simply want this man Alfredo out of my haven. He may not hear well, but his dagger gaze reminds me of a reckless plantation worker of my childhood who could skin a wild boar with a few swift machete swings while we children screamed in terror. "Please, have this man leave immediately, Lupe," I command in a faltering voice.

Lupe quickly answers, "Yes, Missus, he leave, but please no walk under the ladder. It bad luck."

Normally, I disregard Lupe's superstitions with a wave of my hand that tries not to be dismissive, or I smile knowing she meant her warning as a kindness and a protection. But the irrational is filling the house like smoke today, and I snap at her. "The ladder is a little late, Lupe; my bad luck just called! Tell the ladder if it wants me it will have to get in line." I point behind my back with my thumb, indicating the invisible line forming to the rear. Lupe looks confused as a woman should when her calm and impeccably mannered employer seems to have lost it for the first time in her memory. I may even be on the verge of scaring her. I find that I don't care. I have been attacked in my home and the adrenaline buoys me, and I continue with a barrage of displaced aggression. "Next time, Lupe, warn me before the mirror breaks, or if the *cucuy* is outdoors. Yes, please lock all the doors in case the *chupacabras* devours Mademoiselle Latté."

I know it is not her name that brings my little wheaten terrier to me. She comes when called, but more often comes when needed. I bend down to hug my soft-coated Latté. She licks my face urgently, as if to cover up my cheeks, because the anger and the panic are gone and now all I feel is shame. How can I possibly behave this way? Some poor young girl just begged for my help, and all I am worried about is whether I have unwittingly purchased a stolen painting. I look at Lupe, and her expression is one of a person who has already accepted an apology.

It's taken me over a dozen years to methodically and judiciously purchase these works of Spanish Colonial art. At times the search for the precise addition to my art collection has been a minefield bursting with unscrupulous art dealers offering forged paintings; or worse, they want to hand me a stolen painting grenade. I do not allow a dealer to rush me with a purchase because I know that once these paintings arrive at my home, they become more than something to fill the walls of my otherwise cavernous abode. I am not a gullible widow searching to fill my bottomless grief.

What I don't reveal to anyone, ever, is that these paintings are not just an academic exercise for me. They do comfort me, but not with their iconography. I do not worship before my paintings. They are my companions. Like Mademoiselle Latté, they comfort me with their presence. I am made happy by the fact that they exist. There is an energy, a warmth, a devotional fervor that emanates from them. Each work of art is a story, a personality, a voice. They have such wonderful melodic stories to tell me. The 1769 *Adoration of the Magi* calls out in a three-voice harmony as I pass. Prior to purchasing a painting I methodically research its iconography, but I have always wondered why there is so much white in the Virgin's dress in this image. She has the red cloak and the blue mantle that looks like a field of stars as she usually does, but most of her clothing is white from her left knee to her neckline. It could be an emphasis on her purity. The red seems to be downplayed in this image. The clothes of the Virgin speak volumes and they vary only a little.

I pass my Cusco School *Archangel Michael*. When my feet are bare, I imagine I can feel in the floor the vibrations that must be made by the booming voice that drove Adam and Eve from paradise. That voice must be equal to the strength of the Archangel's sword. My 1780 *Divine Shepherdess* comes from the Quito school. The Shepherdess tenderly cajoles her sheep to bleat their chorus of *Ave Marias*. These canvases represent a fusion of European mannerism with style elements of Andean significance. They are the conquerors and the conquered, the glory and the suffering as one. They are truth.

Pacing the rooms of my house, I wonder how the young caller knew my very private, unlisted, phone number. I raise my voice in an accusatory tone and regret it immediately. "Lupe, did you give my private telephone number to anyone?" Of course she didn't. What is the matter with me?

She replies quickly, "Oh, no, Missus. You do not even give me the number, remember?" Latté and I continue with the inspection of my fifty-three paintings. This is how I think best. Whoever gave the caller my telephone number obviously knows about my art collection. It was my vanity that did this. I allowed two glossy magazines to do a photo spread on my house and my art in the last 18 months. It was nothing but vanity. I should have considered more carefully. Now tens of thousands know what is contained within the walls of my sanctuary, and one of them wants what I have. It's small relief to know that I can disregard the caller's claim about the cage and the rape with more certainty—this is the work of a con artist who wants my *Immaculate Conception*.

Still, something doesn't sound the way it should. My ear is slowly adjusting to what it shouldn't be hearing. It's like Vivaldi in the afternoon, but ominous as a storm. I have interpreted something incorrectly. I stop dead in my tracks. Latté whimpers, probably wondering why she is being held so still. I cannot comfort you now, Latté. I cannot comfort myself, because if I am right this time then something horrible is happening to that girl. "Surely she didn't mean sex-slave, did she?" I say aloud. I am not naïve. I know there is a global sex trade that preys on poor women. And I have read of girls from Ecuador who are promised jobs as maids or nannies and then sold for sex slaves. Precious and stolen forever like lost works of living art. But the far more plausible explanation is that I am being manipulated. Logic 101. Occam's razor: all things being equal the simplest explanation is the right one. What is more probable—that I was phoned this morning on an unlisted line by a sex-slave from the city where I was born who happens to be the heir to a painting I own; or that I am being conned; or that perhaps I misunderstood the slavery aspect of her story? That is the simplest. Periodically, my comprehension of the more seedy and mundane expressions in Spanish is lacking. After all, I've lived in Southern California since elementary school, and in the decades since, my diction and expressions reflect a non-country-specific, professional class, pan-Latin-American Spanish. I most likely misunderstood her. Plus, there is the way she quickly transitioned into extortionist mode. It was too choreographed to be entirely believable. Wasn't it?

There is a way to be sure, a way to know that I am the victim of a con shameless enough to use intimate knowledge of a culture to dismantle the work I have done. I will be sure the way I always am—research. I am an expert in Spanish Colonial art, and I have never read about a painter named Isabel Santiago. She would have painted during the Spanish Colonial era in what is now Ecuador and Peru. My library will reveal the truth.

As I walk toward the library, I notice Lupe speaking heatedly with Alfredo, who instead of leaving my property, is up on the ladder outside the house near my master bedroom window. Clearly, Lupe is upset and points to his car out on the street. Alfredo waves a squeegee at her, but Lupe shakes the tall ladder forcefully twice. Alfredo gets the message, comes down, and walks out the side gate. At least I'll have no further exchanges with his menacing scowl.

In my library on my password-protected documents is another kind of treasure. Each document is like a combination genealogy and passport. Where are you from? Who made you? Where do you belong? These paintings and their provenance are a personal cartography, a hybrid geography I have created for myself and for them. This desk in this room is where I solve all things, bring order, restore the past by holding it for the future. So few people, including the girl on the phone and her supposed captors, understand how impossible it is for me to consider these works property though I am their legal owner.

My documents give me a privilege. These paintings honor me with their presence, and I am their protector, curator, steward, and tutelary. I belong to the art and its history the same way the Acjachemen Tribe belongs to the land. I know all about how money and property work, but I understand that there is more to ownership. There are people who think I own an expensive art collection that can be transformed into money with as much consequence as pushing a card into a cash machine. They think paintings are commodities, investments, tax dodges or hobbies. These things are sacrilege and ignorance, and I won't have it. I am fueled by my rage now and not by the guilt I felt for the girl, or by my fear of damaging the reputation that allows me to do this work. This is all a cruel joke. It has to be. I return to myself in my place of refuge. I breathe evenly again and stroke the fur of Latté who knew to climb into my lap when I sat at my computer. She knows not to do this while I am working, but in the way of pets that are companions and not possessions, she knows today it will be allowed. I open the files.

I own five Immaculate Conception of the Virgin Mary paintings, and I have detailed provenance records on all of them. Each dealer listed is among the most respected in the field. The caller only knew about one. Everything is as it should be. My paintings are safe, the details of their purchase above reproach. I am safe. The girl does not exist. It was only a con artist who read those articles, did a little research on me, and knew exactly what buttons to push. It is a fiction for my benefit. There are no sex-slaves in Southern California.

As I sign off from my computer I notice that Alfredo is half-heartedly cleaning the outside of my library window. He deliberately leaves dirty streaks with his helter-skelter squeegee movements. I approach the window and he defiantly stares at me and flings the squeegee across the deck towards the beach gate. He is mouthing words I can't quite understand. He either says, *peligro* or *pendeja*, either way he's spewing danger or calling me a bitch. I close my drapes and call Lupe on the intercom.

"Lupe, why is that man Alfredo still here? Escort him off of my property immediately, pay him, and tell him never to return."

"He already left, Missus."

I yank open the drapes to show Lupe that Alfredo lurks outside my house, but he is indeed gone. I tell Lupe, "Please go outside and make sure that Alfredo has left for good." In the meantime, I call my guard gate and advice him to remove Alfredo from my list of service people.

The guard is puzzled by my request. "You don't have an Alfredo on your list, Mrs. Zubiondo."

"Well, you certainly allowed Alfredo to enter the community this morning."

The guard re-reads the names on my list. He adds, "The guy I let in this morning was Carlos, your usual window guy."

After hanging up, I find Lupe and demand an explanation about Alfredo. Lupe looks down at her swollen feet stuffed like giant burritos into size 5 tennis shoes. "Missus, I sorry. Carlos go back to Mexico because his wife is too much sick. I meet Alfredo at church and he tell me they shoot him in his country and I remember they shoot my brother in El Salvador, too. You see Alfredo's face a little paralyzed. But, my brother, he dead." She wipes her tears with the soiled kitchen towel. "So, I tell Alfredo to say his name is Carlos and to come to clean your chandeliers. I sorry. I think Alfredo no come back. Maybe the shooting make him a little crazy. I sorry."

An hour later Lupe comes into the library and asks, "Missus, you please give me ride to San Juan Capistrano. I no work the rest of the week, remember?" She is meek, speaking demurely, reacting to my mood. I dislike bullies, and I'm sorry for the way I spoke to her. I'm also ashamed about dismissing her brother's violent death.

"Of, course, Lupe," I say. "I'll be ready in five minutes."

I'm glad to leave the house now, because it feels a bit like leaving the scene of a crime. There should be yellow police tape around the loggia, hanging from my rock crystal chandelier, and tied in a bow around that horrible telephone. Driving Lupe is a small atonement for letting a con artist rattle me, a tiny humility for my rudeness, and afterwards I will say my weekly prayers as I always do. My morning routine was a disaster, but there is still the afternoon and peace and solitude of Serra Chapel. If the swallows are back in force today, I will take it as a sign and all will be well. Lupe is anxious to go, perhaps she is afraid I will yell again, maybe she's as afraid as I am that the phone will ring. I've left it off the hook, but anything seems possible today.

Before I leave my library, I have to find just the right book to read in the sanctity of the Serra Chapel in the Mission San Juan Capistrano. I am always careful about what I bring to the chapel to read, but today it is especially important that I reclaim the atmosphere of the day, the feeling and the color of the life I don't live so much as practice. Living well is a practice, and I work hard to get it just right.

I decide to bring an English copy of Baltasar Gracián's 1685 *The Courtiers Manual Oracle, or, the Art of Prudence*. The original was written in Spanish, but his wisdom in any language is the cool salve for my bruises. This book will keep the howler monkeys at bay. While Lupe locks all the doors and coos Latté into her crate, I hold this pocket oracle firmly and find in his Maxim number 47 the comfort and the order I need: "But he that take reason for his Guide, proceeds always with circumspection."

During my weekly visits to the old mission I park my car in the train station parking lot. This mission is known as the Jewel of the Missions. Here in the parking space I have come to think of as mine, I revel in the simultaneous whistling of the arriving train and the ringing of the mission bells. It's a call to the faithful, a measured peal to remind us there is always time for contemplation. I can feel my whole being relax as the bells speak to me. The delicate fluttering of angels' wings emanates from the smallest bells, San Antonio and San Rafael, in the *campanario*. Their 1804 inscriptions long ago faded, but their devotion to the Virgin Mary is eternal and still reverberates. I am reminded of things ancient and sacred and far more important than an annoying phone call.

Usually, I do not acknowledge that the bells are recordings. The four ancient bells only ring on feast days. I said we are all delusional under the California sun, and on most days I am forced to use this to my advantage. But today is a feast day, and the ring of the bells is genuine. The past and the present ring together in harmony, and time seems to fold around me. The screaming train and the call of the bells meld, and I close my eyes for a moment. I feel the breeze and the sun and the emanation of stone and wood and mud saturated with centuries of prayer.

Today is March 19, 2008, the feast day of St. Joseph, and the return of the swallows from their winter home in Argentina. The legend of their homecoming tugs at the collective memory of San Juan Capistrano as hauntingly as the gentle peals of the smallest bell in the *campanario*. Their beloved *golondrinas* are not simply a tourist attraction, but a reminder of spring's renewal of their own dreams and desires, of hope. They visualize their special birds gliding with the winds, beaks open as they feast on tasty insects in flight. The swallows, like the pealing bells, are celestial reminders that we live in an ancient place. Once again, my day takes on the shape I have chosen for it. The ringing of the bells is reaching its sonorous crescendo when I overhear a grandmother or perhaps a great-grandmother say to the preschooler she's holding, "Hear that, *mi hija*? I used to hear the same bells when I was your age in my grandma's arms."

Since this feast day falls on a Wednesday, the streets only have a sprinkling of additional tourists, with their cameras in hand hoping to capture a shot of a swallow in flight. As I cross the street, I see Debbie. She is a regular visitor here too. Debbie sees me and recognition lights her face, and something else, too. Curiosity? Excitement? She looks like a woman with a good piece of gossip to share and she flags me down as I cross to her side.

"Two people were asking about you, Paloma" she says.

The peace I was beginning to feel, the peace I come here for, shatters.

"What did they want to know?" I ask. Perhaps there is too much urgency in my voice. Debbie knows me as a gracious and calm woman.

"They just wanted to know if you were here yet," she says.

I remember Lupe putting Latté in her crate. I visualize her locking every door. I know she locked them, and I am certain that I set my house alarm.

"What did they say?" I ask. This time I am more careful with Debbie. I smile and shield my eyes from the sun, drop my car keys into my purse. A terrified person would grip them tightly. I will be the person people expect. I will let them see the collector, the socialite, the wealthy lady of the bluff. Debbie seems more at ease with me when she answers.

"They had heavy Spanish accents," says Debbie. "At first I thought they said they wanted to talk to you about painting your house, but it's your painting collection they're interested in." Debbie returns my smile, her message delivered. "Listen, it's none of my business, I know, but they were a bit rough looking. I didn't give them any information. Is everything ok, Paloma?"

"It is an unusual situation, and I don't know who they could be."I answer. "But I'm sure all is well. Do you know which way they went?"

"Gee, I think they were heading towards the train station."

I thank her. I turn back to wave, *ta-ta*, as I trip off towards the chapel, away from the train station, and Debbie continues on her way to the parking lot. Neither of us has a care in the world. Right, Debbie? This is just an ordinary day.

Making her way through the small collection of tourists towards me is Lindsay, the thirty-something woman who takes Pilates instruction at my studio. This is the original Lindsay. She is the prototype for all the Lindsay clones I see on the beach who all seem to have her hair and her manicure, her clothes, her mannerisms and words, many of which I don't understand. They also have the same bobbed nose and even more oddly, the same breasts which are pushed into a constant state of cleavage under their workout clothes and don't always move in the same direction they do. I suspect a shared surgeon, and it occurs to me all at once why I am so fascinated by this woman and her clones, why I have paid so much attention to her details and to the ever multiplying versions of her I see here in Orange County and in other cities. Lindsay is a painting, which at this moment brings me relief from the prospect of encountering the rough couple looking for me.

Lindsay smiles at me, rolls her expressive grey eyes towards the heavy-set tourist to her left, and sticks her French-manicured index finger down her throat. All right, so she is a rude painting, but she greets me effusively as if we hadn't seen each other two days ago. "Oh, my God, Paloma, you won't believe it!" she screeches. "I'm auditioning for a new reality show tomorrow." I watch Lindsay bounce and talk and it's all a blur. Her words wash over me, and I feel like she is Pinocchio telling me she is about to be a real girl. "It's about fitness freaks like me," Lindsay continues, and I am grateful she is here because Lindsay is familiar and predictable and there is comfort in that. "Can you believe it?" she asks. "It's so awesome. Orange County is so hot right now, like everyone wants to do a reality show about living down here. Have you been watching them? There's like three shows going on right now. Mine, that is if I get it, would make four shows."

This endless duplication (of what I can only think of now as Lindsay shows) strikes me as a school of painting with all the artists creating endless versions of the assumption, of the annunciation, of the Lindsay. Her image on television would be only a reflection, and I picture her on canvas surrounded by her own set of symbols, especially the spotless mirror. She would be holding it, checking her makeup. Just when I'm about to congratulate her, Lindsay interrupts me with her flawless smile and coos, "Shut uuup, I can't wait for my audition! I just left the stables because my trainer said I wasn't focusing. Well, duh? Hello? I'm so amped up about being a reality show star. Don't you think I'd be just purrrfect? What should I wear? I want to start my own line of exercise apparel. You're so classy, would you help me? I also want to target the older fit woman. Fifty is the new thirty, right? I super want to show off my abs, a six-pack, baby!"

I'm picturing a new painting now. Celestial light highlights Lindsay's stomach. *The Adoration of the Six-Pack.* Is it possible that I am slowly losing my mind? Lindsay is still talking. "But like I don't want to look like a skank. I'm gonna get my fake-bake in a bit, but what if it comes out too orange? Like that happened to me two weeks before I went to Cabo. What a crack up! We flew there on my friend's new pj. Thank God, because we didn't have to go through customs or immigration or whatever. Speaking of immigration, what is going on in town? Did all the gardeners and maids get fired or what? Ugh! It's just too much. I mean what is happening to San One? It used to be full of people like us, and now. Well, whatever. Wish me luck. Love you, bye."

After that barrage of empty shells I don't know whether to laugh or cry. It is just incredible to think that gorgeous Lindsay is a college graduate. I'm relieved to have Gracián's Pocket Oracle with me today since I want to read his exact words about courtesy. I had been courteous to Lindsay, but a part of me regrets not having walked away from Lindsay's stream-of-unconsciousness, but as Gracián writes, "Better too much courtesy than too little."

As I turn the corner I see a large gathering of the Acjachemen Tribe near the mission. After two decades of praying together, I know many of the members. I greet several of the women of my generation. We speak softly, and with the subtle understanding that their bold placards say it all. It doesn't really matter what it is this time, because it is all the same thing. Something was taken, or something was lost, or disturbed, or desecrated. Someone lied to them. Again. And they're right to voice their protest. Some of the younger men appear agitated that we do not seem outraged enough for the current moment. But we four huddle together and talk about this and that, but not about the protest. I wish I could remain in this cocoon of friendship instead of peering over my shoulder in fear of strangers looking for me to ask about my paintings. My friends and I all have lived long enough to know that the Acjachemen roots are so deep in this part of California and will always produce fresh young shoots. Those young shoots are busy now raising the consciousness of the passersby. The women who are my age are pacing themselves for the next time.

Most of the visitors are now leaving the mission. More than likely they want to beat the afternoon traffic home or they want to catch the train back to Los Angeles. I hear minor grumbling about the missing-in-action swallows. Only the scout birds that arrive a few days ahead are here, but most of the visitors seem pleased with their day. As I wait for a large, smiling group of visitors to clear the entrance, I bump into Dr. Garcia, a retired school administrator who is now a docent. Still vain in her early seventies, she wears the black, flat- topped, Early California hat at a jaunty angle. Her thin, grey wisps of hair flutter like native dandelions in the warm Santa Ana wind. How I wish I could have introduced Lindsay to Dr. Garcia, who does not suffer fools, not ever? Their vast opposing verbal powers would have been a match of classic, mythological proportions: the scholarly endurance of the Lilliputian docent queen pitted against the Teutonic arrogance of the sorority princess. After quick reflection, I think they would have cancelled each other out.

I thank Dr. Garcia for teaching the children who come to visit the mission daily in preparation for their fourth-grade California mission project. I'm not just being polite. I *am* grateful. She knows I am sincere because she knows her work is important. This is something we have in common. Quickly, I try to think of something Lindsay and I have in common. I'm about to give up when I realize with some humility that Lindsay locks herself away as much or more than I do. She is hidden by a persona too easily duplicated to be real. I know a counterfeit when I see one. I wonder where the real Lindsay hides herself.

Dr. Garcia answers straightforwardly, "You're welcome. Shall we continue our last conversation from four and a half months ago?" Dr. Garcia knows exactly what we were discussing, where our points of contention were, and where we left off. We jump right into art history lingo, and I subtlety probe her encyclopedic mind about the iconography of the Immaculate Conception. From the scowl on her face, I realize that my question is too ambiguous. She bluntly commands, "I believe a full, academic answer would require a doctoral thesis on the matter. Also, please do keep in mind that I am not a theologian, so limit your questions to the realm of art history. Try again." I take a deep breath, consider my words, and speak very carefully. Another mediocre question and I will miss my chance.

"Which artist delineated the symbols that must be placed around the figure of the Immaculate Conception?"

"Why that was the Spaniard Francisco Pacheco in 1600 in Seville," Dr. Garcia fires back.

"As you know, Dr. Garcia, I own several paintings of the Immaculate Conception of the Virgin Mary, and not all my paintings include all the symbols associated with this image. How many symbols should there be?"

"I hope your first comment was not *braggadocio* my dear Paloma. It's most unbecoming your station." I have a graduate degree in art history, as well as degrees in Spanish and French literature, yet this woman makes me feel like one of her fourth graders. "As for the symbols, let's count, shall we? There is the rose without thorns as a symbol of purity. The tower of David is a symbol of the church. The Virgin as the star of the sea, the *stella maris* based on a liturgical hymn, I believe." She ticks them off on her boney fingers. "The cedar of Lebanon because of its incorruptible substance, and its healing virtues. The olive is obviously an ancient symbol of peace. The sun and the crescent moon beneath her feet symbolize her perpetual chastity.

There are at least seven more, but my group is waiting for me, my dear." She is gone after her noisy group of nine- and ten-year-olds, her black sandals clacking on the floor. I wish I had something to write with. I'm trying to commit the symbols she listed to memory as well as the name Francisco Pacheco.

Finally, I step into the chapel. The red candles flicker in continuous prayer. As I walk down the aisle toward the masterpiece of the baroque, gold leaf *retablo,* I notice a black-haired couple inside the tiny St. Peregrine Chapel to my right. They seem to be deep in prayer, but there is something strange about them. I'm not sure what it is that bothers me about them, but I don't want to be rude, so I tip-toe. I think this day has made me paranoid. I sit down at my usual pew. It takes a few seconds before my eyes adjust to the reduced light. I find a sealed, ivory-colored envelope with my name carefully written in calligraphy: Mrs. Paloma Zubiondo.

I turn to look towards the chapel's entrance. Could this be from Dr. Garcia? But all I see are the two black-haired people who were praying when I came in. They look to be in their late teens or early twenties. They both have dark eyes to go with their dark hair; they could be brother and sister. It comes to me all at once what was wrong with them. They were kneeling in front of St. Peregrine, but they were not praying, they were waiting. I have been coming to this chapel long enough to know the difference between people who are trying to look like they are praying, and those who are begging for help or thanking St. Peregrine from the bottom of their hearts. I have trained myself in the significance of details. I should have trusted my first impulse about these two. They stare directly at me and raise their hands, and I think for an instant maybe they know me and are about to wave goodbye, but instead they gesture obscenities at me, and scurry from Serra Chapel.

My first thought is that I should get away and exit the chapel through the front door, the one leading to the centuries-old cemetery, but I can't seem to move. In front of me is the beauty of the carvings of the *retablo*, so I count cherubs. It's no stranger than anything else that has happened today. There are so many cherubs, each one with a slightly different appearance. I start to count them as a way of calming myself. I listen as I do with my paintings to see if each carving has its own personality, its own song, but they don't sing, they overlap and chatter in my head. I resort to the book I've brought with me. I recall Gracián's maxim on vulgarity and quickly try to find it. This doesn't console me, and it doesn't guide me, and I hear the noise of the cherubs rising in my thoughts again. I wish they would be quiet. They jabber like a phone that won't stop ringing. I look around anxiously then open the envelope. The message reads, "You are an art thief. You must return the *Immaculate Conception* painting." The note is unsigned.

I cannot show this note to anyone. Ever. Reputations are hard won and fragile. This would be an argument with my idealistic and slightly naïve Jen. Take it to the police, she would say. They can't damage your reputation if you've done nothing wrong. She doesn't understand that the accusation is enough, ask any politician. She would insist that people would understand. This is one of the things I love and admire about Jen. She still thinks being right is enough. But I need the respect of the circles I move in to do my work. The best art dealers don't want to be associated with a disreputable client. They live by their reputations as well. Art collectors who are suspect bring the FBI, and scrutiny of the rest of a dealer's clients. I would be career poison to them. They would have nothing more to do with me, and I would never complete my work. Donating these objects of devotion, these unique combinations of European Mannerism and Andean techniques is my legacy to my *alma mater*. I have worked diligently at gathering my collection and now someone is trying to steal everything. They are trying to erase me from history. Even the envelope is a sophisticated attempt at manipulation. I am dealing with someone more intelligent and subtler than these two howler monkeys making obscene gestures in a church. These two are only scouts. There is something else behind them waiting to come in force like swallows to Capistrano.

How can my enemy know enough about me to think a threat written in calligraphy and delivered in a fancy envelope would move me more than a crying girl who claims to be in the worst kind of danger? What kind of person am I if it does? No. The girl was a trick. This threat is even more proof of that. The note doesn't mention her. The strategy has changed and changed quickly. Why? Are they on a timetable of some kind? If there really were a prisoner, I would be offered some proof now. Or the threats against her would escalate in some way.

The scouts are common art thieves, but someone else is running the show. Someone intelligent. Someone who knows me. It's a comfort in a way to know there is an intellect at work here. If winning this, whatever this is, depends on knowledge and on logic, then my assailants have met their match. They can't get into my fortress to steal it outright, so they are trying to get me to just hand it over to them. Do they think me so weak and stupid? Suddenly I think of Alfredo. Obviously I haven't taken the necessary precautions, and have even become careless about my personal safety. This very morning a strange man lurked in my house ostensibly cleaning my chandeliers, while I didn't have a clue who he was or what he had done back in his country to earn a bullet that paralyzed his face. I will have to be more careful.

I must think through all the possibilities. Suppose the culprits are waiting for me outside the chapel or at the mission's gate, take the note away from me, and make a scene to draw attention to me and the note. It would be a bad move on their part. It would take away my incentive to placate them, but these are foot soldiers, not generals. They don't understand what they are doing, and that is what makes them dangerous.

What about the person behind the calligraphy and fine paper? Is this just an attempt to put me off balance by making fun of me? Is it a message to tell me I am not who I think I am? Can this person somehow see inside me to what I really am? I will thwart these intentions. I will not be humiliated or manipulated or diminished by these twisted games. Why did they leave me such tangible evidence? How can they know I won't go to the police, have this envelope dusted for fingerprints, its flap checked for saliva? Fine stationary isn't available everywhere. It could be traced. And yet they gave it to me and provoked me on their way out. The solution seems as obvious as Occam's razor, as A + B = C. This note will not leave this chapel.

I breathe methodically and will myself to concentrate on the beauty in front of me. These people don't know who they are dealing with. I know what is mine, and I know how to protect it. Today I will show them a woman who can hold the land. I look around the altar for comfort and for strength. On the right-hand top tier of the 22-foot altar stands a wood-carved, polychrome statue of the Archangel Michael. The Archangel would be the natural choice for anyone engaged in conflict. He is God's soldier, after all. He is armed and fierce but with a whimsical expression that seems to say he means no harm, but he is what he is. I can't help but notice how finely executed his skin-tone is. It's a prime example of an exquisite *encarnado*, as Dr. García would say. Despite the sword he brandishes or perhaps because of it, Michael is not what I need.

I glance to my left and fix my eyes on the 18th century canvas of the *Immaculate Conception* hanging on the bulging, white stucco wall opposite the golden *retablo*. Here is the strength I need, and I am awed once again at the power of devotional objects. There is something in the act of prayer, in the activity of a human mind focused on a purpose. There is something in the relationship between the supplicant and the object, something cultural, spiritual, and ritualistic. And there is a third thing that seems so obvious to some of the people who come here to pray. It is something I am still trying to grasp and one of the reasons I collect the art that I do. There is something that emanates from the object itself. Perhaps what I sense is the part of the artist that remains in the painting. Maybe it is what happens when a work of art becomes the psychic focus for so much intention over such a long period of time.

On this day, I don't really need to know what it is about this 18th century *Immaculate Conception* that gives me what I need. It only matters that I can begin now. Slowly, delicately, and methodically I tear the note into tiny pieces and chew. The first piece goes down easily. I stare at the painting of the Virgin and can't help but think this is some strange form of communion. I tear and place a small piece on my tongue. I taste chemicals and paste. My mouth is growing dry. I think of notes left in churches. I chew. I swallow. I think of St. Peregrine.

Years ago, while praying at this chapel, I met a withered woman scrambling on her knees looking for something on the floor. Seeing her severely arthritic fingers, I knelt down next to her and asked, "What is it that you're looking for? May I help you?"

"Yes, honey," she said, her pearly cataract gaze roaming my face. "My eyes aren't too good no more, but I dropped my *milagro,* and I just have to find it."

Thinking that she was referring to a celestial miracle and not a physical amulet, I said, "Well, I think it would be ok if you sat down and said your prayers of gratitude."

She spoke to me as if explaining something obvious to a small child. "Yes, honey, I say my prayers all day long." "But today I have to thank my *santito*, because he helped my granddaughter with the delivery of her seventh child. I promised my *santito* that if he asked God for his help, then I would bring him the *milagro* to show him how grateful I am."

I had missed the point just as I misunderstood the girl on the phone. I assumed the meaning, the power of healing, was in the old woman's mind, in words combined with prayer and belief. But for her the meaning was in the thing itself. How had I forgotten this? Wasn't my work always about something I sensed in objects of religious devotion? The meaning resides not only in the person, but in the thing itself.

"Can you please help me find my *milagro*?" she asked. "He's a little baby, a little flat metal baby, not like my plump baby."

I was embarrassed that she assumed I wouldn't know what the object looked like. The *milagro* is a devotional charm. They are small pieces folk art. The most common *milagros* I've encountered here and in both humble churches and grand cathedrals on my sojourns in Latin American are heart-shaped. Throughout the world, a heavy heart, an ill heart, and a broken heart all hurt profoundly. *Milagro* offerings are not an accepted practice these days, but when Mademoiselle Latté was sick recently I bought a dog *milagro* online. I was careful to make sure no one saw me leave my *milagro* in gratitude that my prayers were answered. I felt a little like a teenager breaking the rules.

Together the old woman and I found the metal baby, and she wrestled with her knobby digits to place it at the foot of the saint. Her hands may have been gnarled, but the woman would never lose their grip on what is important. She knew which things were her legacy and which things could be cast off. I could tell by the way she mixed her English and her Spanish.

She said *santito* and not little saint. One is accurate and one is not. She knew the difference. The English version diminishes the *santito* with a modifier holding equal weight with the thing it changes. The elegance of the single Spanish word means he is what he is and not a lesser version of something else. Maybe it is only I who see it this way. I don't know anymore. I speak so many languages in different situations, and usually it is so easy to keep them in different boxes, to switch from one to the other when necessary. Lately, they seem to be blurring, vying for dominance or attention, demanding more of myself than I have given them. Perhaps I was wrong when I said I have no children to worry over.

Since that morning with the old woman, I have discovered a sprinkling of *milagros* at this same spot, albeit fewer and fewer each day since I recovered the metal newborn. Maybe what is happening to me now is penance for all the times I've surreptitiously read the pleas that visitors leave at the St. Peregrine statue. "Heavenly Father, please heal my broken heart," said one. Another note was scribbled in a wobbly cursive and attached to a tiny, tin-armed *milagro*. "*Santísimo, cúrale a mi hijo de las drogas.*" Cure my son of drug addiction. These anguished words were not meant for me, and now my stomach has to digest my accuser's poisonous words.

Visitors start to trickle and meander into the lower light and softer temperatures of the chapel, but I know I have time to finish. People adjust when they cross the threshold. No one can seem to help themselves. The body adjusts to the atmosphere of the sacred. Even the small children stop their running and lower their voices when they enter. The building is simply too old, too revered, its adobe walls too seeped in history and prayer.

I have finished eating the sins of those strangers. The note is gone. I have undone their efforts, and I regain my composure. I soak in what the chapel gives me as I soaked in the sun this morning and concentrate on studying the painting in front of me. Unlike my five paintings of the Immaculate Conception, this image was made in the style of the 17th century Spanish artist Bartolomé Esteban Murillo. The Virgin Mary is wearing a billowy white robe with her blue stole also blowing in the vast, celestial ambiance. She wears clouds and sky for clothes, but there is no red in this painting, and only a few of the Marian symbols are depicted.

But in my paintings, the Virgin Mary's robe and mantle are highly decorated with the Cusco school's gold stenciled patterns. The voluminous mantle of my *Inmaculadas* displays the *adamascado de oro,* the golden damask, so favored by the native painters of Cusco. The stencils reveal the patterns of flora found only in the Andean cordillera. Native Cusco artists had an intense preoccupation with the ornamentation of the Virgin Mary, and depicted her with sumptuous jewels. One of my Cusco *Inmaculadas* wears lengthy emerald and pearl earrings that dangle to her delicate collar bone. I understood the depiction of the precious stone since the mines of what is now Colombia were known for emeralds. But what exactly was this flower that is so prominently displayed? What was its message? My obsession with these earrings led me to climb breathlessly in and around Cusco five years ago to photograph the Angel's Trumpet flowers found only in this microclimate. My local guide finally conceded, "Mrs. Zubiondo, they are not to be found. If I am winded you must be careful, otherwise you might get the altitude sickness. This *soroche* is not a laughing matter. Please let us return to the hotel."

Not wishing to appear dismissive and rude, I acquiesced, but only for one day. We were soon looking again for the Angel's Trumpet model of my *Inmaculada's* earrings. A visit to a young local healer clarified the search. She told us that the *Brugmansia* was of a species that is now most likely extinct. She recalled her great-grandmother's didactic explanation: "This flower is both healer and killer. Its narcotic and hallucinogenic properties are a secret that we must guard since it can also end a life."

This caught my interest. "Do you think that the artist used the flower as a symbol of the deadly temptations we face in life?" I asked.

The healer-clairvoyant looked at me in disbelief. She scratched her hair and shook her head. She was stalling. Finally, she said, "Mrs. Gringa, the artist was like me. To us the *Inmaculada* is Pachamama. Our dear *Ally warmiku*, our sweet mother. We do not talk about symbols or messages. She is the Mother Earth and we do not analyze her. She is our protector. All mothers are very stern and also very loving. Do your children not think so?" She paused and peered into my eyes. She said, "Oh, excuse me, you do not know this universal truth because you do not have any children, do you?" I dared probe no further.

The mission's Immaculate Conception painting no longer has any of the numerous symbols of her usual iconography. The catalog of Marian symbols sometimes seems endless. It occurs to me that these symbols are a small and unique language known only to a select group. I know its meanings and its nuances, and what it means when they are sparse or lacking altogether, when they are silent. My paintings still contain all the Marian symbols, such as the *speculum sine macula,* the stainless mirror. My paintings have always spoken to me, but now I think they have more to tell me. I want to get back to them. There is more there than I thought. Maybe it has something to do with the crying girl and the note. Maybe my paintings can give me the answer. I try to recall the date and name of the papal bull permitting the omission of the Marian symbols. I will look it up when I am back in my library. I can no longer concentrate here, and this is unlike me. I know these paintings, and I know these symbols in particular. Their misuse is sometimes helpful in detecting counterfeits. I need the shelter of my fortress sanctuary. I need my books, and I need Mademoiselle Latté. I need my paintings.

My exit from the mission is interrupted with the pleasantries I must exchange with the usual volunteers and neighboring merchants. I walk at a leisurely pace like a woman trying not to panic while leaving a burning building. Every familiar face, every small exchange about the weather and the swallows, the tourists, and the protest takes an enormous effort. I want to run and to yell at them, "Don't bother me now, I've just eaten a letter for pity's sake!" They would think me more than rude. They would think me insane.

I pick up the pace so I can get inside my car and shut the door. As I approach my parking space, I see the rude couple boarding the northbound train to Los Angeles. They turn around and shout something to me. What they are saying is barely discernable; it is neither English nor Spanish, but I vaguely recall the words. They are speaking in my childhood nanny's language: Kichwa. But unlike her sweet words, they sputter dark fumes. I struggle to understand the toxic words they're shouting, but all the languages in my brain pile up and crash. The man runs his index finger across his neck as if he is slicing his own throat or cutting off his head—a death threat in any language. The couple boards the train. They issued their threats as they ran away towards Los Angeles, the City of Angels.

If I tell Jen about these people she will make me call the police, but I'm not afraid. At least not of these two. They didn't face me in the chapel or in the parking lot. They ran away. So brave in their crudeness and obscenity as long as it is practiced from a distance and in a language they are not fit to use. They are cowards, con artists, and thieves.

I'm angry now and somehow betrayed because parking near the train now seems both frivolous and tainted. I know I will never park there again. It may seem like a small thing, but the things I have chosen for myself are changing, and I feel each small loss. I will go home to my cloister by the sea, and I will sequester myself until I piece together this day's events. There is only one place to start. I must find out if Isabel Santiago really existed, and what she did or did not paint.

1699

Quito, Ecuador

Maxime CCC

In a word, to be Holy

*Virtue is the chain of all perfections,
and the center of all felicity.*

Oráculo Manual y Arte de
Prudencia
By Baltasar Gracián
1647

II

*D*espite the earlier torrential rain that hastened the citizens of Quito to scramble for cover, the *plaza* now buzzes with mercantile haggling. The queen bees in this marketplace are the *gateras* who artfully display their parrot-hued goods for their mostly *mestizo* buyers. The *gateras* dribble honeyed words in a patois of Quichua and Castilian to entice their mixed race customers into buying the tad too ripe papaya along with a bunch of flawless bananas. Each *gatera* promotes the delectable flavor of her goods, but never at the expense of her fellow indigenous merchants. One can hear their sweet-talking words as they encourage the customers to chew a bite of stewed hominy or roasted *cuy* guinea pig. They say, *"Mikuylla warmi ñusta,"* as they flatter a stubby-necked matron by telling her: eat, young princess. Collectively, the *gateras* jealously guard their unique commercial honeycomb for they know their monopoly to sell in this marketplace depends on their good standing with the Spanish royal crown that controls everything in 1699.

Amidst this colorful swarm a perky elfin girl weaves through the stalls. Her cheek-to-cheek smile reveals her misaligned teeth; her perfect-pitch voice perks up everyone's ears. She says, "May the rays of our father sun warm your day, ñañas." She entertains her sister vendors by performing a bygone dance step for a few seconds. Although Quilla Punchalla hears the *gateras* call her name, she waves back cheerfully and makes a beeline to complete her errands in record time. Her presence in the marketplace kindles a glowing anticipation in the *gateras'* otherwise monotonous day. As they deal with their customers they also manage to sneak a peek at Quilla Punchalla, their Shining Star, as she purchases cinnamon sticks.

The *gateras* admire Shining Star's meticulous grooming; from her perfectly symmetrical obsidian plaits reflecting the rays of the equatorial sun to the geometric patterns of the exquisitely woven *chumpi* made of *vicuña* and bat fur which she wraps multiple times around her scrawny thirteen-year-old waist. Without exception, every *gatera* stretches her neck to glimpse Shining Star's delicate feet, which catch the eye due to the red *achiote* dye she applies to her heels. The *gateras* appreciate this understated reminiscence of who she might have been under Inca rule. By extension, her crimson heels remind the market women that under the harsh boot of the Spaniards, their ancient Andean world survives in full color and deep symbolism.

As soon as Shining Star completes the marketplace errands for her mistress, the artist Isabel Santiago, she will visit with the *gateras*. Unlike Isabel's infamous irascible nature that casts a blue shadow in the workshop, the *gateras* buoy Shining Star. She is grateful for the *gateras'* affection, and wishes she could raise her mistress's spirits in the same manner. Shining Star concludes that the long-ago death of Isabel's husband, mother, sister, and young nephew during the Andean pestilence must have formed in Isabel a wound that will never heal.

She's determined to be the soothing salve to Isabel's wound. After all, it is just the two of them working side by side in the renowned workshop.

Last week, when she accompanied Isabel to Mass at the elite parish of San Francisco she noticed a rare rose-colored mood in her mistress. "Come here and clasp the gold chain of my crucifix," Isabel said. "I want to see the *criollas'* emerald faces when they see me walk into their church."

Shining Star inappropriately addresses Isabel as *su merced,* your highness, an honorific reserved for the Spanish elite and their native born daughters, the *criollas,* whom Isabel wants to impress. Since Isabel never corrects her on this wrong usage, Shining Star said, "*Su merced,* the craftsmanship of your gold crucifix is without equal. It corresponds with your stature as the talented artist and daughter of the master painter, Miguel de Santiago."

Isabel's lips curled up in distaste. "Don't bring him up in conversation today. I don't want to be reminded that while I toil in the workshop with endless commissions, he's ensconced in the convent of the Augustinians. It's a privileged and weak sentence for slicing mother's ear off, and then threatening to do the same to the judge. He's been in the convent for ages painting giant canvases on the life of St. Augustine. Meanwhile, I have to paint endless Virgin Mary paintings for which he receives total credit."

Shining Star rushed to amend her mistake. "Everyone in Quito wants to own one of your paintings of our Blessed Mother. Your colors reflect the rainbows Pachamama bequeaths to our rainy city every day."

Isabel seemed to rebound at that colorful observation. She says, "My crucifix is like the precious filigree jewels of Nasrid Spain. I want those snobbish women breathless with altitude sickness when they notice my crucifix."

Rather than causing the women to pant with *soroche* or capture their covetous eyes, Shining Star and Isabel overheard Doña Valencía y León discuss her own massive sapphire and emerald ring without even noticing Isabel's attention-grabbing crucifix. Doña Valencia y León said, "Oh, sweet Mother of God, I do believe that my teensy-weensy ring just slipped right off my bitty finger and into the tiny fountain." The residents of Quito reduce any word imaginable into its most diminutive form, but Doña Valencia's boast is a farce. By adding the required suffix, a word can become a term of affection or intimacy, a minute jewel of endearment. The simple word for water, *agua*, becomes *aguita* or *aguitica*, as if only a drop of dew remains of all the water in the world. By the time the speaker delivers the word, it evaporates. In fact, an artfully jabbed diminutive by a malevolent Quito linguist can cut deeply with condescension. One knows instantly when one has been dealt a fatally dismissive *coup de grâce*.

To further aggravate Isabel's loss of face that morning, she and Shining Star inadvertently exited the church in front of another one of Quito's notorious matrons, Doña Pilar. Her two hefty servants pushed Isabel aside and escorted their mistress on her regal exit from the church. Doña Pilar turned to Isabel and addressed her informally, as one would a servant. "Please do tell your little father to rush my commissioned painting of Our Lady of the Pillar," she said. "And a teensy bit of advice to you: perhaps during rainy season you ought to consider staying in your own wee parish, near the slaughterhouse, would you not agree?"

Cholita had absorbed Isabel's humiliation as if it were her own. But she gracefully turned the table on the ill-mannered *chinas*. She defended the honor of her mistress by humbling Doña Pilar's *chinas* in an eloquent Quichua that revealed her regal heritage. She said, "Elder sisters, our beloved Pachamama regards all her creatures with equal love. She's weeping silver tears because you two must be ill with a poison that is creeping into your heart. Will you not expel that poison by bowing your heads to my lady?"

On that day, as the two of them walked home, Shining Star declared, "Our parish church of Santa Barbara welcomes us with many of your paintings on the walls, should we not go there from now on?"

Isabel, deep in thought, didn't respond. What had she been thinking, trying to infiltrate the center? The aristocrats of the El Sagrario parish, closest to the Plaza Mayor, restricted their churches to the elite who regard them as the *ne plus ultra*, and would never venture beyond its borders. Conversely, they expect the others to remain in the confines of their own lower-class parishes.

In an effort to cheer up Isabel, Shining Star, who has delivered paintings to many homes in this neighborhood says, "*Su merced,* you would be surprised at the spaciousness of both stories, why they even house a dozen *chinas*. And the courtyards are festooned with potted geraniums."

As the errand girl for the workshop of the famous but ill tempered Miguel de Santiago, Shining Star is able to negotiate any environment in the city. She is like a speck of ash from the many surrounding volcanoes or a drop of rain, both in ample supply in this bustling colonial city. She can creep in and out of any of the many monasteries, convents, and churches, and even the bedrooms of the pampered women. She is able to carry any package twice her height and weight, and people in town are used to seeing her twiggy limbs carry the dried oil canvases to their new homes. She is a welcome sight because of her constant lyrical songs and her angelic toothy smile.

Shining Star takes Isabel's silence for interest in listening to the details of the houses forbidden to her. She continues. "You would laugh at the tomfoolery of the capuchin monkeys in the courtyards. I think you might even be entertained by the foul-mouthed *papagayos* since they curse in Quichua and Castilian. When you sent me to that corner house over there, three cats almost caught a *papagayo* who lost his long, pepper-red feathers in his escape."

Isabel clamps Shining Star's bony arm like an Amazonian cayman and says, "You are such an imbecile." The insult is directed as much at herself as at Shining Star. How did she ever think that her father's prestige as the foremost painter of the Quito School of art could elevate her among the elite women? She searched for friendship among a closed link of women who will never add her to their chain. She yanks Cholita's arms and says, "We've wasted too much time, already. Let's pick up the pace."

Isabel recognizes that her workshop and her art are her only sanctuary. She will not divert her focus on anything but the creation of her paintings. It had been the solace of methodically applying pigments to a blank canvas and gradually seeing a sacred image emerge that dulled the grief of burying each of her family members years ago. Eager to return to the workshop Isabel unclamps Cholita's arm and tells her, "I don't want to hear another word from you." Despite the sun's searing appearance overhead they returned home under a grey cloud of disappointment. With their heads turned to the cobblestones they neglect to see a double rainbow that arcs over the many abysmal and impenetrable ravines that separate the social classes of Quito.

Since that misfortunate outing two weeks ago, Isabel has not left the workshop. Today, Shining Star completes her errands at the plaza and stops by to help the *gateras*. The first woman grimaces with pain as she hunches over in her stall. She says, "Shining Star, my sweet sister, can you please pull this tick out of my scalp?" They both step behind a huge heap of purple potatoes the old *gatera* sells. Shining Star tells the elderly woman, "Teensy grandma, lean over and hold your plaits so I can charm this wee bug out of your head." With a bit of flame and her own nails, Shining Star coaxes the bloody tick and smashes it under her heel. The old *gatera* gives Shining Star a toothless smile of her own, and a few purple tokens of her affection.

Shining Star meanders from stall to stall helping the women as she goes along. In her woven tapestry coca shoulder bag, Shining Star carries a range of dried herbs and homemade ointments. She sings a melody that all the *gateras* know by heart and they accompany her by humming or drumming or shaking a dried gourd. Shining Star massages an herb-infused oil in the ear of a young *gatera's* nursing baby. Next, she reapplies a mustard poultice to the congested chest of a haggard-looking *quinoa* seller. Each one of her relieved patients shows her gratitude by giving Shining Star a small quantity of whatever item they sell. Shining Star thanks them effusively and runs down a narrow side street to the workshop of the master silversmith, Don Jerónimo Suárez de Guerrero.

Shining Star wipes her feet before entering the workshop. She bows her head humbly as she softly says to the apprentice, "I'm so sorry for disturbing you from your noble work, but the maestro's wife is expecting me."

From the second story balcony window booms a woman's crude voice. "Tell Cholita to come upstairs and to wipe her filthy feet."

The name Cholita still stings Shining Star; it is the tick buried deeply under her skin. When her own mother gave her away to Isabel Santiago five years ago to serve as her lifelong *china*, she requested demurely to be called by her Inca name, Quilla

Punchalla. Isabel replied, "Don't put on any airs of superiority in my workshop, can't you see that I'm inundated with problems and commissions from every church and snobbish woman in Quito? From now on your name is Cholita."

At that time, Shining Star wanted to enumerate her reasons for the request, but she remembered her mother's sage words. "Shining Star, in the olden days you would have been selected for your beauty and grace to be a *taquiaqlla*, a chaste maiden who brings joy to others through dance, music and art. You would have lived in the *aqllahuasí* just like the nuns live in a cloister these days. The exquisite women in our family lived in the *aqllahuasí* near the temple of the sun in Carangue, and remained virgins all their lives. They brought honor to our clan. Isabel Santiago has promised to protect your honor so I must send you to live with her. She will be your *mamacona*, your *Señora Madre*, the teacher you would have had in the *aqllahuasí*. If you stay with us you will die of hunger. Follow Doña Isabel's instructions at all times." Thus, Shining Star became known as Cholita, the little mongrel.

Cholita wipes her already tidy feet before climbing the stairs of the silversmith's house. Waiting for her is a battle-ax whose swollen legs and twisted maroon toes rest on a wooden stool. She says to Cholita, "Your massages are not helping me at all. Those lying *gateras* told me you were the best *sobadora*, but I think you're making my once pretty legs even worse. Massage me with a lot more force!"

After an hour of non-stop massaging the malodorous feet, Cholita is dismissed with a mule kick. Cholita says, "Doña Conchita, I have purple potatoes and yellow squash as a payment for you. Do you think that my weekly payments and the massages I have been administering to you since the last

Feast of Saint Michael the Archangel are enough to pay for that teensy silver pin, no larger than your toenail?"

The woman kicks Cholita even harder. "Hide your ugly face from me next time you see me out on the city," she tells her savagely. "I never said anything about a silver pin. What would a scarred *india* want with a silver pin, anyway?"

As Cholita limps down the stairs, she mumbles in Quichua that silver is the color of Mama Quilla, the moon goddess and the protector of women. Mama Quilla cries tears of silver when her children misbehave.

Cholita rubs the raised scar on her right cheek. She slowly runs her index finger along the quarter moon and its sparkling stars. On the feast of St. Peter and St. Paul in June, before she came to live with Isabel, her mother whispered in her ear. "This feast day is our ancient *Inti Raymi* when we celebrated our sun god. You will soon be going to live with Doña Isabel and I must make sure that no man will ever want to take your virginity. Already there are men ardently approaching me because of your beauty. We must be strong, Shining Star, and remember that I must do this to keep you pure for the sun for eternity. I am doing this today so that you will always remember how important your chastity is to our god."

Cholita's mother was known in their village for her knowledge of healing herbs, and she made Cholita a delicious bowl of mashed fruit. Cholita did not remember anything else for quite a few days. When she finally woke up, her mother was applying a moist and gummy poultice to her right cheek. In a matter of weeks, Cholita almost forgot about her cheek, except for when she heard the gasps of fellow kinsmen when they first saw her, and their subsequent accusations. "Why did they destroy her face?" or "No one will want her now that is for certain." Though she acknowledged that the scar sealed her fate as an imperfect maiden, she resolved to conduct herself as a lustrous Shining Star.

Cast down by Doña Conchita's dropkick, Cholita whimpers her grievances as she trudges along the cobblestone streets heading to her next errand. A blind, indigenous woman stops her on the steps leading into the Church of San Francisco. "Ñañita, do not say those words out loud," she says, tugging at her tunic. "You must not say Chaska, the name of our goddess of dawn or twilight. I heard you imploring her help. She will protect you for you are a young maiden, but when you step into the church you must say her Castilian name."

The blind woman touches Cholita's lips with a moist index finger and whispers to her. "Our brother painters are clever. They have painted our Chaska, our Mama Quilla, our Pachamama, in all the paintings in the churches. Look at Pachamama's mountain-shaped dress. Our painters remind us that she cares for everything on earth. Find the stars in the paintings and give them thanks for they look after all our alpacas and toucans. Look for the full moon in the paintings so that you remember to sacrifice an animal to our goddess. Stand in awe at how our Pachamama crushes the evil *amaru* serpent with her foot. She is not afraid of anything. Pray to her and she will hear you."

Cholita wants to hear more. She asks, "How can you see the details of the paintings for you are blind?"

"They blinded me for speaking the truth," the old woman says. "I'm grateful to them because now I see everything. God will judge us all. Can't you feel where we are standing, Shining Star? This was the temple of our Inti, our sun. Let your feet absorb the power of the four corners of our empire."

"Elder sister, I don't feel anything except a pain deep in my heart and the scar on my cheek," Cholita whispers back.

"Quito is a powerful center of energy, you will feel the truth. Look at our sisters far away in Huamacucho. The Augustinian friars found their hidden *guacas* and threw them in the river, but our deities prevailed. They try to crush us like *cochineal* bugs. But our blood is permanent like the *cochineal*. They even take our *cochineal* back across the big lake so their artists can do what we have always done; we revere red because it is our royal blood. They destroyed our shrines, they smashed our ancestors, which they called mummies, and they melted all our gold. But we keep everything alive under their hairy noses."

Cholita asks the old woman, "The say in the square that our elder brothers from Cusco wrote great books that will help the Spanish King see how badly we are treated in our land. Have you ever heard of Don Garcilaso de la Vega or Felipe Guamán Poma de Ayala, elder sister?"

The old woman blows her nose on her shawl. "I have heard that they lived in Spain too long," she says. "Their mothers' blood was not as powerful in their bodies as their fathers' Spanish blood. They were concerned with appealing to the king for their own estates and rights. Shining Star, stare at our paintings, touch our sculptures, and admire our silver candlesticks in the churches. You will see with new eyes that our old symbols are there for us to grasp and pass on to our brothers and sisters. The friars love you because you are pure and good. Now you must use them to pass on the knowledge to your sisters in the square." She grips Cholita's arm like a bolt of lightning, and in a flash she is gone.

Unlike other visitors who must make a more formal entrance to the convent of San Francisco, Cholita walks silently and meekly. Jovial Friar José stuffs another sweet *turrón* in his already full mouth as he cleans the side entrance to the library in the convent. The friar's eyes light up when he sees Cholita. He pats her head and says in his lisp-laden Castilian, "My shining star is here. What a perfect day our Lord has made! What brings you here, my daughter?"

Cholita explains quietly and precisely that her mistress requests a temporary loan of the convent's Maarten de Vos Immaculate Conception engraved print. Whether the answer is good or bad, she figures it is always best to be humble and she kneels. The friar smiles at her explanation, and tells her to wait. Cholita does not mind the wait at all. From this angle she has a perfect view of her favorite painting of the Immaculate Conception on the first cloister.

In this large canvas, the Virgin Mary wears a red robe and holds a white stole; effusive gold leaf floral stencil patterns adorn both items. Cholita whispers, "Hail, Pachamama," but stops suddenly as she remembers the admonition of the blind woman. She grows quiet and studies the image. The rays that emanate from the Virgin's head form a solid gold disc that is topped off by a circle of luminous stars. Cholita understands the meaning of the sun god immediately, and smiles shyly at her own name, Shining Star. Yes, the stars are the servants of the moon goddess. And there she is: the large white crescent moon. The two angels kneeling at the foot of the Virgin hold flowers and a silver mirror. Cholita understands what the image is telling her. It is late spring and she must prepare for Pawkar Raymi. She must collect flowers and mix them with water from the Machágara River nearby. She will leave the flowers and the water in the patio of the house. Perhaps she can pour a bit of this flower and water on the crown of her *Señora Madre*, Isabel, and say the prayer for good life: "I hope your life blooms like these flowers." Perhaps, then, her mistress might be able to open her heart a little wider and grieve a little less.

Friar José returns and hands Cholita a wrapped print and places two sweets in her coca bag. Cholita stops to pray in the church, although she knows better than to kneel in one of the pews. She kneels instead on the hard, stone floor right below the giant gold sun carved into the ceiling. She looks around and sees so many paintings with the new eyes the blind woman just gave to her. In one painting the Infant Jesus is swaddled in a red, Inca textile pattern cloth, and in another the Christ Child wears the *mascapaycha*, the red-fringed Imperial Inca Crown. In the private chapel of the most important family in Quito is a tiny Child Virgin at the spinning wheel wearing the triangular shawl with the embroidered hems of the Salasaca people who live near the Chimborazo Volcano. Cholita wishes she could stay in church a little while longer to reflect on the symbols of the numerous paintings. She is mesmerized by the small oval painting of Santa Lucia holding her own eyeballs on a silver platter. Cholita feels like she, too, has walked with her eyeballs outside of her head until now. She is so grateful to the blind woman for teaching her how to see the world with different eyes. Cholita knows that it is almost dusk and Chaska, the goddess of dawn and twilight, will watch over her as she rushes back to the workshop holding Isabel's cinnamon sticks and the borrowed print.

After many days of arduous work making pigments and preparing brushes and canvases, in addition to all her housekeeping work, Cholita misses the company of the *gateras*. While Isabel paints, Cholita weaves the alpaca yarn on her back strap loom. Isabel yells at her, "If you don't hurry up and finish the *paño azul* cloth I'm handing you over to Doña Angélica. She knows how to whip you lazy girls into producing at her *obraje*."

It is Isabel's seesaw nature that causes Cholita such anguish. She tries to read her moods, but inevitably Isabel chastises Cholita's kind actions. Cholita feels a creeping tinge of venom entering her own heart just as the poison surged in the *chinas* at church. Cholita hankers to remind Isabel of her own near miss at the clutches of the *paño azul* transporter. A month ago Isabel had returned home in a fury, and recounted the incident in detail.

Don Melchor Bohórquez had greeted Isabel near the marketplace with a reptilian smile. "My dearest lady, pray tell me that you are not walking unaccompanied this morning," he said in his rapid-fire Andalucian Spanish as he tried to push her into a secluded alley.

Isabel quickly demurred. "Don Melchor, thank you for your concern, but my *china* was ill today, and I am in a hurry to get back home."

"My dear widow, may I accompany you home and light a fire in your chilly hearth?"

Isabel wanted to strike him as hard as he was known to flog his muleteers. These poor men traveled thousands of miles across the Andean *cordillera* hauling the famed *paño azul*, quality cloth and alpaca textiles of Quito. Due to their labor Don Melchor acquired tremendous wealth in inverse proportion to his plummeting character. He was the worst type of parvenu: extreme wealth with dismal refinement. His debauchery is notorious; particularly his predilection for younger women of Isabel's class. He is known to promise these maidens marriage just prior to forcibly defiling them. Isabel cannot wait until the day this hairy swine gets his just reward. She imagines him falling to his icy death on the jagged mountain paths northward to the mines in Popayán, preferably thrown off by one of his downtrodden mules. As a *mestiza* must never insult a Spaniard, she mustered a polite, if biting, reply: "No, sir. I treat my workers decently and today my *china* needs my care."

Don Melchor's rowdy howl drew the disapproving attention of the merchants nearby. The proximity of his putrid breath repelled Isabel. He persevered, and said, "My poor widow, allow me to escort you home. I am still quite capable of, how shall I say it, giving comfort both to you and to your *china*."

That day, Cholita quickly served Isabel her favorite cinnamon tea accompanied by steaming, sweet *humitas,* and thanked God that her mistress had not been attacked by this swine.

Cholita's heart swelled with love at hearing Isabel repeat how she told the man that she was in a hurry to return to Cholita who, indeed, was under the weather. Had he hurt her mistress, Cholita thought of all the ways she would get revenge on this man. She could extract the resinous liquid of the Amazonian liana and make *furari.* Cholita pictured the spasms in his chewing muscles followed by his white skin turning blue as the poison swam in his blood. There is no doubt in Cholita's mind that she has the courage to protect her mistress at all costs just as it is Isabel's duty to teach and protect Cholita.

At dawn on the feast of Corpus Christi, Cholita eagerly plans a way to attend the festivities in the square. Quito is ablaze with anticipation of today's festival. Every segment of society has a stake on how its own class will be portrayed in the hierarchy of the procession. Cholita knows that Isabel dreads attending a feast that only serves to remind her of her mediocre standing in society.

Cholita hatches a plan to entice Isabel to attend, and by extension she'll trail along as her attendant. Isabel storms into the workshop and yells, "Why didn't you set up my flowers so

I can continue painting the garland on the little Virgin's painting? You lazy sloth!"

Cholita maintains her head so low that her pointy chin touches her bony clavicle. She doesn't want Isabel to see her sparkling eyes of anticipation. She answers softly so as to not enrage Isabel. "*Su merced,* you are such a talented artist, but perhaps you should not keep it a secret. Everyone in Quito is talking about a young painter, Andrés Mesa Calderón, who is sketching the Corpus Christi processions today. He was at the square yesterday trying to elbow his way into a better location so he could—"

"Shut your monkey mouth, I don't want to hear your gossip," Isabel screams. A couple of seconds later, she adds, "What are the *criollas* saying about his paintings?"

"*Su merced,* they are going to pay him handsomely for his oil paintings of the Corpus Christi processions. I heard that he is going to include Doña Pilar in his painting. She will be at her balcony throwing flowers down onto the procession carts as they pass by." She's embellishing the facts, but how else can she go to the feast?

Isabel silently arranges her canvas; she will not subject herself to any further social mortifications. She slips on her painting smock. Cholita must entice her further and quickly before she dips her brush in the paint. "They say that the painter uses the engraving of Don José Caudí from Spain as his models," Cholita says. "Then he just adds a semblance of the local *ricos.* I overheard a servant of the Royal Scribe, Don Antonio López de Urquía, say that his master thinks the workshop of Maestro Santiago and his talented daughter paint to perfection; much better than this young upstart, *su merced.*"

Isabel arranges her brushes as if about to start painting so Cholita is compelled to lasso Isabel in any way she can. She knows that either Isabel will castigate her or she'll storm out of the house and head to the square. Cholita chooses her words carefully. "Friar Félix has the engraved prints of Don Caudí and he told me that he would let your highness use them to show everyone in Quito the supremacy and high class of your workshop."

Isabel jumps up. "Get me my *vicuña* black shawl; we're going to the feast,"

The women arrive at the square and Cholita finds a cool shady corner where Isabel will be inconspicuous. Cholita stands atop a gunnysack of potatoes that one of the *gateras* lets her use as a stepladder. She fans Isabel so she doesn't get too warm and leave before the festivities commence. Soon they see the arrival of the *caciques*, the indigenous nobility, wearing their combined costumes that were neither native nor Spanish. The Inca nobles attempt to include some of the Spanish attire, such as breeches, so the Spaniards would understand that they are *machos* and not weak. They also wear brightly colored feathers to remind the indigenous people that they are high-status members of society. The indigenous audience understands the irony of the costumes, which signify neither resistance nor acquiescence. The head *cacique* wears the *mascaypacha,* the Imperial Inca tassel head-dress. He also dons a Flemish lace tunic, which together with the headdress is a riddle to the indigenous crowd. Some see it as a reminder that he still rules over them, even though he usurped the title from the deserving *cacique*. Others wonder if the *cacique* is admitting his subordination to the Spaniards or if he is reminding the native people that the head rules the body.

The Spaniards and *criollos* wait anxiously for the procession carts to make the rounds. As the procession continues with all the various guilds and brotherhoods parading and carrying their respective saint sculptures, Isabel sketches rapidly.

She notices the upstart painter under a nearby balcony also sketching Doña Pilar, who is leaning a bit too forward out of her balcony balustrade. A company of obstreperous, military macaws circles the plaza. Their red forehead feathers mock the *mascaypacha* of the Imperial Inca headdress. Their cries overpower the native musicians and they scare Doña Pilar, who falls from her balcony onto the spectators below.

Isabel laughs excitedly. She whispers in Cholita's ear, and her young page runs to the side of the upstart artist.

She taps him respectfully on his forearm and says, "The artist Doña Isabel Santiago would like to offer you her sketch of Doña Pilar's mighty fall. She said to tell you to use concentrated cow urine to make the correct shade of yellow for the condition of Doña Pilar's bloomers as she fell from her balcony."

Isabel and Cholita hustle out of the square and giggle like young girls on their walk home. They stop briefly to visit Isabel's old aunts in the cloistered convent of Santa Catalina to buy some of their delicious honey made from the *ñagcha* yellow flowers. Isabel knocks on the iron enforced gate of the *zahuán* and asks to speak with her aged aunts. Her aunts' elder brothers have kept them cloistered for decades in this monastery, as they were perceived too ugly and dull to waste any of the family's dwindling wealth on their respective dowries. Together they succumbed to the daily, monotonous comfort of religious life. Each brought her *chinas* to the monastery, along with certain family heirloom paintings, silver candlesticks, and their precious emerald and pearl jewelry. The eldest of the two, Sister Santa Cruz, still reads the most current literature from Seville, and the younger nun continues to embroider and sell her delicate linens. The sisters at this convent survived the decade-long battle over jurisdiction with the Dominican friars. The wagging tongues of Quito say that Sister Santa Cruz took a beating from the ill-tempered friars that bruised her head to toe, but she never capitulated.

Isabel wishes she could see the tenacious faces of her great-aunts, as she is only able to hold their cold, waxy hands under the dividing wood grill of the *parlatorio,* the waiting room. Sister Santa Cruz asks Isabel in a formal tongue, "Dearest Isabelita, my teeny niece, can thou paint me an itty-bitty, oval-shaped, oil painting of the *Divine Shepherdess*? Make the Blessed Virgin as a charming wee shepherdess caring for her flock."

"I would be honored to paint this for thee, but it will be a small oval composition. Would thou like such a painting?" Isabel asks, equally formal.

Sister Santa Cruz squeezes Isabel's hands and says, "I do miss the green pastures of my bitty youth. Can thou please include many wooly sheep, bleating their *Ave Marias* gleefully? Oh, and can thou paint a weensy Archangel Michael in the heavens protecting the sheep?"

Sister Santa Cruz perseveres with other details, but Isabel interrupts with a request of her own. "I would love to accommodate all the details thou would like to admire in the composition, but our teeny atelier costs me a fortune to operate. Would thou gift me the wee emerald earrings that thou can never wear again, sweet Auntie?"

The elderly nun's hands freeze with a feigned stiffness of death, and she floats out of the *parlatorio,* without any further comment. In her silence, the nun's loud response is obvious. She's saying, "You are not worthy of my emerald earrings."

Isabel fights her impending dark mood. She clasps Cholita's warmhearted hand as they walk up the hill to their home. Cholita's love for the world transmits from her heart to Isabel, who doesn't even smell the approaching slaughterhouse. She only smells the rosy fragrance of Doña Pilar's poetic justice. As soon as they enter the sheltering gates of their own *zahuán,* Cholita lights the candles of the altar and thanks Pachamama for giving her the best day of her life.

The next morning Cholita wants to show her love for Isabel. After setting up the paints and the canvases, she runs to the ravine to pick up a range of orchids for the painting Isabel could not complete the day before.

As Isabel steps in the workshop, she yells, "Why did you place those ordinary orchids near my painting, you imbecile?"

Cholita cowers in a corner. "But *Señora Madre,* these orchids have a range of colors without equal in the world. I think that the obsidian vampire orchid would contrast beautifully with the spotted yellow orchid. You are a talented artist and can paint the orchids without following any paper drawings. Why don't you try it?"

Isabel wavers, but does not give in to the temptation. Instead, she snaps at Cholita. "Get me the correct shade of red, now."

Cholita scampers to the pigment cabinet. She knows the exact shade of red Isabel wants. It is the red of the male Andean cock-of-the-rock that she sees daily in the ravines of Quito. These feisty birds eat the ill-omened frogs, so she loves to watch them show off the red plumage on their heads. The male birds engage in aerial battles that make Cholita wish the men in her clan had fought the invaders to their lands with equal success. Although 50,000 died and still inhabit the bloody bottom of Lake Yaguarcocho near her hometown, it was not enough to stop the invaders. Cholita remembers her mother telling her that the men of their race face defeat because they are worked more severely than beasts of burden, but that Pachamama gave woman her own life force.

Isabel's mood is dark and unpredictable. Without hesitation, she throws a wadded wet rag at Cholita's damaged cheek. "Don't tell me any more stories about the raised scar on your cheek," she says, out of nowhere. "It does not look like a crescent moon with two white stars, you moron. Those idiotic *gateras* just tell you that so you will give them some of your worthless herbs. Now go and gather the indigo leaves for the pigment I need, and be back before dusk."

Cholita knows that she must run if she is to be back before dusk. While on the narrow road she hears the wheels of a cart and mule approaching, so she gets out of the way. She notices that the man driving the cart is a light-skinned *mestizo* who could almost pass for a Spaniard except that he has no facial hair and speaks to her in a patois of Quichua and Castilian. Two women are riding on top of some burlap sacks in the cart, and Cholita recognizes them from the market plaza. The man is dressed like a local cowboy, a *chullu,* so he must work in one of the nearby haciendas. The women tell her that they are also going her way so she might as well rest her feet for the walk back home. Cholita gives them all a toothy smile and climbs into the cart. During the ride Cholita tells the women that she is afraid to gather the indigo plants because they are tall and crowded and she can get lost in the wild indigo fields. The women tell her to wait until tomorrow when they can help her, but Cholita is afraid of what Isabel will do to her if she arrives home empty-handed.

By the indigo fields Cholita jumps off the cart and waves goodbye to the women. She runs to the shrubs and quickly cuts the blooms and stalks from the periphery, avoiding the depths of the forbidding vegetation. She bends down to tie a hemp rope around the plant bundle when suddenly two strong hands lift her and throw her like a small sack of potatoes into the thickset shrubs. She tries to scream, but the *chullu* from the cart crushes her throat with his forearm. He bears down on her frail body repeatedly like a savage boar. She feels his teeth like brittle tusks biting her shoulder and his stubbly face scratching her delicate neck. Within minutes the *chullu* finishes his pummeling. He grinds her scarred cheek into the rocky mud and growls,

"Be grateful that I don't end your pathetic life, you damaged rat. No man would ever look at you twice with that horrible scar." The pain between her legs is unbearable, so she tries to squeeze herself into a tight ball that can roll down the ravine and sink into the river below.

In a matter of minutes, Cholita hears women's voices calling, "Shining Star, *ñañita,* we're coming to help you. Make some noise so we can find you!" She hears the scratching sound of their panicky, running feet and she hears their horrified whispering. One voice then another: "We should have suspected his motives when he abruptly dropped us off and turned his wagon around," says one. The other one laments. "She was just a young indigo-gathering virgin."

The women's words help Cholita understand the tragedy that has befallen her. She keeps repeating what the second woman said: she was just a young virgin. Cholita looks to the dusky sky, but the moon is fully hidden tonight, and she realizes that even Mama Quilla is ashamed of her. She doesn't want the market women to find her, so she picks up her bundle of indigo branches and drags herself painfully along the gully near the road. Perhaps once she's home and Isabel beats her, she can blame her cuts and bruises on the beating. Perhaps no one will find out that she is no longer a virgin of the sun. Perhaps she might die overnight and the *gateras* will mourn another lost maiden.

For the next few weeks, Cholita weaves endlessly. Despite her discretion, the loathsome *chullu* has boasted of his conquest, and word has spread of the attack. When she runs errands at the market place, the women now simply call her little sister, *ñañita,* not Shining Star. She overhears the *quínoa* seller say, "She was our pure nectar."

Cholita keeps her eyes cast down and responds morosely. She waits for a sign from Pachamama as to what she should do next, but to no avail. She tries to talk to Isabel about the incident, but Isabel—who has also heard the gossip and feels angry and ashamed of Cholita—cuts her off mid-sentence. "Don't cause me any problems," she says. "Your word means nothing against a Spaniard's testimony." After a silence, she adds, "If the rain is determined to fall, one cannot will it to yield. Accept this truism, you worthless, useless girl."

As is the tradition in the highlands, Cholita had immediately burned the clothes she was wearing the night of the attack. She had pointed her finger at the rainbow in disrespect, but she did not die. The night of the attack she burned the clump of hair she yanked from the rapist, and mixed it with corn meal, blowing the evil mixture to the four winds so that the rapist disappears with the winds. But the rapist still lurches around the plaza with an unfazed lecherous smile, much to the consternation of the feisty *gateras*.

Unbeknownst to Cholita, the *gateras* devise their secret revenge on her behalf.

The rapist has been asking the *gateras* for reduced prices on mineral salt. He's planning to take the salt to Popayán to sell to miners who use it to extract silver from ore. The *gateras* never say a word to each other but they know what to do; they instinctively form a ferocious hornet's nest. Before dusk, as they are gathering their wares, they offer the *chullu* a cup of spiked *chicha*. As he begins to get drowsy, the *gateras* walk with him to the outskirts of town, by the river. He thinks that he is going to partake of another young virgin girl; instead the *gateras* gash him deeply and repeatedly, and roll him down the ravine knowing that by morning the condors will have devoured him beyond recognition. But Cholita does not know that the *gateras* have rallied around her. She does not know the rapist has been punished as if by the moon goddess herself. She feels only that she is alone, spoiled, no longer special, indeed worthless.

Isabel feels off-balance without Cholita's constant cheerful comments. She asks her: "Cholita, how should I paint the hands of Sor Juana de Jesús? The bishop wants her to look like a saint."

Cholita's reply is barely audible. "You know I don't know anything about painting, Señora," she says, and returns to her weaving.

Isabel, for once, does not yell; she simply stares quietly and sadly at Cholita.

Cholita is grateful that Isabel has not sent her on errands the last few days. There is one thing that Cholita knows she can do, knows she *must* do, and she methodically carries out the task. She makes a small brush of squirrel hairs and prepares a small amount of *cochineal* blood-red paint. She takes Isabel's mirror and the Maarten de Vos engraved print, and stuffs these items along with two guinea pigs in her coca bag. Finally, she mixes a brew of Angel's Trumpet tea. She grooms herself in the manner that she had been accustomed to before she was defiled, and she sets off for the monastery of San Francisco. Before going up the stone steps, she finds the blind woman and gives her two guinea pigs and her alpaca shawl, and asks her for her blessing.

The wrinkled old woman raises her arthritic hands and waves them in the air like a condor's wings in front of Cholita. She says, "*Quilla Punchalla, Kalpashum nukanchik wasiman.*" Her hands cup Shining Star's face as the old woman repeats: we will fly home together.

As usual, none of the friars notice her arrival. She silently walks up to the second cloister and constructs a makeshift ladder from a wooden bench and a box so that she can reach the red-robed Immaculate Conception painting. She prays in front of the lower half of the painting and asks the moon goddess to guide her home to the sun. Cholita has been studying Isabel for

five years while she paints, so she confidently brushes a stroke
of red paint along the heel of the graceful foot peering from the
robe of the Immaculate Conception. This is a detail Cholita has
always felt this Inca goddess was missing.

As Cholita climbs to the belfry she consumes the rest of the
Angel's Trumpet tea. She recites the virtues of the Immaculate
Conception in a hodgepodge of words and languages. She says,
"I'm climbing the ladder of Jacob to reach the sun."

Fearlessly, she crawls along the clay tiles of the highest
rooftop and finds the spot where she can see the Pichincha
Volcano and it can see her tiny, framed body. She continues
with her recitation of virtues: *et macula non est in te*, and there is
no spot in thee, like Friar José recites. While lying down on the
convex tiles she takes a shard of the mirror and repeats, "You are
a spotless mirror, spotless mirror, spotless mirror," as she cuts
her wrists.

The poison she has consumed makes her wings grow
strong. She's barely whispering, but she hears herself bellow,
"*Kalpashunchikmi wasiman tantanajushpa!*" Let's fly together, she
shrieks to her alpaca in the sky.

In her bony hand, she still holds the engraved print.
She tries to unfurl it to gaze at the goddess one last time, but it
flutters away. She smiles at the condor circling above, and tells
him, "*Kalpashunchikmi wasiman tantanajushpa!*" Let's fly together.

The sun's rays warm her body. "*Araray*," she murmurs.
It's so warm. "*Kushilla llukshi juni.*" I'm so happy leaving.

March 22, 2008

Laguna Beach, California

Maxime CCXXX

To open one's Eyes when it is time

All who see, have not their Eyes open;
nor do all that look see..

Oráculo Manual y Arte de
Prudencia
By Baltasar Gracián
1647

III

When I arrived home from Serra Chapel, I locked myself in my library. I began my search for the 17th century Quito artist Isabel Santiago with my social history texts on the lives of women in colonial Quito. I spent hours with these women reading about their legal rights, their political activities, and all the minutia of public and private life. I eventually accepted that these kinds of books would take me nowhere near painting or the fine arts. I put those books back on the shelf with the lives of all those women, mostly domestic and generic, and looked elsewhere for my answer.

My Ecuadorian art history book collection is extensive, and I scoured all the sources for any mention of Isabel. Her name was always cited in conjunction with her famous father, Miguel de Santiago. Their work might have become conflated over the years, collectors preferring to think the famous father was the author of a work, but my painting is not attributed to either of them.

Miguel is credited by all sources as the premier Quito painter of that era. Unlike Dutch painter Vincent Van Gogh who cut off a piece of his own ear, Miguel Santiago cut off his wife's ear instead and was sentenced to prison. But an exception can always be made for a celebrity, and the parsimonious monks at the convent of St. Augustine saw an opportunity, divinely inspired I am sure, and came up with an alternative time of contemplation and penance: they would hide him while he painted. Miguel was safe, but trapped in the monastery; he fell into a deep depression. His canvas "*El Invierno*" depicts his personal despondency in the figure of the old, decrepit angel of winter. While in this artistic halfway house of the soul, Miguel's remaining family members perished.

All except for Isabel.

His only surviving heir was his widowed and childless daughter. Isabel took over all his commissions, and she painted. She did exist. She did paint. I found it difficult to be disappointed despite my situation. I would not wish this woman out of existence. She was childless, no heirs, so the horrible phone call of a few days ago remained a hoax. But why? My tormentors must have known Isabel had no heirs. So why the phone call? Why the note?

I pulled out my magnifying glass to analyze the photographs of all the paintings attributed to Miguel de Santiago. I used this heavy magnifier frequently, but still it made me feel like a detective, a little like a spy. A handful of images are attributed to Isabel. I am proud of her. Her work has survived her.

I closed my last book on Ecuadorian art history, and was about to place it back in its home on a shelf, but I couldn't. Putting the books away felt like putting the mystery of the phone call and the note to rest, but I needed to follow this trail to the end, and it was a trail. It was a map. I needed to make that map a physical thing, something I could touch and know everything that was happening was real. I took back down one of my books on the lives of women in Colonial Quito and put it on the corner of my usually uncluttered desk. This was the first piece of the puzzle. I placed an index card on top of it that read, "Ecuadorian Women." Next was the book on Ecuadorian art history. This one got a card that said, "Isabel Santiago, Painter." My first two books were like beautiful paving stones pressed together on my desk, a path leading me somewhere. Next, knowing that Quito artists of this era looked to Flemish engraved prints as sources for their own paintings, I started digging through my books on Flemish prints. Lupe knows not to clear away what I leave on my desk, but I made a mental note to remind her not to disturb my mounting pile of clues and leads. I was gathering intelligence. I had created a war room from which to plan.

After three days I found no connection between Isabel Santiago and my Spanish Colonial paintings. Neither were any of the engraved Flemish prints those of the Immaculate Conception. I hadn't realized I'd been holding my breath while looking at the Marian images attributed to the Santiago's *père et fille*. My Immaculate Conception paintings did not appear in any of the sources. Proof that I am most definitely not an art thief. Satisfied that Isabel did not have an heir, and that she did not paint any of my paintings, my Flemish prints book got the spot next to Ecuadorian art history, and a card that said, "Source Prints."

That dispensed with the horrid phone call. But I am still bothered by the note. That was a threat, and there was the more explicit threat of the dark-haired couple, the slice the man made across his neck with his finger before boarding the train. My paintings are safe, but my reputation is still under threat until I know who is doing this.

When I cannot solve the mystery of who sent me the toxic note, I open all the windows of my house and allow the ocean breezes to clear my mind. I ignore the sheets of paper with my convoluted flowcharts of possible suspects as they flutter aimlessly in the wind. I do not try to gather them. Instead, I join the harmonious zephyr with the close embrace of a tango *milonguero*. Chest to chest, I inhale the salty gusts with a syncopated rhythm, still full of confusion over the threatening note, and the more ominous hand gestures of the train riders. My head snaps with the push and pull of the *bandoneón*-like blast of Laguna Beach air.

I close my eyes and breathe in deeply, letting the longer elegant steps of air lead me. The lush and grandiose sounds of the *bahia blanca* tango breezes work their magic. The composer of this tango, which he named after the white bay of his hometown, must have been entranced by its ocean breezes as I am to those of my own bay. Bay denizens everywhere rely on the curative powers of their own salty air.

I spend nearly two hours in isolation and silent communion with the sun and sea before the knock on the door. Solitude is a refuge of strength when one is often under siege in the world. I am asked to translate for strangers on a daily basis. I try to be polite, to be of service as best I can. But there are so many of them, and I am never left alone. I am thinking of this now, because Dr. Ochanda Arnaz is here, and as much as I hate to admit it, she always wants something. Maybe she will help me today instead. As a curator and an author, maybe she will have some insight into what could be gained by accusing a private collector of having a stolen piece.

When Ochanda and I first met she was a hapless undergraduate interviewing for one of three college scholarships I give annually. Everything about her was awkwardness. She stumbled over the greeting, not knowing if she should shake my hand, and having no idea how to address me. She called me "Mrs. Zubiondo" before blushing and saying, "I mean, Señora Zubiondo." I stepped forward and took her hand, kissed her on each cheek, and said, "Please, call me Paloma." That was eleven years ago. I always thought my financial generosity toward my scholarship recipients would result in some eventual token of gratitude, but it has not yet transpired. Ochanda is the one recipient with whom I have developed some attachment. I began as her patron and mentor, but over the years we became friends.

Today she is here for brunch, and I have a gift for her. There is much riding on this gift.

Giving the perfect gift says: I know you and I understand you. It's an acknowledgement of our common interests and the things that bind us to one another. There has been distance between us lately. Ochanda hasn't had time for me. But today we will sit over tea on the loggia, and I will tell her the story of how I found her present, and we will grow close again as the waves and the breeze dance the *bahia blanca* tango for us. If she doesn't notice the rhythm of the water, I will point it out to her, because I know she likes to tango. She has even taken lessons.

I exit the melodic whirlwind, and I am calm, energized, and ready to enjoy the company of my thirty-three-year-old former protégée. I greet Ochanda with my usual two-cheek-kiss, but I sense she is put off by this ritual. She says, "Hi, Paloma. I hope you don't mind, but the 405 freeway from Santa Monica was awful, and now I'm running late for my meeting in San Diego. So, I'll have to leave in just a bit."

I escort her to my loggia where Lupe has brunch ready for the two of us. Ochanda is dressed in a matte, granite-grey jersey dress that accentuates her slim body. She moves gracefully despite the stiletto python heels. She has become a fashionista as

I am, so I approve of the thought she's given to her attire. As we sit down facing the beach, I ask, "May I pour you a glass of hibiscus tea from Oaxaca? I know how much you love—"

We are interrupted by her cell phone. She waves a one-fingered no, points to her ringing cell phone, and walks toward my beach gate for privacy while she speaks with the caller. I am beginning to hate telephones. Her shoulder-length black hair glistens in the sun, and her naturally tanned skin has a healthy glow that makes me happy to see her so vibrant. On the other hand, I hear her voice, and it is too shrill and loud for someone who tries to present herself as a confident and measured professional.

After a couple of minutes, she returns to the table and does not even apologize for her rudeness. I overlook this behavior and decide she is under some job stress. Perhaps she needs my advice, and this is the reason for her last-minute visit this morning. I ask her, "How is your book on Oaxacan textiles coming along?"

"Oh, it's in its final revision, and should be published by the university press in the fall."

I congratulate her, and try to bring the conversation back to Oaxaca since she has spent so much time in this historic Mexican city. Ochanda is an expert on the textile history of this region, with an emphasis on the natural dyes the indigenous weavers continue to use on a range of fibers. Last summer I underwrote her research trip to both Oaxaca and to Otavalo, Ecuador, which is another significant pre-Hispanic textile center.

With my prodding, she planned to undertake a comparative analysis of the history and significance of the *cochineal* red used by Oaxacan back strap loom weavers, and the natural dying techniques of the almost extinct, hand-made, indigo dyers of Otavalo. Ochanda seemed intensely interested in traveling to Ecuador to collect the necessary data. She even asked me to let her borrow the Inca patterned belts, *chumpi*, I inherited from my great-aunt. For years I had kept them in a *repoussé* silver box from Bolivia in my dressing room. How I cherished shaking the box, lifting the lid by the silver angel handle, and peeking in to see how the *chumpi* had rearranged themselves to show their less exhibitionistic, obverse side.

Ochanda said that if she wore my great-aunt's *chumpi* often before her journey, they would be her personal amulets to keep her on track on this new study. She wrapped one multicolored geometric twill *chumpi* to show me how striking it looked against her narrow black skirt. I enjoyed the combination of the modern skirt and the ancient textiles. It looked so right on her, and I felt vindicated in my belief that her dedication to indigenous textiles was the same as the duty I felt towards my paintings. I had put my scholarship money and my time to good use. I imagined Ochanda would rise to the top of her profession and at the right moment thank me for making it all possible. I was building my own legacy a brick at a time. I even convinced myself that through my connection to Ochanda more of the past could be uncovered and preserved, sent to the future in the time capsule. My work could continue beyond me.

Ultimately, she did not take the work quite as seriously as I do. Perhaps she is simply too young to feel a sense of urgency. Most of us think we have plenty of time. Marrying a much older man changed that for me. On anniversaries, I counted in both directions. How many years has it been? How many more will there be? I wonder if he taught me to live this way, or if it was what drew me to him. I have always thought about what would happen after his death. I have always asked myself: what is the legacy of a woman without children? Shortly after Ochanda modeled my *chumpi* with her black skirt, I lent her three others. She called from New York City distraught because she had left them in a cab. They would never be found.

When Ochanda finally arrived in Otavalo, she emailed me such vibrant and discerning photographs of the secretive indigo dyers as they showed her how they ferment their intense purple-blue dyes. After a museum board of directors meeting, I proudly showed her photos to the curator, who was genuinely impressed. I wanted to get her something that would mean as much to her as those photos had meant to me. When next I traveled to Oaxaca, I traipsed from one textile workshop to another looking for the precise weave and color. Since Ochanda has a doctorate in art history, I wanted to select a *huipil* with an important weave motif and a complex use of color worthy of an art piece.

I thought that since the prominent color of the *huipil* is the deepest shade of *cochineal* red, she as an art historian would understand the symbolism of the color. In the Mazatec region, the color red correlates with the north. Since she is third-generation Mexican American, but still remains intrigued by the culture of her ancestors, she should have understood this personal meaning. What had caught my eye about this specific *huipil* was the butterfly motif of the weave. A local myth is that the butterfly is the soul of the departed who have returned on *Día de los Muertos*. Since Ochanda's ancestors immigrated north to the United States during the Mexican Revolution of 1910, I thought she would be captivated by the correlation of all these historical threads woven into her *huipil* and made physical. Threads. My research of the last several days makes me think this is the most apt metaphor for women's lives, and not because of any domestic connotation, but because finding Isabel Santiago and her work was less an act of discovery than it was an untangling of the facts. Maybe this is a strategy I can use. Look for the places where the threads overlap and unweave them.

I found out a few months ago that Ochanda had hired a photographer from Quito to take the photographs and email them to me while she was perfecting her tango for three weeks in Buenos Aires on the stipend I provided. It had not been my intention to purchase either photographs or dance lessons. When I brought these two misjudgments to Ochanda's attention, she dismissed them as minor *contretemps*.

Banishing these past misunderstandings from today's *al fresco* brunch, I enthusiastically tell Ochanda, "I was in Oaxaca for *Día de los Muertos*, the Day of the Dead, back in November, and I bought you a lovely *huipil*." I attempt to hand her a blood red, hand-loomed dress from the Mazatec region of Oaxaca. She smiles, keeps her hands by her cell phone, and does not take the gift from me. I set the *huipil* gently on the empty chair to my left. And I sit there. She sips her water, glances at the ocean. The *huipil* memorializing her personal journey and that of her ancestors flaps in the wind as if to wave and get her attention. Ingratitude is monstrous. This maxim rushes into my mind unbidden like a bursting blood vessel. I wonder momentarily if blood is pooling in my ear.

I do my best. I steer the conversation back to her career. "Will you be lecturing back in Oaxaca this fall?"

"No, I'm trying to structure a lecture ..."

She does not finish her sentence. She is looking down at her cell phone on her lap, which she has tucked under one of my brightly hand-embroidered napkins. Ochanda is obviously texting while trying, and failing, to carry on a conversation with me. This is common behavior everywhere I go. I have even witnessed retired executives tapping away at their cell phones rather than concentrating on the museum's board of directors' issues. But texting during our private meal, in my own home, with my protégée, whom I have supported through her under-graduate and graduate studies, seems particularly boorish.

I sip the deliciously tangy hibiscus tea and wait for Ochanda to realize we are both silent and disengaged. Even the normally vociferous seagulls fly silently overhead. Ochanda is not providing either the information or the distraction I hoped she would. Other things are creeping into my head. I can't take my eyes off the delicate saucers on my table. I love them, and I don't know why they make me sad. I watch Ochanda's black hair dance in the breeze, I rub my finger around the edge of my saucer and I am back on the day I see my nanny Esperanza, even younger than Ochanda but with the same glistening dark hair, on her knees in front of my parents. She was begging them. I was spying from the door. I didn't hear what any of them said, but they dismissed her, sent her from the room. Her shoulders sagged and she was slow in rocking back on her feet and rising from the floor. She put her head up then, which seemed strange to me because she didn't often look at my parents so directly. I know now that look was defiance in the face of betrayal. I didn't know her father had promised her to an older man, and Esperanza had hoped my parents would protect her. She had lived in our house as my nanny since she was so young herself; perhaps she expected the protection of a daughter. She had misunderstood their relationship.

Looking at Ochanda, I try to break the spell of the distant past and concentrate on her. I recall the girl she was 11 years ago when I interviewed her. Since she seemed very nervous, I asked her to tell me about her unusual first name. She said, "My grandmother is Mexican, but her grandmother was Basque, so she named me after a mythological female wolf since she wanted me to be strong, determined and fearless."

I remember the gleam in her eye when she said "determined." So I asked her, "Are you determined to finish college?"

Her smile was so genuine when she said, "Your scholarship would mean everything to me, Mrs. Zubiondo. You won't regret helping me."

I saw Ochanda frequently in the first couple of years of her college career, but as she continued with her graduate program, she often found an excuse to cancel our monthly dinner meetings. However, she did have a knack for contacting me whenever she needed additional financial support for the seminars and special programs she wanted to attend. I was offended by her brazenness, but I always acquiesced. I knew when I let her in that she was a wolf. How could I punish that part of her when it was what I first admired?

Today, I hope once she concludes her texting, I might get her opinion on the telephone call and note I received three days ago. I would like to hear her educated analysis and her advice for me now that she is a mature and well-educated woman. As I wait for Ochanda to finish texting, I self-consciously adjust the center piece on our table. I am shamelessly trying to draw her attention to the whimsical *alebrijes*, the copal wood carvings from the village of San Martin Tilcajete in Oaxaca. It was carved for me in the shape of the she-wolf of Romulus and Remus fame. I remember telling the carver about my young protégée's name. Ochanda does not notice the *alebrije's* connection to her name, or she chooses not to comment. I give up pretending to fiddle with it. I thought she was in love, as I am, with the connections between things, but here she is a few feet from me and able to create such distance, unable to connect with anything.

Ochanda clears her throat, and seems only slightly embarrassed by her lapse, but she continues, "I've been asked to present a paper at a national meeting in Washington D.C., so I won't be going back to Oaxaca. As a matter of fact, I was hoping that you might want to attend." I am so surprised and delighted by her invitation I nearly gasp with relief. She still wants to include me in her life. For a moment I am both honored patron and proud parent. I'm already thinking of schedules and airline tickets. "I hope that you will be able to underwrite a multimedia presentation I want to utilize at this meeting," she says. "It will be something you can be proud of, with such a wow factor that it will make all the right people at the national level notice me. Do you think that you could underwrite it, Paloma?"

I push away the instinct to feel like an ATM machine, which is how I'm afraid she sees me now. There is more at stake here for her than not getting her funding, though she doesn't know it. Perhaps I have neglected her education too much, entrusted it too much to others? I thought she understood innately when she told me about her name so proudly. I thought she understood the difference between valuable and expensive. Expensive will cost you, and not in any of the languages I speak is there any such thing as a "wow factor."

This young woman has a doctorate and a name that would not appeal to the producers of reality shows, and discounting the ubiquitous cell phone, she looks nothing like her, but there is a Lindsay at her edges. Was it there the last time, or is this a new addition to her personality? She is a hybrid now, an intellectual ambitious Lindsay who still doesn't value the right things. Do I have the right to decide what is of value in the world? Does anyone? Isn't that what Ochanda does as a curator? Decide what is worth keeping? Am I losing hope for her, or for myself that my project didn't turn out as well as I wanted? Is it hubris to consider a person a project? All I want for her is quality, success, excellence, significance. In these things I assumed she would find happiness. Perhaps it was just another one of my sun-induced delusions thinking I could choose to keep children from my life. They find me anyway and gather to themselves the power to make me proud or disappoint and confuse me, or break my heart.

"Let me think about it," I say. "In the meantime, I would like your opinion about an unusual telephone call I received."

As I start to reveal the facts about the bizarre telephone call, I notice that again, Ochanda is texting and not listening to me at all. I am embarrassed to utter the word sex-slave in front of her. She doesn't notice my discomfort, and I don't think anything I have said is registering with her. Ochanda remains engrossed in her texting. I feel like I am the girl on the phone. I don't understand why no one will answer. No one is listening. I can't connect. I have never felt so confined out here on the loggia surrounded by beauty and the negatively charged ions of the fresh ocean breeze. It makes people feel good, but I feel like I'm choking. I cough, and excuse myself from the table. I tell her I'm going to the kitchen to refill the tea pitcher. Did she nod her head? Half-smile? I can't tell because she hasn't lifted her face. Where is that awkward girl who wanted so badly to greet me the right way?

From my kitchen window, I look out towards the white-water waves crashing by my deck. I see a man peering through my beach gate. Curious passersby will do this once in a while, but I'm alarmed when I see his hand turning the door handle. Thankfully, it is locked. I grab my binoculars on the kitchen counter and focus on the man. I gasp: it's Alfredo's distorted face. I refocus the binoculars but Alfredo is nowhere near my house.

Ochanda is now speaking to someone on her cell, and has her car keys and purse in hand, ready to leave. My visit with Ochanda in the ocean air has made two things clear: I know that I must talk to someone about the hysterical caller, the threatening note, and now Alfredo. I will have no peace until I know who is out there and what they really want. And second, I chose the wrong person to talk to. Ochanda is not who I thought she was. I got our relationship wrong, but it is not her fault.

I text my lifelong friend, Jen, who lives in Los Angeles. I should have done this in the first place.

"Feeling untethered. Unusual experiences lately. Need your opinion. Can I come over and spend the night? Will you pick me up at Union Station?" Jen's immediate text response both reassures and puzzles me.

"SLAP. UR my BFF. CFN."

I am gratified I was heard and answered so quickly, but I have no idea what these acronyms mean. Jen and I are the same age, but she is current and hip, which are things I am not often accused of. She knows about popular music and social networking. In that world, Jen translates for me. I am heartened by the thought of spending time with the electrifying Jen.

Ochanda is now standing in my kitchen tapping her toe with impatience. She says, "I really have to go now. Thanks for brunch, Paloma. When will you be able to let me know about underwriting my presentation?"

I respond, "Well, Ochanda, I would love to think about it. But for now, what does this text message mean?"

She looks bothered and quickly answers, "It means: Sounds like a plan. You're my best friend forever, Ciao for now." She adds, "And, I have to say ciao, too. Oh, by the way Paloma, I prefer for people to call me Andy now. It's not as foreign-sounding as Ochanda, and since I'm determined to get a high-level post on the East Coast, I don't want my name to be an impediment of any kind."

I am reminded of cultures where people have real names to keep secret and false names for everyday use. The true name contains power and is guarded closely. This wolf-woman has dropped her secret name on the floor in my kitchen like a dish towel and may step on it with her snakeskin heel on the way out. An expensive choice. I hope it doesn't cost her too much. I will preserve her secret name here with my other treasures and keep it safe against the day she will want it back again. I know she will want it back some day, and I forgive her in advance for leaving without the red dress, which is currently dancing a gentle tango with the sea from its chair on my loggia. I watch the dress from the kitchen window for a long time after she leaves. I imagine the ancient dyes, the patterns, the hues infused in this garment responding to their counterparts in the sea. Chest to chest. It's beautiful, and I'm glad she left the dress. It would have been sad and confused to be forgotten in the back seat of a Washington D.C. taxi cab.

I think about her beautiful discarded name and all it means and now more than ever, I think that the name Ochanda suits her perfectly. She's become so fierce and feral that she would bite the hand that feeds her. No regrets—just pure animal instinct. I still wish her the best in her career, but I realize that our relationship is strictly a monetary one. I am to Ochanda what Esperanza was to my parents: a means to an end.

The word "impediment" is tugging at me as if once again I have missed something. This is the feeling I had in Serra Chapel when I knew there was something off about the dark-haired couple pretending to pray at St. Peregrine's Altar. There was a time when I underwrote a presentation for Ochanda. I searched the program for some mention of my support, but it was missing. It is customary to acknowledge a project's funding, and at that point I had considered her a friend. I was expecting something a little more personal than the usual corporate thanks. I wrote the omission off to inexperience and immaturity at the time, but perhaps she knew what she was doing even then. Maybe she already had the East Coast and her high-level position in mind. Could it be possible that Paloma Zubiondo was too "foreign-sounding"? Have I become an impediment in her mind? I remember young Ochanda's stumbling greeting when we first met, the way she tried calling me *Señora* as a bid for solidarity, and I realize Ochanda came to me already understanding the power of names.

The chasm between Ochanda cannot be closed. I need Jen and her sage interpretations. Who did Esperanza have to turn to when my parents turned out to be only her employers and not the family she took them for? I am ashamed when I realize she had only me. It's an irrational feeling. I was only a child of five, but she asked to be saved, and no one helped her. I did nothing to save her. What could I do?

I return to my library to gather some of the art history books I would like to share with Jen. Perhaps Jen's clear insight and good judgment about people will help me determine if the caller's claims of being held as a sex-slave could be true even though I am no longer in doubt about the provenance of my painting. Jen is like the red-tailed hawks in the canyons. She has the keen sight to detect danger and the sharp talons to get things done. And like the hawks, whose tail feathers do not turn vibrant brick-red until they are very mature, Jen's wisdom intensifies with age. But don't be fooled by age and grace and beauty. The elegant hawk can generate sixty-five pounds of pressure with its talons. That's enough force to crush a mouse or a rabbit, or any bone in the human body. The red hawk can act in defense of herself or another. And that is Jen. She saves people. Jen is saving the world one person at a time and she plans to get to everyone eventually. I have told her on numerous occasions that her goal is unrealistic. Her answer is always the same.

"It's not a goal," she says. "It's a plan."

"It's a plan with no chance of succeeding," I say.

"It works for me," she says.

"Incorrigible."

"I love you too." She usually finds a way to kiss the top of my head at this point. That's my Jen, and that's what I need.

As I am closing all the windows of my house, my private telephone line rings. Thinking it is Jen confirming my train arrival time, I pick up the receiver without thinking. I've forgotten to be afraid of that thing. I hear the same antiquated Andean-Castilian of my childhood, but it's a different voice this time, and I really do not understand all the specific words. The caller is female; the voice is mature, sonorous, and trembling. My response is automatic: *"Esperanza, Esperanzita? Sois vos en el aparato?"* When there is time for shock, I realize have said, "Esperanza, little Esperanza, is it thou on the device?" I am afraid that I might cry along with the weeping caller, and I don't know what I'm doing. I don't know why I said it. So I switch quickly to English. "Sorry, wrong number." And I hang up.

I no longer have control over when I answer the phone, who I talk to, or which language I use. I have lost control of my life. What has happened in my brain that I am instantaneously speaking a form of Castilian with Andean intonations that I didn't even know I remembered?

The fact that intonation and cadence can trigger a past mostly dormant since I was five is both amazing and terrifying to me. I've known for some time that second- and third-language acquisition is often more formalized and rationalized by the learner, whereas a person's mother tongue is useful in recognizing unconscious thoughts, desires and early emotions. But I understood the caller without knowing the words. I could hear the subtext, with all its dismal and murky shades. I don't have this language the way I have the other ones. What I have is the residue it left in me. Somehow I know I have retained the unique *patois* of Kichwa even in this shadow form only because I was a child when I first heard it, and because it was spoken by someone whose face I loved before I had language. I store her somber messages in my finely compartmentalized linguistic brain, moving them from the sub-conscious to conscious. I'll contemplate her words when I have the time to absorb and interpret them accurately.

I park my car in the lot of the San Juan Capistrano train station and try not to stare as the *migra* immigration officers tie plastic handcuffs around the wrists of six young Latino men. I disregard their slumped defeated looks, but instead of turning away from me, one of the young men recognizes me and greets me very politely in Spanish. "Muy buenos días, Doña Paloma. Que Dios la bendiga." He greets me good morning and hopes that God blesses me.

I reply in kind while trying to avoid any eye contact. I am not embarrassed by him, it's just that his smile is so youthful yet crestfallen, and my eyes are welling up. I recognize him as one of the busboys from *The Forge* restaurant nearby, and his genuine courtliness toward me in his time of distress is breaking my heart. As I walk toward the train platform he shrugs his shoulders as if to say, *"qué será, será,"* but he keeps on smiling at me. I imagine him as a young boy not so long ago, sitting on his mother's lap smiling while she feeds him a piece of whatever delicious fruit is local and in season. I have witnessed this scene of mother and child again and again in the towns and villages of Mexico. A modern day Madonna and Child. She would have tousled his shiny black hair and kissed his dimpled cheeks. I'm sure his job at *The Forge* produced a weekly remittance he could send her. I'm sure she was proud. Today, he is shoved into a green van by a burdened immigration officer. His fate and dreams dead on the vine.

A few hecklers shout at the young men. "Adiós, beaners!" shouts a burly grandmother. She has managed to abuse a discouraged group of young people and mangle two languages all in two words. Such economy. She must be proud of her accomplishment. Another slightly-built man wearing a blue cap with the Christian Ichthys logo stammers, "Gggg,gggo back to stinkin' Mexico!" He should see a good speech language pathologist for that disfluency. I don't know who can help him with his other problems. There are supporters too. A couple of young surfers walk by with their boards in tow. The short one with the golden shag haircut speaks in a gentle voice and tells the men in handcuffs, "Sorry, bros, hope you can come back, okay?"

The young immigrants look down in resignation, except the busboy. He's just smiling at a distant point past my head. I hope he sees his mother in the horizon since I've turned my eyes away from him and am now gazing at the sky. I have honed a polite and distant persona when interacting with Latino service employees. I encounter them daily in South Orange County, and I've become good at putting on my please-don't-bother-me face. I tell myself that this emotional detachment is mental assertiveness and not the inability to connect emotionally. Now, I am the wolf. I pass a reflective window and I'm looking in a mirror. Time seems to slow as I walk past and look away. I usually have a book open so they realize that I am reading, or I'll have my cell phone next to me as a shield that I pick up the instant when they start to talk to me.

In the past, I was gracious and friendly, but ultimately these young immigrants started to perceive me as their own personal problem solver. As a waiter served my chicken salad at *The Forge* I would have to endure his bit-by-bit tale of woe. At the coffee shop, the busboy tells me another chapter of his mother's botched operations. I helped here and there whenever I could. Now, I always have a twenty-dollar bill ready to tip them for leaving me alone. I decided that unlike my friend Jen, I am not a hands-on do-gooder. Her world-saving plan would kill me.

I absolutely cannot bear another heartfelt request for help. "Mrs. Zubiondo, can you please try to get my cousin a job at the garden shop on the weekends, his daughter is really sick," implored one man. Another young woman begged me to adopt her yet unborn child. All I want to do while these poor young people are divulging their sad requests is to be enclosed in my house with my books and paintings or walking my dog as I listen to the consistent crash of the waves. No one can save them all. There are simply too many of them.

There are other kinds of strangers, too, especially on the train, the ones who just want to engage in an inane form of chit-chat. It is generally tedious and repetitive since the topics of interest in this beach community are primarily the weather, and how wonderful it is; followed by the individual's fitness or athletic interests and or excellence; with the finale being their verbose pride over their very gifted child or grandchild. I have come to ignore both the tragedy and the pointless chatter, and it pains me to treat their words as if they are equals. I put them in the same bag and they exchange arms and legs until they are monsters of expression: my family is starving, have a nice day, the waves were awesome, and we don't know if the baby will live. I've prayed for help, and God has sent you to me, have you seen my latest pictures of my grandchildren, the boy is on the honor roll, and his sister was sold to a brothel just this morning, we are all so proud. Can you help me? Can you save us? He is old. Save me. My love of word play has turned on me. I need some peace.

As I board the business-class car of the northbound train, I am glad for my habit of paying for two seats. I have made myself a space to be in, to think in. This has become something of coping and something of survival for me. My public persona runs interference between me and the constant demands. She sits here in the empty seat beside me. I'm not sure I like this companion, but she is a necessary protection. I am tempted sometimes to give her a name just to be sure that she isn't me. But you have to be careful with names. A name can give a thing power or take it away. Names can be tricky.

Heaving an audible sigh of relief, I sit down and set my book bag in the seat next to me. The northbound train passes the verdant hills full of sagebrush to the west, and I'm already missing the approaching sunset-at-the-beach beyond these hills. I breathe deeply and watch the native California landscape out the window and after a time, I regain my balance. Homeostasis returns, and I can finally allow myself the time to reflect on the tidal wave of emotions I felt earlier upon hearing the caller speak in the same *patois* as my cherished nanny, Esperanza.

The analyst in me tries to deconstruct my brief yet intense interaction with the caller. First, the timbre of her voice was similar to the lower-tone *quenacho* flute, just like Esperanza's voice. The child Paloma doesn't want to analyze with the adult. She makes herself comfortable in the empty seat next to me and remembers how Esperanza and I would sit on a mossy bench in my family's vast garden, under the canopy of the *puma chaqui* tree. She would warn me that the *chaqui*, the claw of the puma tree, would scratch me if I did not finish my afternoon *naranjilla* fruit snack. It was a gentle kind of teasing and she never frightened me. I've always been a finicky eater, so she would temp me with her sing-song, deep-voice. She would say in her oddly accented *patois*, "*Comá, Mikuylla warmi ñusta*" eat young princess, and I would spit the fruit into her hand. She would eat what I had spit out, and tell me it tasted even sweeter. The caller addressed me this way, too.

Second, the caller's inconsistent inflection patterns were identical to Esperanza's. My mother often scolded me for interjecting Kichwa phrases into my long-winded stories. She would say, "Palomita, a young lady uses the appropriate *bon mot* to accent a tale, not ordinary Kichwa." My conspiratorial eyes would catch Esperanza's disheartened gaze at mother's advice. As soon as we were alone again, Esperanza would purposely unload Kichwa words like honey bon bons from a clay *piñata*. Today's caller chided me on the phone by saying, "Don't be such a little lying *amaru*, you know you have the stolen painting."

Finally, and these are the words that stung the most and brought out unconscious thoughts and strange words, she said, "You never loved me. You let them take me away, but I still have your precious gold necklace."

There are only two people who know what happened that day fifty years ago: Esperanza and me. I remember what she said. Her last resolute words to me were, "Now, I'll never forget you or your family."

On that day, I found Esperanza crying as she bundled her meager belongings in a large hemp sack. I had a stack of religious cards with me. Since she could not read, she used to concoct stories for me about the angels and saints. That day, she did not even glance at the cards. She hugged me tightly and whispered candy-coated words in my ear. She told me gently, "Young princess, I must leave you. My father married me to some man."

I remember asking her, "Is he a young prince?"

Esperanza's trembling voice, just like the one on the telephone today, cried out, "No, he is old and cruel. Please, save me." I didn't know what to do. I didn't know how to save her. I was only five, and all I could think of was to give her one of my prayer cards. I gave her my favorite image, *The Assumption of the*

Blessed Virgin Mary, in soft pastel blues. In my usual bossy voice, I said, "Pray every day, Esperanzita, and the little Virgin Mary will bring you back to me because I need you to brush my shiny hair every day! And that's an order." Between our sobs, and the words in Kichwa, which I want to recall right now, but cannot, she told me to stop crying. She stroked my light chestnut hair, delicately removed my oversized, 18-karat gold medallion and necklace from my skinny neck and took it with her.

I do not blame her for taking my necklace. She must have thought it was the least my family owed her and the most she would get from us.

The train is now approaching Union Station in Los Angeles, and I realize that hurt and conflict are stored in the mother tongue, even if such a tongue is already a mixture of two languages, as was mine. I gather my heavy book bag with my book of Flemish prints to show Jen, and regain my composure knowing that nothing is hiding in my intellectualized second language.

CHAPTER FOUR

March 22, 2008
Los Angeles, California

Maxime CLVI

Friends by Election

We judge of men by the Friends he hath.

Oráculo Manual y Arte de
Prudencia
By Baltasar Gracián
1647

IV

I lug my bag of books and my overnight bag off
the train and into the once opulent waiting
room of Union Station. It's such a shift of
being, leaving the closeness of the train and entering the great
room of the station where the high-beamed ceiling goes up
forever. It's a mix of architecture and materials. The ceiling is
a warm brown wood; the long rectangular windows go from
ceiling to floor and let in tremendous amounts of sunlight.
Travertine creeps halfway up the walls and speckles the inlaid
marble aisle running down the center of the room. The rest
of the floor is terra cotta tile and on these sit row after row of
stuffed brown chairs.

The arrangement of these chairs is what pleases me. There
is a variety of configurations, threes, fours, longer rows. I always
look for a set of chairs, just two together, one for my bags and
one for me. Someone looked past the function of this place
and forgot about moving herds of people from place to place in
an orderly manner and thought about the travelers in ones and

twos and threes. The architect knew that some people need more help than others to be alone in a crowd.

Jen glides down the waiting room to meet me with arms open. She's not even carrying a purse, which means she parked close, probably illegally, and left the purse sitting on the front seat. She always does that, and I always scold her for it. We have a routine, Jen and I. It is like a dance, our own special tango. The sun creeping through the lobby creates a backlight halo effect around her head. On anyone else it would be a cliché. Her thick, shoulder-length curly black hair bobs up and down as she waves. I freeze her image in my mind and encircle her with symbols of her own. There is a mirror because there is always a mirror, and there is a cell phone too, a protest sign, a diploma, purple sweater and blue hair ribbon. There are croissants from Paris and souvenirs from her family's shop on Olvera Street. These are her totems and her signs. The castle representing the church is for her a homeless shelter where she volunteers, her dogs are there at the bottom as guards, and the evil delicately stamped out by her stiletto-clad toes is represented by a pile of vanquished pimps, drug dealers, and gang bangers. This makes me laugh. I think I must be over-tired. I hope Jen has wine.

I smile back and shake my head. She looks like she belongs here, which is not surprising. Jen looks like she belongs wherever she is. We are the same age, and yet she still turns heads in her tight jeans and fitted turquoise tank top. I put mine away years ago shortly after I started dating my husband. I was uncomfortable with the looks we got when we were out in public together. I wanted to protect his reputation, and I wanted to know it was real. I wanted everyone to know that he was a good man and not a cradle robber on his third or fourth wife.

I never considered this may have been a mistake. Charles would never have asked me to dress my age instead of his, but it might have pleased him if I had. When did I start caring so much what other people think? I hope he didn't think the conservative clothes were a test to see if he really loved me. I knew.

Jen knows the impression she makes, but it isn't calculated. It's just her. Jen does not dress for the occasion. The background shifts to accommodate her. This is a person who has never strayed far from the place where she was born. For Jen, traveling is for fun. It isn't exile or culture shock. She trusts the world not to change too much. She must be the only Californian for whom the ground doesn't move.

"Hey, girlfriend, give me *un abrazote*," she commands me. She embraces me, kisses both cheeks, twice, and hugs me again, and I am reminded of Ochanda so uncomfortable this morning with me touching her in just the same way. Jen giggles, yes, giggles. A woman of this age should not be giggling like a fourteen-year-old girl. But we were fourteen-year-old girls together so perhaps that gives her an exception. "We gotta roll, cuz," she says. "I've got my homey watching my illegally parked car right outside the main doors." Nor should she park illegally or even know what the word "homey" means. But this is Jen. Eternally twenty. She knows the clothes and the secret words, and they let her in, the young people. They let her help them. Maybe if I had tried to enter Ochanda's world instead of dragging her into mine things would have been different.

When my family and I first arrived in Silver Lake from Ecuador in the spring of 1962, I was petrified to attend a coed school. I'd been pampered like a princess at home by my nanny, and I obeyed all the rules at my convent school. The morning of my first day in public school I was dressed in my prim and proper robin's egg blue alpaca sweater set and matching grosgrain bow precisely placed in my bobbed hair. All the kids in my class laughed at my curtsy to the teacher and my attempt to shake hands with my classmates. All but Jen, who not only shook my hand but held it tightly during recess while hurling insults right back at the others on my behalf.

Her predilection for certain expletives, *pinche* among them, used to get her into weekly trouble at catechism. She always apologized to the nuns, except for saying that Judas was a *pinche* traitor. Jen did not back down on that one, and she did not go on our class field trip, either. She shouted at our departing school bus, "*Y qué?*" so what, which is one of her more acceptable expressions.

By the end of that first day at school, she had my ribbon in her hair, and I was wearing her purple sweater.

Jen takes both my books and my overnight bag off the chair before I can stop her swinging one onto each shoulder as if they are weightless. I trail a few steps behind, because I'm sure there will be a policeman writing her a ticket when we get to her car. I am equally sure she will talk her way out of the ticket, but if I'm standing next to her she will expect me to know how to back up her story as she makes it up. I used to be good at this. When we were in Paris together we would play off one another half in English and half in broken French manufactured for the occasion.

Sure enough, as we exit the building there is a tall dark-haired officer complete with mirrored sunglasses and ticket book. He is standing in front of her car to get a better look at the license plate and is prepared to start writing, but there seems to be something wrong with his pen. He keeps shaking it and scribbling in the corner of his ticket book. I sneak into the passenger seat while Jen puts my bags in the car.

"Thanks, Manny," she says to the officer. "Give your mom a big hug for me."

In a city the size Los Angeles, Jen acts like she lives in a small town. She knows everyone, or everyone's mother. And she parks wherever she wants. Jen pulls into traffic and we head for Silver Lake. We are silent for a time. Then she does what she always does. She tells me in her way to lighten up. It is her favorite piece of advice.

"You wanna stop in Chinatown and see if Billy is visiting his mom?" she asks. Billy was my junior high school boyfriend whose family still owns a restaurant in Chinatown. We both laugh. She isn't serious. She is reminding me that I was once young, and that I once dated beautiful young men. I think she is telling me where we are too, helping me to acclimate to where I used to live, where I grew up. It makes me a little sad to think that it has been so long Jen thinks I need a tour guide. She may be scolding me for hiding at the beach for so long. Jen turns the volume on her car radio up too high. I don't recognize this music, and I am being generous with the word "music." Jen knows all the lyrics. She winks at me and keeps on singing.

A few miles into Silver Lake, we stop at her favorite coffee shop on Sunset Boulevard. As we go in, Jen tells me, "Tuck the bling into your t-shirt so you don't look so rich-bitch, bitch." How does she make a thing like that sound affectionate? She puts her arm around me, and says, "I'm just kidding, you know you always look very put together."

I know she's calling me conservative, but who isn't compared to her? I decide to try and surprise her with something Ochanda said once when I hinted she wasn't dressed appropriately for a luncheon. I spread my arms to showcase my outfit and say, "This is just how I roll."

"Nice try," she says. Jen shakes her head and feigns pity. She has chosen a corner table to give us a little more privacy. Jen puts on her serious face, holds my hands, and says, "I want to hear all about the *pinche* idiots who are bothering you. Tell me all the details."

I describe the two foul scouts at the mission, the note they left me, and the dreaded phone calls. Jen has heard far, far worse in her counseling practice, but she takes everything I say seriously, asking a few questions here and there. She shakes her finger at me. "I told you not to spend so much time locked up in that beach house. If you got out more your calls would be more like mine." I know she's setting me up, but I ask anyway. I have always been her straight man.

"All right, what kind of calls do you get?"

"I, on the other hand, received a very welcome booty call two nights ago."

I flinch at the thought of what this expression might mean. "Please tell me it doesn't mean what I think it means."

Our twenty-something waiter has arrived with menus and glasses of water, and Jen takes the opportunity to involve him in our conversation. "Babe, what does 'booty call' mean to you?"

He roars with laughter, and tells Jen, "Better watch out, Jen, I'm into cougars, and if you give me your digits I'll show you what a for-real booty-call is!" The people at the surrounding tables, some of them "cougars" themselves, howl at the waiter. He winks at them all before taking the menus back from Jen. She simply pointed at something on the specials board, held up two fingers and handed the menus back un-opened. When the waiter brings our food it is sort of a salad, but heavier on mango salsa and shrimp than greens. There are wedges of lime and cilantro, and another herb I can't quite identify, but its flavor is bright like lemon. She ordered perfectly.

I tell her everything, and she listens and processes it all. It's a relief to know all I have to do for the next hour or so is eat a lovely meal with a lovely friend, and reminisce about our favorite rowdy café on the boulevard St. Michel in Paris during our college days. I ask Jen, "Remember when we thought we could change the world? We would sit for hours drinking espressos in that smoky Café Chaud with all the international students and make big plans for the future."

"It was easy then, we were young and idealistic," Jen says. "Now, I just pick one person at a time or that one cause I can affect, and I focus on that. For a time, that one thing becomes the whole world and I can be that young dreamer. It's exhilarating and rejuvenating. You see?" She puts her fork down next to her plate and uses her hands to hold back her hair so I can see her whole face. "No wrinkles," she says. "You should try it."

I don't want to deflate Jen's boundless optimism. If this is what wisdom in later years sounds like, it is just one step away from youthful naïveté. My stubborn vocal chords refuse to comment. She has found her answer, and it bothers her that I don't follow. I think this is one of the major points of contention between Jen and her daughter, Chantal, who stayed in New York City after law school. When I last spoke with Chantal a few months ago, she told me, "Sorry *tía* Paloma, but you'll have to keep mom company. I don't have any plans to circle her bohemian orbit in L.A." Chantal doesn't want to replicate Jen's life or her work. I think Jen felt diminished by this. As if anyone who wouldn't join her doesn't acknowledge the validity of her work.

Jen snorts. "Some of us are still trying to change a small part of the world, and one of us has turned into a scholarly monk in expensive clothing."

I don't try to defend myself. In fact, I rather like the visual of me with a tonsure and a boiled wool habit toiling in a scriptorium.

Besides, there is some truth in what Jen is saying. In the short time Jen and I have spent together this afternoon, how many people has she addressed by name? She is so engaged with life and with other people. All ages, colors, and shapes come up to her while we eat and hug her, talk to her, make plans to see each other later in the week. These are not acquaintances or contacts. Each one appears to be a friend. People know Jen from her volunteer work around the neighborhood, from her counseling practice, or from teaching English as a Second Language at night school. I'm impressed at Jen's recall of specific details about each person she talks to. Her compassion is as genuine as the stray gray hairs she does not dye and the wrinkles she pretends not to have.

Inevitably, one person or another thanks her for her intervention on their behalf or they try to recruit her for another non-profit event. Jen says, "I can't make the walk for diabetes research until 9 a.m., but I'll recruit my two neighbors. We'll have a great time." Her warm voice is like the steaming Mexican hot chocolate and *churros* the waiter is serving to another table. Jen's voice does not cower in a book or hide behind a tall painting; her voice fills the coffee shop with love and humor. Not once does she yell, "wrong number," and slam down the phone. What kind of person does that? Jen would not be fearful of any crank calls or threatening notes. She would have chased the two obscene black-haired scouts in San Juan Capistrano right onto the train and taught them some manners. She knows how to deal with a city leader or an errant gangster. She trusts her intuition about people because she is a great listener who accepts the failings of all people. Even me.

A handsome thirty-something young man stops by to chat with Jen. He doesn't look unusual in the parade of visitors we have had at our table, and I'm expecting more of the same. But there is something different about this one. His body language is wrong for either gratitude or a request. He is agitated, rocking almost imperceptibly from foot to foot like a prize fighter. His hands are on his hips and he keeps looking over his shoulder through the glass at the side of the café at a car double parked and clearly waiting for him. He is nervous, defensive. No one acts this way around Jen. He sounds very proud of his recent job giving private lessons in foreign accent reduction. This is when I know he is a fool, and I wonder what he has to do with Jen.

Jen finds his job hilarious. She says, "Everyone in LA has an accent from somewhere else. You're going to make millions,

Larry." She raises her long aquiline nose toward the ceiling, and with an air of false arrogance, tells Larry, "Everyone has a foreign accent, except me, that is. My California roots go all the way to La Placita, even before there was a placita." All three of us chortle at her reference. The old Placita church and square were built in 1861 in downtown Los Angeles and are only three miles from where we sit on Sunset Boulevard. Her family has never strayed more than a few miles from La Placita, a fact Jen loves. She has always thought being a "native Californian" (I have tried to explain to her how absurd this phrase is) should give her special privileges. Larry seems to take this as a challenge.

Larry adds, "Whatever, Jen. You know I can always trump you in the oldest roots in California bragging game. Besides who cares about who was here first? The only thing that matters now in Southern California is who has the most money and the most connections, and neither one of us has that. I'm just glad I gave up teaching that cheesy ESL class, and now I'm making tons of real cheddar teaching my private clients."

Jen is no longer enjoying this. She ceases their verbal jostling and introduces me to Larry. He runs his long fingers through his dense, dark hair, and does not shake my hand. He tells me, "My full name is Lorenzo Saens, Mrs. Zubiondo. I read all about your collection of Spanish Colonial art in one of my sister's magazines when I went back home to San Juan Capistrano last month." He quickly adds, "In fact, I told my beautiful girlfriend about your collection since she used to be an art conservator in Madrid." He reflexively looks over his shoulder at the silver-grey car still double parked outside. So it's his "beautiful" girlfriend. Why didn't he bring her in and introduce her? And why the hell did I let those magazines into my house? I look at the girl waiting in the car and all I can see is brown hair and dark sunglasses in the rearview mirror. All I know of her is the back of her head, and she has seen my art collection. She could be anyone. I wonder if she was really a conservator, or if Larry's incessant bragging is just out of control.

"It's a pleasure to meet you, Lorenzo," I say. "Are you from the Saens family who are members of the Acjachamen Tribe?"

Now it's Larry's turn to look curiously puzzled. I know things too, Larry. Why doesn't he just change his name to Andy and get it over with? His jaw tightens up and he responds, "Yep, same family from the same tribe. Who gives a damn about California history, right Mrs. Z?" He is baiting me, and I am reminded of the beautiful boy in plastic handcuffs sitting on a concrete curb who addressed me with such dignity just a few hours earlier. He had none of this boy's anger or his bitterness, and he had a right to. Larry pushes his shoulders back as if he has something important to say. "I moved to L.A. because I was tired of feeling like an outcast in my own land. All those grotesque mansions taking up every piece of spare land. What about the fake-it-till-you-make it hordes that think they control South County, I think you know what I mean, don't you Mrs. Z?"

Those young people on the curb, hands bound with plastic, left this morning by force because of nothing more than an accident of birth. And Larry left because the mansions were bothering him. I am a civilized and well mannered woman, but I would very much like to slap Larry. If he calls me Mrs. Z one more time, I might. I find myself a little excited by the idea. I am half hoping he gets even ruder than this.

Jen is ready to intervene, but I want to hear what else this tightly wound man wants to get off his chest. I say, "Well, Lorenzo, it's so beautiful in our neck of the woods that I guess everyone wants to move down there."

"Are you kidding, Mrs. Z?" he snaps back. "It used to be beautiful until the *faux-nouveaux* moved in. They're total trash. They treat all the immigrant workers badly." He feels wronged. Someone has cheated him. Larry lives in a constant state of injustice, and I wonder how he can be one of Jen's circle, because he is all the things she is not. Maybe this is the secret to Jen. She is a naturally grateful person who found so little injustice in her own life she was compelled to fight it for others. "And they treat us like aliens, when all of it used to be our land! Can you believe that some little grommets told me to go back to Mexico when I was surfing at Gravels last month? Don't get me wrong, L.A. is no panacea either. My girlfriends is really well connected in Hollywood, and believe me, L.A. is segregated into pockets of rich bastards, too. The only difference is that the *gabachos* in L.A. have enough sense to keep their bigoted mouths shut. What do you say, Mrs. Z?"

I can't slap him. My upbringing just won't allow it, and I'm starting to feel sorry for him. I try what Jen does. I'll take things back out of the serious realm with a joke. "You know, if you were to say your name backwards, as in San Lorenzo instead of Lorenzo Saens, it would be the name of the patron saint of chefs, and then you would be able to tolerate all the hot grilling?"

Jen is shaking her head in pity again, and Larry just looks confused. I should not try to tell jokes. It's quiet for too long, then Larry concludes I must be trying to insult his intelligence in some way.

"Yeah," he says. "I went to Catholic school, too, but I don't believe in any of that martyr crap then or now. Later, ladies." He hurries out of the café.

Jen calls after him. "Come back to volunteer at the homeless shelter. We really need you, Larry." Jen shakes her head in disbelief. "That is not the Larry I know. What's made him so bitter, now? I haven't seen him in a few months, but I wonder what triggered such a drastic change?"

"I think Larry might have been directing his criticism of the *nouveau riche* at me," I say.

"You think?" asks Jen.

"It was obvious wasn't it? I know many of his family members in San Juan Capistrano, and they are courteous to a fault."

Jen keeps looking out the window of the coffee shop as if she could read Larry's problems in the exhaust fumes of his girlfriend's gunmetal convertible. Jen adds, "You would have liked the way he used to be: charming, articulate and kind. Something is going on with him."

"Maybe it has something to do with his new beautiful girlfriend who was both an art conservator in Madrid and really well connected in Hollywood? He made such a point of giving us her resume when he didn't even introduce her."

"He was probably just making it all up to impress us. I'll let him cool off for a few days then give him a call. I'll even stop by Larry's house and have a little *tête à tête* with him, if I have to."

Jen is concerned for Larry, but her French words are for me to let me know she's defending me too. She combines her languages to say more with less. She takes joy in her hybrid ways of talking the way she takes joy in most things. This is how she rolls.

"We gotta change into our gowns before we foxtrot with Antonio," says Jen as we park in her driveway and lug my books and overnight bag out of the car. "You can make us your famous Rusty Nails." Jen's house on Micheltorena Street is inhabited by the ghost of Antonio Moreno, a silent-movies Latin-lover who lived next door in the 1920's. She inherited the Spanish Colonial Revival house from her grandmother, and she knows all the quirky social history of Silver Lake and Echo Park. These are the homes of old Hollywood, and they are all haunted in one way or another. There is a story, myth, scandal, or fable to go with each one. I guess this is what happens when too much drama is concentrated in one place.

Jen's neighborhood hospitality extends to the front gardens and the gazebo. Beyond this point sit her intimidating sentinels: two pepper and salt Bouviers des Flandres dogs. Hope and Charity deter any intrusion into her home. Her family has always owned this breed of dog because they are rational and loyal watch dogs. Jen has her two canine guards, and I have my dozen cameras and alarms. Even Jen's burglar alarms have heartbeats and give her hugs. Jen has a practical wisdom. I know she can help me with my own intruders.

We sit down at her grandmother's rustic hacienda dining table, and I spread out all the books I brought with me. Hope and Charity sit on the oversize hosts' chairs and lick Jen's fingers while she eats chips and salsa. We go through several books that have photographs of Isabel Santiago's works, and we cross-reference them to the anonymous paintings of the Immaculate Conception Isabel might have painted. Jen is an astute art critic. She says, "Okay, so Isabel worked like a *pinche* art slave at the workshop, and her father got all the credit. *Y qué*, what's new?" I know my friend needs to speak of the injustice of it first. We both know that female artists were often not credited for their work. But Jen needs to honor Isabel by saying it out loud, and she needs to vent before the critical analysis will come. "But I think while her father's work is more somber in color and theme, Isabel really conveys the goodness of a young Madonna."

Jen pushes the open book towards me with her left hand, the one that isn't covered with salt and dog slobber. She knows better than to leave finger prints on my books. "The gentleness of the one on this page," she says, and taps gently with her index finger on the Madonna's chin. "It's very similar to the downward gaze of a Zurbarán Immaculate Conception I saw at the Prado last fall. In fact, I think that Isabel conveyed the delicate hands of the Virgin Mary much better than the almost impressionistic large hands of the Zurbarán, which made the composition very dissonant."

She's right, and she knows it. Jen puts her hands on her hips, her pose of victory. And she makes room for me to study her conclusion. "That's a great point," I tell her. "According to Francisco Pacheco, the Immaculate Conception is to be painted in the flower of her youth. All her features should be innocent, kind, and perfect to remind the faithful of her absence of original sin."

Jen hands me one book and says, "From what I gather, there are only a few paintings that art historians agree were painted by Isabel Santiago. This five-foot-tall canvas of the *Virgin Mary Visiting Elizabeth*. Then, there is this enchanting *Annunciation*. By the way, that shade of brick red on her gown is not apparent in any of her father's many paintings. That guy was the king of the somber, umber, murky compositions. My God, look at all the death scenes he painted: who would want to gaze at his six-foot-tall *Death of Saint Agustin*? Poor Isabel, her father's got me depressed 300 years after he painted."

Jen leaves the table for a couple of minutes to step down to her cellar. She brings up a bottle of our favorite *fino*, sherry from Jerez, Spain. She toasts her grandfather who built the cool cellar away from the prying eyes of the prohibitionist way back when. She raises her glass. "Here's to my *abuelito: Salud, dinero y amor y tiempo para disfrutarlos.*" I envy Jen who joyously toasts to health, wealth, and love and the time to enjoy them with a loving ghost who still watches over her and his sturdy stone cellar. We are in a home that has always been filled with familial love and laughter. My problems may seem nebulous, but together in this old house with the thick uneven white stucco walls, we will find a clear course of action.

While we share our bottle, I spread photographs of my paintings across the dark wood of the table. Jen has seen them before, but I want to jog her memory. There is something nice about seeing my Immaculate Conception paintings in this setting. Jen has always treated her late grandparents as a presence in this house. It's not that she actually believes in ghosts in the occult sense or any of the clichés they engender. It's her deep connection to history and place and her need to honor what she loves by speaking it out loud to make it real. She keeps the memory of her loved ones alive on a daily basis and in a joyful way. I can almost feel her grandmother over my shoulder looking at my photographs. I hope she approves of the images I have chosen.

Jen and I get to work and make a list of the features that identify my paintings as being from the Cusco School. We go about this methodically and tick off those characteristics we know of. But our research reveals more than is in the books.

"Did you notice?" asks Jen.

"There are other similarities," I say.

"Besides the gold stencil patterns of the robe."

"And the excessive bejeweled adornments of both the Cusco and the Quito style."

"In both cities the Immaculate Conception was portrayed without the Child." We are speaking rapid fire now, finishing each other's sentences. We are on to something, and we are excited.

"And her hands—"

"They're held together in prayer—"

"To teach the faithful to pray for her intercession!" We laugh together as we make this final observation in unison and loud enough to get the attention of Hope and Charity who had retreated to the kitchen where it's warmer. Jen calms them down, and refills our glasses. We recover our composure and continue with our discussion.

"Additionally," she says. She raises one finger like a professor giving an art lecture, and we both bust out laughing again. It's all I can do to keep from spitting my sherry out on the table. She sits back down and takes a deep drink from her glass. She starts again. "Additionally, unlike European paintings, the Andean Immaculate Mary paintings did not illustrate the billowy clouds in the sky." Neither one of us is laughing now, because the conclusion is this: it is possible that a painting attributed to a Cusco artist could have actually been painted by an artist from Quito. One of my paintings. We don't say this part out loud. You only speak it in Jen's house if you want it to be real.

Jen is the first to speak. She doesn't want to alarm me. "Even if artists from both cities used similar gold leaf techniques and composition, your paintings clearly state they are from Cusco." We both know that is no guarantee. Unscrupulous art dealers can falsify these things to get a sale, or to increase the value of a piece. Jen is up and pacing. She makes one full circle around her grandmother's table. Then she puts both hands flat on the table as if she has come to a conclusion.

"All right," she says. "Let's focus on the qualities that define the Immaculate Conception images painted in Quito. That is where Isabel Santiago painted." She pulls out a chair next to me instead of across from me. "In both cities European monks brought engraved prints to train the indigenous artists to paint the same iconography."

I see where Jen is going with this line of thought, and she is right. The Quito artistic tradition owes its inception to Fray Jodoco Rijcke from Flanders. He traveled from Antwerp to Mexico City, and eventually settled in Quito. He and his fellow

Flemish monk, Pedro Gocial, who had been a member of the artist's guild of Saint Luke in Antwerp, founded the San Andrés art school in Quito in 1552. The monks brought Flemish engraved prints of the Virgin Mary to utilize as models for the production of paintings by the local artists they trained. Antwerp had the reputation of having the most expert engravers and the most advanced printing presses in the world. In particular, the *Officina Plantiniana* produced exquisite books for the Spanish crown since Flanders was Spanish territory.

It occurs to me that in addition to searching for text references and photographic images of the Immaculate Conception painted in Quito during the early colonial period, we should look at the Flemish engraved prints on the same subject since they might shed some light on our main question: did Isabel Santiago paint any of my paintings? Jen is game to follow this line of research.

We both find Flemish print sources of the Immaculate Conception, and we try to assess which ones might have served as models for the Quito artists. Jen is the first one to identify a likely print source. "Bingo!" she shouts. "It's gotta be Hieronymus Wierix, don't you think? Here's one with all the Quito attributes we're looking for, but with saints or God above the Virgin's head."

I'm inclined to favor the two Maarten de Vos prints. I tell Jen, "Any of the four prints could have been the prototype for the Andean artists. They do form a correspondence. What really astounds me is the artistic originality of the Andean artists who embellished the garb of the Virgin Mary with the symbol of their sun god: gold, lots and lots of stenciled gold."

Jen giggles like a schoolgirl and punches me in the arm. Then she rubs the spot she hit. She can't help herself. She says, "You are such a princess. Gold, my butt! I'm more impressed by the Andean artists' defiant inclusion of their indigenous styles, textiles, and landscapes, and, like you said, their own religious symbols right under the nose of their conquerors! Now, that's true genius!"

As we continue our research over wine and more wine, and frequent visits from the dogs, Jen and I quickly deduce that although the Quito artists painted the Immaculate Conception often, they used a different range of Marian images. We both notice that several books mention paintings of the *Immaculate Conception with the Eucharist* by Miguel de Santiago. In this image, the Virgin Mary is holding a splendidly ornate gold monstrance, a detail that is absent from all my paintings.

I hold back bringing up the marvelous jewels and goldsmith talents of this monstrance, knowing that Jen might fling one of my treasured books at me. Jen adds, "It appears that Miguel de Santiago also created the iconography for *The Virgin of Quito*. It is an image of the Woman of the Apocalypse with two wings of a great eagle attached to her back. I wish I could remember more of my catechism, but didn't the Virgin of the Apocalypse precede the Immaculate Conception or was that the Assumption of the Virgin Mary? Oh well! Miguel's Winged Virgin seems to have created a following by the artists of Quito for centuries. In 1979 the city of Quito even constructed a 148-foot-tall winged Virgin of the Apocalypse, its own Virgin of Quito, on a hill not far from the 16th century San Francisco Church. In your paintings the Virgin Mary is never depicted with wings, is she?"

I shake my head. "I think I own every art book on the Quito School printed in the last two hundred years. The details on my paintings are not typical. Do you think the first caller was just fishing for information on my specific paintings?"

"Didn't the paintings appear in those magazine interviews I warned you not to do?"

I ignore her scolding. "The magazine articles did not describe any details in depth, and the photographs were of the paintings and the interior decoration. None of them were close enough for this level of detail. Perhaps the caller wanted me to somehow describe my paintings to her first, and then she could figure out what to do with the information? There is just simply no mention of either a Miguel de Santiago or an Isabel Santiago Immaculate Conception painting that looks like mine in any of these books."

Jen concludes, "That is precisely what that *pinche ladrona* was trying to get out of you. This bumbling thief was probably trying to intimidate you into revealing the number of paintings you have on the same subject and the details of each one. Why she mentioned the obscure Isabel Santiago is perplexing, but it does indicate the caller has some knowledge of Quito art. Something else about this has been bothering me. There's something very opportunistic and devious about the phone calls. I've treated my share of sociopaths and this behavior is starting to sound familiar. A simple criminal who wants to profit can at least be understood, but we may be talking about a person without a conscience of any kind, someone who is incapable of empathy. They ingratiate themselves to their target any way they can. You can't imagine the financial and psychological scars they leave on their victims. You won't allow another magazine to do a photographic coverage of your art collection again, right? It's astounding the information thieves can assemble with all the electronic information available to their sticky fingers." She can see her description of the sociopath is beginning to frighten me. She slaps her thigh and changes the subject. "Speaking of sticky, my grandmother's voice is telling me to take the *enchiladas* out of the oven, now."

While we have our dinner overlooking the twinkling lights of Los Angeles, I attempt to bring the conversation back to art, but Jen has a different agenda. She has been waiting for the right time to confront me with this, and I am grateful for her gentle brand of frankness. She begins by asking if I am satisfied with our research. "Don't you think that we've concluded it's highly improbable that you have a stolen painting?"

I nod, feeling a bit like I'm on the witness stand answering charges.

"And, do you agree the magazine printed several photos of your Immaculate Conception paintings which could have led a potential extortionist to identify this specific imagery during her phone call to you?"

"You know I do, Jen. Get to the point. I feel like I'm on trial here."

She ignores my defensiveness and plods on with her interrogation at her own pace. "So, we've applied tons of deductive reasoning to the claim of a stolen painting, right? And, since it is common knowledge that you own several Immaculate Conception paintings, all of which have the correct provenance records, we can assume the caller wants something else."

"I don't understand. What else could they want from me?"

"I don't know. But it seems to be tied to your old nanny and to a young woman who claims to have been trafficked as a sex-slave. What I want to know is why you don't feel compelled to discuss the claim by the young woman? Why is she of secondary importance to you, my Palomita?"

She's a skilled therapist and a good friend, and she's aware of how I can retract my head like a Galapagos tortoise. Jen knows my life is a Swiss watch requiring a few adjustments here and there. Through the years we've analyzed our respective lives with and without therapists. We counterbalance each other with acceptance and respect for our different personalities.

Jen pours us another glass of *fino*, and says, "I'm going to quote your favorite Latin cliché: '*In vino veritas*,' little buddy. We need the truth right about now, don't you think? Enough with the books, all sixteen that you brought here. Why don't we table the scholarly discussion, okay? Don't you think we need to talk about the human trafficking part of the message?"

I ask her, "What do you want to know?"

Jen puts it simply. "Why didn't you believe the hysterical first caller? You do know there's a sex trade out there. You can't be that naïve."

I reply, "No one has addressed me in Kichwa in decades. She called me *ñañita*, little sister, and I was elated with this gift. Then she interjected *su merced*, your highness or your mercy, in Spanish, which reminded me of the way our household help addressed us, and I was ashamed that this young woman still used this form of verbal subjugation in this day. It was like hearing an enchanting fugue followed by clanking noise."

"Okay, so her choice of words and the way she said them played havoc with your emotions and your equilibrium, but why didn't you simply ask her who she was?"

I sigh and tell Jen, "She was weeping. And in a cage and getting raped! I just could not process this information. That's the only way I can explain it. It was like knowing what the words meant but not understanding them. Does that make any sense?"

She nods and encourages me to continue. I need to explain, so I can understand as well.

"First, I was elated, then ashamed, then confused, and finally, utterly shocked by the caller. It did not occur to me to ask her who she was." This is the worst part. How could I not even have wondered what her name was? All I cared about were her intentions. All I felt were different versions of fear.

Jen nods in agreement. "Yep, it is a lot to process. So when the caller switched to her extortionist mode, you said you noticed a change in voice and tone. Do you think that it could have been a different person who was speaking then? And did that voice, the extortionist voice, sound like the second caller?"

I'm struggling with my memory. "I think the first caller was just one person, although she did recover instantly to tell me she's the rightful heir of Isabel Santiago's painting. I did wonder how anyone could recover that quickly. But the second caller's voice was identical to my nanny, Esperanza. That's why I called out her name."

Jen leans close to me and touches my arm. "If all she said to you was, 'eat, little princess' and 'don't be a lying snake,' why do you refer to her words as dark and disturbing? What did she really say to you, *comadre?*"

By calling me *comadre* she reminds me that I am her daughter's co-parent. Our ties are eternal, and I can trust her. I look down and admit, "I was afraid that my nanny had become demented in her old age, and was calling me to ruin all my precious memories of her. I'm sure it was her voice I heard. No one can imitate that deep timbre, and the words she select-ed could only come from her."

Jen squeezes my arm gently, and prods. "And, what were those hurtful words?"

"She didn't just say: 'eat, young princess,' like when I was a child," I admit. "No, she said: 'eat crap, young princess.' Then, she called me a lying snake. The workers at my grandfa-ther's hacienda detested snakes more than anything. They would urinate on them before killing them. To call someone a lying snake meant you would kill them. Finally, the caller hissed: 'I never loved you, either.' It was like I was five again, and she was taking away my memories of my nanny one word at a time."

"I'm sorry the caller wanted to ruin your memories, but you know memories are a fusion of facts, senses, and emotions. The love you had and have for your nanny can remain intact. In fact, is it possible that it was not your nanny calling since she must be near eighty by now, and you know women's voices deepen post menopause?"

This possibility revives me. Now I just blurt out, "It couldn't be Esperanza! It must be someone who's heard Esperanza's recollections of me as a child in her care. Could it be a young female relative with a similar voice?"

Jen is pacing the room now, followed by her two shaggy guards. She says, "It could be. But, more importantly, we still haven't addressed the hysterical caller who could be a sex-slave this very minute while we sit here enjoying our *fino* and ruminating like in a *pinche telenovela*. Suppose there is a young *Ecuatoriana* being held by the second caller or her associates. I've known you since we were snotty *mocosas* in elementary school, and my gut tells me that your gut is telling you there IS a grain of truth to the hysterical first caller's claims, right?"

"Well," I answer, "there may be some truth to the sexual abuse allegations, but not about the stolen painting." Jen looks at me with disappointment. I don't think she has ever looked at me this way before.

"I did some research on human trafficking when you first told me about this," she says. "And as a matter of fact, *Ecuatorianas* are trafficked as sex-slaves in Spain, so why not in Southern California, too? Let's go into my office so I can show you some painful reporting on the web. Can you handle it?"

Of course I can handle it, even though I don't want to. The world can be horribly cruel. Gracián reminds us of that in so many of his maxims. He exhorts us to behave honorably despite the evils of the world. Up to this point in my life I thought that I could filter all these horrors by adhering to a disciplined life, but these demons have managed to infiltrate my fortress.

Jen is at her computer growling at the images. "Every reputable site I've searched has so much data on sex trafficking of Latin American women," she says. "We could spend days researching the topic."

For a moment, I lose my nerve. "But how can you stand it? How can you go on with your day knowing this is happening on a scale you can't even make a dent in? What good does it do anyone to open yourself to that kind of information? Do you think they will suddenly stop? Don't you think people have been selling and stealing daughters since the beginning of time?"

"Listen to yourself, Paloma. Humans are kidnapped, not stolen. Women are not paintings. You've lost track haven't you?" I have no idea what to say.

She finds a site that is particularly well informed. It is from a Madrid television exposé. We hear a Spanish journalist describe the treacherous journey these young immigrants undertake. The female journalist traveled to Ecuador to visit one of the small hometowns of the girls who were trafficked as sex-slaves throughout Spain. The *modus operandi* of the traffickers is to have a local woman who has lived abroad, in this case Spain, return to the hometown and rave about the financial gains she's made by being a domestic worker or a waitress in reputable establishments in Spain. She tells the eager listeners that she can probably take a few younger women back with her if the girls can pay their way to Spain. The trafficker assures the families she will handle all the passport issues and will watch over the girls as if they are her own. Despite the severe economic downturn faced by these village families, they gather the required two to four thousand Euros from their extended families knowing that through their daughter's diligent hard work they will recover this money in a few months, and then the girls' subsequent salaries will support the entire family for as long as their daughters can stay abroad.

While we watch the screen, Jen is chewing on her ebony curls. She says, "You would think that these families would have had some suspicion about the financial claims. But, here's this unassuming, middle-aged frump, assuring the Ecuadorian villagers that their lithe and energetic daughters could do much better economically than she did in Spain. All parents in the world want their children to do well, so, of course, they fall for this trap." Jen pushes the space bar with one long fingernail and freezes the image on the screen. "You know who I blame the most?" she asks. For one irrational moment I think she will point at me, and I will die here on her floor from this accusation because it will be true if Jen says it. "Her." Jen's fingernail clicks on the glass screen as she points out the middle-aged frump, and she names her out loud. "Judas," she says.

And then my steady Jen finally loses control. "Women have always been dispensable throughout history!" she screams. "Any accomplishment is forgotten by time. Look at the artist, Isabel Santiago, whose life and art you've had to unearth one obscure citation at a time from even more arcane art books. Even now, 300 years after Isabel painted her Marian images, the chaste Ecuadorian girls are exploited by depraved monsters. And who is documenting their plight? How can we know how many have perished? Their potential accomplishments, their innocence, are plundered. These young victims become another bleak statistic that gets buried along with all the massacres in history. I still say there is a *pinche* hypocrisy at every level of the human trafficking network, starting with the girls' families right up to the legal systems of each country. Everyone looks at these humble young girls and says, Y *qué*, it's just another poor expendable girl. I'm so exhausted of the *pinche* world, Paloma."

Jen leaves the office and drags back to the succor of her grandmother's table. I remain a while longer in front of her computer screen. The journalist interviews some of the Ecuadorian girls who work as streetwalkers in the heart of Madrid. She describes how the traffickers take the girls' passports away, lock them up, rape them, beat them up, and ply them with drugs until they submit to the daily life of a sex-slave. Some girls work in bordello night clubs, but an inordinate number of them walk the streets under the evil watch of their abusers. The journalist interviews the few victims who are now in shelters trying to recover. The girls are broken spirits; they don't know who or what they are or where they belong.

As I approach Jen, she looks up and asks, "Did you read those dreadful statistics? Human trafficking for sexual exploitation is ranked right up there with illegal arms sales and drug trafficking, and art theft is not far behind." I nod yes, and Jen continues in her most sympathetic voice. She is calmer now. "Whoever targeted you for this scam is an odious person or persons. You do realize that you have to consult with your lawyer, security experts, and law enforcement, don't you?" This is clearly not a suggestion. I think Jen would carry me there if she had to. "And, you know I'll be with you!" Of course I do. That is why I came here in the first place.

I sit next to Charity and bury my face in her warm fur; she licks my ear in return. Jen and I both sit at the table and silently flip through the art books, one Marian image after another consoling us. We chit chat in French in a mutual effort to regress to a more carefree time in our lives, a time when all good things seemed possible. I'm rarely a comic, but I slide my reading glasses to the tip of my nose, in the manner of our old French professor in Paris, and tell Jen, "Mademoiselle, *revenons à nos moutons*." Jen chuckles and perks up at the memory.

We should get back to the point or maybe I'm just getting better at telling jokes. We both sigh deeply, ready for what comes next.

"Can we talk about my favorite missal now?" I ask.

"Is it the one you bought in Mexico City? I went with you on that book-hunting trip, didn't I?

"Yes, but you left me with the booksellers while you sipped margaritas, who knows where and with whom?

"Thanks for the memory! The margaritas were sweet, and so was he."

"Seriously Jen, Look at the amazing detail of this engraving of the *Assumption of the Virgin* in this 1613 Missal printed by the greatest press in Antwerp, the *Officina Plantiniana.*"

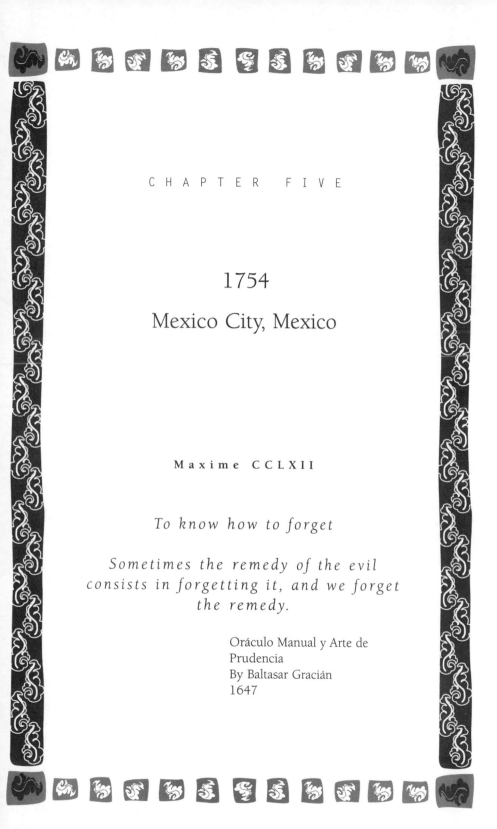

CHAPTER FIVE

1754

Mexico City, Mexico

Maxime CCLXII

To know how to forget

Sometimes the remedy of the evil consists in forgetting it, and we forget the remedy.

Oráculo Manual y Arte de
Prudencia
By Baltasar Gracián
1647

V

oña María de Rivera Calderón y Benavides descends the *cantera* stone stairs from the second story living quarters barking orders at her servants, Xochitl and Tomasa. As always she scolds the elder of the two first. "*Apúrate*, Tomasa, you're so slow in your old age." What Doña María doesn't realize is that she is the laggard while browbeaten Tomasa gently holds her hand down the steep stairs.

Despite serving Doña María hand and foot for over fifty-five years, Tomasa remains patient, but somewhat sarcastic. She utters under her breath, "*Siquiera yo vuelo con mis propias alas.*" At least I fly on my own two wings.

Doña María doesn't wait for a later date to reprimand Tomasa. She doesn't even wait for the pause at the first landing of the stairs. On the contrary, Doña María knows all about managing employees. She regards herself as Mexico City's most venerable publisher and book seller because her management acumen supersedes that of any three men. Her father made this observation in the strictest confidence to her before he died forty years ago in 1710. Doña María castigates Tomasa. "You're testing my patience with all your folk proverbs. This is a literary house, not a barn. I don't want to hear anything having to do with animals or animal parts, do you understand?"

"Clear as a bell," Tomasa answers.

"Let me remind you, Tomasa, that you've been supremely privileged to work for the greatest publishing dynasty in Nueva España," says Doña Maria.

"Thank you, ith been a bed of rothes," responds Tomasa. Due to gaps between her missing teeth, she can no longer enunciate certain consonant sounds like she could in her youth.

Doña María has heard enough and must now reprimand Tomasa corporally. She swats her with the missal she is holding in her left hand. In the process of executing this maneuver, they both stumble, but Tomasa lifts Doña María with agility rarely seen on a woman sixty-eight years old. She is thirteen years older than Doña María, yet her braids remain jet black, whereas Doña María's fine gray hair barely knots into a flimsy chignon. Tomasa always volunteers to groom Doña María's hair because she cherishes having a bit of the upper hand on her *patrona*.

Doña María feels remorseful about striking Tomasa, yet she remains true to herself. It is her duty as her boss, her *patrona*, to instruct Tomasa, so she adds, "Tomasa, I have told you numerous times that the illustrious Miguel de Cervantes Saavedra wrote that a proverb is appropriate when aptly and reasonably applied, but to be forever discharging a proverb results in an insipid and vulgar conversation. Can you comprehend what I am saying?"

"Yeth, Doña. I've been hearing your commandth thince the day you were born."

Xochitl, the other servant, waits for both of them on the first floor by the bookstore entrance to the large corner house.

She is a stout indigenous woman from Oaxaca. Today she wears a threadbare *cochineal* red *huipil*. She is as proud of her straight white teeth as Tomasa is vain of her thick black braids. Xochitl remembers the days the notable printing presses worked like beasts of burden. This morning the presses are as quiet as a church mouse, as Tomasa would say. Xochitl predicts that this morning the trio will be on another counterproductive espionage stroll around the *zócolo,* the main square, to determine the burgeoning printing competition.

As soon as Doña María reaches the first floor, she barks another command. "Xochitl, take this book back up to the library in the *entresuelo,* and bring me my favorite Flemish missal. Run up those stairs now!"

"Ay, Dios mío, Doña María, I'm sixty years old," Xochitl whines. "I'm not the fifteen-year-old who arrived to this house forty-five years ago."

Doña María claps her hands jovially, as if she was at the theatre. "I applaud your accurate observations on the passing of time," she says. "But please remember this is not just a house, Xochitl, this is a publishing empire. Don't ever forget that."

Tomasa can't help herself. "Doña, did you just thay a *non thequitur?*

"Insolent beast!" Doña María answers.

The Seville style house on Empedradillo Street is located three blocks east of the *zócolo* in Mexico City. Doña María maintains a small book store at the street level and operates a more select book store for her long-time clients on the mezzanine floor. She cultivates a veneer of continued business success despite witnessing a gradual and unrecoverable decline in both the production of books and in the esteem among her printing patrons. She rehearses a series of activities that she executes punctiliously in order to create the illusion that her family's publishing empire still glows. Periodically, she even fools herself into thinking that she remains a prominent publisher.

On a regular basis, she commands two errand boys to rush out of the corner house as if they are discharged on the most urgent publishing matters with various Spanish Crown or church officials. Doña María published New Spain's gazette, *La Gazeta de México*, from 1732 to 1737, a fact she wants to keep on the minds of her competitors and her clients. She obligates Tomasa to open the windows of the print shop while Xochitl and the errand boys clank the presses and make noises as if the shop were still in full swing. She convinces her few remaining print shop employees that they must maintain the presses in tip-top shape since an impending book order is right around the corner. She knows that this concocted activity will reach the nosy ears of passing pedestrians who, in turn, will stir gossip around the *zócalo* about the resurgent production at the *Imprenta Real del Superior Govierno* of Doña María de Rivera Calderón y Benavides. She will leave no stone unturned in her search for ways to keep her business alive. The day she accepts the decline of her illustrious family printing heritage is the day she will stop breathing.

In 1631 a young printer from Spain and his clever wife, Paula de Benavides, started a printing business in Mexico City. Bernardo Calderón arrived from Alcalá de Henares with dreams of establishing himself in this wealthy city. He and Paula kept the printing press busy during the day and at night they pressed against each other to produce four sons and two daughters in record time. By 1641, Paula was a widow with five of her six children in the religious orders. Thankfully, their intellect and familial responsibility impelled them to promote their mother's printing business and book store to their respective religious superiors.

Paula ran the business with an iron fist that produced just over one thousand documents such as hagiographies, sermons, dictionaries, and devotional books. She was partial to printing devotional *villancicos*, the poetic songs she would sing fervently at the high feast of the Immaculate Conception. Before Mass started, Paula could be seen rejoicing in the theatre and costumes that entertained all the social classes. She proudly printed the *villancicos* written by Sor Juana Inés de la Cruz. Paula could be heard singing, "tumba, la-lá-la, tumba la-lé-le, wherever Saint Peter enters, no one remains a slave."

Paula's forays into pleasure were few and far between. She preferred to keep a tight grip, albeit at a distance, on all her children. She coerced them into landing her the exclusive printing rights for religious cards, both large and small. Her children knew better than to disappoint their mother, and one after the other petitioned the Count de Alba de Aliste to grant their family's establishment printing privileges. In record time, Paula enjoyed the exclusive license to print the highly desirable large religious cards in Castilian and the indigenous Nahuatl language. More significantly, Paula relished in the accompanying decree prohibiting any other printer from this lucrative field on the threat of confiscation of their typeset and a fine of two hundred pesos.

Paula's obnoxious affectation of holding up her right hand to show her five inky fingers resulted from the fact that no fewer than five viceroys granted Paula the exclusive privilege of publishing their edicts. Paula repeated the five-finger hand gesture to accent any of her constant commands. Her pomposity reached a most disagreeable level when she pronounced her establishment as the Antwerp Press and the Plantin Press of Nueva España.

Upon Paula's death in 1684, after forty-three years of single-handedly managing the printing enterprise, her daughter María inherited the business. María had also married a printer, Juán de Ribera, back in January 1655. As was the style of that era, María went by the name of María de Benavides, her famous mother's family name. Unlike her mother's prolific production, María de Benavides concentrated on maintaining the suspension bridge between her business and the Holy Office of the Inquisition free of any weak ropes. On the one hand, María had the monopoly on the local printing for any documents originating from this efficacious and much feared office. On the other hand, she also dodged any inquiries into her own selection of books for sale, which luckily escaped the judgmental bonfires of the ubiquitous censors.

Juán and María kept up the family traditions and spent countless nights amorously producing eight children, two of whom entered the religious orders, enabling them to champion the family business in influential circles. After Juan's passing in 1685, María honored his memory throughout her lifetime by printing every title page with his name: María de Benavides, widow of Juán de Rivera. One of their sons, Miguel, advanced the family business on Empedradillo Street. In this main-line home Miguel basked in the warmth and wit of his favorite daughter, María, named in honor of his mother.

Like her father Miguel, Doña Maria has a long memory and a short fuse. When Xochitl breathlessly arrives to the ground floor with the wrong missal, Doña María tells her, "Such incompetence! I said the Flemish *Missale Romanum,* not this one. Run back up to the mezzanine and find it now."

Xochitl's bronze face drips with perspiration and exhaustion. She is about to run up the stairs when Tomasa says, "Doña,

I'll find it. I won't go on a wild goothe chathe." Tomasa ducks Doña María's thump on the head. She runs up the stairs cackling at her own wisecrack. Under her breath she says, "That Doña can't alwayth be *el gallito del lugar*."

The three women drape their black shawls over their heads and shoulders and exit the house. Each one knows her role in their private street drama, and they shuffle into position. Doña María is the summit of their roving isosceles triangle. Xochitl and Tomasa guard her flanks and attend to her every step. Although Doña María knows each and every cobblestone on the streets surrounding the *zócalo*, her declining eyesight sees obstacles where the street is clear. Conversely, she bumps into people standing directly in front of her. It is Tomasa's duty to shout out, "Make way for Doña María de Rivera Calderón y Benavideth. She is on important busthineth for the *Imprenta Real del Thuperior Govierno*."

Doña María stops dead in her tracks and waits for Tomasa to continue announcing all her publishing privileges. With every additional decayed tooth that falls from Tomasa's mouth, she dreads public speaking more and more. She clears her throat and hoarsely cries out, "My lady ith altho the printer of the *Nuevo Rezado*." The meaning of this recent privilege eludes Tomasa, but nobody seems to care. The street urchins nearby snicker at Tomasa since they assume she is putting on airs by pronouncing her words with a Castilian lisp. Once they recognize Doña María, they spring out of her way.

In the past, Doña María's reputation as a publishing giant and as a *beata* opened doors and cleared paths for her. Now, the only respect she receives is from the lowest denizens in Mexico City to whom she is always charitable, and from the benevolent Franciscan friars who are planning their missionary voyages to the Californias. She accepts the moniker of a *beata*, as these pious laywomen were universally respected for leading an ascetic and charitable life. In her case, her acceptance of the label is more practical than religious. After her father's death, she wore her *traje de luto,* mourning attire on a daily basis, and as long as she is chaperoned by her two servants, she can conduct publishing business throughout the city like any man. She makes sure to attend mass daily and to be seen giving alms to the poor. Doña María relishes the gossip about herself. The scuttlebutt around the *zócalo* is that she's given up all worldly pleasures. The idle talk amuses since it is so far from her truth.

Rather than turn right towards the *zócalo*, the women turn left and weave their way west toward Doña María's nemesis: the *Colegio de San Idelfonso*. All three grimace once they approach the stone façade of the headquarters of the black-robed Jesuits. Doña María does not admit to anyone that the purpose of this reconnaissance promenade is to ascertain the extent of the damage the black crows have in store for her printing business. How she wishes she were still printing the *Gazeta de México* under its erudite editor, Juan Ignacio María Castorena Ursúa y Goyeneche. She would be able to influence him to encapsulate the headlines in such a way that everyone would know the harm the Jesuits were inflicting on her printing business. In her mind she can already see the broadsheets she would print with headlines such as: "Thieves in Black Habits Steal Doña María de Rivera's Clients," or "Historic Publishing Family Decimated by Omnivorous Crows." She pictures the gazette flying from hand to hand in the *zócalo*. Everyone would sympathize with her instead of regarding her as a faded relic from a long-gone era.

In her reverie Doña María actually sees time fly by on the rainclouds rolling into the square. She mumbles to herself a tad too loudly, "Ah, *tempus fugit.*"

Whenever Xochitl hears Latin, she answers, "*Et Cum Spiritu Tuo. Amen.*"

Xochitl's inappropriate response flies by Doña María, but not Tomasa, who smirks, "Jutht my luck, Xochitl is gone to the dogth and the other one never thtops putting on the dog."

Doña María's frustration at the relentless competition from the Jesuits turns into rage. She walks perilously close to the main entrance to the Colegio de San Idelfonso, but her servants approach her stealthily on each side and guide their *patrona* toward the *zócalo*. Their tactic almost succeeds until they hear the tinny voice of Baltasar Troncoso. He greets Doña María with a bow. He attempts to kiss her hand, but Tomasa refuses to release her lady's right hand. Troncoso is left with his pursed lips in midair. He finally says, "It is always a joy to greet a *doncella* and her attendants."

"A *doncella* is a maiden, and although I've never married, I am far from naïve or young, or have you forgotten?" their *patrona* responds.

Troncoso is perturbed. He can't recall any disagreeable past events. All he can say is, "If I have in any way displeased you, my esteemed Doña María, I extend to you my profound apologies."

"Apologies accepted. Now, let's take a moment to discuss a new commission I would like to offer you," Doña María responds.

He answers, "At present, I am terribly preoccupied with other commissions." Troncoso begins to back away as if ready to flee, except Tomasa and Xochitl have cornered him against the sumptuous wall of the villa of the Marqués del Apartado.

Their *patrona* continues, "Indeed. I commissioned you to engrave the Virgin of Guadalupe back in 1740. You did not honor my commission. Yet you turned around and embellished my idea to include the *matlazáhuatl* and the miraculous intervention of our Lady of Guadalupe that was printed by the house of the widow Hogal, instead of my press. Did this engraving not make you remarkably famous?"

"I fail to see—"

"Is that so?" Doña María says. "Your engraving was a masterpiece; no one can argue that point. But you know full well that both you and the author disparaged too many fine citizens in Mexico City with that publication. How could you blame them for the pestilence and fevers? How many of the books were burned, after all?"

Troncoso attempts to put two and two together, but can't grasp her point. He simply elbows his way past Xochitl, and says, "My best wishes to you. Good day!"

"How quickly they all forget my family's grandeur! Our dynastic name ends with me. I am but a shriveled vine," Doña María acknowledges.

Her servants hate to see her so depressed. Xochitl's eyes fill with tears, but Tomasa concludes, "Ay, Doña, thour grapes, that's all it ith. Or ith it thcapegoating, Doña?"

Doña María doesn't answer.

Xochitl says, "Doña Maria, please allow Tomasa and me to say the lines from *La Viuda Valenciana*. It's your favorite comedy from Don Lope de Vega. If we make a mistake you can strike us. You start, Tomasa."

"Ay, I'm a dead duck, I don't remember the lines," Tomasa says.

Doña María ignores Xochitl's suggestion. She still stings at the memory of being bypassed for the illustrious printing and engraving that describes the *matlazáhuatl*, the epidemic of 1736 and 1737. Troncoso finally had time to engrave another Virgin of Guadalupe for a title page for Doña María in 1750. Regrettably, the fifty-three-page eulogy authored by an official of the Holy Office of the Inquisition was not a best seller. She blames

Troncoso for the decline in her publishing. After his insult of bypassing her press, she was regarded as a minor publisher. She recently heard that the prolific president of the Academy of Painters, Miguel Cabrera, was going to publish a definitive book on the Virgin of Guadalupe and had asked the Jesuits to publish it instead of her.

"The affront! Don Cabrera didn't even consider me," she says.

As they near the cathedral, Xochitl takes the initiative and delivers the first line. "Ah, what a rich print!"

Tomasa's grudgingly recites the next line. "Show me! What ith that print or ith it paper? Ay, I forget."

Doña María declares, "It is *Adonis* by Titian, whose divine hand—" but she doesn't continue with the game that she and her servants have played since her childhood.

Xochitl attempts to keep the game alive. "And don't forget the wonderful line about your favorite artist, Martín de Vos."

Doña María cheers up at the mention of the Flemish artist. "You're right, Xochitl. Let's stop by the cathedral and admire his painting of *Tobias and the Angel*. Have I ever told you that Maarten de Vos was a student of Tintoretto, who in turn was a student of Titian?"

"Only one thousand timeth," answers Tomasa.

"Well, this will make one thousand and one, so pay attention. Like I was saying, Titian and Tintoretto were known for their genius with composition and color, especially their application of crimson red that was made from our very own *cochineal* insects. I've always wanted to commission a small painting of the *Miracle of the Slave* so I can admire Tintoretto's *magnum opus* in shades of carmine red on the walls of my home. Wouldn't it complement the reds in my painting of the *Assumption of the Virgin?*"

Tomasa and Xochitl nod disinterestedly.

The trio enters the cathedral and makes a beeline for the side chapel of Our Lady of the Agonies of Granada. The servants busy themselves lighting the votive candles, and Doña María pays her respect to Maarten de Vos. She studies *Tobias and the Angel* as if Tobias might have the answer to her gnawing question. How could her establishment ever reach the glory of the *Officina Plantiniana* in Antwerp?

She alternates between staring up at the youthful Tobias and looking down on her lap at her *Missale Romanum* printed by her paragon and idol, the Plantin Press. With her eyes fixed on the engraving of the *Assumption of the Virgin Mary*, she compares the trajectory of the Plantin publishing empire to that of her family. Her great-grandmother Paula was a lioness in her pursuit of favorable privileges from the crown and church. Christophe Plantin was a transplant from Paris to Antwerp in 1555, and he simultaneously courted the Spanish courtiers and their enemies. Both Paula Benavides and Plantin printed books as well as sold books and prints. They both endeavored to hire the best designers and engravers, and left an admirable legacy to their offspring, to the extent that Paula Benavides was often referred to as the Plantin Press of Nueva España. However, where Plantin and his son-in-law, Jan Moretus, continued to improve their presses and typesetting technology, her grandmother and namesake continuously dodged the Inquisition. Moretus developed relationships with designers of the caliber of Maarten de Vos and Peter Paul Rubens, whereas her grandmother ensconced more and more books listed on the Index of Forbidden Books. Her loving father Miguel's scholarly temperament allowed competition to creep into his territory. Out of his eleven children, he saw the determination and intellect required to continue the family business in the inquisitive mind of Doña María. She regrets that such a stellar legacy fell on her weak shoulders, and she denies the eventual conclusion of her inheritance.

Doña María returns her attention to the painting and the missal. She sees the meticulous details of every corner of the engraved page. On the lower level, she admires the Apostles' astonished expressions as they witness the Blessed Mother's empty coffin. To their right there stands a stone bridge with undulating water streaming beneath. She feels the coolness of the water through the details of the engraving. On the contrary, she remains unmoved by any of the colorful details in the oil painting of *Tobias and the Angel*. Not by the vanishing point of perspective in the curved road leading up to a mountaintop castle, and not by the dominant wings of the angel. Her vision idles on her missal's engraving of the Blessed Mother and the angels surrounding her. She can count the strings on the lutes of the musician angels as the fluttering folds of the Madonna's gown elevate her to heaven past the four angels. She hears their strings exuding a celestial tune that she has never heard in the vast space of the *Catedral de la Asunción de María*.

Her guilt over mismanaging her inheritance gets the best of her, and she hangs her head in disappointment. She acknowledges the forward thinking of Jan Moretus. Not only did he hire Maarten de Vos for the illustration of the missal, but he also engaged Adriaen Collaert to do the engraving. Doña María had also planned for a great future when she ordered all the new printing presses in 1733. She had even ordered the Hebrew and Greek typeset, but in short order she lost the rights to publish the *Gazeta*.

The *Officina Plantiniana* enjoyed the luxury of replacing the engraved plates once the number of impressions negatively impacted the clarity of the printed page. Doña María's economic constraints forced her to print unclear impressions. If only the turncoat Troncoso had engraved what she had commissioned years back, she would not be in such despair. The opportunist seized his chance to work with the design of José de Ibarra and created a copper engraving of the plague and the miracle of the Virgin of Guadalupe that is heralded as a national treasure.

Xochitl notices that her *patrona* is causing a stir by shouting unintelligible outbursts from her pew. She approaches Doña María and looks over her shoulder at the missal that her *patrona* strokes as if it were a puppy. She says, "Doña María, it seems to me that the engraving you are looking at is not as clear as the one in your other missal. Shall we go home and retrieve it?"

Doña María reads the title page to confirm what Xochitl's eagle eyes detected. This missal was printed in 1613, probably at the end of a three-thousand-run impression. She realizes that strings of the angel's lute in this edition blur into the background. It was her imagination counting each string. Her own servant saw the lesser quality of the engraving, yet Doña María didn't detect the inferior quality to that of her 1596 edition. She can't hide her chagrin. Her standards have declined substantially. At one point in her life she arrogantly attempted to copy this very same *Assumption of the Virgin* by Maarten de Vos. The engraver she hired assured her excellent results, but he left the city mysteriously after selling his burin. Her poor judgment progressed to the point that she allowed a mere wood whittler to produce a crude woodcut of the Virgin Mary standing on a large spiny cactus instead of the regal bearing of the de Vos engraving. Because of all her past transgressions, she starts to flog herself with the missal. She cries out, "*Mea culpa, mea culpa, mea culpa!*"

Tomasa glares at those who stare alarmed at her *patrona*. She shoves a couple of jeerers as she escorts Doña María out of the cathedral.

Both servants speak loudly in an attempt to camouflage their *patrona's* ramblings. One minute Doña María asks for her father and next she commands Xochitl to fetch Maarten de Vos. She instructs Xochitl, "Tell Don de Vos that I must have the engraving in copper plate no later than the feast of Saint Michael. Tell him that I've waited long enough for the *Assumption of the Virgin Mary* engraving."

Tomasa can't tolerate witnessing her *patrona's* deterioration. She tries to revive her the best way she can. She says, "Ay, Doña, *no le busque tres pies al gato*, you're always looking for trouble. Let's go home and enjoy a hot tea; the way only I know how to make jutht for you."

Doña María does not respond. Xochitl catches on to Tomasa's strategy. She says, "Let's forget about printing for an hour. Let's have a whale of a time here in the *zócolo,* shall we?

Both servants expect a reprimand for spouting animal proverbs, but their *patrona's* mind wanders elsewhere. Tomasa devises another way to restore Doña María to her former ornery persona. She tells Xochitl, "Leth walk into the eye of the thtorm."

She doesn't wait for Xochitl's response. Tomasa leads the trio toward the sleazy vendors of both cheaply printed playing cards and their companion lewd prints. The vendors see Doña María approaching their stalls and scramble to hide or cover their products. In the past, they've had to endure her lectures. One vendor calls out to the others, "Here comes that beastly *beata*! Hide your playing cards! You know which ones I mean."

The nearby vendors of cut-rate printed religious cards also gather their wares and escape the area. She had previously denounced them to the authorities, and within days their cards had been confiscated and burned. One or two of their fellow conspirators still linger in jail. Doña Maria used to defend the royal privilege to print these religious cards with a fury, but in the past few years these printing pirates and their hawkers have chiseled away at her business. This morning, she looks at their products with disgust, yet she walks away without a fight.

Xochitl wants to prevent her *patrona's* collapse in the *zócalo,* where the gossips will tear down her *patrona's* remaining dignity. She tells Tomasa, "Thith could be the thtraw that breakth the camel'th back. I am taking her home."

Tomasa agrees, and they usher her home on Empedradillo Street. As they enter, Doña María picks up her pace and bolts up the staircase. She chippers like a schoolgirl, "Papá I'm home! I have a superlative suggestion for a colophon. Let me design it for you. I'll meet you in the library."

Xochitl shadows her *patrona,* and Tomasa closes all the shutters and drapes. All they hear inside the house is Doña María's humming of a censored *villancico.* Tomasa concludes, "At leatht she'th picked a happy tune for her thwan thong."

Xochitl believes she can coax the old tiger hiding inside her *patrona's* mind. She says, "Just wait and see, Tomasa, our lady is a fighter, she'll be strong again tomorrow."

Tomasa retorts, "You're thuch a pain in the neck with your conthtant optimithim."

After a few minutes, Tomasa brings her *patrona* a tray of steaming hot *té de canela.* Both servants leave the library momentarily to allow Doña María to surreptitiously pour a bit of *manzanilla* sherry into her tea. Xochitl questions Tomasa's alcoholic solution to her *patrona's* depression. She says, "Ay, la Doña is just like her father, ay."

Tomasa simply says, "She needth to thleep it off."

Doña María pretends to be asleep to get rid of the two fossilized albatrosses that have been at her beck and call since childhood. Once they are downstairs she lights up her cigar and sits in her father's chair. She relishes his favorite *puro* and his *vino de Jerez oloroso,* as he did at the end of a productive day. The aroma of both brings forth memories of this very room with her father trying to civilize her unruly siblings. His discourses ranged from literature to the price of printing paper, but it was to no avail. One by one, her siblings would scamper out of the library as their father meandered from one subject to another. Once he was fully inebriated, they would all dash out of the library. Except María; she remained engrossed in his erudite tales and in peering into his prized books.

The library is modest in size by any standard. This was an intentional design by her ancestors. They regularly kept five times as many books hidden in various rooms on the top two floors of the house. Although her father deemed that she was still too young to know the exact location of the precious books, she could predict where they might be hidden in the deep custom-designed armoires. Her father would smoke his *puros* in various rooms throughout the house. He had the habit of leaving one or two unlit cigars along with a heavy sprinkling of pepper to keep the hairy Mexican book beetles a bay. Late at night, the young María would sneak into these armoires and read the forbidden books.

Although her father revered the work of the Plantin Press, he never wanted to discuss their exceptional qualities. He simply nodded as she showed him the detailed engravings of the title pages, or the fine typesets in Hebrew and Greek of the Plantin Press. Periodically, she would ask, "Papá, it would be wonderful if we could create and use our own colophon. Look at this beautiful design with the words '*Labore et Constantia*' that the widow of Christophe Plantin of the *Officina Plantiniana* used in 1591."

Her father humored her and asked, "What would be the motto and the design of our colophon, daughter?"

She wanted to shout her answer. It would be: *Excellentia super omnia.* But instinctively, she knew this comment would hurt her father since he also had aspired to be excellent above all, so she abstained. Her father had given in to many compromises in print quality in order to keep up with the increasing printing competition in Nueva España. He was an astute man and a scholar, but not a determined publisher. She decided to simply say, "I am still thinking about the colophon, Papá."

"Daughter, it will be up to you and your determination to continue our legacy. Out of all my eleven children, you have the intellect and the business acumen of three men. You are as persistent as my grandmother, Paula." As he poured another glass of sherry, she understood that it was her responsibility to shift the conversation and change his disheartened mood.

After a few quiet minutes, she adroitly asked, "Is Lazarillo truly so sly, Papá?"

"Absolutely, daughter, Lazarillo was a crafty *pícaro* who lived through many adventures," he answered.

Leaning on his tall hide chair, Miguel acted out another chapter from the picaresque novel *Lazarillo de Tormes,* where the young Lazarillo suffered at the hands of the blind man. Her father's inebriated condition helped him bump convincingly into the armoire that served as the stone pillar of the story. Lazarillo gets his revenge on the vicious blind man by giving him wrong directions. The blind man crashes into a stone pillar in the same way that poor Lazarillo had suffered earlier in the tale.

She applauded his performance and said, "Papá, please act out chapter four and five."

"Impossible. Let me jump right to the end of the story," he replied.

"But I want to see you act as the pardoner. Please, Papá, sell me a papal indulgence."

Her stunned father asked, "How do you know about these details, María?"

She proudly confessed, "I know that these two chapters are in the *Index of Prohibited Books*, but I read them in the book you have hidden in the linen armoire. How did you buy such an old copy from Antwerp, Papá?"

"My God, don't ever repeat such things! Our whole family will suffer. Do you understand me?"

She quickly reasoned that Miguel had overlooked an important fact. "But we don't have to fear the Holy Office," she said. "Your mother was the printer for the Inquisition in 1647. She even printed the documents for the *Auto de Fé* at the Plaza del Volador. We don't have to worry, Papá."

He screamed, "Who the devil would tell a child such tales?"

She miscalculated how far she could push her father. Yet she persisted. "I know that all my uncles would not allow our house to be inspected for any forbidden books. I heard you tell your cousin, Father San Juan, to rush to the docks before they unload the shipment from Seville. Do you think that we will soon have more swashbuckling tales to read?"

Her father slapped her across the face and left the library. Soon thereafter he passed away and she never regained the magic of reading together with anyone else again.

Doña María ambles from room to room in the house. She peers deep into one armoire after another. She gathers a favorite book from here and there, inhaling the musty and addictive aroma of the old leather and glue. She laughs at a snippet of Quevedo and cries at a sentence from Cervantes. These men have been her companions since childhood. Their ideas and exploits are forever lodged in her mind. She finally locates her spectacles and titters at the fact they are commonly called *quevedos* in honor of one of her favorite writers. Once her *pince-nez* rests comfortably on the bridge of her nose, she reads a few of Gracían's maxims. In the past she had practiced what he preached. Now she puts his book in the bin of books she plans to sell to gain some income for her business.

The fact that Gracían was a Jesuit, albeit from one hundred years ago in Spain, doesn't exempt him from her own list of forbidden and soon forgotten books. She's determined to cull all the hidden crannies to extract the books printed by the Jesuits and her traitorous fellow printers in Nueva España. Decisively she acclaims, "I shall never be fool enough to turn my business around!"

Tomasa and Xochitl have been shadowing their *patrona* in her drunken stupor. They both come forward from behind one of the armoires. Tomasa boldly asks, "That ith a line from Don Cervantes, ith it not?"

Xochitl adds, "I don't remember it expressed quite in those exact words. Which edition of *Don Quixote* shall I bring for you to read to us, Doña?"

Doña María adjusts her spectacles and regards her maids with fuzzy eyes but crystal clear vision. Perhaps this is the first time that she sees them for the clever and caring souls they are. She tells them, "We will get to reading soon enough. First, I want both of you to bring up the leather travelling trunks. We will fill them with these useless but profitable editions. When the errands boys return, you two will accompany them to our friend, Don Gonzalo. He'll sell them for us. We're not on our last legs, yet!"

"I can lift the trunks myself, Doña, I'm ath thtrong as an ox," Tomasa says and runs down the stairs to get the trunks.

Doña María knows that both her servants have the fortitude she lacks. She resolves to finish what she started in 1749. On that January 21st, the trio left early morning mass at the *Catedral*. On their way across the *zócalo* they were entrapped by a mob hankering for a burning. The Holy Office's officials, Doctors Estrada y Escobedo and Juan Saenz de Mañuca, decreed that a stand be built for the upcoming *auto de fé*. The crowd cheered in anticipation of roasting more heretics. The three women failed to find an escape route from the violent mob. Instead, they witnessed a virtual auction for the sale of the candle that would ignite the savagery. As soon as the trio returned home, Doña María packed a trunk of valuable books and donated them to the Franciscan friars who planned a missionary trip. She wanted to save her books from the same fiery destiny.

Today, Doña María caresses both editions of her *Missale Romanum* for the last time. She allows her bony fingers to feel every bump in their spines. She closes her eyes as she absorbs the texture of the vellum. She wipes her spectacles in hopes that the clean glass will enable her to etch all the minute details of the engraving of the *Assumption of the Virgin* by Maarten de Vos into her mind. She sighs with satisfaction knowing that the Maarten de Vos engraved prints continue to serve as prototypes for the native artists in Nueva España and in the Viceroyalty of Peru. His designs and exquisite engraving for the *Officina Plantiniana* represent the apex in publishing she couldn't climb. Doña María begins assessing all her past errors in judgment, but stops herself. Out of thin air, Gracían's maxim comes to her mind: The world recognizes the final failure and forgets any previous diligence. As much as she desired to detest him, she also agrees with his astute perceptions of human failure. His words echo in her head: A good end gilds everything.

She wraps her beloved books, and prays that once the Franciscan missionaries reach the Californias, they will put the missals and the engravings to good use with their new flocks. She surveys the rest of her inventory of books lying on the junk pile. She extricates her own flawed copy of the rule book for the cathedral's boys' choir. On its title page is the woodcut of the Virgin of the cactus that makes Doña María shudder with embarrassment at her own low standards. She never wanted to hear her printing describes as "quaint," but this is precisely the adjective she would use to portray her title page. She squeezes this thin volume in the same leather chest that she will send to the Franciscans today.

Tomasa and Xochitl heave the trunks up to the mezzanine. Xochitl says, "Ay, Doña, I hope you don't expect us to carry the full trunks downstairs."

Doña María says, "The big trunks can wait, but do take this chest to the San Francisco convent and give them to Friar Felipe. He will make sure to pack them for their eventual destination in the Californias. The books will be of service there instead of getting eaten by our Mexican beetles. Take the books to him immediately before I change my mind."

Tomasa says, "We never leave you alone, Doña. I'll take the chetht of bookth by myself."

"I know you're strong as an ox, but you're also stubborn as a mule. I command you both to take the chest, and that's final," Doña María responds.

Both servants see a gleam of humor in the eyes of their *patrona*. They both see her as the playful child who loved word games and books. They lift the chest and quickly depart before Doña María's mood reverts to desolation.

Doña María pours herself a large glass of *fino de Jerez*, and continues reading the forbidden *Lazarillo de Tormes*. She walks around the many empty rooms trying to pantomime the travails of poor Lazarillo. She opens armoires and drawers, and finally locates Paula Benavides's old gloves. She manages to slip on the right-hand glove and lifts her hand close to her eyes. She smiles smugly at the traces of indigo ink on the index finger of the glove. Her ancestor knew how to inspect the printed material coming from her presses.

Doña María walks up the stairs to the rooftop *azotea*. Every house in the city has a similar *azotea* that serves as a garden and storage area. She sees several women on a nearby *azotea* with their faces covered as their long hair gets bleached by the sun and the lemon paste their servants apply to their tresses. She's grateful her father didn't allow such ludicrousness in her family. She takes a swig of the carafe she carries in her left hand and smacks her lips. She tries to re-light the *puro* but the wind won't allow it.

The daylight in the *azotea* illuminates the pages of Doña María's book. In her drunken stupor, she daydreams that she is riding an Andalusian stallion. Its thick gray mane of the breed's inherent *Pura Raza Española* sways in front of her saddle. He gallops toward a country estate in Oaxaca, and she laughs buoyantly at his zest. She feels a gust of air in her long and abundant, auburn hair. The neighbors from the nearby *azoteas* wave frantically to her and shout warnings. Instead of yanking back on the leather reigns with fear, she wants to show the waiting staff of the *hacienda* that she's a decisive *patrona*. She commands the horse with a swift kick of the spurs, and together they leap across the ravine to blaring welcome-home cheers.

March 27, 2008
Los Angeles, California

M a x i m e   XIII

*To proceed sometimes cunningly,
sometimes candidly*

*Man's life is a conflict with the
malice of man himself.*

Oráculo Manual y Arte de
Prudencia
By Baltasar Gracián
1647

VI

The traffic on Sunset Boulevard is unusually light for a weekday morning as Montserrat weaves in and out of the westbound lanes. She does this because it makes sense. Most of the time she doesn't even register the cars around her except to see them as obstacles and the spaces between them as obvious opportunities. When she does think of the people in the metal containers moving past her, it is to wonder why they don't take advantage of the spaces themselves. Why aren't they swerving? Why not take advantage of even the smallest opportunity when it's right in front of them? Why are they all so stupid?

In an honest moment Montserrat might admit the anger comes from her inability to understand any of them, but Montserrat rarely has honest moments. She is not evil, just lacking in certain things. Humility is one of those things and a conscience is another. And that is Montserrat. She has her good qualities as well. She is intelligent and not at all deluded. Montserrat understands she is different, but she chooses to see this difference as superiority. And when she can trick them, and most of the time she can trick them, she knows she is not different so much as special. The anger is back at her own misfortune to have been born so far above the peasants who surround her. They bore and confuse her. They are toys: fun when novel, entertaining for a while, and when they turn boring she breaks them. Next they are forgotten. Most anyway. She remembers Fernando. Fernando tried to win the game, which is against the rules. Montserrat wins, or no one does.

Sometimes she is angry at the cars for being in her way, for driving too slow, for using the particular road that she wants to use when she wants to use it. Montserrat's consciousness expands to include the people in other cars at intersections where she can see them. Like a small child playing peek-a-boo they come into existence in front of her, and now she can play with them. New toys! She could grace them with any number of crude or suggestive gestures, smile seductively and then drive off. Sometimes she just enjoys their confusion when she yells things like, "I warned you I would kill you next time, no?" She drives off and instantly, a flustered and confused stranger is forgotten.

Three months ago, what's his name loaned her the gunmetal convertible for a couple of days and she's been driving with the top down ever since. Finders keepers! Today Larry is in the car, so she reaches over and starts rubbing his inner thighs instead. He gets aroused instantly. Larry is such a boy, so easy to control. All it takes is a caress, but Montserrat is already bored. Bored, bored, bored. She returns to her favorite subject: ways to get rich quickly. This is never far from her mind. People like her were meant to be rich, and since she was not born into it like some, and has not found a way to marry into it, she will just take it from someone else. It's easy enough. This is how she gets most things. She wanted the car, she took the car. It's easier with men, but not much harder with women, especially women she can interest sexually. There have been a surprising number of them. Montserrat has a natural disdain for women who don't seem to know what their bodies are worth. She tells Larry beside her, "You can't believe how innocent these dumb peasants are. We could make so much money if we—"

Larry, who has been quiet and contemplative up until now, interrupts her. "You cannot call people 'peasants' in California, Montserrat. It's degrading, do you understand?"

Degrading? And what doesn't she understand? It's Larry who understands nothing. He is a peasant, no? She wants to slap him when he scolds her like a child. He should know by now that she is definitely not a child. Yes, my Larry. You stupid, stupid, boy. I understand. She punctuates her thoughts with a sudden and violent swerve to the right and she laughs as if they are on a rollercoaster together and not in traffic. Larry is forced to grab the dashboard with both hands. Montserrat straightens out the car now that she has his attention. It was sort of like slapping him. It was quite satisfying.

"Sure, baby," she says. "In California everyone is so kind to strangers. They just like to make people work so hard, like peasants, but they call them 'undocumented workers.' Is that what you mean, Larry?"

Instead of answering her, Larry leans his head on the headrest of the passenger seat. His fingertips are still on the dash in case she tries it again. She is so frustrating because there is always a logic to the things she does and says. It's a twisted logic sometimes, but other times it's so close to being right it confuses him. Maybe he is a hypocrite for thinking "undocumented worker" is a respectful term for a human being. It does imply a certain illegitimacy doesn't it, a certain drone-like value to their lives? Maybe he is being an elitist when he tries to control the words Montserrat uses. But still. Something about her logic and her explanations are always off just a little.

At the stoplight, Montserrat massages his neck and kisses him passionately. He's having trouble remembering what it was he thought she did wrong. She says, "Okay, *amor*. It is not my fault if my English is not that good. I had a bad teacher, no? Mr. Teacher?"

She always gets to this point eventually. Larry is beginning to notice the pattern, but doesn't she have a point? He was her teacher, and he knows the same words can be polite in one culture and rude in another. Is he only making excuses for her? He doesn't know. It's hard to think when Montserrat drives, and she won't let him drive the car, something about only her being covered on her friend's insurance. Words *can* have slightly different meanings, different connotations when spoken in the context of a local history. Some things don't translate at all. This is what Montserrat is like. She doesn't quite translate. Something is lost in the transmission, and Larry doesn't know how to read the static.

He does remember the evening Montserrat walked into his intermediate-level ESL class. The entire class, including the quintet of Sri Lankan monks in saffron robes, turned around to stare at her. She smiled at all of them but she focused on Larry, and she stood too close. He tried to remind himself of the differences in personal space between cultures. He felt vaguely like a soldier trying to remember his training now that the battlefield was real. He'll never forget her first words: "If you are my teacher," Montserrat softly said, "I would like to learn everything from you. You to help me, no?" He nodded, yes, and pointed to an empty chair.

It was at the university in Quito that Montserrat learned how to get what she wanted from teachers. It was an accident really, just a reaction to something her grandmother said. Montserrat had received a local art award, not her first, and her grandmother had been elated. She hugged her and said, "I told you, *guaguita*, you have art in your blood, just like your ancestor, Miguel de Santiago." Montserrat shared this artistic lineage with her art professor in Quito. Dr. Sforza ridiculed her. He said, "Miss Joa, be cautious about posturing yourself as more than what you are, a mildly talented provincial girl. For your edification, please know that the great 17th century Quito artist, Miguel de Santiago, had only one remaining offspring: his daughter Isabel, and she died childless. Therefore, if you know anything about genetics, this means that Miguel de Santiago did not have any descendants. Please do not repeat such a preposterous lie. You may leave my office now." This was not how it was supposed to go. Montserrat was special, talented—he should have recognized this. Instead, he humiliated her and tried to throw her out of his office like trash. Montserrat knew all about humiliation and shame and revenge, and she knew what was called for. She was frozen for only a moment before turning the tables on this stupid man.

Montserrat threw some books on the floor. He looked down at them startled and she waited until he looked back up at her to slap herself hard across the face. She cried out loudly, "No, please, don't Dr. Sforza, no!" She smiled as the old man's mouth fell open and she scratched him on the face. He grabbed her wrist instinctively to protect himself and she twisted against it hard enough to leave a bruise. Montserrat ran out of his office with a torn blouse. It was thrilling. The best game she had played yet, and that horrible old man would never insult her again. Montserrat felt powerful, so powerful. She was special after all, she knew it.

Of course, she had no choice but to denounce Dr. Sforza for his inappropriate sexual advances. When she presented herself before a university investigative panel, she wore her simplest alpaca sweater in a celadon green that highlighted her mesmerizing eyes. Her long brown hair was pulled back in a ballerina chignon that accented her buttery skin. While letting a select number of tears escape down her lovely cheeks— she had spent hours learning to do this on cue—Montserrat described Dr. Sforza's beastly behavior. The deep bruising on her wrist was having trouble healing (she had been keeping it fresh by banging on it with a rolling pin when she was bored or angry), and she assured the panel it was a terrible reminder. Not the descendant of Miguel de Santiago? We'll see. During the next term, she meekly approached all the members of the investigative panel for an endorsement to study abroad. They were delighted to unanimously vote for her, and she was announced as the winner of the scholarship to study art conservation in Madrid.

Montserrat drives more judiciously now as she tries again to explain the obvious to Larry while not getting angry at his stupidity. She still needs him for a while. "So, these country girl virgins, they are very stupid," she says.

"How can you say that?" asks Larry.

Montserrat sighs and waits for his objection. What did she say wrong this time? She assumed "country girl virgin" was more acceptable than "peasant." Larry has become so tiresome, always telling her to keep her voice down, to drive slower, to not say this or that.

"Just because people are poor," Larry continues, "doesn't make them stupid."

Montserrat ignores this because it is so obviously wrong. If they are so smart, why don't they figure out a way to become rich like she has? She files it away with all the things she doesn't understand, doesn't believe could be true, but might come in handy later. She may parrot Larry's pronouncement one day that poor and stupid are not the same word, but she will never believe it. It's ridiculous, no? She goes on to explain, to justify, and to take the edge off what she said which is what she does when she gets a reaction like that from Larry. She has to find a way to make what she has said palatable, logical, not really so bad after all. I didn't mean it. You misunderstood.

"All I mean is they work long hours at their sweaty factories downtown. It is my English again. 'Stupid' is not the right word. I mean their lives are bad, no? They return to their stinky apartments, shower and clean up like school girls, and come to learn English in ESL night classes."

"They are just trying to better themselves. It's the American dream. You can't blame them for wanting that."

"The American dream is to be filthy rich, no?"

Larry used to know what the American dream was. It was something he connected to like a reflex every time a new student walked into his ESL class. But something had happened to him. He had become so jaded.

He doesn't answer her right away, and Montserrat mistakes his silence for agreement. She may be able to ramp him up into her plan if she can just explain to him how much better her plan would be for the girls and for the two of them. He liked it when she got him private clients and more money. Maybe Larry is not so stupid after all. She knows there are lines other people will not cross things they will not do. She does not know why, so she has difficulty seeing them coming.

"Why?" she asks. "Why they better themselves? To get better job. I tell them: 'Why don't you come to work with me three nights a week, and we can clean rich men's houses instead?' They are so afraid of working at night in private homes. I tell them, look at me, I have a university degree from Quito, and I still have to clean houses, but at least I charge lots money, and I make the old men happy, no?"

Larry sits ups stiffly. Is she actually talking about prostitution now? He gets a sick feeling in his stomach as he wonders where she was when he was giving those accent reduction classes she set up for him.

"What have you been doing on the nights I teach?" he asks.

"I just told you, *amorcito,* I take these little virgins and we go to clean rich men's houses. They clean and I, how do you say it, Larry?"

"I know how I would say it. I want to hear you say it."

"I just small talk with the old men. That's all."

Larry is not remotely satisfied with her response, but her hand under his t-shirt feels so good.

Again, she thinks he is softening towards her plan. "Larry, why not to get many pretty girls, country virgins, and introduce them to rich men? They can decide what they do together. I just charge the men two thousand dollars for introduction to clean girls, no?"

Larry pulls her hand away from his groin, and says, "You're insane, you know that?"

Montserrat has been called insane before, she has been called crazy when things go badly with a mark, and she does not like it. Larry has ceased to be her favorite toy, but she had such plans to make so much money off him.

"Introductions?" says Larry. Maybe there is a language problem here after all. "All right, first of all you're talking about being a madam, a pimp, and it's illegal. It's called pandering, and it's a crime in the United States." Larry tries one last time to give her the benefit of the doubt, to be the teacher he was supposed to be. "I understand prostitution is not illegal in every country, and there are places where it is tradition for the police to turn a blind eye. It is not like that here. You could go to jail, and I could go to jail, and I do not want to spend any time in jail, ever."

Jail, jail, jail. Larry is a coward. He is like a little boy afraid to be in trouble. Police are stupid. There is nothing wrong with introducing people, and what they do is their own business. Larry is afraid to be rich. Montserrat is disgusted by this. Larry is still talking. She wishes he would stop.

"Second," he says, softening his voice, "and please listen carefully."

He's begging, but he knows the futility of his words. It seems he has known for a long time, but was afraid, or just too lazy to admit it. He was having so much fun. He was making money. It was just too good to have Montserrat on his arm and know strangers were thinking, how did he get a woman like her?

"Second, what you are saying is evil."

Montserrat understands how prostitution works, because Fernando explained it to her. It is not evil, it is supply and demand. Everyone knows that. Fernando taught her this and other things as well, and like Dr. Sforza he thought he could humiliate her; thought there would be no penalty for trying to throw her away.

One year ago in March 2007, Montserrat was strolling around the Plaza de las Ventas bullring in Madrid. Rather than preparing for one more day of art classes, she wanted to be noticed at the opening of the bullfighting season. In hand, she had the professional camera she took from the art school's media cabinet. She pretended to be taking photos of the Neo-Mudéjar bullring while she assessed the crowd. Among a gregarious group of cultivated business men, she noticed a slender, athletically built man wearing a discreet antique watch. Rather than make eye contact with him, she dropped the camera and looked distraught, practically in tears. When she bent down to pick up the pieces, she made certain that her silk dress rose high up on her slender thigh. Her magnetic legs and her sad mien attracted his attention. As she walked dejectedly away from the scene, her cold-blooded third eye confirmed that he was following her. If he could forgo the pageantry of opening day to coyly pursue her, she would reward him with an arduous hunt.

"*Señorita*, excuse for bothering you, but you seem so upset about your broken camera. Are you here with the foreign press covering the opening *corrida*?" The man spoke with a polished, deep Castilian lisp.

Assuming the role of a reticent South American damsel, she did not turn around to look at him. When he approached her, she gave him her best deer-in-the-headlights expression, and demurely replied, "How very kind of you to notice my distress. I am a South American photojournalist, but today I came to the bullring to gather information for my blog. Unfortunately, my friend just texted me and said that she was unable to bring my entrance ticket to the *corrida*. It's been a dreadful day. You are a gentleman for asking. Thank you, and goodbye." She walked away, but of course, he followed. What easy prey!

His confused expression amused her deeply. He followed her and said, "Please, *Señorita*, be my guest at the *corrida*. My family has the most select seats on the shady side. I would be honored if you would accompany me. Plus, I would love to hear an explanation about your work. I am dying to know what a blog is. Please do me the honor? My name is Fernando."

She agreed, and soon they entered the bullring just as the trumpets of the *pasodoble* march-like music amped up the crowd. She could not hear what Fernando was saying, so he leaned over and whispered in her ear, "I gather you are not aware that wearing yellow to a bullfight is bad luck? May I remove your scarf for you? If you'll allow me, tomorrow I will buy you a gold necklace worthy of your beauty."

Ignoring his comment, Montserrat advanced to the select seats, letting her curves and regal bearing draw the attention of the throngs of male aficionados. Fernando took her hand possessively and explained the pageantry of the bullfights as if she were a neophyte. How could he have known that in Quito and all its surrounding towns, the bullfights are the center of social activity during fiesta season? Montserrat thrived on the blood and gore at these country bullfights. She had even attempted to jump into the ring once to have a stab at the playful young bull, but her grandmother yanked her by her long braid. Montserrat knows all about the three stages of the *corrida*; they parallel her movements during her hunt for prey.

Her affair with Fernando was as predictable as the first stage of the bullfight: the bullfighter performs a few passes to assess the bull's tendencies and ferocity. Her bull, Fernando, appeared easy to figure out. His generosity and wanderlust took her from St. Petersburg to Marrakesh in just a few months. At each city he bought her expensive tokens of his affection, but he never asked for her opinion on anything. He was often dismissive of her. His dominance tested her patience, but she reminded herself that she was still assessing this testy beast lest he be a man-killing Mura bull.

As they spent more time in his luxury properties all over Spain, he told her unequivocally, "*Chiquita*, my little one, don't tell any of my friends at the yacht club that you are from Ecuador."

She wanted to stab him with a *banderilla*, like the bullfighter does to a bull in the second stage of the fight. Nobody told her what to do, ever. Instead she giggled innocently, and said, "*Amor,* you say the cutest things. Quito is beautiful, emerald and lush set against a cerulean blue sky. Rainbows appear magically every single day. Now that I've seen so many world capitals, Quito's old town and prodigious colonial art is remarkable, no?"

He responded flatly, "No, probably not. I don't really care. All I know is that all the streetwalkers in Spain are from your green paradise. Now get over here and show me what those luscious lips can do."

Once back in Madrid, Montserrat needed to confirm if what Fernando said was true. She walked to the Puerta del Sol, and in broad daylight, smack in the middle of historic Calle Montera, she spotted the hookers. She recognized the Andean facial characteristics of the girls: the peanut-brittle-colored skin and the narrow, almond-shaped eyes. Their natural jet-black hair now dyed unnatural shades of orange and bottle blond gave them a clownish appearance. Their plump thighs bulged out of their tight miniskirts, and the uneven soles of their platform boots were a testament to the many kilometers these streetwalkers had ambled looking for a few Euros at a time. Their furtive glances fluttered from this corner of the street to the other, and were full of fear since they knew their pimps were shadowing them.

Whereas other fellow South Americans might have felt embarrassment or at least pity for these juvenile hookers, Montserrat wanted to crush them like bugs for being so stupid. Just looking at them was starting to bore her. She thought that if she were to charge for sex, she sure wouldn't stroll any street. She would increase the arsenal of sex tricks and she would only perform them for a select clientele. After a quick calculation of what she would charge for each of her sex acts she realized that she would not yield the profits she sought. But, if she were to groom these hookers and train them like they train the capuchin monkeys back home, she might be able to meet her financial goals.

That night, she circuitously asked Fernando why the streetwalkers didn't charge more money for their services.

He yawned and said, "Are you sure you have a university degree, *chiquita*? I'm beginning to have my doubts about you. It's an elementary principle called supply and demand. Lots of people pay for sex; therefore, we need a supply of prostitutes. Prostitution is legal in Spain and we call the hookers 'sex workers.' Hilarious, but accurate, don't you think? Pimping is definitely illegal, and that is why you didn't see the pimps trailing their hookers. What you saw on the street is the lowest of the low. Do I need to say more?"

"Where do the better looking hookers work, then?" she asked.

Fernando sat naked on the off-white lamb leather sofa and ran his well-groomed hands through his close-cropped grey hair in frustration. He responded, "This is so tedious, *chica*! Why don't you surf the net and educate yourself? Whatever happened to your blog? Never mind, I'll give you a primer on prostitution and economics in one minute. There are millions of scrawny girls from impoverished paradises, like yours, whose families are in desperate need of money to live. They send their girls here or the United States, or whichever country demands their services. I suppose some of the incredulous girls might think they're arriving to work as maids or to be caretakers for the elderly. But come on, everyone knows that these girls arrive to these countries to provide sexual satisfaction. Here's the twist: international organized crime controls the human trafficking market because they want to reap the profits. Demand. Supply. Profit. End of lesson."

She whined, "But *amor*, why don't these girls work for themselves if prostitution is legal in Spain?"

Fernando sprawled suggestively on the sofa. "You are as obdurate as a bull, and you're breaking my back! Do you think these cartels are going to share their profits? They don't pay the prostitutes a salary! They beat them, drug them, take their passports away, and threaten to tell their parents back home. These stupid girls are sex-slaves. Period!"

He grabbed Montserrat by her hair and forced her down. Montserrat saw this act for what it was: the third stage of the bullfight—the stage of death. The bullfighter fights the bull with a small red cape in one hand and a small sword on the other. She labored at the small sword for ten minutes. Fernando pushed her off and said, "Don't be so concerned about your fellow Ecuadorians. They are being replaced by Romanian hookers, as we speak. The novelty for indigenous girls has worn off."

His comment threw her off balance. She was the bullfighter in this relationship, was she not? She orchestrated what they did and what he bought her, not Fernando. At every stage of their four-month *corrida,* the band had struck up the *pasodoble* march at her adroit controlling moves, not his. The trumpets heralded her success at dominating this well-bred bull, didn't they? I am never the victim, she wanted to screech like a Yellow Headed Amazon parrot.

Montserrat needed to swim off all this sweltering awareness in the Mediterranean Sea. She had been a fool to think she might make money off of these dumb hookers. She'd been a bigger fool to allow Fernando the upper hand in their tryst. All she needed was a weekend to retrain him masterfully, to regain her smell for the hunt. Fernando was in the bedroom, so she shouted, *"Amorcito,* can we go to your house on the Costa Brava this weekend?"

He shouted back, "Let's go out now. Get ready."

In a few minutes, Fernando was at the main door of the penthouse with her small duffel bag in his hand. He yawned theatrically, and called her over. He opened the door and his threatening driver was waiting for her at the elevator landing. Fernando said, "Sorry, *chiquita,* but your novelty has worn off, too."

Montserrat had accumulated a stash of treasures, both the ones Fernando had gladly handed over and those she lifted from his *hacienda* outside Seville, his yacht, and the beach house. His scion friends were equally careless with their wallets, jewels, and valuable trinkets so she'd managed to pick up easy-to-fence items here and there. She loved living on the edge, but by July of 2007 she yearned to shine on a large stage. Spain was too small for her dreams. She knew she had to find a way to California.

❦

Montserrat continues to slalom from lane to lane under the Los Angeles sun in her grey convertible. Larry knows the "clean girls" Montserrat is talking about. And he knows what "clean" means. Men are looking for girls they believe to be virgins in a misguided and ineffectual way of avoiding diseases. He knows the girls' innocent faces from his night classes. They are so young, so naïve and full of promise and hope. The idea of anyone wanting to harm them begins to bring Larry back to himself; he is once again the person Jen would recognize. He is the man who volunteered in the homeless shelter. He is the man who helped others to have a better life. He feels the bitterness slipping from him. He wanted more money, he wanted to have fun, but he draws the line at hurting anyone. "Do you understand?" he asks Montserrat. "What you're talking about *is* evil. It hurts people."

"I understand that you do not understand me. I am just kidding you. I like to tell you tiny stories; that is all," she pouts.

Larry wonders how anything so beautiful can be so poisonous, and yet when she pouts like that she looks like a child herself. Larry wonders for the first time what happened to her. Who was it who broke her when she was one of those young faces so full of hope? Larry is caught between compassion and self-preservation. He is no longer buying her excuses, but she is so beautiful and so damn erotic.

"Larry, *amor,* not every man is lucky to have a hot girl like me," she says. "You forget there are many lonely rich men. Why don't we just manage girls who are not virgins, then it is not so evil, no?"

So beautiful, so destructive. Montserrat will preside at the end of the world and shed no tears. There is a name he remembers from somewhere deep in his catechism: apocalypse woman. He never quite understood this aspect of the Holy Mother. She had wings and she watched the world end. She did not save anyone. As a child he had considered the apocalypse woman to be the Virgin Mary's evil twin. His mother discouraged this interpretation, but it was the only way he could understand it. Sometimes she would appear in his dreams, the sound of enormous eagle wings waking him in the dark. Power, beauty, and destruction. This also is Montserrat.

"If you ever bring that subject up again," says Larry. "We are finished, do you understand me?" But he knows already that they are finished, because he knows she will bring it up again. He wishes money weren't so important to her, and this too feels like his fault. Larry let her win him over to her way of thinking. How could he have been shallow enough to change who he was for a pretty face and some extra money. It was less effort tutoring people who didn't need his help the way his ESL students had. He should have tried harder to bring Montserrat into his world instead of drifting into hers. It took him too long to figure out just how obsessed she was with money. In the past few months she's come up with some ridiculous get-rich-quick schemes. Larry laughed at all of it because he thought she was being sarcastic, telling her "tiny stories."

When they first started going out together, Larry noticed Montserrat was simultaneously attracted to and repelled by the wealthy people she saw spending thousands of dollars at bottle service at the latest clubs in Hollywood. She would say, "My God, Larry, are all these people millionaires? How do they get so rich in LA? They are all about our same age, no?" He was never quite sure why she brought up their ages, but he took it to mean that he was late. That he should have found a way to be rich by now, and that he had already failed her. He could see now all the small ways she had of making him want nothing but to please her, to turn himself into what would please her. She pointed out his deficits whenever she could, but in a way that was not insulting but shaming. It seems to be a lesson she learned well, what shame can do to a person. He wonders again what her childhood was like, and he is ashamed he never asked. He has been as selfish as she.

Within a matter of weeks after he met Montserrat in his ESL class, she started driving this late model convertible she said her wealthy uncle from Quito bought for her. Then, she got invited to some ostentatious parties in the Hollywood Hills. On the nights Larry was free to join her at these parties, Montserrat declined to attend, preferring to spend time in his house in Silver Lake, so he overlooked the inconsistencies in her explanations and her behavior. After all, her actions are unorthodox, but it was Montserrat who initially got him his first private clients in accent-reduction coaching. She had been right: the extra money felt great. He now has so many private clients that he resigned from his ESL teaching job. A few weeks after her first class, she moved into Larry's house. His life became a passionate, yet confusing whirlwind, totally unlike his bucolic life in San Juan Capistrano.

Larry is glad they are going to the beach today. They can sit together and look at the sea under the comfort and searing warmth of the sun. He will ask her all the questions he should have asked. He will go slowly, and maybe there will be something to salvage. Maybe something of the real Larry will appeal to her as much as the Larry she created. Maybe there is still hope for Larry and his apocalypse woman, and if there is not, then this will be the last day. He smiles as her, puts his hand on her thigh and squeezes in a way he means to be reassuring, but she clearly thinks is sexual. His heart is sinking again.

Montserrat gives him her megawatt smile and makes a harsh left turn onto Sweetzer Avenue. This is not the way to the beach. On another day, he might ask her where she was going, but today it seems important to let it play out in front of him. He needs to convince himself. He needs to know without a doubt that he is right about her. Montserrat parks outside a two-story condominium building. "I'll be out in a few minutes," she says. "I have to pick up a book from a friend to read at the beach." She is already out of the car and on the sidewalk. She has developed a habit of throwing her long legs over the door of the convertible instead of opening the door.

"No, Montserrat, you can't just leave me in the car and traipse after a book," he calls after her. "We are having an important discussion here. Don't you care? Don't you care about anything?"

She stops walking away from him, and when she turns there are tears threatening to crest the edges of her eyes. Her voice is a little shaky. "Why do you think I need the book? It will take my mind off what you really think of me. Don't you love me, *amorcito?* How can you say I am evil?"

"That's not what I said." Larry feels guilty and exhausted. "I'm sorry, go get your book."

After a forty-minute wait, Montserrat returns to the car looking disheveled and with a strong musky odor on her clothing. No book. "What were you doing in the condo, and where's the book?"

"Oh, Larry, my friend is the sloppiest gay guy I know. I have to help him look for the book inside his filthy closet. We can't find it."

"What was the title of the book?"

"How should I know? He said it was good book. He said, I loan it to you. Books are expensive, and you won't help me make money, so what else do I do?"

Larry moans and ignores the accusation that this too is somehow his fault. "Looking for a book does not result in that odor." He wishes he hadn't said it out loud, there was no point, but he couldn't help himself. An accusation of any kind is like the firing of a starting pistol for Montserrat.

She gets out of the driver's seat and starts to take off her blouse. She tells Larry, "I smell like a *puta* hooker because his closet is stinky. If you don't believe me, let's to go inside, and you ask him." She throws her blouse down on the sidewalk. She isn't wearing a bra, but Larry has the sneaking suspicion she was wearing one at some point earlier in the day. There are faint impressions on her skin. He wonders where it went. At what point in the day had it left them?

She is standing on the street bare-breasted, so Larry jumps up and hands her his sweatshirt to put on. He demands, "Don't you have any shame, Montserrat?" He is sorry to have asked this question. Despite her behavior, he feels he has hit on something far too personal.

She cries again for a few seconds. "I have feelings, you know." This sentence is from the file she keeps in her head. Montserrat pays attention when couples fight in public. "I have feelings" is a phrase that seems to pop up a lot, and about half the time it has the power to admonish. It usually comes from the female half of the couple, and it seems to shame the man for his insensitivity and neglect.

"I'm sorry," says Larry, astonished to hear these words come out of his mouth again. He is becoming more and more aware of the extent to which he has been manipulated; conscripted seems a better word. How many times has he apologized to her over the past months? But awareness isn't everything. He seems unable to stop himself. "I know you have feelings." Her tears turn off like a water faucet. She laughs her usual throaty chortle and returns to the driver's seat.

As far as Larry is concerned their plan to go to lunch at Santa Monica beach is ruined. But Montserrat drives as if nothing has happened. At every stop light, she zips and unzips the sweatshirt he put on her. She purrs, "I like the way you take care of me, *amorcito*. I take care of you, too. Before we get to the beach, I am taking you to meet some *rusos* or *turcos*, I do not know what country they are from, but they want to hire you as a language coach. You are happy, no?"

"No, I'm not happy." He's going to defend himself, give her some ground rules and see how she reacts. "You have to let me know ahead of time, and let me speak with the prospective client first." She continues playing with her zipper and weaving in and out of traffic. "I am not feeling at all comfortable with this pit stop, or with the last one." Montserrat responds by driving ten miles an hour faster than she already was. Larry feels helpless to control the direction of this day at all, and he feels something else. He realizes she scares him a little. Unpredictability and impulsiveness can be exciting, and it was as first. But now Larry is beginning to feel vaguely kidnapped.

Montserrat parks in front of a seedy bungalow off the Sunset Strip. She maneuvers her way through a series of overgrown shrubs completely obscuring the entrance. She must have been here at least a few times before to maneuver this labyrinth so well. What kind of people disguises their front door? This is not good. "Are you sure about this?" asks Larry.

He used to feel safe in the cocoon of her confidence. Now he feels vulnerable.

An elderly man opens the door. Larry can't tell either if he is Turkish or Russian, Eastern European he thinks. The man looks at Montserrat in a way that is both acknowledgement and invitation. These two know each other well. What in the world has she been up to? Without a word, he guides them through the house. Most of the rooms are empty of furniture and the windows are covered with blankets. Every bit of floor space except for a narrow path for walking from room to room is taken up by cardboard boxes, and unidentifiable bulkier items covered with painter's tarps. Larry wonders if he asked Montserrat what would she tell him was in the boxes? His worst fears are guns or drugs. He's hoping for counterfeit designer purses. Montserrat would probably tell him it was food for the poor.

Two middle-aged men politely ask Larry into the kitchen. They also seem Eastern European. They introduce themselves and an elderly woman who turns out to be their sister. Larry does not understand their names. This is a moment that takes him back to his ESL classes and why he taught them. It is frustrating to hear the sounds and not be able to assign either letters or meaning to them. He tries to always remember this feeling when an attempt at communication is completely lost on him and imagine how it would feel if that attempt came from his boss, or the policeman who had just pulled him over. All the important information of your new life kept from you in a blur of sound. He understands the sister's name. It is Sofia. Larry shakes all their hands courteously.

Sofia points to a chair, so Larry sits down and begins to explain his method of helping foreign speakers of English to reduce their accents. As he is explaining, he realizes these strange four have positioned themselves to block the entrance to the kitchen. They are all intent on listening to him and nod frequently. It would be rude to push past them to look for Montserrat. This thought comes automatically to him in a way it has not since he has been with Montserrat. Courtesy used to be one of his primary concerns in his daily life. Then Montserrat became primary. She became everything. She re-wrote his DNA. Did he abandon everything?

Larry is momentarily mortified as he remembers how he spoke to Jen and Mrs. Z in the café. He was deliberately rude. His family would be so ashamed. He continues to explain his methods out of simple politeness and becomes less and less concerned with where Montserrat has gone and what she is doing. She will do what she wants, and when she is done she will return with half a story that would have satisfied him at any time in the last three months. But not today.

Montserrat is inside the ramshackle studio apartment behind the bungalow straddling a very heavy set woman with a pronounced, gray mustache. Montserrat tells the woman, "Any cheap hooker can to do a little lap dance, but I tell you juicy stories that make you so hot, no, *mi gordota?*" This is not Montserrat's first lesbian encounter by far. She barely registers most of the things she does with her marks as being sex. She relishes the fact that the gross woman thinks *mi gordota* means my gorgeous one instead of my fatso. There is no fool like a horny fool. The woman fondles Montserrat and tries to kiss her lips. Montserrat reprimands her, "*Mi gordota*, I can't kiss you and tell you stories. Listen. We are secret business partners with secret benefits, no? The woman slobbers all over Montserrat's lithe and flawless body while Montserrat's masterful fingers make the woman moan, but Montserrat isn't even looking at the woman. She stares at the wood partition hiding her and her fatso's secrets in a compact panic room. The woman finally asks in a heavy Eastern European accent between her moans and sighs, "When you taking your merchandise out of here? I no want trouble."

Montserrat stands up and zips up her sweatshirt. Taking herself away is punishment. She wants to strike the grotesque woman for asking her any questions at all, but she refrains since she still needs her for a few more days. Instead, she bends down and cups the woman's large face in her hands and plants wet kisses all over her wrinkled face. The woman melts at the tenderness Montserrat displays. She tries to kiss Montserrat on the lips again, but Montserrat tells her, "We will have more time for all the French kissing in a few days. I told you, that one virgin hanging on the walls of the rich-bitch's house is worth a fortune. Your brothers, they make millions with many virgins, but you and me, we are too clever, and we make millions with just one virgin. Trust me, I know all about art, because I am an art conservator trained in Madrid. You believe me, no?"

The woman nods yes, but demands, "I need more, now." They always want more. It's predictably the same with all her targets. She knows exactly who and what she wants. Fernando wanted more just before he kicked her out. The men in the village wanted more before her grandmother came to live with Montserrat and her mother. Before that, what happened to her was predictable. It was what happens to every village girl who is alone with no one to protect her. Montserrat learned that she could use her body very young, but she also learned she could leave it behind. She could go to the mountains and stay there, wait until they were done with her physical body. It stopped when her grandmother came, but Montserrat had learned and a few more pieces of her were gone. Perhaps she scattered them on the wind in mountains by mistake and forgot to bring them back to her sore and beaten body.

Not all the men were cruel, but most of the men in the foggy hamlet of Saquibamba near Quito treated her with desire. With them she was able to charm her way out of any problem. That is how she learned to detect a person's palpitations, their pupils dilated with desire, as their sweat emanated with their intentions. She could smell that they coveted her, and she became a feral hunter.

On the day she was seen stabbing the *cuyes* that were being fattened for an upcoming feast, her grandmother gave her a sound spanking. That was enough for Montserrat. She wanted out of Saquibamba. Montserrat's subsequent severe headache and her complaints to the doctor that her mother's suitor was making unwanted advances toward her landed her a plum stay at a convent school in Quito. The doctor had to be enticed a teensy-weensy bit, as they say in Quito. It was not difficult; she had discovered that men wanted only two things from her, to protect her or to have sex with her. In the doctor she was able to play both ends against the middle and she was soon traveling in his comfortable car to the convent. It was in the convent school where she discovered her artistic talent. In her twenty-three years, Montserrat has learned that once she ensnares her targets into her unpredictably erotic world, they beg for more, every last one of them.

During her four years at the university in Quito, Montserrat studied diligently and received awards for her art work, but her sights were set on the major art capitals of the world, and not this pious city devoted to its archaic Spanish Colonial art. She loved to surf the net: studying what other beautiful women her age were wearing and doing around the world. She could already picture herself in a turquoise Grecian goddess gown walking up the steps at the film festival in Cannes. She was ready for her close-up; all she needed was another plan.

The art conservation program in Madrid was difficult. It was harder than she had counted on. She tried to transfer her coursework to painting or photography but was denied by the dean. There was no glamour in wearing a baggy lab coat and analyzing layers of paint *ad nauseum*. Montserrat does not love paintings. All her preconceived ideas of wearing alluring dresses and traveling throughout Europe expired like the old tubes of paint she was asked to empty out by one of the harsh teaching assistants. To aggravate matters, her fellow students were nose-to-the-grindstone types who maintained a focused lens on their future careers. She stole the school's camera to punish the dean for not letting her change programs and headed for the bullring.

Montserrat has been killing time pleasuring the *gordota*, when she'd rather be pursuing her new quarry. She must see the rich Ecuadorian art collector in person today. She has to be close to her to smell her fears and her desires. She must know how far to push her, so she'll release her money without alerting the police. The worthless stooges she sent to scare her at the mission returned without one perceptive observation about the widow's reaction to the note. Instead of being on the ball, these two dimwits were stoned again, their surveillance meaningless.

Finally, the *gordota* reaches her spasmodic climax and Montserrat jumps off again. She tickles the *gordota* under her bountiful triple chin, and says, "That is all for today. Please try to keep your hands off my jewels while I'm gone. I'm still trying to figure out what to do with them, and we still want to keep a little shine on them, no?

The woman replies, "No want trouble. Please. You take them out. Please, come back soon."

Montserrat slips on her metallic gold sandals. "You are smarter than your brothers, no? They treat you like a guard dog not like the shrewd woman you are. So trust me, with just one virgin we will to make millions of dollars. I just have to push my little *burro*, Larry, to help me with the rich Ecuadorian."

Larry sits fatigued and dejected in the car. He doesn't know how to reach Montserrat. How can he be so vulnerable to experience supreme elation one day with her and abject repulsion the next? Montserrat drives in her usual erratic fashion west on Sunset Boulevard. She is talking incessantly and incoherently. Fortunately, her blather is putting Larry to sleep. One minute she's explaining that the younger nephew of the kitchen quartet is the owner of a dance club in North Hollywood and is doing great business with dancers from Romania. She says, "Do you want to invest in the Romanian girls?"

He interrupts her babble. "Please shut up. You trapped me in that disgusting kitchen with people who didn't know what the hell I was talking about, Montserrat."

Larry feigns sleep in order to figure out how to deal with her. Six months ago he was with his biking team on the weekend. One night, Montserrat blew in like the Mistral wind that creates havoc in her namesake region of Spain, and his life is now off kilter. Unlike his usual brooding and analytical self, he got swept up by her interest in him. In fairness, Montserrat empowered him to boldness. He feels confident in any situation now, and he has been making five times more money with his clients. Early in their relationship she told him she decided to cross the Atlantic without any plan because she was certain that her soul mate was waiting for her in California. Knowing that Larry was an altar boy at heart, she said, "The Black Madonna at the Shrine of Montserrat near Barcelona told me to come to L.A. and look for you, *amorcito.*"

Larry replied, "Don't exaggerate so much, but I appreciate you saying that."

She recounted how she made her way from Madrid to California as part of a group of art students who first traveled from Madrid to Mexico City for a landmark exhibit on Spanish Colonial Art. This same exhibit then traveled to Los Angeles in the fall of 2007, and as she put it, "And, here I am in L.A. with my handsome soul mate in his warm little bed." Even back then, Larry had an inkling that Montserrat was a habitual liar. He reiterated, "Really, Montserrat, you don't have to embellish all your stories."

Not one to accept an admonition, Montserrat expanded her claim. She said,

"You don't have any faith, Larry. Not like my grandmother. Before I left Quito, she said, "*Guaguita*, you're going to be so far from Quito, go to pray at *La Moreneta*, Our Lady of Montserrat, and sing her the song I always sang to you. 'April rose, dusky Lady of the mountain. Above all, listen to Our Lady's advice." Montserrat added, "I'll even download this choir song to convince your skeptical side, Larry."

What she didn't tell Larry was that her grandmother's piety fatigued her immensely. On feast days she had to rise before dawn to make the trek to the Shrine of the Virgin of Guápulo to pray. While her grandmother's devotion to the patroness of the shrine bordered on fanaticism, Montserrat liked to kneel and study another painting.

This painting depicted an indigenous woman who was said to be possessed by demons until she was saved through the intercession of the Blessed Mother. Montserrat admired Miguel de Santiago's imperfect strokes that had captured the essence of the demonic woman, and his selection of opaque ochre for the altar to create an impressionistic counterpoint. The church was full of tourists on this feast day. There was one tourist Montserrat will always remember, because he was the one who put it in her mind that everyone in the United States was rich and their walls were all hung with collections of rare art. They bought them like souvenirs to match their furniture or their curtains. He was the one who made her think it was art that would make her rich. Her tourist was a tall man wearing a faded Texas t-shirt who said to the rest of his tour group, "Y'all, look at that one. Wouldn't that look purty at my ranch? This good old boy, Miguel de Santi-whatever, beat them Frenchie impressionists by 200 years. Shoot, I'd pay fifty g's for that crazy filly."

His bubble-haired wife cheered his offer. She added, "Well, you go ahead and make an offer, Chuck. It worked for you in Mexico, and we got that ol' painting of that sword-toting angel St. Michael practically delivered to us in Austin."

Chuck replied, "Everything has a price, momma! Everything has its price!"

Montserrat stared at their rapacious eyes and understood enough English to know that this type of art fanatic could make her very wealthy.

Today, after another quirky and vaguely sinister day, Larry is so tired of everything Montserrat says and does. He falls asleep as Montserrat drives south on the 405 Freeway instead of going to Santa Monica Beach. One hour later, Larry wakes up to a familiar sound, and it takes him a confused moment to place himself. It's the train near the mission in San Juan Capistrano. They are parked on Los Rios Street near his family home. For a moment he thinks he may be dreaming, and then Montserrat leans over to kiss him and he remembers their day together. He is instantly on his guard. What is she up to this time? What happened to the beach?

"I miss not going to a real *barroco* church; you told me the altar at the mission is baroque gold-leaf, no?" She says this as if it is an explanation, as if it is perfectly reasonable to drive an hour out of your way without consulting the other person in the car. Gold leaf? What is she talking about? Is that what she thinks the mission is? Larry is still blurry from sleeping in the car and for an insane moment he pictures Montserrat lifting the enormous ceiling to floor gilded altar and trying to hide it under her coat.

"What are we doing here?" he asks, rubbing his eyes and trying to wake himself up with deep breaths of ocean-laced air.

Montserrat smiles sweetly and explains, "*Amorcito*, you were asleep, so I thought, why not drive all the way to San Juan Capistrano? You can show me how you surf. I bet you look so handsome on your surfboard. You surf in front of where the rich Ecuadorian art collector lives, no?"

Larry wonders how this day would have been different if Montserrat had kept her word just one time and taken him to the beach as she promised. She thinks she has brought him closer to the thing she wants by bringing him here. She has made a fatal mistake. She brought him home. Montserrat has never known a love for a place. She has never been connected to the land or to history. She doesn't know how much strength she has given him by bringing him here where the tall willow and euca-lyptus trees share the narrow road with the California succulents trying to escape their front yards. The pace is so much slower here. Even in its heyday, when his ancestors built the mission, this was a tranquil haven for its residents. She takes his hand and walks toward the train tracks and the mission.

Even now, she might win him back for a day or two, if she says the right thing, shows some humanity, offers him anything but sex and one more chance to serve her. But Montserrat cannot read the emotional or spiritual landscape around her; this is a language she does not understand, so she tries another lie.

She tries to use him one more time. To trick him. It is really all she knows.

She coyly asks, "Larry, a friend of mine in L.A. is auditioning for the part of an FBI agent for a television show. You remember, I told you about Eddie?"

Larry does not remember Eddie. He is fairly sure already that there is no Eddie. She should not have tried this here, but this is not something she is capable of understanding. This knowledge fills Larry with sadness for her and remorse for himself. He cannot change her. She would only change him.

She continues, sure that she is gaining ground. "Eddie is a little nervous about saying his lines." Of course he is, thinks Larry. "I told him you would call him and read his lines in his answering machine so he can —"

This is too much. It is too ridiculous and too sad. Larry laughs out loud and it is a relief, but there is no joy in it. Larry laughs and shakes his head, no. He would like the luxury of thinking he was blinded by love, but he was selfish, and he went along willingly because it was exciting. He's more like Saint Lucy and not Saint Lorenzo, as Mrs. Zubiondo had told him at the coffee shop back in Silver Lake. He is perplexed as to why Montserrat is so set on seeing where Mrs. Z lives. But he knows now he was very close to putting her in Montserrat's sights. He wonders now just how dangerous Montserrat is. Her cons and schemes seemed mostly harmless, but what about what she said that morning about her prostitution scheme? And why so anxious to get to Mrs. Zubiondo?

Larry's disappointment in himself is immense. In exchange for false affection and sex, he had become her pawn. If his ancestors were here this moment, they'd whip him with welt-sprouting nettles and make him run the warrior gauntlet. And he would deserve it. He wishes life was that simple now, that he could purify himself in the eyes of his community in a ritual and be done with it. But this is modern life, and Larry will have to live with his mistakes. If the warrior gauntlet was not enough, his ancestors would have taken him into the nearby canyons and let him fight the potent mountain lions, *mano a mano*. Perhaps this is what he can still do. He'll hike into the national forest to find himself again. There are still plenty of mountain lions left to teach him all about vindication. His ancestors knew how to hold onto themselves, and Larry is once again proud to be who he is. When did he start being ashamed of not having money or connections? It was when he thought those were the things that would make Montserrat love him. Had he always known she didn't? It wasn't until today that he knew it wasn't because of what he lacked, it was because she couldn't.

Montserrat is unsuccessful in reading Larry's eye-opening laughter. She kisses him a bit too passionately in front of the tourists waiting for their train. Last week, or yesterday, or even that same morning, he would have found such pleasure in both her kiss and the fact that it was public. He would have thought everyone who saw was jealous of what he had. Now, he is repulsed. Awareness cannot be undone, especially not under this piercing sun on this historic street in his ancestral homeland.

There were so many questions he never asked her, so many absurd explanations he just accepted. He thinks of the story she told him of how she got to California. Her stories always had so much detail, and he didn't know why she wanted to make things up. Larry had never dealt with a pathological liar before, and it took him much too long to recognize it. Who else could have come up with such a cliffhanger as to how she earned money to pay for her expensive art excursion to Los Angeles? She told him she was part of a team of conservators repairing Byzantine mosaics in Sardinia. She rescued a child from the waters off a pier, and the child's father, a mafia don, no less, rewarded her handsomely. Knowing Montserrat as he does now, the real story is probably just as ludicrous, but he wonders who she hurt on the way. Somehow he feels responsible for her victims. He has been a sort of accomplice, a willing sidekick to her cruelty and insanity. He wishes he could reach back through time and apologize to the person who really got her here.

Before leaving Madrid Montserrat hand-delivered the video she had taken of Fernando in explicit sexual scenes. She'd staged them while he was in a drugged and euphoric state. Revenge is best served with high resolution and crisp audio. Fernando's estranged wife had bewilderedly asked her to come in for a cup of tea when she showed up unannounced at her home. After all, hospitality had been an integral part of her well-bred upbringing. Together they viewed the video a few times, until his wife's perspiration gave her away. Fernando's submissive wife simply asked, "How much do I owe you for the video and the memory card?"

Montserrat replied, "Fifty thousand Euros, but I must have them now."

Fernando's wife wiped the sweat of her brow, and said, "I'm sorry, but I only have around twelve thousand Euros in the house. I don't suppose you can come back. No, of course not. Fernando is right: I'm really quite dense in difficult times. What do I do?"

Montserrat's predator instincts prevailed, and she gently grabbed the wife by her useless breasts and made out savagely with her for a while, until she got bored. Soon thereafter, she left Spain with what Montserrat considered a treasure trove of money and a life lesson on how to always remain on top.

As they wait for the train to clear the tracks, Montserrat rubs herself against Larry's arm. This perverse sensual behavior might as well have been an icy slap in the face. With granite conviction, Larry knows what he must do. His grandmother often told him, "Trust the angel on your shoulder, he whispers to you when there is evil near." At that instant, he heard his angel in the howl of the train whistling its departure. It was a warning and a call to truth. He has to let her go now. He tilted his head back into the mild Capistrano breeze, felt the warmth of sun on his face and smiled.

He looked happy, Montserrat knew how to read that. It meant she was winning. She could get him to do a few more things for her.

Montserrat hangs on Larry's arm and talks faster. "*Amorcito*, all you have to say into Eddie's answering machine in your perfect *gringo* English is: 'This is Agent Williams of the Federal Bur— "

The train's prolonged whistle muffles the rest. But Larry has heard enough. As they start to cross the train tracks toward the mission, Larry unwraps her hand from his arm. For an instant Montserrat looks bewildered. Her amber eyes no longer reflect Larry's love back to him. In its place, tiny sparks strobe from her eyes. Larry doesn't care what they mean. He turns around and heads back to his home, and leaves Montserrat on the opposite side of the tracks. His primordial California sun is already fading her out, bleaching her outline until she is only a silhouette and then nothing.

CHAPTER SEVEN

1889

San Juan Capistrano, California

Maxime LXXXVI

To arm against Calumny

*The vulgar hath many heads and tongues,
and by consequence more eyes also.*

.

Oráculo Manual y Arte de
Prudencia
By Baltasar Gracián
1647

VII

I hate you chickens so much! You're keeping me
away from the fiesta at the Rancho Boca de la
Playa," Modesta Ávila crowed as she watched
her hens run and scratch in the sunshine of San Juan Capistrano.
Others criticize her flighty and flirty nature, but she accepts her
responsibility to her flock and her family with equanimity. Back
in the time when everyone in town shared and bartered whatever crops they had, the Ávila clan was able to make ends meet.
Now, Modesta and her sister live in the tiny shack next to the
chicken coop counting eggs as if they were worthy pearls.
Her mother, father and brothers live and toil on the other end of
the three-acre lot they've owned since way before the Yankees
swaggered into town like the cock o' the walk.

Modesta learned about the Treaty of Guadulupe Hidalgo in
school, but all she knows now is that after the treaty the *ricos* got
richer and the rest got poorer. Even the owners of the huge ranches scrambled to marry off their daughters to the scheming
Yankees in order to hedge their bets on the future of their lands.
She will have none of it. She prances confidently around her plot

of land and talks to her hens. "The Californios should all learn to read and write in English and Spanish, like I do. The teacher said I was the smartest girl in school. I didn't need him to tell me that, I know I'm clever and I know how to take care of what's mine. I don't need to marry no Yankee. I should be dancing a *fandango* with Rigoberto, but no, I'm henpecked by all of you!" Her last statement startles the hens, which flap their wings in a tizzy.

"Shout all you want, Modesta, you're stuck in town just like me," answers Chola Martina as she peeks over the overgrown cactus that serves as a fence between their properties. "Your Rigoberto replaced you long ago for a better dancer."

"Jealous old bat, fly away on your broom!" Modesta screeches. "What do you know about love anyway? Juan Flores used you to help him rob the storekeeper. You were a dumb girl in 1857 when you became an accomplice to a crime, and you're a crazy old woman now. You don't even know what accomplice means, do you? How old are you anyway? Your skin is tougher than a desert tortoise!"

"Old enough to know all the *chismes* in town. Do you want to know what they're saying about you? It's not pretty, my lovely," cackles Chola Martina.

"They're all envious of me. I take care of myself and my family, I'm a graceful dancer, I write and read in English, and I don't let the Yankees push me around. *Y qué*, what's it to you? You don't think people don't gossip plenty about you?"

"This is what you should learn about gossip, my lovely: sometimes it is better if people fear you. Yes, indeed," Chola says, and spits out her chewing tobacco. "The stories about me are scary, aren't they? What if what they say about me is true and here you are all alone with a *bruja*?"

Modesta turns her back to the witch. Her huge brown eyes open wide as she figures out her next step. "Prove it, you old bat. They say you're a shape-shifter so why don't you turn yourself into a toad and hop right into Aliso Creek, for all I care. I have work to do; leave me alone."

Modesta turns around to watch the *bruja* walk away, but all she sees is a crow glide by low above her head.

Instead of brooding about witches and gossip, Modesta walks to the mission singing a love ballad. She can't remember which handsome ranch hand sang this song to her, but the memory warms her body like the bubbling hot springs up in the hills near the Mission San Juan Capistrano. Is it her fault that all the single men ask her to dance? Last month, she danced with all the sons of Don Pablo's *mayordomo,* and now the envious *chismosas* say that she kissed all of them, too. So what, how else could she decide which one was the best kisser? "*Mentirosas!*" she shouts at the liars of the deserted town.

Modesta doesn't care what they say about her. She's just pretty and poor, not like the rich and pious Señora Rosa Modesta Ávila. Now that lady married into the right families: the Pryor, Yorba, and Verdugo clans. But Modesta doesn't care about highfalutin' names because she knows the Yankees are going to control all the ranches, anyway. She not only knows how to read, but she's better at reading between the lines. When she took the wagon to Santa Ana last month she read in the *Weekly Blade* that Don Bandini lost his legal battle over the land title to his ranch. The newspaper listed all the other land grant families who couldn't prove their ownership to the land, as per the new Yankee laws. What difference does this make to her? The *ricos* can all lose their lands, for all she cares. All her family owns is a dusty three-acre parcel and some jittery hens.

Modesta walks into the mission as if it were her own house. The old caretaker barely notices her as she whistles by him.

She walks around from room to room pretending to clean up, but who really takes note of her? There hasn't been a resident priest here in months, the ruins of the stone church are overgrown with weeds, and the olive mill hasn't crushed an olive in years.

She peeks in the leather chests the Franciscan friars brought from Mexico City long ago. She's looking for the missal with the Immaculate Conception print on the front. "Did the Father Mut tell me that it was called the frontispiece of a book or was that the colophon?" she asks of no one. It doesn't matter if no one is there to listen; all she needs are a couple of books to read while she wastes her time taking care of the chickens. She rummages in the chest for the other thin book with a pretty Virgin on top of a *nopal*, just like the big cactus on her land. Father Mut told her that this book was printed by a woman printer in Mexico City, Doña María de Rivera. He said, "If we ever have a print shop at the mission, you will be able to check all the English and Spanish words for us, would you like that?" That was years ago and now even the vineyard has shriveled up.

"I'll just borrow the books for a while," Modesta says as she puts them in her apron pocket.

She walks reverently into the chapel and makes the Sign of the Cross. She kneels and quickly says her prayers of penance for stealing the books. Once that's out of the way, Modesta admires the paintings on the walls. Her favorite painting is the one of the Immaculate Conception because the Virgin Mary looks like she's dancing. She admires the movement of her delicate feet and the manner in which the robe flows up in the clouds as if the Virgin Mary was waltzing with the angels in heaven. She made this observation in front of Father Mut three years ago and he scolded her for being sacrilegious. Since no one is around, she starts to sing another love ballad.

She hears a voice say, "Don't be sacrilegious, my daughter!"

Modesta figures it's just her vivid imagination, so she continues humming. She doesn't believe in any ghosts or in La Llorona, either. This crying woman frightens everyone in town with her nightly laments along San Juan Creek.

"I said, don't be sacrilegious!" dictates the old voice.

Fear creeps up her back, but Modesta decides to stand up and face the voice. It's just old Polonia Montano, the resident pious biddy.

"I know what you're praying for, and it's blasphemous," Polonia says. "You wish you were dancing with the *vaqueros* at the *fiesta*, don't you? Listen to me, my daughter, you have to change your ways or you're going to spend your days lonely and far away from San Juan Capistrano. Don't think I don't know about the month you spent in jail in Los Angeles last year."

"You're hearing fibs from the illiterate *chismosas* when you should be out healing the sick," Modesta says. "You're making slanderous allegations. Shall I define those words for you? Or would you prefer that I spell them?"

"Your arrogance and wild ways will be your downfall, my daughter. You are a clever girl, there's no doubt about that. You have to learn humility; otherwise, I can see you ending up in a dark and cold cave. I help those in need and you need my counsel, my daughter. You cannot fight against an iron monster, but you can control your inner demons. Your reputation is all you have in this town, and yours is starting to stink like the slaughterhouse."

Modesta doesn't need another decrepit tongue wagging lies about her, so she feigns docility. "Doña Polonia, everyone in town says you're a devout and kind healer. I know you led a long procession with the statue of San Vicente covered in *milagros* for many, many leagues. On that day we got our much needed rain."

Modesta smiles bashfully at Doña Polonia. She anticipates seeing a compassionate smile on the old biddy's face; instead she detects a self-righteous grimace, and Modesta's hubris and ire get the best of her. "Look here, Polonia, your old ways worked for you under the old Californio code. We're under the bootstrap of the Yankee now, so you'd better learn to stand strong or die. As for the other rumors, I am simply a happy woman who enjoys life; that is all. If you want to busy yourself with prayers then please pray for the needy. Good day."

The next morning fog rolls in from Capistrano Bay, and her lazy hens don't lay enough eggs. This is June and by now the many days of sunshine should have encouraged the hens to lay abundantly. Modesta's little shack rattles and shakes as if there were another earthquake of 1812, but this jolt is not from Mother Earth. It's the cursed railroad trespassing on her land. "You chicken-shit Yankees, get your infernal iron monster off my land!"

She runs to the mission and borrows all the indigo ink she can find. She doesn't stop by the chapel to say her penance for theft since she has some urgent business to transact with the robber barons. She's read the *El Clamor Público* newspaper from Los Angeles. The Yankees don't honor their treaties, they don't respect property rights; the only things Yankees respect are the almighty dollar and the written contract. And that's exactly what Modesta Ávila will give them.

"This land belongs to me. And if the railroad wants to run here, it must pay me $10,000." Modesta felt incredible power writing these words. She checked for spelling errors, she confirmed the dollar amount, and she re-read it for correct word usage. It's a direct demand, but she's noticed that Yankees admire the blunt approach. They don't embrace graceful words in their salutations and they never embellish their tales with charming and subtle expressions. It's always: give me; bring me; I want; move; I'll pay you this amount and no more. "You want to play chicken, Yankees, I'll play chicken," Modesta yells with exhilaration.

Modesta sits admiring her commanding sign when she notices the postmaster and express agent for San Juan Capistrano waiting for the train. She knows about Max and his litigious ways. Everyone in town still talks about how he took Señora Pryor to court, and won. Poor lady, she didn't know how to write or read in English or in Spanish. She was under the impression that her word was good enough, as it had been in the old system. Max, on the other hand, was a creative record keeper and he kept written records of what she and her ranch hands owed him in his own special way.

Modesta hears Max's thick Polish accent, but she's not sure if he's speaking to her in Spanish or English. What she understands unequivocally is that he's telling her to move her sign, and from her own land, no less. Her anger rises and she tells Max that once the railroad pays her for her land, they can pass by. "This is my land," she says. "You're the interloper, Max!" She relishes seeing Max's face inflate the size and color of a summer watermelon.

The power Modesta feels at humbling the agent representing the distant robber barons raises her spirits so high that she jumps up and dances the *fandango* all by herself while pounding a tambourine. The clucking of the chickens to the brassy beat of the tambourine makes her laugh uncontrollably. "Give me my ten thousand dollars, you chicken-shits!" she yells. "Do you want to see me write it down again and again for you? I have plenty of indigo ink and I'll keep writing my demands until you pay me."

Chola Martina, her prying godmother, pokes her head over the cactus fence. "Don't count your chickens before they hatch, my lovely. You'll never see one single dollar from the railroad. I felt your same elation when I helped Juan Flores escape from the law, but what did it get me? They killed my Juanito, and I'm the town pariah. Go apologize to Max or do you want to end up a hard-shelled tortoise?"

"I'm not breaking the law like you did. I read about my rights, and I have the right to demand payment from the railroad for trespassing on my land. I won't rest until I see those Yankees eat crow!"

Every day the train thunders by her land, her hens produce less and less. Even the overly dominant rooster cowers in a corner of the coop, neglecting his duties. "You're killing my business, robber barons!" Modesta hollers at the rattling iron monster. "It's always about business, isn't it? If that's the only thing you understand, I'll talk business."

Minutes later, Modesta storms out of the shack with the determination to resolve this business and legal matter today. She wipes a hint of indigo ink on her index finger so that the Yankees she has to deal with will understand that she is a literate woman. No one is going to push her around anymore.

When Modesta walks into the bank in Santa Ana, she tries the direct approach. "I'm expecting $10,000 from the railroad company," she says. "They will be paying me for the right to pass through my land. How soon will I be receiving my money?"

The clerk passes the buck to the bank manager, who not only dismisses Modesta's request but brusquely asks her to leave. Not one to take no for an answer, Modesta perseveres Yankee-style. "Look here, my good man, I will be making a $10,000 transaction at your mercantile bank, and as such, I demand an answer to my question: when will I receive my money?"

"When hell freezes over, I expect," says the lanky man as he walks away with long and languorous strides.

Humiliated, Modesta tries a different approach at the sheriff's office. The County of Orange was founded just three months ago and she doesn't know much about the new sheriff. She approaches the officers timidly, covers her head with a *rebozo,* and smiles like a shy *señorita.* "Good afternoon, officers. With which one of you gentlemen shall I inquire about the appropriate permits that are required to host a *fiesta?*"

"Why don't you have your men folk come in and talk to us, *comprende?*"

"Yeah, we love to talk to greasers," howls a walrus-mustached lackey.

Beyond her boiling point, Modesta judiciously leaves the sheriff's office to their parting cat calls and derogatory comments. As she walks dejectedly in town she meets some ranch hands who remember her vivacious dancing and lively conversation. One or two of them might also recall an additional kiss or a heavy caress, but they're *caballeros* and don't mention it among the assembled friends. "*Señorita* Modesta, *felicidades!*" says a handsome olive-skinned *vaquero.* "You bring us the sunshine and the sounds of the bells from San Juan Capistrano. Congratulations on receiving $10,000 from the railroad. We heard you're going to host a *fiesta* and share your winnings with your friends."

"Please do tell us the date of your party," says another *vaquero.* "If it meets your approval, beautiful Modesta, I would like to bring my brother Rigoberto; he mentions you fondly."

Modesta decides in a split second to host the party, with or without the $10,000. "I'll be hosting it on the feast day of Saint Teresa of Ávila."

She always remembers this day because the saint's native province of Ávila in Spain is the same as her last name. Modesta sings the lines written by Saint Teresa of Ávila with conviction as she heads home: "Let nothing disturb you. Let nothing make you afraid. All things are passing. God alone never changes." Modesta deliberately omits, "Patience gains all things," because after all she's no saint. She giggles with pride at her own keen play on words.

Lickety-split, the sheriff shuts down her *fiesta* and hauls Modesta to jail. They rough her up to show everyone they mean business; take an unflattering mug shot that still can't conceal her alluring face; and contact the newspaper.

"Listen here," the sheriff says to the rookie journalist sent by the *Weekly Blade*. "The district attorney is filing charges against Modesta Ávila for the felony of attempted obstruction of a train."

The journalist looks stunned. "But that's a preposterous charge. She didn't do anything of the sort. Besides, who ever heard of such a felony in Orange County?"

The rookie journalist stands up to leave the office and several men shove him to and fro. "What? Is you one of her lovers? Do you like them black-eyed *señoritas*?"

A whale-sized Yankee grabs the rookie by neck and grips very tightly. "You'd better toe the line, college boy, or yous gonna find out how cold the Pacific Ocean really is, you hearing me?"

Two days later on October 17, the Santa Ana *Weekly Blade* prints a playful account of the case. It states that Modesta spread her laundry on the railroad tracks without any consideration of the grave consequences.

Meanwhile, Modesta waits anxiously for someone from San Juan Capistrano to come to her rescue. She learns a tragic and lasting lesson: nobody cares about a poor and assertive woman. On the contrary, the rumor mill churns endless innuendos about her past indiscretions and poor judgment, which add more stains to her already murky reputation. She's forlorn at her own sister's rejection. Granted, Lourdes had accosted her after her incarceration in Los Angeles a year ago. "Don't pretend you don't know the meaning of the word 'vagrancy,' Modesta. You were arrested on a charge of vagrancy. You pride yourself on an extensive vocabulary, so what do you think this word means?"

Modesta kept on counting chicken eggs and placing them in the basket. She finally replied, "It simply means wandering from place to place. I was lost in Los Angeles."

Lourdes didn't want anyone to hear, not even the chickens, and certainly not Chola Martina. She stretched her head near Modesta's ear and said, "You know that it means. You were wandering around looking for a man to pay for your, uh, your uh, services." As soon as she uttered her words, she retracted her head to avoid touching Modesta in any way.

Modesta dropped the basket. "It was a false accusation then and that is why I was released in no time. Think about it, Lourdes. If there had been a kernel of truth, if they could have proved it, I would still be in jail."

Lourdes reflected on Modesta's reasoning, and she had to admit that she was probably correct. The Yankee jailers never pass up an opportunity to lock up the impoverished Californios, and throw away the key. Instead of commiserating with Modesta, Lourdes says, "Well, even if what you say is factually accurate, think of how your suspicious ways are tainting my reputation."

That slanderous conversation took place a year ago. Today, not one single person comes to Modesta's defense, with the exception of her defense attorney, a man burdened by his own unsavory personal history. He must smell his own, concludes Modesta, but what other choice did she have? She went along with whatever her defense attorney recommended.

On October 22, 1889, Modesta's trial results in a hung jury. Feeling the sting of her incarceration and abandonment by everyone she has ever known, Modesta returns home and writes a well crafted letter to a woman she admires from afar. Chola Martina hovers behind her and startles Modesta.

"Now you show up, you old *bruja*," Modesta says. "I could have used your help last week."

"I've been busy brewing some *yerbitas* for you to take with you, my lovely."

"I don't need any herbs from an ignorant witch. I'm writing a letter to Doña María Amparo Ruíz de Burton, she's written several books in English and in Spanish. Have you ever heard of *The Squatter and the Don?*"

"Everybody is a squatter or a don, as far as I'm concerned. Take you, for example, you say this is your land, but my ancestors lived right where you're standing."

"Shut your crow beak. Let me concentrate on the proper words to address this lady. Do you know that she lived in Washington D.C. and knew President Lincoln? When her husband died she came back to Rancho Jamul in San Diego, and guess what?"

Chola Martina spits out a river-rock-sized wad of chewing tobacco, and cackles. "Let me guess! When she came back a widow, without her fancy Yankee captain husband, did she find her land full of Yankee squatters? Did she think that her knowledge of English and her fancy lawyers could kick the squatters off her land? Am I ever going to wear a fancy ball gown? Is the district attorney ever going to let you go free?"

The witch's prophesy came true. On October 22, one week after a hung jury, Modesta's second trial rendered a guilty plea and she was sentenced to three years in San Quentin State Penitentiary. On the long way to the San Francisco Bay, Modesta wonders if Chola Martina will do as she promised.

"Don't worry, my lovely," she had said. " I will fly like a red-tailed hawk and drop your letter on the famous writer's desk. Just read me the letter, I need a good laugh."

"Pay attention to the main supplications of my letter, just in case you drop it, so at least you'll remember what to say to the lady. First, tell Doña Ruíz de Burton that I admire the irony of her sentence: kiss the foot that tramples us. Can you remember that?"

Chola Martina bent down as agile as a twelve-year-old, kissed her own filthy calloused feet, and crowed, "Go ahead."

"Second, ask her to write to Congressman Andrés Castillero to intervene on my behalf. Third, ask her to send me one of her books. Last, extend my condolences on the passing of her beloved husband."

Chola Martina pantomimed the entire letter. Then, she had a few demands of her own.

"One, if you are with child, you'd better tell me this moment so we can make the little being go back up to heaven. Two, hide my *yerbas* into your warm female parts because you're going to need them. While you're at it, you might as well roll up the paper pictures of the Virgin Mary from the books you stole from the mission, and hide them inside the hem of your skirt. Third, can I have one of your chickens, I haven't eaten in days."

San Quentin prison greets Modesta with an excess of fog and a multitude of lecherous eyeballs. Keeping her head low and her dignity intact, Modesta marches up to the women's cellblock ready to face whatever comes her way. The three dozen women stare at her with some interest. It seems her reputation as a bullheaded girl fighting the giant railroad earns her a temporary reprieve from harassment by the female felons. Although in very tight quarters, Modesta makes do since she's used to her miniature shack and the tight chicken coop.

In the evening the guards, whose rooms are just one staircase down from the isolated female inmate block on the top floor, stroll licentiously among the women and yank whomever they please for a nighttime interrogation session. The working girls from the San Francisco brothels tag along in a stupor as if the local fog had replaced their brains.

Modesta laughs too boisterously at the irony of her life. "Even in prison I'm in a stinking chicken coop. Instead of one mean rooster with fierce spurs, I'm going to have to deal with several malicious *gallos*."

Two tiny hands wrap around Modesta's face and cover up her laughter. A tiny pipsqueak voice says, "*Ma chérie, tais-toi* or the guard will slice your pretty face."

"Do you not find it comical that the foxes live below the chicken coop?" Modesta says.

"*Oui,* I am a *comédienne. Je m'appelle, Yvette.* Last year, I was the star attraction at Madame Johanna's on the Barbary Coast. Every day and night I acted the part of a virgin girl to the satisfaction of the men who paid to deflower me. Watch how I act the part."

Modesta and Yvette share their lives' stories candidly, and they jointly conclude that they must escape from this place.

Modesta tells Yvette the ironic tale of Saint Quentin, the saint and not the prison. "Do you know that he escaped from prison twice in France? How stupid are the men who name a prison after a saint who is remembered for escaping from prison?"

Yvette squeals with joy. "It's a sign for us to plan our escape. Do you think we can do it?"

"Sure we can. Juan Flores, the boyfriend of my godmother Chola Martina, escaped many years ago and so did Tiburcio Vasquez. I read that there have been fifty-six escapes, especially on foggy days. When shall we try?"

"Is it true you are with child? If so, we have to escape right away, no child should ever live in this snake pit. Look over there, between the men's cellblocks: that is Crazy Alley. All day and night long the insane prisoners are left alone to become irreversibly insane and savage to each other. Fortunately, more than half of all the inmates are *habitués* to the opium, so it is quiet at night. Well, almost quiet since you can still hear the guards ravage their *poules*. Are you truly able to read?"

"In Spanish and in English. I bet I could even read in French," Modesta brags unabashedly.

Yvette shakes Modesta's hand. "I like your confidence. Are you sure you are not a little *Française*?"

With Yvette as her friend, life in San Quentin prison is almost bearable. The Lively French Flea, as she had been billed at Madame Johanna's parlor house, gets a hold of a book. Modesta reads to the female inmates, who in turn shield her from the foxes that steal into the chicken coop nightly. It isn't so much that the female inmates care for Modesta, but they sure appreciate her delivery of the story and Yvette's acting of the scenes from the book. When Yvette's cunning schemes cannot yield another book, Modesta pretends to be reading to the women. She recounts endless tales of life in San Juan Capistrano. The *fiestas* full of games, exquisite food, and dancing the *fandango*. They relish her tales of horse races, cock fights, and the small bull ring where the local youth showed their bullfighting skills. They cry with remorse for their sins when Modesta recounts the Divine attributes of the glorious painting of the Immaculate Conception hanging on the walls of Serra Chapel. Finally, she tells them about Rigoberto's tender caresses and the baby they will all soon cuddle.

Due to Yvette's curious prowling around the prison, the female inmates find out that the new chaplain, Reverend Drähms, who apparently is a well-known scientist, decided to measure all the inmates' head circumferences and other facial characteristics. He wants to prove that criminals have beady eyes. Yvettte tells the crowd of laughing women, "Modesta, you are not a criminal and they must release you *tout de suite*; your eyes are as big as the cows' eyes on the pastures."

Modesta laughs along with the women. "My godmother, Chola Martina, says the exact same thing. She's a known healer and gives me helpful counsel."

Yvette continues mimicking the reverend. "According to his theory, the eyelids of sex offenders are very congested. I think I'll invite the reverend to come and study the eyelids of the guards."

Two foxes lunge from their den, knock Yvette out with a single punch, and drag her down the stairs. The inmates try halfheartedly to come to Yvette's defense since no one else could entertain them with her antics. Modesta lunges at the guards who swat her soundly with their batons. When Modesta regains consciousness her fellow inmates appear to have smoked more opium than usual to block out the rampage in Crazy Alley. As Modesta looks out through the cell's window she sees three bodies being carried to the prison's graveyard. Yvette's lively pipsqueak voice is never heard again.

Modesta's melancholy cannot be lifted by any of the antics of the women. She unfurls the rolled-up title pages with images of the Virgin Mary that she stole from the books in the antique leather chest at the mission. She says her prayers fervently, but the foxes attack her nightly anyway. She's like her hens back home who lose all their feathers due to the constant mounting of the rooster. Her stories no longer make sense to the women; even the ones foggy on opium no longer listen to her gibberish. One minute she's praying and the next she's shouting at the crow flying by their block window. "Chola Martina, did you get the letter to Doña Ruiz de Burton? Your *yerbas* are all gone, fly in here and bring me some more."

Modesta feels a tiny foot kick her in triple-time beat inside her belly. It's her little daughter dancing a *fandango*. She tries to dance along with her in the cramped cell space. "What shall I name the baby?" she asks her cell mates, who mercifully do not reply. Her only previous worth to them was her reading and storytelling, now she's a pathetic nuisance. Unlike the hardened inmates, Modesta does not comprehend that San Quentin is not purgatory; it is hell.

"Isn't my little girl taking a long time to arrive? She must be waiting for summer in San Juan Capistrano. If it's too warm, I'll take her to the beach so she can dance on the sand while the sea breezes cool her down."

"Enough with the talk about the baby please, Modesta," moans one of her cell mates.

The other cell mate is less diplomatic. "Crazy Mexican. There is no baby. You are not pregnant, *comprende*?"

"I'm excellent at reading and writing, but I am not so good at arithmetic. I probably miscounted the number of moons."

"Shut up or I'll kick your brown ass all the way to hell!"

Modesta understands how difficult it is for her new angry cell mate to adjust to San Quentin. Tomorrow she'll try to convince her to escape just like Yvette did, did she not? Modesta refuses to lie down. She prefers to stand and daydream while gazing at the moon that glistens over the bay. On top of the lookout tower she sees a giant California Spotted Owl hooting her ear-piercing, four-note calls that can be heard throughout the prison. "Hoo, hoo, "hoo, hoo."

Modesta understands every word the owl says: "It's me, Chola Martina."

"Hoo, hoo, hoo, hoo! How is the baby?"

"What is her name? Hoo, hoo, hoo, hoo!"

Modesta rubs her belly rhythmically. She must decide on the baby's name instantly. She's been considering girl names for over twenty moons, and it would be immensely rude not to share the good news with Chola Martina. Only a Yankee would turn a friend away without offering a simple glass of lemonade or at minimum, a kind word. Modesta is a modest woman now, and she doesn't forget the old Californio code of hospitality: "Mi casa es su casa" is the welcome one extends to a guest. But the Yankees took it literally and appropriated our houses. Appropriate, why that's the word that she spelled when she almost won the spelling bee at school. Modesta spells it out loud: "A-P-P-R-O-P-R-I-A-T-E."

"That's the last time I'm ever going to tell you to shut up!" screams her homicidal new cell mate. "If you say one more word, I'll crush your face."

All the children clapped for Modesta that day, except for Billy Norris who was in second place. The teacher said, "Modesta, please use the word in a complete sentence."

"The Yankees will appropriate all our lands."

The teacher's nostrils flared like a bull when he announced, "The winner of the spelling bee is Billy Norris. Modesta lost on a technicality."

"Hoo, hoo, hoo, hoo! Modesta Ávila, my lovely? Hoo, hoo! What is her name?"

Chola Martina has flown all the way up north to pay her a visit. But Modesta can't decide between the name Asunción, like the Virgin of Assumption on the title page she's gripping, or just María of the *nopal*, like the big cactus back home.

Modesta's elation at the sight and sound of her old friend overwhelms her with joy. Chola Martina notices the tears in her eyes and flies closer to her cell window. Modesta can't believe what she's seeing. It's Chola Martina's dark brown feathers and serious black eyes staring lovingly back at her. She's so fortunate to have a true friend from back home. As Modesta looks at the shimmering ocean, she remembers the stars on the painting of the Immaculate Conception in Serra Chapel. She recites the Virgin Mary's attributes in a soft voice. "She is fair as the moon, she is the olive branch," she says, her voice becoming louder and louder. "She is the rose without thorns, the gate of heaven." She screams with such force of delight at the last attribute because of its coincidence with her daughter's name. Modesta is in fool's paradise and she doesn't notice the short-fused assassin rising from her cot. Modesta shouts, "She is the star of the sea."

Modesta can't admit to Chola Martina her daughter's obstinacy; her twenty-month refusal to leave her mother's warm home. She rather likes that her daughter is true to their old Californio ways. She's decided to stay in her mother's cozy womb; *mi casa es su casa,* after all.

The assassin is an expert in the ancient Spanish garrote art of strangulation. She lurks behind an oblivious Modesta who inhales deeply and wails thunderously from her fathomless soul. "Hoo, hoo, hoo, hoo! Chola Martina, beloved godmother. Hoo, hoo! She is Stella Maris!"

CHAPTER EIGHT

March 28, 2008
Laguna Beach, California

Maxime LXXXII

*Not to pry too much neither into
good nor evil*

*The Orange that is too much squeezed,
yields a bitter juice.*

Oráculo Manual y Arte de
Prudencia
By Baltasar Gracián
1647

VIII

*I*t's been ten tumultuous days since the feast of St. Joseph and the Return of the Swallows to San Capistrano. On that morning I woke up thinking every facet of my life was symmetrical, balanced, everything in proportion to everything else. My crisp linen dress and white phalaenopsis orchids, my house, my library, my art collection, my reputation, were all brilliantly polished and perfectly in place. But lives change forever in seconds and now everything is different. One phone call has changed everything. What was once a tiny crack in my relationship with Ochanda is now a chasm. The provenance of some of my paintings may be cloudy. My memories of my childhood nanny are blemished.

I still have the same images in my head, but the captions under them have been re-written in a stranger's hand. Nothing is what I thought it was. Past, present and future: all the facets of me. My childhood with my nanny in Quito, the artist I tried to create in Ochanda, the art collection that was to preserve the Cusco school of painting and be my legacy. The enemy has attacked on all three fronts. Worse, I've had to look closely at everything that is me and everything that is mine. My life does not hold up under 10x magnification.

Mademoiselle Latté brings me her chewy toys in an effort to cheer me up. We've resorted to playing chase all over the house instead of our brisk walks with the ocean breeze as our companion. I have abandoned my reading spot in the shade on the cliff. I look out through the glass doors to my empty deck. The humming birds venture closer to the house. They hover at the edges of the door where I can barely see them. This seems important, this suggestion of a bird that my brain accepts as being the whole bird. There's a lesson in there somewhere, but I'm not in the mood.

Even in my guarded gate community, I've become fearful of the outdoors. It's ridiculous. On my usual walk with Latté two days ago, I caught myself looking over my shoulder apprehensively. Behind every bougainvillea or olive tree, I thought I saw those horrible scouts from the mission. Their spiky black hair poking out from the birds of paradise orange blooms; ready to jump out and kidnap Latté. It's paranoid, I know. But they seemed interested in ruining my life, so losing Latté would be the final step.

I picked up my dog and cradled her in my arms, which she is used to. Latté is always receptive to a spontaneous hug, but then she expects to be put down again. But I didn't let her go. I found I couldn't. She tolerated me a bit longer before beginning to struggle against my arms. I held her tighter and she started to twist her body. I was losing my grip on her, so I bent at the waist using my thighs and knees to keep her from slipping out the bottom of my grip. I was on my knees in the sand clutching Latté and burying my face in her fur when I felt more than heard someone behind me.

I froze with fear and stayed where I was as I realized how stupid I had been to have brought Latté into the line of fire.

I knew I could not run and hold Latté at the same time. I didn't know if I could outrun them in any case. I stayed where I was with my dog, and waited for them to reach me. I should not have been alone on that beach. I shouldn't have to go through any of this alone, and I realized as I shivered and held Latté that I am angry with Charles for not being here to protect me. Wasn't that the deal we made? Wasn't he supposed to take care of me? Where was he now that I really needed him? A hand on my shoulder, a familiar voice.

"Paloma, dear, are you all right?" It was only Hannah, my meddlesome octogenarian neighbor. She was panting. She must have been running to catch up to Latté and me. "Is there something wrong with your dog?" she asked.

"Oh, no, we were just playing," I said. Latté finally slipped my grip and ran off down the beach.

"Are you sure?" she asked. "You don't seem your usual upright self these days."

I wanted to commend Hannah on her selection of the word: upright. It was the *mot juste*, as mother would have said. I wanted to reply, "*Touché*, Hannah, you are so perceptive. The incorruptible, principled, and high-minded."

I might have told her the life I've been living since March 19th, but Hannah has a propensity to broadcast rumors. When Jen visited me in February she went skinny dipping in my patio hot tub. Within minutes, Hannah had tipped off the guard gate, and I received a call from the timid young guard asking me to speak with my "awesome" guest about her late night foray in the tub. Jen now calls Hannah "that *pinche chismosa*." With that admonition in mind, I simply replied, "I've been struggling with my allergies. How have you been, Hannah?" This open invitation to hear all her woes was a temporary distraction. It was like hearing the buzzing of bees at a distance; I was benignly on guard. I kept my gaze on Latté for the rest of that walk and resisted the urge to scoop her up and run back to the house with her in front of Hannah. Latté and I exercise indoors for now.

Today, this frisky terrier wants to win at a game of tug o' war with her rope toy. I'm surprised how strong she is, or maybe how much my heart is not in the game, and when she jerks the rope from my hands, I stumble and hit the table where I've angled a white orchid in a white porcelain pot towards the glass doors so it gets just the right amount of sun during the day. The orchid and its pot of black soil fall together as if in slow motion. I am overly dramatic these days, but I know the orchid is me in midair still perfect but about to be hit by the reality of the floor. Gravity has won out, and we will both go to pieces.

In the time after the orchid has been knocked from the table and before hitting the marble floor, Latté runs to hide under the grand piano. Why would she do this? Is she afraid of being blamed, or is she just afraid of me? But why be afraid of me? I never lose my composure. Do I? Have I? I don't know. I married Charles before I figured out who I was, and I still don't know. Today I am not composed. Today I am having a conniption. The orchid strikes the floor, the pot shattering like an egg. Black soil rich with white grains of perlite spread out from the center of the crash in concentric circles.

My plant and I erupt as one, and Latté backs away from me further under the piano, because I'm sitting on the floor laughing and crying pathetically and then choking and coughing when I try to do both at the same time. What an *á propos* visual of my present life! One day intact and the next a soiled mess. Latté has never seen me react this way, and neither have I. I take great pride in controlling my emotions. Don't I? Who taught me that? I can't remember anymore who told me that big girls don't cry. I believe that tears from an adult are only acceptable at hospitals and funerals, and now I can't remember if those were my own thoughts or if it was something Charles said, something I knew he expected and so I made it part of me. He wanted a second wife who wouldn't give him any trouble. I suppose he felt he had earned it.

Here I am on the kitchen floor crying. I am breaking the rules, but I don't know whose rules they are or why I ever thought they were important. Poor Charles, I think. And I find myself wailing, "Poor, poor Charles!" He would not have thought himself poor, not in any respect.

Twelve years after his death am I finally outwardly grieving for the gentle and loving man who indulged all my whims? Was that really what he did? Would he have indulged this behavior? This conniption on the floor surrounded by pot shards and dirt? Everyone at his funeral expected me to wail like a stereotypical Latina, but I disappointed all of them, except Charles. I knew how much he admired my composure, and I paid him my respects by behaving exactly the way he would have wanted. I dressed the part. I wore my black mourning outfit as they do in Seville. I look good in black lace, and I was dressing for Charles. Not for his funeral, but for him.

Charles loved to attend the lengthy ceremonies of Holy Week in Seville, where the *Sevillanas* wear their *traje de luto* mourning dress with grace and glamour. Day and night, we would sit in the premier seats outside the cathedral and admire the processions of the religious brotherhoods carrying statues of Christ and the mournful Virgin Mary on their shoulders. On the crisp 2 a.m. processions Charles would readjust the collar of my sable coat and wrap his arms around me to keep me warm. Once the impromptu singers belted out an intensely sorrowful *saeta* from one of the nearby balconies, Charles kissed my hand and told me, half in jest, "Sweetheart, I could almost convert to Catholicism."

I walked down the aisle alone at his memorial service. My black lace mantilla of the *traje de luto* sat stoically on the tall tortoise shell comb like a crown and screened my eyes from the obsequious would-be mourners. I was amazed at how many of them where obviously just sniffing for crumbs from Charles's estate. Every other detail of the funeral was handled with perfection and brevity, and I never saw those parasites again. I stayed in touch with that small cadre of true friends who remained loyal to his memory, and by extension to me. Ultimately though, I realized they were Charles's friends and not mine.

I lie on my back on the marble floor and look at the ceiling. Still crying softly, and mumbling Charles's name, I do nothing about the broken flower pot. This has not been a catharsis. I do not feel cleansed, purged, or healed. I feel sick. My mind and soul are spiraling into doubt. Wasn't there a miracle about a spiral staircase? I can't remember now. My mind is everywhere at once. I question whether Charles really loved me or whether I just provided the elegant and exotic theatre for the third act of his life. Act one: his wastrel trust fund days. Act two: the first wife and adult children, a successful career in finance. Act three: he felt deserving of the excitement of a cultured young wife. After all, he had earned it. He often said, "What would I do without you?" This observation surfaced romantically after men of his generation and class eyed me yearningly. I would keep him feeling as young and entertained as possible for the last part of his life. Can you love someone for this service? Did I give away the first part of my life to fit into the last part of his?

Was even my marriage less than I thought it was? If I am honest, did I marry him only for love? What about my own dark motives? The dirt on my floor has unearthed this nugget of truth: I was nothing but a skillful goldsmith. Charles was the noble metal that I forged in my own style. I am no better than one of Lindsay's gold-digger buddies. I can just hear Lindsay now: "Well, hello? A girl's gotta look out for number one, duh!"

I sit up and begin to clean up the mess I've made. This must look safer to Latté, more familiar. She comes closer and licks the back of my hand. I push her away gently so she won't step on the shards. I begin painstakingly picking up the pieces of the flower pot by hand, and I find I am sorrowful for not creating a family that would be supporting me now. Our deal was fine while he was alive, but I never really thought there would be a time after Charles. I pity the ineffective hermit I've become. Above all, I fear that once I open Pandora's Box of regrets I will never close it. I was much younger than Charles. I have lots of time left to live with regret. What if the clichés are not true, and hope is not preserved in the box?

Dirt has crept into my cuticles and nails. "I'm down and dirty now, Latté." Latté cowers near the piano bench in hopes I don't command her to come to me. "I'm going to hell in a hand basket, girl; I'm on a course for disaster!" I shriek, and I roll in the dirt on my floor. Gracián advises us to allow ourselves some forgivable sin lest our every perfection causes envy. I laugh out loud, as if anyone has only one sin on their record. I shout, "Baltasar baby, ain't nobody gonna be envious of me now!"

My sins have found me out, Gracián, and I have no need for your bull's eye maxims. Like a matador, I can leave my cape on the horns of envy or sloth or any other vice, for that matter, because nothing can save my immortality. There is nothing enduring about my existence and I leave nothing to posterity. No foster daughter, just a feral she-wolf, no prime art collection but probable stolen paintings, and no public esteem, just ridicule. I'm skulking down a dark alley holding hands with villainous sins.

My extortionists knowingly and deliberately committed mortal sins, which is a grave matter in the eyes of God and society. If indeed they kidnapped the young caller, raped her and prostituted her, they are assured a prime seat in hell. But now that I'm joined to them at the hip as we stroll down sin alley, I must acknowledge my own participation in at least one of these capital sins.

The theft of the *Immaculate Conception* painting weighs most heavily in my heart. Did I unwittingly participate with a gang of art thieves when I asked every art dealer in the country for a Cusco School Immaculate Conception painting? In retrospect, I *de facto* placed an order for this specific image with an organized crime syndicate. And, lo and behold, within months I had my pick of Spanish Colonial Immaculate Conception paintings. Was it serendipity that all of these paintings came on the market or did I virtually transmit a sin of lust to thieves waiting anxiously to accommodate my greed and fill my exact order?

I finally stand up and sweep the mess off the floor. I see my reflection on the hand-etched Murano mirror, and it disgusts me. I follow Jen's lead and strip naked in a symbolic gesture of shedding my old skin. But I am not as brave as she is. I don't walk out under the sun and use the hot tub as Jen did. The feeling of being watched is too strong. It seems to be coming from everywhere now. I walk into the indoor tub to wash off the grime, and I smile as I hear Latté's delicate paws following me. I wonder if there is such a thing as doggie therapy. This dog has a crazy mother, and she's going to need a shrink. Maybe we both will.

While soaking, I recall a theft in July of 2006 of a 1570 painting of *Our Lady of Pópolo* from the La Compañia Jesuit church in Oaxaca. I had flown down to visit Ochanda who was an eager scholar two years ago. After our lunch near the *zócalo* square, we stopped at this baroque church. The painting was stolen in daylight from a fenced sacred place. I spoke to the priest who was a restorer trained in Madrid. His sad commentary on the disappearance of his church's masterpiece was that it had been warm in the restoration room, and he left a window open. *Voilà*, the painting was gone. Does the priest share guilt with the thieves I wonder, for letting them in? What is the penance for a sin of negligence? From my readings, I remember the national director of anthropology and history connecting art theft to other kinds of crimes. He said that art smugglers are as organized as any crime organization, and they use the same trade routes as drugs and arms dealers.

What if a similar gang snatched some or all of my Immaculate Conception paintings? In my shopping frenzy I over-gorged and purchased all of the Immaculate Conception paintings that came on the market. What I didn't do is examine their provenance thoroughly. By glossing over the detailed provenance records the art dealers provided me instead of asking much more pointed questions about the painting's prior ownership. I am as guilty of premeditated sin as the sleazy thieves. I am the one who left the window open.

Too ashamed to ask for forgiveness out loud, I submerge my head in the tub and pray that my sins may be forgiven. Despite a sense of calm brought on by a long soak in the tub, I walk around my house seeing my paintings with inquisitorial eyes. I don't hear their music anymore. On previous strolls through my galleries, my adoring eyes focused on the Madonna and Christ. Mother and Child.

Today I am pursued from room to room by the evil eyes of the demons, the snakes, and the devils in these paintings. Their eyes seem to follow me. Where I used to hear the strong flutter of St. Michael's wings as he descended to execute the dragon, I am now hypnotized by the glowing eyes of the cast-down beast. It's looking at me.

Like me, the Andean artists feared the devil and never uttered its name: *supay*. Prior to the Spaniards' arrival they knew a devil with tail and claws who tempted the divine Inti with an alcoholic glass of *chicha*. The artists' abhorrence of *supay* was greater than their fear of repercussions by the rulings of the Third Council of Lima of 1583. My paintings date from one hundred years beyond the decrees of this council, yet the artists persisted in including Andean details to warn their people that demons still lived among them.

To better warn the people, the indigenous artists quickly learned the importance of perspective, light, and shadow to create the impression of depth and distance. However, as I move around the room I don't acknowledge their ingenious optical illusion for I am convinced the amber eyes of the dragon are mocking me, winking at me and hissing in all my languages. I get the message loud and clear: "Welcome, *bienvenida, ñañita*. May we pour you some *chicha?* No need to rush in, we're enjoying your drama. *A bientôt, ma chérie.*" I see blood and death and the fires of hell, and I am terrified. I finally admit to myself and to God the thing that has been haunting me since Charles's death.

I look at the jeweled crown of the Virgin Mary, and I remember the diamond choker Charles presented to me in 1984 when we were taking the waters at Montreux. As the dull companion to this sparkling bribe, Charles made an appointment to have my tubes choked, too. The fact is that Charles did not want any more children with me, his new wife. I have been lying to myself for years that it was my choice not to have children. Today I see my husband's wrinkled and lusty face on the snake approaching the prayerful lambs gracing the *Divine Shepherdess* painting, and I don't miss him at all, wherever the hell he is.

I sold my fertility for a trinket and an easy life. All my future generations are stillborn. The most I can hope for is to do time in purgatory. My ocean fortress feels like a prison now. I'm incarcerated in my gilded cage surrounded by accommodating evil eyes. The demons are my prison guards. Instead of showcasing sacred art and rare books, my palazzo hides a multitude of sins. I yearn for the peace that can be found in Serra Chapel. I close my eyes and imagine dipping my fingers in the cool Holy Water. Enlightened St. Teresa of Ávila wrote about the power of Holy Water to ward off evil. As I make the Sign of the Cross I will repent my sins and beg for protection from evil. I'm in dire need of Holy Water for I can sense the demons will soon attack.

Next time I'm at Serra Chapel I'll sit in a different pew so as to not weigh down the old wood bench with my even heavier heart than the one I had the day I ate the vicious note. The pew closest to the painting of the Fourth Station of the Cross will welcome me. In this small painting Jesus meets his mother. Her sadness at his suffering is palpable; I can feel her moist tears and those of the artist who painted them. I will clasp my hands just as the Blessed Mother is doing, and implore her to intercede for me.

With these thoughts of maternal love and baptism, I am reminded of all the baptisms I attended in my childhood. With over one hundred and thirty cousins living in Quito, there was always a baptism, a Holy Communion, or wedding to attend. For mother and all her competitive sisters it was an opportunity to show off their children and the expensive European clothing we all wore. Esperanza loved to dress me. As she lifted my arm into a silk sleeve she would sing a song with my name: *ñuca wawa urpikulla*, my little girl dove.

On these festive occasions, Esperanza also donned her finest white blouse embroidered with an explosion of bright flowers. She tucked her blouse into a deep indigo wrap skirt and tied an equally colorful *chumpi* belt around her waist. I was in awe of her beauty and grace, but in my selfishness I would cling to her neck during the entire event to prevent anyone else from admiring her. The other nannies would catch the eye of the chauffeurs or ranch foremen and manage a few minutes of flirting without their charges hanging like sloths, but I demanded Esperanza's complete attention.

At the next religious ceremony, Esperanza would hear that one or another of the nannies had married and moved on to form her own family. Poor Esperanza got stuck with our demanding and insensitive household that never let her forget she was just the hired help. The gold necklace and pendant she removed from my neck are a pittance of what I truly owe her.

Several minutes after inhaling the curative sea air from my deck my forlorn mood is pushed back to the depths where I have been keeping my secret regrets for so many years. I have a fundraiser tonight. I will be the old Paloma, the one who wears the evening gown and makes smart conversation and has never committed a sin in her charmed and perfect life. I am the woman who doesn't mind never having children. In fact, I planned it that way knowing my legacy would be a perfect marriage and a perfect art collection. I wave to friends walking by on the sand. All of them have a healthy glow from walking on the beach. A group of women wearing floppy hats and giant sunglasses waves back enthusiastically. One of them shrills in a high-pitched baby voice, "See you at sunset at the gallery! I want to introduce you to a hunky silverback!" They laugh together and wave as they keep speed-walking.

There's still a tinge of grime crawling under my skin. I've allowed myself unbridled introspection, and I'm depleted. I'm tempted to take another bath. Is this why I've always surrounded myself in white? Is it because I never quite felt clean?

Since I have a few hours before attending the fundraiser at one of the galleries near the beach, I return to my library and check my emails. Ochanda's message is lengthy and conciliatory; she's human after all. I accept her invitation to attend the museum conference in Washington D.C. and ask a few logistical questions. Her enthusiastic reply almost fools me. In the post script, she bares her fangs. "Since you'll be attending the conference, I'm assuming that you've decided to underwrite my presentation. I've already notified the media company that you'll be paying for their services. The costs are $8,350. You can wire the funds to my bank so I can pay them directly. Best, Andy." Ochanda's fangs have elongated in inverse proportion to her name.

Shame on me, she's fooled me more than twice. I want to congratulate Andy for executing a *coup de grâce* with brutal force. Dejectedly, I write: "I'm afraid that I won't be able to help you financially." I resist the temptation to close my message with the curt and evasive word, "Best," as she has done.

Andy's best bite drew blood, but I won't retaliate. Esperanza taught me that. As a spoiled brat, I often bit her arm. My guilt would get to me, and I would start to cry. Esperanza scolded me in her singular way. She would say, *"Ama wakaychu wawaku,* don't cry little girl. You are turning into a regal *mashu* vampire bat. You'll grow up to be as bloodthirsty as your people." Perhaps Andy is my daughter after all, the daughter I deserve. Gracían warns us not to deal with dishonorable people because there is no true friendship with them since they have no feeling of honor. I heed his advice and close my email to Andy with the simple words: Sincerely, Mrs. Zubiondo. Although Andy does not reply, I think I can hear a distant howl.

Now that I'm in the calm sea of my library, I have to be aware of the siren song of my books. I can easily lose track of time in here, so I set the alarm on my cell phone for four p.m.

Although I promised Jen I would consider contacting my lawyer about the threats, I want to review them *vis à vis* the facts about my paintings. I start filling out my flow chart of facts and threats with the cautionary title, Make Haste Slowly. Haste is the failing of fools, Gracían comments. I must deliberate and delay my judgment on what action to take. I can just hear what Jen would say. "A flow chart?! You made a flow chart? What about calling the police? Didn't we say police?" Shut up, Jen. I'm tired of doing what other people want me to do. I'm tired of it to the point of exhaustion. I don't want to go to the gallery tonight. But I know I'll go anyway. It's what is expected of me, and so I will do it, and I will dress the part as I always do.

With so many art galleries located in Laguna Beach, art theft and art fraud are not entirely uncommon. I recall numerous police cases from the past dozen years, but none of them mirror my dilemma. My collection of Spanish Colonial paintings, and more specific Cusco School or Quito School paintings, is so specific and out of vogue in this region that there aren't any dealers carrying my preferred genre in Laguna. Yet, organizations such as UNESCO and Interpol address the increasing number of art thefts from Latin America, especially Ecuador, Peru, and Mexico, the historic centers of production of Spanish Colonial art. Obviously, if such august entities are sounding the alarm, people must covet these works for their artistic merits.

If you have an eye for Rafael's Archangel Michael, but know you could never afford one, you might fetch an expertly executed 17th century Cusco Archangel for fifty thousand dollars.

A collector can afford to satisfy a craving within a more realistic budget. Ultimately though, what I want to understand, what I must know is this: why do collectors yearn for these highly religious and idiosyncratic works of art? More specifically, what is it about the Virgin Mary's gaze in these paintings that makes her image the most irresistible to fanatical collectors and to the henchmen who satisfy those desires? Why these paintings?

I clear the round table in the center of my library to create a gallery of nothing but Andean Madonna images from dozens of books. I rearrange other tables to make a labyrinth; each mini-path leads to the center round table and back out. I travel like a well trained white rat back and forth through my maze viewing the Marian images. I want to clear my mind of everything but these images. If I induce a receptive state I might understand the magnetic pull these Andean Virgin Mary images still have on American collectors hundreds of years after their creation by native hands.

What first catch my eye are the symmetrical features of the faces of the Marian images. The eyes are large and look down ever so slightly at the viewer. The proportion of the large eyes, small chin, and nose seem to follow mathematical formulas. The features I see on all the images are still considered universal traits of female beauty today. Their eyes hold the viewer's attention, and they seem to say, "I have all the patience in the world to listen to you, my child." Perhaps this sacred gaze between viewer and image satiates the spiritual hunger of collectors who demand more and more Andean Virgins despite strict export laws.

I pace to the center of the labyrinth and back out several times. Sometimes I cross my arms and touch nothing. Sometimes I trace the edges of the tables with my finders. If I find the right angle, the right incantation, I can learn the secret. The second obvious feature of the Andean Virgins is the bell shape of their gowns. Through the use of this shape the indigenous artists advanced the veneration of mountains, which were representative of the deity Pachamama, mother of the earth. The gown is festooned with gold patterns, flowers, jewels and feathers, all of which contain profound devotional meaning to the pre-Hispanic people of the Andes. The paintings include an excess of flora and fauna depicting the beneficence of Pachamama. Any viewer would understand that she is the protector of everything on earth.

My mini-labyrinth is proving ineffective. I start bumping into tables. I'm searching for the intangible factor that moves collectors to buy these paintings at all costs. Instead of walking a contemplative labyrinth, I'm stuck in a maze with dead ends and trick turns. I command myself to focus. I stop walking so I can't even hear the sound of my footsteps on the floor. I keep asking, "What force pulls fanatical collectors to overlook fraudulent provenance records, engage with shady art dealers, and link to art theft rings?" I only come up with academic possibilities.

First, there is the armchair anthropologist collector interested in impressing his coterie of art dilettante friends in ways that he never did when he was in retail. Too late in the game and not wealthy enough to collect European impressionist painters, he settles for something he can afford. He has confidence in his selling skills, and he knows he can sell his friends a story. He will invite friends over for an evening of cocktails and art. I can already hear his shallow lecture, "Dear friends, let me call your attention to the robe of this maaarvelous *Virgin of Pomata*. As you know, the Inca *caciques* or chiefs wore the finest woven cloth called *cumbi*. Nowadays it is spelled *q'ompi*. But I digress. As I was saying, since only nobility could wear *cumbi* cloth, its high–status was transferred to the Virgin Mary. However, the patterns of the Inca *tocapu* signs are not as evident in this painting as the profuse utilization of the *ñukchu* lilies is, which as you all know, were the sacred flower of the Incas." The dilettante downs one strong Pisco sour after another, and continues: "All in all, the native painters continued their pre-Colombo, excuse me, I meant to say, pre-Columbus religious motifs well into the colonial era." He notices his audience drifting toward the bar and seafood *ceviche* station. His old retail savvy kicks in. He knows how to engage his customers. "Who would like to guess how much dough the Spanish crown got out of the trade in cloth from Quito? Take a stab at it? And remember, they didn't have any damn unions to cut down on profits. Any takers?"

For every pseudo anthropologist-collector there are two quasi-historians. These omnivorous collectors actually make it a point to collect a wide range of interrelated items and know the facts of each item at a molecular level. Never satisfied with just one painting depicting the *Virgin of Lake Titicaca*, they amass as many *titicacas* as they can. Then, they must collect the types of pearls depicted in the paintings. Not satisfied with that addition, they commission a contemporary wood carver to carve, gold leaf, and antique the Madonna's crown so that they can display it under the paintings of the same subject. They spend countless hours reading anything related to their collection. They become experts in the myth of *Virachocha*, the Inca deity who rose from Lake Titicaca and created the sun, moon, and stars. All these facts and artifacts add depth to their otherwise unfulfilled lives.

I see nothing but selfish motives behind every collector, present company included. I keep adding to my list of bogus collectors: there's the ecologist wanting to prove her point. Her accusatory tone rings in my head. She points to her *Virgin of Bethlehem* and condemns her listeners, "Look at what you've done. All these orchids in my painting, they're extinct now. Look at these birds, you won't ever see them flying in the ravines anymore."

The ecologist's abysmal woe is not as unfathomable as the religious fanatic collector. She's a raving mental case. She has candles burning day and night under her paintings. She swears there are actual tears in her painting of the Virgin of the Rosary.

In her overzealous state she even feels a stabbing pain to her own heart when she sees the knife in the heart of the Virgin Mary in her *Dolorosa* painting.

I've given up on the labyrinth and sit down with my terrier on my lap. She's licking my face as if to say, "Chill out! You're on the verge of being committed yourself."

I reserve my biggest contempt for the adventurer-collector. This deep-pockets spendthrift pays for first-class expeditions high up in the Andes and deep into the Amazon. He travels with a retinue of handlers who ensure his expeditions are as comfortable as his private jet. Along the way he buys or issues an order to purchase whatever he covets at each location. He dictates his notes into his phone or shouts them out to the lackey who'd better be writing them down.

While in Quito, he says, "Buy this painting of *Our Lady of Mercy*. I like her story. Actually, I like the story of Saint Peter Nolasco who initiated her order; he sounds just like me. He was in the military, like me. He was a born leader, ditto me. He had balls of steel when he was on a military mission, definitely me. He and his men ransomed Christian prisoners from the Moors; remind me to do that or at least to make it look like I did that." This type of collector doesn't even notice the compassion in the Blessed Mother's eyes. For this hulk it's all about accumulation; last year it was Timbuktu and next year will be Bhutan. When he finally tires of jetting all over the globe, he'll hire a ghostwriter to write his opus: *A Humble Explorer for the 21st Century*. He'll print as many copies as he damn well pleases to ensure that his book will be a huge bestseller.

In my litany of duplicitous art collectors I neglect to include the bogus blue-blood who can be heard at every society gala saying, "*Au contraire*, I've never had to buy a painting. I grew up admiring nana's art collection, so naturally when she passed on, she left it to me."

I also know why I almost forgot to mention the bogus blue blood. It is because, disgracefully, I am its perfect specimen. With a kernel of truth of three inherited Cusco Virgin paintings I fertilized my story until I could account for a golden field of paintings. I suppose that hyperbole is embedded in my DNA. My ancestors from Iberia tormented themselves trying to prove their *limpieza de sangre* despite their prominently hypnotic Levantine eyes. They fabricated documents to prove there wasn't a drop of any foreign blood in their Spanish bodies. With such proof in hand they pursued their fortunes in the New World. They evangelized and subjugated the native cultures, and in the process accumulated riches and honorific titles they did not have in Spain. At best, they were *hidalgos*, the fourth or fifth sons of very minor nobility who had no choice but to try their luck in the New World since they were on the losing side of the laws of primogeniture. The irony of my ancestors is that once they collided with the native Andean people they fused to create remarkable art that beckons collectors to this day. Something new was created in that fusion. Something powerful. Something perhaps unintended.

I know why the labyrinth isn't helping. To be a meditative experience, walking a labyrinth requires reflection, and prayer. I haven't done any of this. All I did was mock other collectors. Dissatisfied with my mean-spirited contemplation, I give the labyrinth one last try. I pace to and fro, and yet my observations on the allure of the Andean Virgin Mary are elementary and pedestrian. The essence of the power of the images evades me. Lindsay would have understood as much as I, and in record time. She would conclude, "OMG, Paloma. The Virgin of whatever is so awesome. She's got lots of bling and everything around her is abundant. Not like the freakin' depression we're going through. Sucks, big time. If the Virgin is a good luck charm, I gotta have one. I already have a Buddha and an evil eye, too. Whatever works, girlfriend!"

Of course, that's it. When the viewer of these paintings is desperate or lonely or somehow in need, a whatever-works mentality actually works. The indigenous people saw their ancient spiritual landscape in these paintings and they venerated the images for reminding them of the civilization they lost. How odd that venerating what was lost could become an act of creation?

American collectors look at the images and see sincere maternal love, empathy, and the deep connections missing in their lives. Whatever works to make the viewer feel loved, actually works. At the end of a hollow and hectic modern day, these paintings of the Andean Virgin Mary gaze down with sacred eyes at their new owners and exude solace and forgiveness. Who owns whom in that moment, I wonder? People crave a tangible contact with the divine in the confines of their home; in exchange they'll withhold asking questions about how these paintings came into their homes. It's an easy thing to justify. After so many years have passed, after all the original owners have been dead for generations, who really has the best claim on one painting or another? It's an excuse I hear often, but there is a grain of truth in it.

As I put on a champagne cocktail dress and accent it with the Angel's Trumpet gold and emerald earrings I bought in Cusco, I exhale a sigh of relief. I feel as if I've aged a decade in the last ten days, but somehow I look oddly refreshed. My old life is back for a night! I've dressed the part. In a few minutes I'll see all my sandlot buddies, as we call ourselves since we inevitably bump into each other at the beach or at one fundraiser or another. The economy is tanking around us, but we aren't terribly worried. The gallery that is hosting this benefit for a new foster children support group always serves the best. Not to the foster children, of course, to us. Was that a mean joke? I don't know anymore. You can't just ask for our money, you have to coax it out with an evening of perfection. Everything will be like a Parisian macaroon, light, airy and momentarily satisfying. That's exactly what I need tonight. I need to be beautiful and shallow and make conversation that doesn't matter. I need to be spoiled into generosity. I need to be Lindsay.

As I hand my car keys to the valet outside the gallery, I feel my cell phone vibrating in my crystal evening bag. On Jen's advice, I haven't answered any calls in days, and I won't do it now. I do check to see who is calling, but it's a text message from Ochanda. Instead of reading her text, I exchange pleasantries with Luis, the valet. He shakes my hand gallantly, and says, *"Muchísimas gracias, Señora Zubiondo. Mi hermana está muy contenta con su empleo."* Luis thanks me for finding his recently widowed sister a job. Who wouldn't help a widow with four children, regardless of her immigration status?

I'm glad I haven't edited or deleted Ochanda's name from my cell phone contact list, as I was tempted to do earlier today. I read her text over and over to see if by repeating it in my mind I will decipher it. Surely people don't text with this many acronyms unless they're in military intelligence. Ochanda texts: IMHO URVE UNADR BTW AFAIK the conference is SRO SBT.

I don't really need a text message translator. In any language, the deeper message is actually briefer than her acronyms. What she's really saying is simply impudent: no money, no love. Andy is not howling at the moon; she's howling an ultimatum: "You're old and out of touch, and I don't find you interesting. I can pretend to be your foster child, but you'll have to buy my love." This is one foster child who doesn't need a support group. She's going to do just fine on her own. I don't have time to feel the pain since the wave of arriving friends pushes me into the gallery.

Everyone greets me as if I've been away from Laguna Beach for months. I join the book club cluster of women as they discuss the new book for next month's meeting. As I grab a glass of champagne I chit-chat with the horse set. They're disappointed with the closing of another stable due to hard times. We all flit from group to group and exchange pleasantries. Cindy, a statuesque blonde, is telling her small audience about her upcoming romantic April-in-Paris vacation. I catch the tail end of her discourse. "…and can you believe that my college senior set us up? He said, mom, you two will be the perfect pair: a hot cougar and a rich silverback!" Everyone finds this hilarious, except me.

I'm definitely a pop culture dinosaur if even my book club friends know the meaning of silverback. Whatever could it mean? I hope Cindy's silverback is not the same silverback I'm supposed to meet. I ask Elaine who is standing next to me the meaning of the word. She responds, "It refers to wealthy men in their sixties who are alpha males and who behave as if they're still out on the prowl. Why are you asking? You're not dating one, are you? Of course you're not; they only date the flashy ones, like Cindy."

Perhaps it was meant as a punch to the stomach, but I don't think so. Elaine has three college-age kids so she's used to brutal honesty. In fact, I think Elaine just paid me a sincere compliment. The last thing I need is a man who collects available females instead of Andean Madonna paintings. I take advantage of her knowledge of current lingo and ask, "Elaine, how good are you at understanding all the acronyms kids use to text?" Without skipping a beat, she pulls out her cell phone and shows me her most recent texts from her kids away at college. She asks, "What do you think?"

"I think I need your help with this text," I answer, and then I show her Ochanda's text message. Elaine has to read it a few times. "You sure you want to hear this?" she says. "This isn't from one of us here, is it? If it is, I'm going up to that person immediately."

I assure Elaine it's from a disgruntled person I once helped out. How can I tell her that it is from someone I consider my foster child? The irony of discussing an ingrate child at this benefit for foster children reeks of inappropriateness. Elaine clears her throat and says, "The text reads: In my honest opinion you're very emotional. You need a doctor. By the way, as far as I know, the conference is standing room only. Sorry about that."

Elaine recommends that I text back with a simple: BM. "Absolutely," Elain says, "just tell this animal: bite me."

I'll ignore Elaine's recommendation. Andy's grandmother might have been more perceptive about her granddaughter's true nature than I previously believed. As they say in Oaxaca, you don't mess with a shape-shifter werewolf under any circumstance. You evade this *nahual* at all costs, and I will. Whatever money I have left after legal fees and security personnel costs to defend myself against the evil forces that are approaching me, I'll leave to Jen. What was I thinking when I opened my home and my heart to Ochanda? Every child knows that the big bad wolf will blow your house down.

Near the martini chute bar, I see my neighbor Bob chatting with a group of men in their relaxed Hawaiian print shirts. He pulls me over and asks, "Hey Paloma, you look gorgeous as always. I know this is politically incorrect, but we're friends, right? You're originally from south of the border, aren't you? What do you think about building a fence along the Mexican border?"

I think I need Gracián's wisdom now. I stall by saying, "Bob, you look fabulous yourself. Gentlemen, good to see you all. Well, Bob, what do you think about the proposed fence?"

Clearly he has something to say, and he's using me as an excuse. He thinks I'm his Latina poster child. If I agree with him he must be right, isn't that how it works? I bet he's already told these men that some of his best friends are Mexican. He wants to vent and he wants to see who among us agrees with his point of view. "Well, I think it's the five-hundred pound gorilla in the room, and we have to recognize that it's a huge problem, right?"

To keep from rising to the bait, I picture Bob's suggestion in my head. There is his five-hundred-pound gorilla standing in the middle of the Rio Grande waving his arms and pounding his chest. I don't know whether to drape him in an American flag, or dress him in a Hawaiian shirt like Bob and his pals. I almost laugh, but Bob might misunderstand.

So far, so good, I'm staying out of the fray. I don't want to discuss a problem so complex and controversial with a nitwit while we all admire the fiery sun setting over Catalina Island. It's almost the exact same sunset our desperate Mexican neighbors are watching from the not so distant Baja coast as they wait for their coyotes to bring them across to our golden state. I give Bob a little more rope. I can't help myself. I say, "It's undoubtedly a complicated problem."

Bob is in full gear now. He thinks I'm agreeing with his anti-immigrant rant, and he goes on and on. I'm not listening to this fool; I'm listening to Gracían's advice so I don't look like a fool, too. Gracían writes that a wise person is not known by what she says in the public square.

In fact, he says that a prudent person avoids swimming against the stream, and should retire into silence until she decides when to come out of the shade. I notice that some of the men are disagreeing with Bob, and they're starting to walk away, as Gracían advises. One thing I do know, I'll come out of the shade at election time to answer Bob's question.

There are enough good-hearted people in various clusters here and there at the gallery, so I join a group talking about the needs of a food bank. I know what to expect in social settings in South Orange County. One has to step lightly until one knows the location of the social landmines. Now that I know Bob is waiting to explode, I'll avoid him. There are plenty of others here tonight who want to make this community a better place and that's a good enough goal for me.

I set my purse down on a small table while I eat a tasty hors d'oeuvre, and listen to Phil tell me about his latest diving trip. I notice that my small evening bag is moving on its own ever so slightly. Despite the temptation to open the purse and see who is calling or texting, I cannot be rude to Phil, and besides he's a funny storyteller.

We're both approached by Estelle and Dave. Estelle grabs my left hand as if it were a lucky rabbit's paw and pulls me toward them. She says, "You wily fox, you! Dave and I just got back from Machu Picchu. We didn't realize the value of the Spanish Colonial paintings you collect. How did you ever amass such a vast collection?"

"It's taken me years to find my paintings. What did you like about the ones you saw?" I ask.

Dave interjects, "Hell, everything else we like, like Monet or Van Gogh, is impossible to buy."

"Don't you mean it's impossible for us to afford, Dave?" asks Estelle. "Anyway, we thought those archangels with the muskets, whatever they're called down there, would look great in the new Tuscan style villa we're building. You have a couple of impressive angels, don't you? I saw them in the fall issue of one of the magazines." Those magazines again. They're always getting me into trouble.

"They're called *ángeles arcabuceros*, meaning archangel with a matchlock gun. These images depict military angels under the command of the Archangel Michael. The Andean painters loved these *ángeles arcabuceros* because they were said to control the stars and other heavenly phenomena, which the ancient Incas also revered. Did you notice —"

Dave pretends to be snoring. He guffaws, "You're a doll, Paloma, but I don't care about ancient Inca anything. Their descendants still eat guinea pig, for God's sake. They actually tried to serve us those rodents for dinner, so I don't give a rat's ass about their religious beliefs. I simply don't want to pass up on a potential art investment. If I had listened to Estelle years ago, we would have bought more California Plein Air paintings. Now there's an investment."

I'm squashed between Estelle and Dave. Time to try ending this conversation. "There are still superb Plein Air paintings available," I tell them, but it falls on deaf ears.

Dave and Estelle have been married decades and they apparently communicate telepathically. They both lean into me like mafia accomplices. Dave says, "They told us in Peru that their patrimony laws prohibit the export and transfer of ownership of cultural property.

"So, who do you know down there?"

Estelle leans in even closer and adds her two cents. "They said only cultural property that has the proper documentation, which includes the written permission from the institute of culture, I think that's what it's called, can be exported. You sly fox, how is it done? You can trust us." She is so close to me that I can smell intense greed and garlic on her breath.

This being Orange County, I make my getaway by sounding bubbly. I say, "To be continued, my darlings, I gotta tinkle ASAP." I grab my *minaudiere* and I dart past them to the restroom.

I lock myself in the bathroom stall to plan my next move. I want to avoid Dave and Estelle, but I don't want to leave the benefit just yet. My cell phone is vibrating again, so I glance at the screen. It's a long text without any acronyms. This is not a relief. It reads: "We know you have the stolen painting of the *Immaculate Conception*. The FBI has also been looking for it. If you don't believe me, look at their website. It's the same painting as yours, no? We can keep secret for one million dollars. And, I want your fancy little purse, too. ha!ha!ha! About the other virgin, you don't want to save her, no? We know how to deal with her. My phone is stolen. We reach you."

There are over one hundred persons outside this bathroom and there isn't one whom I can trust. I rehearse my soliloquy of woe silently in my mind. The whole saga of extortion, art theft, and trafficked young women for sex exploitation. I don't think they would be interested. The goal of living here is to avoid wretchedness in all forms. We live in paradise. Up until a few minutes ago, I might have revealed my predicament to Dave and Estelle, but there is no investment in this, and Dave might not give a "rat's ass." I dismiss the idea of sharing my story with anyone. I exit the bathroom, look around for any new faces who might want to harm me, and I make my exit.

Luis has spotted me leaving the gallery and has my car ready for me. He senses something is wrong and asks, "*Señora Zubiondo, la puedo ayudar con algo?*"

Holding back my emotions, I thankfully accept his offer to help me. I ask Luis to please follow me home and make sure that no one else is following me. I finally say the words that I've been wanting to say for ten days. "Luis, *el diablo me persigue!*"

Luis reaches in his pant pocket and puts his Holy Rosary around my neck. He knows the devil is real. He saw him when his fellow villagers died in the California desert after their coyote smuggler left them without water. He saw him again when militiamen chased him in the darkness. There is no doubt in Luis's soul that *el diablo* is real.

Luis runs to his assistant valets and tells them something, and in seconds he is following me on his old-style bicycle at full speed. It's dusk now and the sun we so crave in Laguna Beach has set. In its place the sky expands with slate and charcoal clouds. I look in my rear-view mirror and I see Luis's white valet jacket flapping in the wind like archangel's wings; the chrome on his high handlebars become avenging swords. I'm careful to keep my speed low so he can keep up.

When we are stopped at a red light, I see Luis on his cell phone, and a siren goes off in my head. Could he have been the person who texted me? Luis saw what I was wearing and the purse I was carrying. Did I just invite my extortionist to my home? Of course not, I tell myself; only a handful of close friends have my cell number. The light turns green and my escort and I continue driving south on Pacific Coast Highway. I take a suspicious look in the rear-view mirror, and I see Luis making the Sign of the Cross.

Following his lead, I say, "By the Sign of the Cross, deliver me from my enemies. O Lord." After we pass the hotel on the ocean side, two young men on bicycles join Luis. All three men cross themselves, and I'm certain that I hear a choir of angels asking God to watch over me. I could not have hoped for a better honor guard to see me home.

The guard at my community's entrance gate is suspicious of my guardian angels. He asks, "I didn't realize you were having a catered event tonight, Mrs. Zubiondo. Will the rest of the staff be arriving in cars?"

I tell him not to allow anyone else to enter but my friend Jen who will arrive later on. He smiles. "It will be a pleasure to see her again."

Luis and his friends enter my house, but don't ask me any questions. They are praying together and going from room to room. They kneel in front of a small silver crucifix that is hanging on the landing going into my library. Finally Luis speaks for all three. He asks my permission to stay watching over me for the evening. I nod my agreement, and he says, "*Que la paz sea con usted, Señora Zubiondo.*"

"Peace be with you, Luis," I respond.

They all step into the gusty ocean wind. Luis assigns one friend to my beach gate area, the second one is stationed by the garage side gate, and Luis stands guard at my front door. Luis is a practical guardian angel, he knows the devil can take any shape, but in his experience it's usually in the shape of a person. I pace my house with Latté at my heels waiting for Jen to arrive.

My childhood friend must have driven at breakneck speed. When I was hiding out in the toilet stall of the gallery, I texted her to come to my house right away, and I forwarded her the text message from the extortionist. I hear Jen's bilingual cursing at poor Luis. When I open the front door, there's a muscular woman holding Luis to the ground while Jen is screaming at his two friends, "*No se muevan* or I'll shoot you."

I tell Jen and the Amazonian that Luis and his friends are taking care of me. Both women apologize profusely to Luis. Jen begs for his forgiveness in her singular foul mouth way that makes all of us laugh. She says to Luis, "How could I recognize that you were *un pinche angelito*? All I ever meet are SOB *cabrones.*"

She gives all three men a bear hug. Luis shakes it off and rubs his neck trying to look *macho* next to the Amazonian. Always logical, my buddy announces, "Paloma, you'd better dismiss your guardian angels before that *pinche chismosa* neighbor of yours calls the cops. She won't rest until your angels get deported." I thank Luis for all he has done and try to give him back his rosary. He insists that I keep it saying it is the least he owes me.

Jen practically drags me by my ears back into the house. She demands, "What the hell is the matter with you, Paloma? Why didn't you call the cops? Why didn't you call them days ago?"

She doesn't wait for my answer. She turns around to the Amazonian and says, "Annette, didn't I tell you she wouldn't call the cops? And why wouldn't she call the cops? Because she doesn't want to cause a scene, that's why. What would you call having three *pobre Mexicanos* guarding your house in their bus boy uniforms?"

Annette asks my permission to inspect my property. She looks like she could take down anyone in her path. I'm almost reluctant to ask, but I do so anyway. "Who is Annette, Jen?"

"Do you remember Tiny Mapu from the football team in high school?"

"Who can forget that gentle giant?" I reply.

"Tiny married that mean girl, Sandy Torrez. Remember?" asks Jen.

"Poor Tiny," I comment. Unlike other parts of Los Angeles, people stay in Silver Lake in their original family homes for generations.

"Annette is their daughter. Thankfully, she inherited their best traits. Annette is a former cop. She was also a bodyguard for that snotty young actress, who cares what her name is. Anyway, Annette got tired of babysitting that destructive nymphomaniac, and now she's training for a body-building contest. Luckily for you that Annette and I were boxing some donations at the food bank when you texted me. Paloma, you're killing me. Come here and give me *un abrazote.*"

I walk over to her and we hug. I ask, "Jen, where is your gun?"

"What gun?"

"Oh, never mind. What do you think of the text from the extortionist?"

"What text? You didn't forward it to me, Paloma," she answers.

"But I did forward it. Let me get my cell phone," I reply.

I try to recall the extortionist's text, but there's only Ochanda's text. I say, "I can't access that text, Jen. What could have happened to it?"

"Don't panic, we'll figure it out. Why don't you write down what you remember. Meanwhile, let me look at your call and text history," Jen says.

I have total recall of that text, so I quickly write down the extortionist's choppy demands. I also remember pressing the delete button, but I can't admit it to Jen. Gracían's sage words also apply to technological glitches. He writes that folly consists not in committing folly, but in not hiding it when committed. So, when Jen says, "Paloma, you must have erased the text," I deny it unconvincingly.

Gracían understood that even in a solid friendship it's hard to admit one's failings. Jen stares at me with her piercing Spanish eyes. She figures out that I somehow botched this critical text message, so she says, "*Pinche* erase buttons. *Y qué!* Show me what the text said."

Jen doesn't stall for a second. "Sign on to your computer with all your passwords so we can check the FBI website," she says. "First things first, let's take a real good look at the description of the stolen painting."

We type on the search engine: FBI stolen Immaculate Conception painting and it's the first site listed. The FBI Art Theft Program website describes the painting as: *Painting - Central Panel of a Triptych, "Immaculate Conception," oil on canvas,*

170 x 130 cm, Stolen September 7-8, 1993 from the convent of San Francisco in Quito, Ecuador. We both stare at the photograph of the painting. It's a black and white image, and we are unable to enlarge it beyond its 3" by 2" on my screen. My screen is 22" yet we have to resort to a lighted magnifier to look at details.

Jen recites all the similarities between two of my Immaculate Conception paintings and the stolen one. "Brace yourself, Palomita, the Virgin Mary's pose and the rest of the composition are identical to the two in your living room and possibly to the one by your staircase."

"No, you're wrong," I say. "On the one by the staircase the Virgin Mary's head tilts to her left shoulder, whereas on the stolen painting her head tilts right."

Jen sounds relieved. She adds, "Your approach is better that mine, let's just look for the differences." We are down to two possible matches to the stolen painting. We count cherubs and the attributes. Jen shouts, "The mirrors are not identical. See, one of yours has a more ornate handle."

I disagree, the mirror is identical; it's just that my screen and the magnifying glass distort the image. I instruct her, "Let's just look for the glaring differences, ok?"

Jen slaps her forehead. "Paloma, the most obvious difference has to be in the dimensions. What are the exact dimensions of the two possible suspect paintings you have?"

My best friend just called my paintings suspects, and is forcing them to stand up for a police lineup. Now I'm getting shaky. I can't stand the inevitable confirmation that one of my beloved paintings is stolen. I try to access my provenance records, but I keep opening the wrong files. Jen's hawk talons glide over my trembling hands, and lift them as if they were lifting the near-extinct Dana Point Pocket Mouse. She admonishes me, "Palomita, let's don't inadvertently erase any more files, ok. Girlfriend, you have to face the music, and we have to call the police immediately."

"You're wrong, Jen. I don't think the measurements of the stolen painting are the same as mine," I tell her.

"Okay, prove it."

"The provenance records on my two paintings are listed in inches," I morosely tell Jen.

"*Y qué!*" she hisses. "Please, Paloma, let me convert them to the metric system." She does so quickly. "The dimensions of one of your paintings are too big by four inches in height. I suppose that art thieves could join pieces of old canvases to try to foil the FBI," Jen speculates.

I say, "That's a relief. I've read that art thieves will cut out a painting from its frame and then further trim the canvas to permanently change the painting's size and remove peripheral details."

"But the dimensions of the one painting by your grand piano are 67 inches by 52 inches. Sorry, Paloma, that converts to 170 centimeters by 130 centimeters, which are the dimensions of the stolen painting," Jen concludes.

"The width is actually 51.2 inches, not 52."

"Gimme a break, Paloma. You know that it's close enough."

I walk over to my beloved painting. Its vertical lines lead my gaze to the Virgin Mary's all-understanding eyes. I whisper, "Please Blessed Mother, tell me what to do?"

Jen is in the kitchen feeding Latté and pouring three glasses of Cabernet Sauvignon.

"*In vino veritas!*" She toasts me or mocks me, I'm not sure.

She's at the kitchen laptop that I use for surfing the net. She tries to lure me into the kitchen by telling me a series of facts about art theft in Latin America. She knows that otherwise I'll stay in my library trying to avoid the inevitable truth about my painting. She reads aloud, "According to this newspaper article, Ecuador reported 469 works of art missing from 1998 to 2001, making this small nation the second hardest-hit in South America. Does this make sense to you, Paloma? Listen, this website says that between 1996 and 2000 over 2,700 works of art, valued at more than fifty-eight million dollars, is estimated to have been stolen in the Cusco region alone. Yet when I search the FBI list by country, Peru only lists Two Funerary Masks Representing Jaguars dating from 100 to 600 A.D."

I tell her, "Peru, Ecuador, and Mexico are making a heroic effort to inventory all the sacred art work, but it's extremely expensive. I suppose that some of the smaller village churches haven't received the funds to catalogue their cultural property."

Jen lures me in little by little. She says, "The Interpol website lists the recent art thefts, but the items are not categorized by country or genre. So far I can't find any stolen sacred art from Ecuador on its website. How did you cross-reference your purchases to verify that they were not listed in any of the art registries?"

I'm angry at Jen's veiled insinuation that I was not forthright in my purchases of art works. I step into the kitchen and snap back, "Jen, I only deal with the most reputable dealers. All my provenance records are impeccable. In case you didn't notice, several of the art registries you're referring to are for-profit registries. I don't want to receive countless emails from these registries selling me products I do not need. I just want to be left alone to live with my paintings, Jen."

She's at the refrigerator taking out some cheese and vegetables. She pulls out a chopping board and says, "I'd better offer Annette something to eat before we call the police. She follows a rigorous body-building nutrition routine. Look at her out on your patio. She's doing push-ups."

"Jen, I'm so grateful that you're here, but I'm not calling the police. Let's just hold off a couple of days."

"No, I disagree with your decision. It's as plain as can be, Paloma. The FBI website says that people with information regarding this theft should contact the nearest FBI field office," she tells me.

I'm looking for any reason to stall calling the police. I continue surfing the art theft websites. I find an article about a recent heist of a jewel-encrusted, 18-karat-gold chalice stolen a few months ago from the city of Riobamba, not far from Quito. I tell Jen, "Call it the power of suggestion, but I swear I remember that chalice. My nanny took me to her village, near Riobamba, and we went to mass at that church. I remember the priest's hands were shaking when he held up the chalice. The precious stones were like a kaleidoscope reflecting colors on the white stucco walls of the church. It's unbelievable that I recall that!"

Jen responds, "Little buddy, you've always had a remarkable memory. I'm surprised you don't remember how the church smelled, too."

"But I do. Besides the usual incense, I recall that there was a farmer's market vendor sitting in the pew in front of us. She had a basket of overripe cherimoyas that nobody had bought. My nanny said, "*Ñuka wawa urpikulla*, my little girl dove, I'm overripe fruit, too. Nobody wants me and nobody can save me."

Jen simply says, "Poor nanny, she was only in her twenties, right? If there is a young woman held as a sex-slave here in Southern California, as we speak, I wonder how old she is?"

It's a cheap shot at empathy, but I don't say anything.

Jen continues, "Look, it's Friday night, so I suppose you don't have to call the FBI, but you must call the police. Don't you remember what the extortionist texted you? You're in danger. Do you want to call your attorney and ask his advice?"

"Absolutely not. Do you know how embarrassing that would be for me? I see him at all the social events in Orange County. He's always regarded me in high esteem. I don't want him to see me as a shady art collector!"

Gracían advises us to avoid notoriety in all things, especially discreditable eccentricities. After tonight's discovery, my entire Spanish Colonial art collection falls into the category of foolish excess, and I'll be the biggest fool in Laguna Beach.

Jen's reaches her breaking point with me. "It appears that we are staring at the stolen painting on the FBI list," she says. "The extortionists are knowledgeable about this painting. They know how to contact you. They knew how to find you in San Juan Capistrano. For God's sake, one of them even sounded like your old nanny on the phone. These are cunning vipers. Unfortunately, you have no proof about the phone calls or the text message, but it doesn't matter. What is the most critical thing that we keep overlooking?"

I nod because although Jen and I process information differently, we agree on the important facts. Jen says, "That's right: the extortionists know a whole lot about you. If the painting we're looking at on your wall is the same one on the FBI website, the extortionists know more than you realize. They understand your motivations, Paloma. They recognize that you will do anything to avoid being dragged in the mud. They're banking that you'll even cave in to the million-dollar demand."

"Everything you say makes sense," I acquiesce.

Jen looks puzzled. "There are a few inconsistencies about the extortion text, though. They interchange the word "we" and "me" as if it's just one extortionist who is trying to convince you that there are more people involved. They assume that you only care about the painting and safeguarding your reputation.

It's very chilling how they dismiss the girl victim. Are you sure you wrote down everything from their text?"

"I did leave out one demand," I admit. "The extortionist wrote: 'I want your little purse, ha!ha!ha!'"

"You're unbelievable. That means that the *pinche ladrona* was stalking you at the gallery," Jen says.

Jen sets her glass down and concludes, "In my opinion, this discussion must continue with your lawyer and law enforcement. Paloma, listen carefully. If the stolen painting is the one we're looking at this moment, then there is a pretty good chance there's also a poor girl being pummeled by who knows how many beasts right now. Isn't saving her more important than your reputation? Plus, I'm feeling vulnerable here in your house. We either call the police, your lawyer, or you're coming with me back to Silver Lake. I'm making a phone call and then I'm getting Annette and Latté in my car NOW."

Jen's right, of course. But I just can't face the humiliation. I go into my library and look frantically through my Ecuadorian art history books. In a few minutes they're scattered haphazardly all over the floor and tables. I have to trust my prodigious memory; there's a hummingbird fact fleeting in my mind.

When others are under stress they drink alcohol excessively, take tranquilizers, or binge on retail therapy. My release is bibliotherapy. I love my books because they are a door to someone's world and yet remain a window to my own. The words and images in my books have been the building blocks of my life. Their ideas flow into my mind and alter it. Granted, at times I've had an exaggerated preoccupation with the acquisition of books bordering on bibliomania. Right now, I hope that my frantic mining in the Ecuadorian art books will yield that one gold nugget of truth. I allow my mind to accelerate into divergent roads. My mind is revving up, and I cheer it on: "Come on synapses, don't fail me now!" Instead, I look up and see the stern and impatient expression on Jen's face.

She uses that calm, methodical, therapist voice and says, "I've just spoken with Triple J. I'm sure you remember her, we were the only three Latinas who were invited to every Bar Mitzvah and Bat Mitzvah all through junior high school. Triple J is a high-power attorney in Downtown L.A. She is at an awards banquet tonight, but is willing to meet with us later this weekend. Is that all right with you?"

"Sure, thank you. I remember her because of her brains and her name: Ximena Jurado Jauregui. It irritated me that people called her Triple J when her first name started with an X not a J, like the old Spanish spelling."

Before Jen rushes me out of my house, I hold my ground as I always have. I tell her, "Kindly allow me a few minutes to let my memory do its job. I'm onto something important about my painting."

Jen remains standing in my library. She's never seen it in such disarray, and I know she's assessing my emotional well-being of the last ten days. It's a therapist reflex. She's on the verge of saying something, but stops herself. Instead she approaches the center table of my makeshift labyrinth and looks through the brittle *Arte Quiteño Colonial* book.

Gracián must have had a friend like Jen in mind when he wrote that it is a sign of a noble heart to be endowed with patience. She's not going to lose her way in useless discussion or going over in the brushwood of wearisome verbosity, as Gracián writes. Jen follows a silent timeline she deems as appropriate, and then she'll act.

I startle her with my cries, "I love my books; I truly do! Look here, Jen, on page 59 of this old edition of *Quito Eterno*. It's a photograph of the exact stolen painting on the FBI website.

It says here that it is the central panel of a polyptych located on the top floor of the first cloister of the San Francisco Monastery in Quito."

Jen sits next to me and we both peer at the FBI website and at the book. Jen notices a tiny caption on the opposite page of the photograph in the book. "Well, now we know for sure that the *pinche ladrona* was wrong about who painted this *Immaculate Conception*," she says. "This painting is attributed to an anonymous painter from Quito in 1590. Her supposed ancestor, Isabel Santiago, was born around 1655."

Our brief elation crashes when we realize that my painting could still be the stolen one. All we've proven is that Isabel Santiago did not paint the *Immaculate Conception*. According to Gracían, lies always come first, dragging fools along. Truth always lags last, limping along on the arm of time. Suddenly, I'm energized. I won't allow the extortionists to yank me here and there. I'll face the truth this very second. I grab my book and rush out to the living room. Jen and I look up to the painting and down to the book. The photograph in the book is in color, and we both shout out, "The Virgin's robe is red!" We look up together at my painting where the Virgin's robe is an indigo blue more incandescent than the Southern California sky.

CHAPTER NINE

March 29, 2008

Los Angeles, California

Maxime CXCVII

Never to be hampered with Fools

*It is dangerous to keep them Company,
and pernicious to admit them
to our Confidence.*

Oráculo Manual y Arte de
Prudencia
By Baltasar Gracián
1647

IX

After last night's tense evening in Laguna Beach, the women rebound into light-heartedness. Their mood Saturday morning mirrors the playfulness of their four dogs that have made a small canine family at Jen's house. Her fleecy guards paw gently at Latté, who gallops after Annette's shelter rescue, Fuzzy. As the women prepare breakfast together, Annette says, "Both of you are eating all the wrong foods, and don't think it doesn't show. One has too much junk in her trunk." Annette cracks a raw egg into the blender and avoids looking at Jen. Paloma is dripping thin crêpe batter into a hot pan the way she did almost every morning when she lived in Paris with Jen. Annette is right. Crepes with fresh cream and fruit are indulgent, but they have had a rough night and they all feed their souls in their own ways.

"I don't need to eat all that protein to be a lean and mean fighting machine," says Jen. She punctuates her words by sparring with Annette and even manages a good left hook. Jen, who is a foot shorter than Annette, swats at Annette like a pesky mosquito.

Paloma laughs at Jen's friskiness. "When are you going to act your age, Jen?"

"When I'm six feet under, that's when," Jen answers and turns up the volume. She's dancing solo to a *salsa* beat because this is what makes her feel good. Her dogs are accustomed to the dance routine, but Latté and Fuzzy hide under grandma's table. Fuzzy acclimated to the other dogs quickly for a rescue. They are usually defensive, accustomed to abuse and neglect, and often can't be introduced to homes with other dogs. But not this small bundle. Fuzzy seems to have always been a part of this patchwork household of women and dogs. Jen yanks Paloma onto the dance floor and twirls her round and round. The crêpes will be overdone. They have to be turned at precisely the right time.

"I don't dance with wild women," Paloma demurs and rushes back to the stove. Her crêpe is saved. Perfect. Just right. This is what calms Paloma and holds back the chaos.

Jen sways her hips in quick *merengue* steps to distance herself from Paloma. "You're not dancing wildly or alone for that matter. Isn't my *abuelito* a great dance partner? And, look at me, I've got Antonio Moreno leading me with gusto!" Jen has the physical joy for life she finds in the body and she has her memories.

Annette asks, "What are you two *locas* talking about? Who's Antonio? And, didn't your grandfather pass away years ago, Jen?" Annette is young and still finding her way. She looks for control in bodybuilding, police work, being a bodyguard, but she cannot protect her heart. The older women know she will get there in her own time, and they will make sure she doesn't fall too far.

Jen is now shaking her hips rhythmically to a Brazilian *samba*. She pounds her heart with her fist and says, "He's always right here, baby. We always carry those who we've loved with us forever. Come on, show me what you can do," and she pulls Annette onto the dance floor.

Annette cries out, "Is this the sad state of affairs that I have to look forward to in my fifties? I'd better escape this bedlam now." Annette smiles and begins to dance.

Jen pants, "It's all good, baby" and continues dancing with total abandon. "It beats the alternative, right, *abuelito?*"

Paloma's cell phone rings and the dancing stops. Even the dogs seem to stand still. Paloma glances at the number. "It's just my car service confirming my schedule today. I have a meeting at eleven about a new art exhibit." Jen gives her a scolding look. "But I'll be at Triple J's office at two." Jen is satisfied with her promise, but it's impossible to recreate the vibe in the house. The women finish their breakfast in silence. Jen returns to her laptop. Paloma gathers items for her purse, and Annette looks through Paloma's antiquarian books.

She points to a title page and asks, "How old is this book? I've always been terrible at reading roman numerals."

"That's a Flemish missal from 1613," says Paloma. "Isn't it beautiful?"

"These images are so detailed," says Annette. "Tell me why you bought it."

Jen looks up from her laptop. "You're opening a can of worms, Annette. Paloma has dragged me to every funky book store in Europe, Mexico City, and Buenos Aires. It's her obsession; make that *one* of her obsessions."

"It's a benign obsession," says Paloma.

"All the more reason I want to know," says Annette.

Paloma is glad to answer Annette. "This missal is one of my favorites because the designer of the engravings was a remarkable artist from a family of artists in Antwerp.

He was responsible for redecorating the churches of Antwerp after they were destroyed during the Reformation iconoclasm. His engraved prints made their way to all the corners of the Spanish Empire during its heyday, and the indigenous artists used them as models for their own creations. There's a brilliant de Vos painting of *Tobias and the Angel* in the cathedral in Mexico City, which Jen loves. Right, Jen?"

"Yep, I love that painting. That's exactly how I picture my guardian angel: wide open wings ready to pounce on evil; tall, strong, and with a mop of curly hair, like my little goddaughter, Annette." Jen stands on her tippy-toes and plants a kiss on Annette's forehead. Annette is painfully aware she has no image for her guardian angel. Fuzzy seems to sense her distress and nuzzles her leg. She strokes the soft head with one hand while she looks at Paloma's book.

An image rises up in Paloma's mind unbidden. She sees Luis and his friends riding behind her at breakneck speed. The hosts of heaven bringing her home. She shakes away the image and returns to her professorial manner. "Besides the missal's remarkable craftsmanship, I cherish it because it has been touched by so many devout hands as their previous owners said their prayers and responses at Mass throughout the years." Paloma believes these objects to be radioactive with the energy of prayer, the living legacy of the devout. No one remembers their names, but their hearts are here beating inside these paintings. Perhaps it is not possible to live and leave nothing of yourself behind.

Annette looks disappointed. "It's a pity I don't read Latin, I could use some religious exercises to mend my broken heart. Not that your counseling isn't helping, Jen. You know what I mean, don't you?"

"No offense taken, baby," says Jen. "The truly wise say that in prayer our hearts and minds can be focused on the eternal truths of God."

Annette nods in agreement. She scratches Hope and Charity behind their ears, and soon all four dogs convene around Annette. They nuzzle and lick and vie for attention, and Annette giggles at their impromptu love fest. "Thanks for letting me stay in your home," Annette tells Jen. "This is a good place to pick up the pieces of my life." She exhales plaintively, and adds, "When will the heartache end, Jen?"

"It will subside, and I'll be here for you along the way. Sometimes we just can't reach into another person's heart to rekindle their love for us or peek into their mind to figure out where our relationship with them went wrong. I'm pretty blue myself. I've been trying to talk to my daughter all week, but Chantal never returned my calls. This morning I sent her an email and got an automatic notification that she's out of the office for two weeks. Go figure."

Paloma says, "Jen, you always said you wanted to give Chantal wings to fly."

"Fly, yes. But not a condor gliding in the airstream of the New York legal world. I'm afraid she may never want to come back down."

There is a knock at the door and the women stiffen again. All four dogs bark at once and run for the door. The two smallest, Latté and Fuzzy, are in the lead. It takes a few minutes to call all the dogs off for Paloma's driver.

Jen tells her, "Ok, I'll meet you at Triple J's office downtown at 2 p.m. Please don't answer any calls from numbers you don't recognize."

Annette adds, "I'll be glad to tag along with you this morning, Paloma."

"Thank you, Annette, but I think everything is okay now. I've known this driver for years, so I'm in good hands. Now that we've confirmed my painting is not the stolen one listed on the FBI website, I'm proceeding with my life as usual. I refuse to allow some lunatic to manipulate me and dictate my life. I've had enough," Paloma answers.

Jen raises her eyebrows quizzically and asks, "Perhaps you should wait to hear Triple J's advice on this matter? I'm still very concerned about the possibility of human trafficking in this whole degenerate scheme. Aren't you, Paloma?"

"That goes without saying," Paloma snaps back. "Actually, no, do you know what? I am not concerned. I'm sure that will turn out to be a hoax, too. I'll see you at Triple J's office in a few hours." Paloma walks out the door.

Jen shouts back, "Someone reminds me of an ostrich burying its perfectly coiffed head in the sand!"

Jen leaves Annette at the house with the dogs and within minutes she is down on Sunset Boulevard at her regular coffee shop. She makes the rounds greeting the regulars. She joins a table of friends who are planning their summer long-distance bike trip down the Pacific Coast over almond biscotti and foamy oversized cups of coffee. One of the men says, "I just asked Larry Saens to rejoin our bike club, but he turned me down. It's a bummer, he's a great guy to have around."

The petite redhead to his right stirs her coffee with half a biscotti. "No kidding," she says as the biscotti dissolves and leaves crumbs. "He really sets a good pace, and he's genuinely kind to everyone. Maybe Jen should ask him." Everyone at the table seems to agree this is a job for Jen. "He's sitting at the back table," continues the redhead whose name is Shelley. "You have your ways of convincing people. You talked me into volunteering at the food bank, as if I don't have enough work in my law practice."

A man in a cropped Afro adds, "I've seen Larry at a couple of Hollywood clubs with a fine brunette. I'd say he'd rather spend time with her than this grungy group."

"Well, I saw him arrive here on his bike, so maybe he's back to his riding routine," adds Shelley.

The group of friends leaves the coffee shop together. Before leaving, Shelley leans close to Jen and tells her, "Go up and talk Larry into rejoining our biking group. I kinda had a thing with him last year, and I'd love to hook up with him again. Okay, Jen?"

Jen replies, "No worries, I'm your wing-man."

Jen approaches Larry's small table cautiously since his posture speaks volumes about his mood. He's slumped on a wooden chair ignoring his full cup of coffee. He's staring at a blank wall in front of him, motionless. Jen's experience as a counselor tells her to be gentle with Larry. She recalls his last show of bravado at this same place a week ago. He was out of character then, being rude to Paloma and today's body language screams woefulness. She softly greets him, "Hi Larry, may I join you?"

Larry looks up at Jen but doesn't seem to recognize her. Granted, it's dark in Larry's corner, but not so much so that he would be blinded. After a few seconds, he answers, "Sure, Jen, but I'm not very good company right now." She's already sitting, but he didn't seem to notice.

"Did you hurt yourself on your bike?" she asks. She's giving him a chance to volunteer something more, but he doesn't answer. "Or is it something else?" she asks.

"It's a big something else, Jen. A huge mistake I made a couple of days ago."

Jen relaxes. He's going to open up to her. Now she just has to be patient and listen. "My grandma always said that talking things over a cup of *cafesito* is good for the soul," she says. "Can I get you a fresh cup?"

"Nah, thanks, anyway," Larry says. "I listened to my grandmother's voice last Thursday, and now I don't have a girlfriend. I'm through with all that ancestor crap. It holds you back instead of pushing you forward, know what I mean?"

He needs the validation of her agreement, which means he doesn't really believe it himself. Jen goes carefully and tries to be non-committal. She doesn't want to lead him, or frighten him back into silence. Part of her job as a therapist is to make her clients feel heard and understood without either endorsing or dismissing their statements. She goes for the middle ground. It's a fine line.

"Sometimes it can appear meaningless, and sometimes their wisdom helps. What advice do you regret following?" Jen wishes she had a cup of coffee and some of that biscotti herself, but she doesn't want to do anything to interrupt Larry's flow.

"It's so convoluted, Jen. I don't know where to begin or even if I should."

Time for a nudge. "Is it the ancestor angst or the breakup that is most pressing right now?" asks Jen.

Larry shrugs and slumps even farther down on his chair. He's virtually splayed apart in his ill-lit corner.

"Do you want to rescue your relationship with your girlfriend?" Jen probes. Rescue is a word Jen likes. It puts a positive spin on trying to get something back even if that thing is destructive. It's not a trick but an attempt to remove judgment.

"You hit the nail on the head, Jen. A part of me wants to be back with her so bad my heart actually aches." Jen had forgotten how young Larry is. This is worse than Annette. Larry sounds like a teenager. Someone really did a number on him. "What a freakin' wimp I've become!" Larry goes on.

"But another part of me knows with certainty that she has some pretty reprehensible qualities that were intolerable." Jen is relieved. The adult Larry is still here.

Before Jen decides what approach to take, Larry unloads a barrage of information about his ex-girlfriend. "Montserrat could be so passionate and fun one minute and manipulative and cruel the next," he says. "You would not believe some of the complex and pathological lies she could conjure up."

It raises Jen's suspicions when a lay person uses a phrase like "pathological lies." "Tell me about the lies that finally led to your breakup," she says.

Annette takes the four dogs out to the front garden overlooking the city. It's an unusually warm morning for March, and people walk by cheerfully waving to Annette. She sits inside the small gazebo reading Paloma's missal out loud. She pronounces the Latin words phonetically and finds that this task calms her. The words continue to roll off her tongue as if the incantation originated directly from her soul. She's practically chanting words she doesn't understand, but the innate and melodic sounds her heart emits bring her peace. She remembers what Paloma said this morning about devotional objects and wonders if understanding what she is saying is necessary. The two smaller dogs sit at her feet, but Hope and Charity remain serious sentinels on their watch. She feels safe here. Annette closes her eyes to allow this sense of calm to permeate her entire body.

Hope's growl and Charity's bark interrupt her serenity. There is a beautiful young woman smiling at her about ten feet away from the gazebo. "I hope they don't bite," she says. "I'm here to see Genevieve."

Annette loves the woman's musical accent. Between the missal's magic and this woman's smile, Annette feels transformed. She says, "Sorry, Genevieve doesn't live here. Are you sure you have the right address?"

"Yes. Can you please ask someone inside the house?"

"No one else here but me," Annette offers. Annette almost winces at this mistake. Personal safety 101: never volunteer information about who is in the house. Never admit to being home alone. At the neighborhood watch meetings she used to facilitate, Annette would tell people, "As far as the stranger at the door knows you have six guys in the back room cleaning their shot guns and taking the muzzle off the Doberman." That always got a laugh.

The woman's smile glistens with moisture as she wets her lips with her delicate pink tongue. She removes her sunglasses and sparks of sunlight reflect in her cat-eyes. She replies, "I'm a friend of Paloma Zubiondo, and she told me to meet her here. I thought she said her friend's name was Genevova Uriarte. Maybe I am confused, no?"

"No, you're not confused. I suppose Jen's first name is Genevova, but her last name is definitely Uriarte. You're welcome to wait for her here. She'll be back soon."

"I would love to wait next to you. You are strong athlete, no? I'll just go and get my sketch pad from my car; I'll be right back," the woman says.

Annette senses no danger from this woman. She is surrounded by dogs and she towers over her. If she wanted to, Annette is sure she could snap this strange and beautiful woman in two.

Annette waits eagerly for the woman to return, but Hope and Charity growl again when they see her return to the garden. She glides next to Annette and says, "My name is Montserrat.

Thank you for letting me to wait here for Paloma. Do you mind if I sketch the garden?"

"So that's how you know Paloma. You're an artist?"

"Yes, I am an artist, but I would love to sketch you instead of the flowers. Your musculature would be the envy of Michaelangelo. You are a muse to many artists, no?"

"No," says Annette. "Absolutely not. But sketch away."

"If you are not a muse," asks Montserrat. "Then you must be a stunt woman, no?"

"No, again." Annette is aware that Montserrat is digging for information about her. But she just can't see the harm in it. She will be sure to speak only about herself. "I was a bodyguard," she says. "But now I'm training for a bodybuild-ing contest."

"Yes, you should show your perfect physique to the world," says Montserrat as she looks Annette up and down and scribbles in her notebook. "Do you make lots of money?"

"Sadly, no," says Annette. Montserrat's staring is beginning to make her uncomfortable. It was flattering at first. But this look isn't quite like admiration or appraisal. It's something else. "I sound so boring, don't I?" Annette asks, trying to discourage this discussion of her life.

"On the contrary, you're intriguing."

What could be intriguing about me? thinks Annette.

"Did you carry a gun when you were a bodyguard?"

This is a red flag. Annette is silently glad that the cop in her rears its suspicious head every once in awhile. She should have fought harder to stay in the force, but she wasn't in the frame of mind to do anything pro-active in her life after Jim left her. The truth was, she never carried a gun, but she's not going to let Montserrat know it.

"I was always properly outfitted," says Annette. "Why do you ask?"

"I'm afraid of guns, that is why I asked," Montserrat says. "I was kidnapped in Mexico a couple of years ago, and I was pistol whipped. See my scar." Montserrat slowly pulls her blouse so Annette can see a tiny scar on the middle of her back. "You can touch the scar," Montserrat suggests as she leans back catlike on Annette's arm. "I was painting like a slave for an art gallery in San Miguel de Allende when I was kidnapped. After I regained consciousness I had a sort of vision—I felt that I would meet my soul mate in California, so I came here. Do you believe in a soul mate?"

"Not anymore," says Annette.

The truth about the scar would be much more interesting to a cop.

When Montserrat ditched the traveling student group from Madrid in Mexico City, she accepted the invitation of an art collector couple who owned a *hacienda* in the Bajio Mountains near the colonial gem of San Miguel de Allende. At first, Montserrat luxuriated in the decadent *ménage à trois* due to its generous spending privileges. Within days their post-coital conversation evolved into a full-fledged art forgery scam.

The husband, Nick, a retired American contractor, concocted the plan with Beatriz, his elegant Mexican wife. "Hell, yeah! We can do this right here in town. While the Mexicans are busy killing each other over drugs, we'll just take a chunk out of the art theft business and nobody will notice. Besides, I got me my own Mexican." Nick slapped Bea's rump and continued with the details. "Bea knows all the specific paintings hangin' in them churches that collectors stateside want, but can't buy. And we know you can paint, Monty.

That was a nasty painting you did of my Bea undressed like a queen in a fairy tale and showing me all her jewels. How did you make the painting look so antique?"

Montserrat and another local artist named Chui, who had a severe hearing impairment and an uncorrected facial deformity, painted copies of *The Virgin of Sorrows* and *St. Anthony of Padua*. The original paintings were hanging on the stucco walls of a small church in Santa Rita Tlachihualpan. All the men in Chui's family were outstanding artists and carvers. They had been since colonial times, but the younger generation left their village to work in the United States. Their families counted on their remittances to survive in the abandoned and economically deprived village. The only young man left behind was Chui, and he toiled day and night as a painter for Nick and Beatriz. Periodically, Montserrat would make out with Chui, just for the novelty of sucking his malformed lip. He began to tremble in anticipation anytime she stood near him, so she enjoyed petting him like the cats she briefly tinkered with as a child in Saquibamba. One by one she tired of the cats back then, and preferred to hear their screeches as she put them out of their misery in innovative ways.

Beatriz had a firm order for both of these paintings, and she daily canvassed a number of churches for the ever-growing requests. Montserrat felt like she could paint the *Dolorosa, The Virgin of Sorrows*, with her eyes closed. The painting showed the requisite tears rolling down her cheeks and the seven arrows piercing her heart. Her grandmother would say her fervent prayers to the Virgin Mary's Seven Sorrows on a daily basis. The parishioners back home in dusty Saquibamba would carry statues of Our Lady of Sorrows in processions on the days leading to Good Friday. The memory of her grandmother's unyielding devotion made her jittery. She wanted to stab a *cui* or at least throw a broken bottle at a stray cat. Instead, she pushed Chui to work harder, so she could collect her money and seek her fortune in California.

"You are talented in so many ways, Montserrat," purred Beatriz when she walked into the hidden studio on her vast property. "How do you do it?"

"I am bragging, but it is true. This type of work requires masterful technical expertise and deep knowledge of art history. Don't get too overconfident on the quality of our forged paintings, Beatriz, because a laboratory analysis with infrared reflectography and X-radiography can detect a phony immediately."

Beatriz laughed uncontrollably. "You are hilarious! These little churches have treasures that nobody is guarding. The federal government plans to take a national inventory of all the valuable paintings, sculptures, silver, even the antique books in all the churches. But that will be *mañana;* today these little churches can't even afford a digital camera. When they do have a clever priest, he doesn't want to take an inventory or a photo because he's afraid the central government will claim the church's paintings as national treasures and keep them warehoused elsewhere. It's always *mañana* in our countries, don't you think, Montserrat?"

"Who cares!" snapped Montserrat, already bored with this woman. "Just remember that a technical examination can detect modern paint. For example, the *Dolorosa* at the church in Santa Rita was painted with indigo pigments, not this." She held up a tube of paint. "Same thing with the *craquelure* that Nick liked so much in your sexy painting. The cracking pattern can be detected very easily."

"You worry too much, Montserrat. I have the antiqued frames ready. You'll go into the church at Santa Rita Tlachihualpan at night and replace their paintings with these two; those dumb peasants there won't notice anything different. The originals will be in Florida in some rich collector's home in a matter of days."

Beatriz was over-confident and thinks nothing can possibly go wrong. Montserrat knew better. It was always the thing you don't expect that gets you. She decided she has stayed with Beatriz and her husband too long. After she gets her money it will be time to go.

"When do I get my big cut of this deal?" asked Montserrat.

"You love excitement so much that you're the one who will make the switch at the church, and the coyote will pay you your share. Nick and I get our cut from the dealer in Florida. Don't worry!"

Beatriz continued describing their plot: "Our dealer is even going to have an American laboratory examine the two original paintings for all the qualities you just described. Once collectors have faith that our dealer only sells authenticated works, we can start selling the forged ones instead. We'll be in Brazil by the time any doubts arise."

The night Montserrat and Chui attempted to make the switch, they were attacked near the church by two henchmen. Chui valiantly protected Montserrat, who escaped with surface stab wounds to her back. As she ran away she heard the henchmen brag about how their confederates had killed Bea and Nick, as they both finished off Chui. Montserrat managed to flag down a driver who took her to his apartment for payment due. She was gladly ensconced there servicing him for a few days before making her way to California.

Once Larry opens the floodgates of his heartache to Jen, he reveals the many bizarre and inconsistent stories Montserrat has told him. Jen has managed a coffee and biscotti for each of them by this point, but Larry has let his go cold a second time. He moans in the back corner of the café. "But despite her lack of remorse and her lying she made me feel so powerful. I've always hated the buzzword 'empowered' because politicians use it to mess with their constituents. Now I get the true meaning: Montserrat delegated power to me. She made me feel in control of my life, my future, my place in California. I'm so ashamed to admit this, Jen, but up until meeting Montserrat, I had a chip on my shoulder about my roots. I thought they held me back with an invisible grip. You know what I mean, you're a native-born Latina. We're constantly tested by other people's negative stereotypes of us, and in our freakin' homeland, no less! Then, we waste time trying to prove to them that we don't fit whatever negative stereotype they perceive in us. On the other hand, our guilty conscience bows down to our ancestral pride, and soon we're the monkey in the middle."

"I do see your point, although not all of us react that way, Larry. There are many ways to cope, to advance, to achieve self-acceptance, and also to maintain one's dignity," Jen counsels. She reminds herself hat Larry is still a young adult who is learning about intimacy. His loving relationship, at least he perceives it as such, has collapsed and he feels lonely and isolated. She gives him time to reflect on what she's said while she sips from her cup.

Larry needs to let loose. "Just the other day in Beverly Hills I was waiting for Montserrat to come out of an art gallery and some jackass called me 'chief' and tried to hand me his car keys to park his car. In the past I would have either cussed at the guy or blushed in humiliation. This time I thought of Montserrat and I just let the guy's keys drop to the ground and dismissed him entirely. When I told her the story she said, "*Amor*, you were perfectly right to ignore the imbecile. Do you pay attention to every trashcan that you pass?"

Jen sees a lot of problems with the way this Montserrat thinks. What bothers her the most is that she didn't relate to Larry's feelings at all—she simply dismissed them as if they were unworthy of her time and consideration, as if she had never felt that kind of pain herself. "What do you think of that kind of reasoning?" Jen asks.

"It sucks to think of anyone as trash. I was brought up to respect all living things, to turn the other cheek with fools like that. It worked when I was a kid, but as a man it pissed me off to hold back. That's what I mean—Montserrat made me feel powerful in all situations. Like I could reach any goal. And believe me, she had some huge goals for both of us."

The phrase "huge goals" becomes "grandiosity" in Jen's trained ears. She is beginning to get that nervous feeling in her stomach that tells her a client may have a more serious pathology than she thought. But if she is right about the signs here, then Larry has been manipulated by an expert and an outright accusation will only make him defend Montserrat and then probably storm out. At the least she will have lost his trust. Jen decides to turn the conversation towards Larry and away from the girlfriend.

"It seems to me that most of the behavior you've described, such as her manipulative actions towards others and her pathological lying, contradict your values, right?"

Larry suddenly sits up. "Jen, you don't know what the poor girl has gone through! She was sexually abused as a child, then her college professor molested her, and in Spain she was accused of stealing camera equipment from her art school. Poor Montserrat! She was even kidnapped and pistol-whipped in Mexico; she still has the scar on her back. It's a miracle she made it to L.A. and that she's maintained a positive outlook on life."

Jen remains non-committal. She sits back in her chair, opens her body language because Larry's is beginning to close.

His arms are crossed now. He is practically daring Jen to say anything negative about "poor Montserrat." Jen sincerely doubts that anything Larry knows about this woman is true. Larry has been in the hands of a master manipulator and right here under her nose. Jen is sorry she didn't take better care of Larry. She should have been looking out for him instead of whining about Chantal who can clearly take care of herself. Jen takes a sip of her coffee, says nothing, and gives Larry the space he needs to tell the rest.

Luis arrives for work at the gallery in Laguna Beach. Saturdays are busy days, but between parking cars his co-workers tell him some alarming news in snippets of conversation. One valet finally summarizes the events of the previous night. "After you left to follow Mrs. Zubiondo home, a hot chick asked me if that was Mrs. Zubiondo who just left. I say, yeah. Then she tried real hard for me to tell her where Mrs. Zubiondo lives, so I told her I wasn't sure but it's one of the guarded gate communities down the coast. I'm sorry, man. I screwed up, didn't I?"

"Maybe," says Luis. "But right now I need to borrow your car to check on Mrs. Zubiondo. She's a kind lady, and she's in trouble."

Luis drives into the community and the goofy young guard allows him in because he sees his valet uniform. He tells Luis, "You're too early to valet cars, dude. The party at number 135 starts at four this afternoon."

Luis enters through the side gate and peers into Paloma's windows. He calls out her name and whistles for her dog. While he's inspecting the beachfront decks, he hears a woman yelling at him. "Are you authorized to be in Paloma's yard? You're not her usual gardener."

Luis looks around and finally spots an elderly neighbor on her balcony looking at him.

"Hey, I know you from the lot on Pacific Coast!" the woman said. "Hey, what's going on over there? Paloma's had more new people at her house than ever before. Last night I saw two Mexican fellas freezing to death outside her house, then there was a very tall and athletic woman doing pushups on her deck, and finally there was a flirty young woman in tight jeans with her midriff all exposed poking around, just like you're doing. What's going on?"

Luis replies, "Madam, I am so sorry to disturb you. Can you please tell me more about the young woman? What did she want?"

"How should I know? I thought maybe she was related to that bohemian friend of Paloma's, the one from Los Angeles. I think her name is Jean or Jane. They both have that curvy Jezebel figure that drives men crazy. Glad I was always reed thin. At any rate, the young Jezebel said she was at the wrong house. It bugged me all night, so this morning I called the guard gate and they sent someone to look around. "

Luis wants to leave, but doesn't want to be rude. "Thank you for...."

"Don't thank me yet! I can tell a mean Mexican a mile away. Did you know that Paloma had a known criminal working at her house as a chandelier cleaner? I read in the paper today that the cops caught him breaking into a house that he had earlier cleaned. And guess what? This ugly-faced criminal was a known paramilitary assassin in one of those banana-cocaine republics in South America."

Luis stammers, "I, I, I'm so sorry, Misses."

Hannah cracks a smile and says, "Nah, I know you're no criminal. Hey, do you have time to wash my car? I'll pay you three dollars."

Luis is stumped by the words and inconsistencies of what he's just heard. He sits in his borrowed car saying the Rosary. He prays to the Virgin Mary to shed light on all these events, and to protect Mrs. Zubiondo. He spots a gardener up the street and decides to tell him about the devil dressed as a beautiful young woman who is hunting down Mrs. Zubiondo. The gardener says, "Ay, Diós mio! I understand. It's the same *pinche diablo Jezabel* that took my father away from us." He tells Luis that Mrs. Zubiondo's best friend lives in Silver Lake in Los Angeles, that her name is Mrs. Genoveva, and that she works at a food bank near her house.

Luis takes off to Los Angeles without a clear plan, but with a profound conviction that the Virgin Mary will guide him.

Annette looks at the sketch Montserrat has drawn. She's flattered by how physically attractive she appears, but her face looks tragically downcast. "Do I really look that sad, Montserrat?"

Montserrat feigns empathy while restraining her total contempt for this weak iron woman. "I think I know why you're despondent. You are still looking for your soul mate out there." Montserrat gestures expansively at the city below them. "But that person might be sitting right next to you, no?"

Annette doesn't know what to make of that comment. She's still has her doubts about this lithe creature. She simply tells Montserrat, "I'll be right back. I have to feed the dogs." Hope and Charity bare their teeth at Montserrat, but they follow Annette's command to get in the house.

Montserrat salivates at the control she'll soon have over her new muscular victim. While Annette is inside, she takes the opportunity to return the many calls the *gordota* has been making to her since last night. The woman speaks cryptically. "Our two birds are dying. You must get them out of the cage."

Montserrat can't believe that such a strong woman could be so emotionally weak. She encourages her. "You are stronger and smarter than your brothers, no? They have many birds in smaller cages. Just give the birds a little something to help them to relax. You must come over to where I am now and help me load one or two older birds to put in the cage."

"Sorry, you must to come here and empty the cage. I must leave now. I never forget you," the *gordota* mumbles and hangs up.

Feeling her anger rise like a volcano, Montserrat speeds up her plan of action. She gathers her sketch pad and steals the ancient missal. She loads them in her car, and brings out the roofies, which she carries in powder form for moments just like these. She walks up to a side of the house and gently opens a door. It's her lucky day, she's in the laundry room where the four dog bowls are full of food. She manages to sprinkle some of the roofies in a couple of the dog bowls, but stops when she hears Annette approaching. In her most melodious voice she asks Annette, "May I please use your restroom? I'm afraid I must leave now."

Annette is holding onto the four dogs by their leashes. Hope and Charity growl and bark incessantly. Annette apologizes about the dogs, but she'd like to investigate Montserrat further. She asks, "I was getting ready to take them for a walk, would you like to come along? I think these two big growlers will calm down soon."

"I'd love to spend more time with you—I probably have time for a short walk. But may I please have a glass of water first?"

"How about a protein smoothie instead? I'm making one for myself."

Montserrat sweetly suggests, "Sounds delicious, but perhaps the big dogs should eat before our walk."

Annette agrees and closes the laundry room door so the dogs can eat.

Sociopath is the word that won't leave Jen's mind as she sits with Larry in his corner of the café that seems to be getting darker as he continues to describe Montserrat: displays an intoxicating superficial charm which she uses to manipulate and con her victims, rams through anybody and anything that gets in her way, has a huge ego, displays shallow and insincere emotions. Sociopath indeed, Jen thinks, and she'd bet Montserrat is quite possible a danger to herself and others. Kindhearted Larry didn't stand a chance. As a mental health professional, Jen does not believe in possession or that her clients have demons in their heads. But she has dealt with sociopaths before and this ailment is the closest thing she has seen to true evil. Jen doesn't know if Montserrat can be helped or not, but the young man in front of her is in a more fragile and perilous spot than he knows.

Jen's goal is to help Larry come to his own conclusion that Montserrat's character is the polar opposite of his own. He must decide for himself that he should break off from her permanently. Any pushing will send him in the wrong direction.

Once again, Larry slumps down on the chair. "Jen, I haven't been totally truthful with you nor with myself," he confesses. "When Montserrat recounted her tale of misery while she was in Mexico, her details seemed contradictory, so I went online."

Jen is relieved. Larry doubted Montserrat enough on his own to take action against her. He sought to verify her story.

"I cross-referenced some of the places where she said she painted. It turns out that in all of the towns she mentioned there were thefts of valuable and historical paintings. In the parish church of Tepeyanco thieves stole the figures of San José and San

Martín de Porres. Soon thereafter, thieves stole paintings of the Virgin Mary in the towns of Tlaxco, Zitlaltepec, and San Lorenzo Tlacualoyan. I asked her about her connection to these thefts and she said, 'I just copied some original paintings, that's all. I did the same type of work in Quito. It's not my fault if other people sell forged paintings and claim they are the original ones.' Jen, I'm so disgusted with myself. Even after she admitted that she was involved in the theft of these sacred works, I kept on hooking up with her. And listen to this, a couple of weeks ago I admired a painting she was restoring in my apartment. It was called *Souls in Purgatory*, and it had a bunch of people with deeply anxious faces floating on the canvas. So I told her that I saw my face in one of the people in the painting, but not hers. Do you know what she said? 'My gorgeous face is in the Inferno painting!' Her comment distressed me so much that I looked online, and guess what? The Dominican church of San Vicente in Chimalhuacan near Mexico City had a recent theft of its *Souls in Purgatory* painting."

Larry's confession switches trajectory rapidly. "Montserrat has so many talents. When she dances she clears the floor of any nightclub; all the men ache to be with her. So, yeah, okay, I'm the sleazy guy who overlooks her repugnant behaviors. Maybe it's because she can make me laugh like no one else—granted, her humor is at the expense of others. But she's so gifted in languages, and you should hear her do impressions! She can mimic any female voice. She would mock the country bumpkin girls in the ESL class I taught. She could imitate their indigenous inflections and even the timbre of their voices. I'm so ashamed that I laughed along with her at their naïve comments."

Annette drops red strawberries into the blender as it is whirling. As she serves two glasses, Montserrat drops the remaining strawberries on the kitchen floor. As Annette stoops to get them, Montserrat drops the rest of the roofies into Annette's glass and takes the safe smoothie for herself. They both take a sip of their respective smoothies. Montserrat tells Annette, "Let's finish our smoothies, I think we're going to need lots energy to walk those active dogs. I like the music you're playing. I love to dance, just watch me."

Annette wishes she could be as carefree as Montserrat, who is a remarkable dancer. Annette delights in the taste of the strawberry smoothie. Soon she feels like she's floating in a cloud of sweet honey. She doesn't hear the dogs barking or the phone ringing, all she feels are the nibbles on her glutei muscles, and she closes her eyes.

Paloma's meeting about the new art gallery ended earlier than anticipated. Her driver waits for her a few steps away. Once in the car, Paloma checks her phone. There are a couple of messages from her guard gate and her alarm company in Laguna Beach. She decides that Lupe probably forgot to turn the alarm off when she went in this morning to clean. This is the best explanation. This is the scenario she wants, and only the smallest part of her still thinks she can decide these things and the world will fall in line. She calls the guard gate to make sure she is right. If she is, this can be the first step to everything going back to normal. Normal is books and paintings and walks on the beach without fear. Normal is everything in its place. The guard gate finally answers after eight rings and Paloma asks, "Did my housekeeper forget to turn the alarm off, again?"

The young guard answers, "It's a little more complicated than that. Let's see. I let your young friend in last night 'cuz she said you looked sick when you left the gallery. Then she came by again on her way out of the community and said that you forgot your medicine when you left with Jen. She showed me the prescription medicine bottle, so I gave her Jen's address in L.A. Hope it was ok?"

Paloma asks the driver to pull over. The guard's message has made her instantly queasy. "How do you know Jen's address?"

"Uh, well, uh, I stopped by to see her after the spa incident a couple of months ago. She's awesome, can you please have her call me again?"

"You're saying that Jen gave you her address and phone number?"

"Yeah, she's really cool. Did you get your medicine?"

Paloma wants to choke this kid in a guard costume. "Did you get the name and phone number of the young woman who had my medicine?"

"No, I didn't, 'cuz she was in a hurry to get it to you. But, apparently this morning the gardener for the party at house number 135 was asking for Jen's address, too? Jen's really into young dudes, isn't she?"

❧❧❧

Larry's ambivalence is leaning toward salvaging his relationship with Montserrat. He makes a final pitch in support of her. "You know Jen, maybe I ought to accept Montserrat as an eccentric artist like Vincent Van Gogh or Pablo Picasso. Take the good with the bad, as my grandma used to say. Montserrat came from a line of well known but notorious artists in Quito. Her ancestor Miguel de Santiago cut his wife's ear off. His daughter Isabel Santiago was pretty famous in her time, too."

Jen grabs Larry's hands and pulls him up straight in his chair. No more time to be gentle and draw him out. "Larry, listen to me carefully. This is no longer about a break-up, and it isn't about your feelings. Are you listening to me?" He nods, stunned. "This person you call Montserrat may be involved in human trafficking and in an extortion attempt that involves my friend Paloma Zubiondo."

"What? No way. What are you talking about, Jen? All I know is that after Montserrat saw the magazine article about Mrs. Z, she was real interested. I thought it was an Ecuadorian pride thing. She wanted me to show her Mrs. Z's house because I surf right in front of it. Then a couple of months ago, she told me that one of the young maids who worked cleaning houses with her was somehow related to Mrs. Z. Listen, Montserrat lies non-stop, but she's not an extortionist." Larry gathers his bike helmet and gloves.

Jen quickly back pedals. She'll give him a chance to go back into denial if that is where he will talk. "What I mean is that Montserrat may have heard something about an extortion plot. Someone accused Paloma of owning a stolen painting that is on the FBI list. Larry, please don't leave and listen to me. A young Ecuadorian girl called Paloma on the phone and begged for help. She said she was being held as a sex-slave right here in L.A." Jen takes his hands and makes him look her in the eye. "I volunteered with you at the homeless shelter, Larry, and I know you have a heart of gold. Help me, please."

With his head down on the table and his arms covering his ears, Larry cries out, "I love her, Jen." Then he lifts his head, and Jen knows she has broken through. "But she might have some connection. She told me that one of the little maids—oh, man, she used to call them the little virgin maids—was learning English in order to impress Mrs. Z. Apparently, the little maid's grandmother used to take care of Mrs. Z when she was a young kid back in Ecuador. Montserrat used to laugh like a hyena and mimic the little maid, she'd say: 'When I to talk very good English my godmother, Mrs. Paloma Zubiondo, will to pay my university studies. My grandmother Esperanza too much love for her like her own baby. When I am ready I have her secret telephone number."

"Larry, can I follow you to your apartment?" asks Jen. "I'd like to wait there and meet Montserrat. Perhaps she might help clear this up."

"Sure, I need a lift anyway; my bike has a flat tire. I doubt she'll be there."

"Can you call her and ask her to meet you there?"

"Are you kidding, she loses all her phones. Let's just go, please."

While Larry loads his bike in Jen's car, she texts Paloma telling her to go directly to Triple J's office and to wait there.

Paloma texts Jen to tell her that an unknown woman has her address. In her nervous state she sends the text to Lindsay who says, "OMG, Paloma's losing it. Sucks to be old," and deletes the text.

⁂

When Jen and Larry arrive at his apartment they find the place in disarray. "She must have been here looking for something," he says. Larry walks around assessing the mess. He shouts, "She's gone for good, Jen."

Jen walks into Larry's bathroom and they both freeze in horror. There is a message written on the wall with a marker. It says, "*Amor*, you're right, it's dog-eat-dog in Southern California. Tell that bitch Paloma I'm not finished with her. About Jen's dogs, they're dead, ha!ha!ha!"

Jen dashes out of Larry's apartment. Larry looks at the tub and sees clumps of Montserrat's silky chocolate hair. He grabs her long strands and inhales her scent. He remembers that day in the parking lot of the mission in San Capistrano when he let go of her hand and she looked at him for a moment as if he was the enemy. Had she been planning her revenge since that day? The angel on his shoulder fiercely commands him to chase after Jen. He jumps in her car and they drive up the steep hill to her home.

Within minutes of their arrival, Jen's home is a beehive of paramedic and police activity. Jen accompanies Annette as they load her into the ambulance. Hope is acting dopey, Latté and Charity quiver, and Fuzzy is lifeless. Larry and Jen's neighbor Enrique take the four dogs to the vet down the hill. Jen shouts from the ambulance, "Please have Dr. Lopez keep them at the clinic until I pick them up. Only Latté can be released to Paloma, got it?"

Paloma meets with Triple J as scheduled. She's relieved to divulge all the details of the extortionist's demands to a lawyer who is capable of disassembling this hornet's nest. Triple J listens acutely as if her ears can detect a falsehood buried in a sound wave. She asks an insurmountable number of questions, most of them mildly accusatory, such as: "Who has a reason to hate you?" and "which art dealer do you still owe money to?" Paloma wants to be in control of this interview; she's the client, after all. She does acknowledge that Triple J is a person who plumbs the most profound depths, as Gracían says. Triple J dissects the anatomy of Paloma's character with her questioning scalpel. Ximena Jurado-Jimenez judges Paloma's deepest fears, and this infuriates Paloma. She wonders why she ever listened to Jen.

Triple J adjusts her glasses, and stares at Paloma. "It seems to me that your primary concern is not your personal safety but rather you would like to confirm that your paintings are legitimate in every way, am I correct, Paloma?

"That's correct," says Paloma. And why shouldn't it be? "After all, I don't want to be involved with the FBI since my painting is absolutely not the one listed on the website."

"Do you truly attribute all the personal facts the extortionist knew about you to random coincidence?" Triple J is looking at her as if Paloma is a child or a fool, as if her position is laughable. Paloma is thrown off balance and she wants to end this meeting. Her painting is not the one on the FBI list. Period. End of story. She refuses to jump into the filthy trough of police investigations, possible sex-slavery, stolen paintings, and all the related media attention. She's wealthy, extremely wealthy, she's in command of her life, and she's had enough of this line of questioning. How did she let things get to this point? The world will be what she wants it to be. Life will be what she has made it. She let the world into her fortress and it all went wrong. Never again. Time to pull up the drawbridge. She'll hire a bodyguard if she needs one, she'll hire a driver, and when she needs a lawyer she'll pay for one—like a plumber or a manicurist, or a maid. Paloma has had enough of this chaos. She wants order and solitude. She wants all the things Charles promised her and all the things she has negotiated with the sun and the sea. She wants to be safe and in charge of herself and her world. She wants the royal blue sky and the guard at the gate, and she doesn't want to feel responsible anymore. She didn't make the world the confusing and violent and ruthlessly unjust place it is, and she can't fix it by herself. No one can. She wants to go home. Paloma composes herself as always and makes another person believe the incredible lie that she just doesn't care.

"Thank you for seeing me on a Saturday." Paloma tucks her purse under her arm, hands over a business card with a jangle of bracelets and the glimmer of a perfect manicure. Her manner says, go ahead, find something wrong with me. Look for the flaw if you dare. You won't find it. You don't speak my language. You don't even know its name. "Here's my accountant's contact information." And she walks out the door alone.

CHAPTER TEN

April 12, 2008
Laguna Beach, California

Maxime CCLVIII

*To look out for one that may help carry
the burden of adversity*

*Be never alone, especially in dangers,
else thou wilt charge thy self
with all hatred.*

Oráculo Manual y Arte de
Prudencia
By Baltasar Gracián
1647

X

We sit mesmerized by the fluidity of the surfers as they weave in and out of the majestic waves in front of my house in Laguna. In their agility and swaying motion I detect a choreography that can only be orchestrated under the Southern California sun. The surfers of all ages and ethnicities comprise the violins and violas that carry the melody of the coastal lifestyle.

The sonorous cellos impersonate the waves; without them there would be no drama or energy to the music. The versatility of the brass section can be heard in the songs of the piccolo sandpiper and the French horn dolphins. This being a California musical composition, the *sitar, zampoña,* and Chinese zither replicate the cacophony of foreign languages spoken by the beachgoers.

Larry, who rides the waves on a traditional long board, unifies the composition with the percussion of the conch shell and the wooden rattles of primeval California. Jen waves to Larry who is perched on the nose of his board and hanging ten. Jen applauds his talent and struts around the deck in her Brazilian string bikini singing a silly refrain, "Farewell and *adieu* to you, ladies of Spain."

"What is that awful song you're singing?" demands Annette, who lies motionless on the lounge chair.

"It's a Yankee whaling song," replies Jen. "But I don't remember the rest."

"You're a month late," I tell her. "The whales swam by in early March; they're in Mexico by now. But I need your help. I'm stymied by the rest of this Shakespearean sonnet: Like as the waves make towards the pebbled shore, so do our minutes hasten their end. What comes after that, Jen?"

"Death," she whispers and points to Annette.

We have to tread lightly on the subject of death ever since Fuzzy's demise. As best as Jen can put together, Fuzzy's stray dog instinct must have compelled him to lick all four bowls of dog food that Annette dispensed two weeks ago. He ingested a lethal dose of flunitrazepam thereby saving the other three dogs from a similar fate. It was what he learned to survive on the street, in the wilderness, outside of a family. But in a home, in a place of love, it was fatal to him. Jen explained to Annette how that love was made manifest by the permanent presence of her grandparents and hoped it would help her to believe that the souls of kind people had held her dog and stroked his fur while his sleep deepened.

After Annette's release from the hospital for roofie intoxication, she single-handedly dug a deep grave next to a tall cypress in Jen's garden. Annette's palms bled from blisters, but she would not stop digging until Jen ceremoniously wrapped Fuzzy in her grandmother's prized *rebozo* shawl. Jen lit *luminarias* that glowed from the front door through the curved garden path leading to Fuzzy's grave. We three ambled solemnly at twilight to put Fuzzy to rest. Jen and I laid dozens of marigolds over Fuzzy's grave in the style of Oaxaca on the Day of the Dead. It was an earnest tribute to the intense love we share with our pets. There are those who would say Fuzzy was "only" a dog, and our tribute goes too far. Fuzzy was not, after all, a person. It seems to be the lack of intellect that confuses people. But isn't that the point? Imagine a lifelong relationship with a living being and the only language you share is emotion. Every command, every touch, every look pure emotion bereft of the cold of logic, intellect or debate. Annette blames herself as she grieves for Fuzzy, for her incomprehensible break-up with Jim, and for her lack of judgment with a cunning sociopath. She was a bodyguard, a trained police officer, and she couldn't protect a sweet stray dog. She is only too aware that it could have been her friends in the house instead of the dogs if the timing had been just a little bit different. As she adjusts herself on the lounge chair she still moans with pain for the vicious bites to her buttocks inflicted by the human maniac.

Always cordial, Lupe glides by each one of us with a tray of hibiscus tea and tasty slices of papaya and watermelon. Jen is in the hot tub soaking her barely clothed body. She invites Lupe to remove her shoes and dip her feet in the warm whirlpool. Lupe eyes bulge out. "No, thank you, Señora Genoveva. I have too much work to do."

"*Y qué,* you can take a fifteen-minute break. I know the boss." Jen winks at me.

Lupe is tempted, but one glance at my facial expression and she gathers her tray and skulks back in the kitchen.

"Would it kill you to let her have a little bit of fun?" asks Jen.

"Please don't start with your leftie, union rules diatribe. Let's enjoy this glorious—"

I can't finish my sentence because Hannah shouts from her balcony. "The minute you let them think they're your equal, you've lost control, Paloma!"

"*Pinche metiche*, I don't care how old you are, you're going to learn a lesson," hisses Jen. She exits the whirlpool and walks right under Hannah's balcony. By the time she opens her mouth I can tell that she already feels sorry for Hannah.

"Hi Hannah, we've had many brief conversation in the last dozen years, haven't we?"

"Probably, and most of them have been a real pain the ass, if I recall correctly."

"I would categorize them as ineffectual," says Jen. "I'm glad that you keep an eye out for my best friend's welfare. She lives all alone as you do, so it's good to know that you have a neighbor who cares for you, isn't it?"

"How would I know, everyone here is waiting for me to die so they can tear down my house and put up a hideously huge monstrosity on my lot. So what do you want from me?"

"I hope that we can begin by being polite to each other. I don't want to make you angry every time I come over and take a dip in the hot tub. You and Paloma are very fortunate to live at the beach. When I come over to visit her I love to feel the ocean breeze against my skin, and I like to get an all-over tan. Did you like to tan?"

"I'm not dead yet," shouts Hannah. "Why are you talking to me in the past tense, damn it?"

Annette and I are stifling giggles. Jen's perfect record of being able to win over anyone is about to be shattered. She tries another tack.

"So what do you enjoy doing?" Jen asks. "What makes you content?"

Annette whispers to me from her lounge chair, "She seems to enjoy spying and shouting pretty well."

"How should I know?" answers Hannah. "I spent my younger years yelling at my kids. A lot of good it did me—they're all failures and they hate me, to boot. My ex-husband is dead and all the people I knew in Laguna are either dead or in a senior home. What is there to be happy about?" Hannah seems to have stumped Jen for a moment.

"You look to be in good health," Jen finally says.

"Nice save," I whisper.

"Your hearing and eyesight are excellent!" adds Jen. Annette laughs out loud and has to put her hands over her mouth. Jen winks at Hannah.

"Why are you winking at me?" the old woman yells. "I'm not gay. I don't understand you people. Why didn't you all just stay in Mexico?" Hannah storms inside her upstairs bedroom and draws the drapes.

Jen comes to sit next to me and looks like she's about to cry. "My God, poor bitter Hannah! I wanted to yell at her, 'This is my land!' but then I would be equally guilty of xeno-phobia. What a way to end your years. She views her life as unproductive and a failure. She must be suffering from despair and depression. Is there anyone she gets along with here?"

"Just me, I'm afraid," I admit.

"Keep it up, then," says Jen. "Poor Hannah feels hopeless. Her decision to age badly reminds me of the end of that Shakespeare sonnet you quoted. The sonnet is about the passage of time and the ravages of time. But at the end of the sonnet the speaker declares that his poems will remain immortal."

"Ah, so we're back to the topic of legacy," I say.

"This is our golden opportunity to decide between follow-ing a path of generativity versus a path of stagnation." She points to Hannah's balcony. "Your philanthropic contributions have helped many people, even ingrates such as Ochanda, and you also should be proud of your intellectual accomplishments." Jen gives me a high five. I do have things to be proud of.

"But what?" I probe.

Jen sits up straight and lectures me. "No buts, just opportunities to grow. Here's what you're doing right: You use your leisure time creatively, you've adjusted beautifully to the physical changes of middle age, you have an incredible home, you're bequeathing your art collection to your *alma mater*, and you share your wealth with your friends." She kisses me on both cheeks. "*Merci beaucoup, ma copine.* Here's what I would suggest: we both need to nurture things that will outlast us. We have to plunge deeper in the world and seek new levels of insight and fulfillment."

Always suspicious, I add, "Would those new levels of insight include my getting involved with the human trafficking victim?" It seems so cold to hear myself refer to her that way, but she has not told anyone her name.

"It would be an opportunity to selflessly bestow your efforts toward the welfare of a young woman who wants to talk to you," says Jen.

But for me it's not that simple. For Jen it is simple to do the right thing. She has always refused to accept complexity. That is why she thought kindness would work on Hannah. The world is not so simple, and I am not heartless. There are injustices in the world that cannot be fixed with kindness, or stability, or resources, or love. Sometimes things stay broken because we don't even have the words to begin to repair them.

"Surely, Triple J didn't tell give that advice, did she?" I ask Jen.

"Triple J decided not to get involved in this situation whatsoever," says Jen. "You dismissed her summarily, is what she said."

"I behaved imperiously, I'm afraid. I admit it."

"She didn't phrase it quite that way," says Jen. "Let's just say she's not so eager to take my phone calls anymore."

"Well, I'll give you the number of another one because I've been up to my ears in attorneys. Each one advises me not to talk to anyone about anything that happened. You're my only family, so I'm ignoring them."

"So you ignored my lawyer and yours. Why do you even hire them?" asks Jen, clearly exasperated with me.

"The attorney who was searching for the whereabouts of Luis gave me sad news yesterday," I say. "The attorney described all the steps and forms, I-203 and I-247, and on and on. Bottom line, Luis hasn't been cleared of criminal charges and he's still being detained."

Annette, who dozed off, sits up suddenly. "Ouch! That viper didn't attack him, too, did she?"

Jen and I haven't told her the details of the whereabouts of my guardian angel, Luis. Annette has been through enough. I glance at Jen, who walks over and sits on the edge of the Annette's lounge chair. "This is what happened to Luis," she says. "He went to Paloma's house and discovered that the she-devil had been there."

We've made a pact never to mention the sociopath's name again. She doesn't deserve to have the same name of the sacred cathedral near Barcelona. Both Jen and I remember the heavenly choir music and exalted spires that epitomized the noble efforts of the builders and musician monks throughout the centuries.

Jen wants to yank off the bad-news bandage in one swift motion. "He found out more or less where I live and drove up from Laguna in a borrowed car. He asked many of the merchants on Sunset Boulevard, many of whom have known me since

I was a teen, for a Mrs. Genoveva, but everyone knows me as Jen. Then, Luis walked to the food bank where I volunteer. The center was crowded with needy people, and he politely waited in line outside. Unfortunately, the *migra* was rounding up undocumented workers and they nabbed Luis."

"Oh no," Annette says. "So please tell me he's out now and back with his family?"

"No, baby. It took his sister several days to finally get a hold of Paloma," Jen says.

I shake my head in disbelief. "As you know, I decided to cut off all communication with everyone except Jen and my attorneys. I hired an expert in this matter, but Luis is in a lot of trouble since the car he borrowed was a stolen car and it contained traces of drugs and incriminating drug paraphernalia."

"Oh, *no*," Annette moans. "He'll definitely get deported!"

"We'll see what we can do," I assure her. But I know there is little hope.

Annette stands up and stretches out her bodybuilder physique. Some passersby howl and whistle. "Morons!" Annette shouts back, and heads indoors. "I can't take any more," she says. "Show me the new painting you bought, Paloma."

Resting on a hand-wrought iron easel in the library is an 18th century painting of San Isidro, the farmer. The art restorer, who was working on him for months, just delivered him last week. His full body covers the center of the composition, but I want to expand on the minor details instead. Annette sits cautiously on my leather divan, and Latté snuggles on her lap. "Tell me all about this painting."

"San Isidro is the patron saint of day laborers and field workers since he was a field hand working for a wealthy man near Madrid back in 1100," I say. "His co-workers turned him in to the owner of the farm because he arrived late to the field since he went to Mass daily before arriving to work."

"Yeah, co-workers will turn on you for any tiny misdemeanor and then turn you in to your sergeant. I can relate to this saint already." Annette pulls on Latté's oatmeal-colored beard and makes my dog's head nod up and down in agreement.

"As you can see in the background of the painting, there are three angels working the field. They helped San Isidro so that at the end of the day he produced more than his co-workers."

"I didn't have any angels on my watch, that's for sure." Annette makes Latté nod in disagreement.

Jen storms in the library like the tornado she is. "Professor Zubiondo, do tell us the bigger significance of this painting."

"The indigenous artists of the Quito School wanted to remind and instruct their people about the upcoming solstice festivals that were so important in the Andean calendar. If you pay attention to the landscape, you notice that the wide farmland is framed by a mountain range that is very similar to the ring of volcanoes that surround Quito. On the left there is a dominant red-orange sun ubiquitous to the equator, and the dark gray thunderclouds remind the viewer that this scene is taking place in Quito, not in Madrid. The three angels work the field in bare feet wearing robes similar to the robes traditionally worn by the Andean males prior to the Spanish conquest. A painting of this size would have hung in one of the churches so the faithful could, in essence, read the story of their ancestral traditions. It's like a book for the illiterate."

Annette asks, "Where's the religious instruction in the painting?"

"I think that the instruction is a fusion of both the Catholic and Inca religions. The native feast surreptitiously depicted here is the harvest festival that took place before the June Solstice.

The native feast coincides with the Catholic feast for San Isidro celebrated on May 15th. The stormy clouds with lightning tell the indigenous people to prepare for the reappearance of celestial events, the Pleiades in this case. The angel on the right is pouring *chicha,* not water, onto the soil from a ceramic vase that is Inca in design. Look closely and you will see the *tocapu* abstract designs. The Incas always poured the fermented drink, *chicha*, as a tribute to Pachamama, their Earth Mother."

Jen chimes in. "I can vouch for how generously they still pour that *chicha* elixir. I loved every mug of it. They call the mugs *keros* and they're made from hard jungle wood. Please continue, Professor Paloma."

"Some would argue that the blood-red color of San Isidro's clothing might be a cautionary note to the viewers. San Isidro should have been painted in simple worker garb of grey or brown. By painting his clothing a vivid red, which to the Inca was essentially war attire, the native artists might have been saying: Beware of the Spaniards, although the natives didn't really need reminders. The fusion of both religions is in the solid gold disc signifying sainthood to the Catholics, and the sun god to the Incas. The faithful amalgamated Catholicism with whatever they could glean of the old Inca religion from these images."

"So, the indigenous artists are a prime example of the positive elements of generativity," Jen remarks. "They were concerned for the welfare of generations. They were highly involved and inclusive. The artists wanted to create and accomplish something of artistic value and of cultural significance for the benefit of future generations. They promoted their ancient values despite the yoke of Spanish rule."

"Jen doesn't give up, does she?" Annette groans.

"Paloma is at a threshold of deep understanding," Jen says. "Plus, sorry, please don't get mad at me: I've spoken with the director of the center where they are taking good care of the trafficked girl. The director and I worked together years ago. She contacted me after she saw my name in the file."

Annette perks up. "Hey, this is my territory. Jen, be very cautious about what you divulge about the victim, the circumstances, or the center where she is detained."

Jen answers, "Of course, you're right, Annette. Here's what I can say: The victim has comprehensive case management, including legal, medical or mental health services. But the director is very worried that her mental health is deteriorating. She's not making progress in individual and group therapy. Her despondency exceeds the psychopathology for the trauma she's experienced. Apparently, she's unable to recall important aspects of the trauma. She's mostly silent and withdrawn, but will experience outbursts of hysterical weeping, where she speaks in a blend of Spanish and Kichwa. That's when the counselor heard the girl calling Paloma's name." Jen gives me another significant look.

I walk around the library touching the spines of my books hoping their tactile messages speed directly to my logical mind and not to the heartstrings Jen is plucking. I ask her, "Are you sure your middle name isn't Diana or Artemis? I know you're the strong protectress and the nurturing helper, but set the bow down for a while." Granted, I'm stalling, but according to Gracían, in dealing with people it is necessary to look within. He advocates that people must be studied as deeply as books.

Annette sees the opportunity to introduce a temporary truce between Jen and me. "Paloma, I've been meaning to apologize for leaving your priceless missal out on the gazebo table. The engravings made the beast's eyes glow. She seemed so knowledgeable about copper engravings. She even told me that the *intaglio* plates, I think that's what she called them, wore down rapidly due to the great pressure that was used to print the image on paper."

But Annette's peacemaker role goes awry. She sinks in the chair and berates herself. "How could I have let her deceive me so easily? My sweet Fuzzy suffered for my mistakes! Why didn't I recognize a con? No wonder I got thrown off the force; I'm so inattentive. How will I ever pay you back for your lost treasure?"

"The book will resurface, and we'll track it down," I say. "We'll be a three-person, book detective squad. We'll go to antiquarian bookstores in New York and Mexico City. Do you know that the first print shop in the Western Hemisphere was established in 1535 in Mexico City? And the longest printing dynasty there, the Calderón-Benavides-Rivera publishing powerhouse, was primarily run by women from the same family from 1625 to 1754?"

"Why did they stop publishing?" asks Annette.

I try to recall the facts. "María de Rivera Calderón y Benavides, who was the last scion of this eminent family, left no heirs."

Jen gets a jab in. "I recall that our guide at the museum of the first printing enterprise in Mexico City said that good old María couldn't keep up with the competition. She thought she could just rest on the laurels of her inheritance. Although, I do love that one book she printed, the one with the Virgin Mary standing on top of a giant *nopal* cactus. It's a rustic woodcut, do you recall?"

"That book is a 1734 rulebook printed by María for the operation of the boys' choir at the Cathedral of the Assumption of Mary in Mexico City," I say. "I believe that María de Rivera was introducing the image of Our Lady of *Los Remedios* as her colophon since this image was appropriated by the Spanish during their conquest of Mexico. It's believed that during a fierce battle with the Aztecs, a young maiden threw dirt in the eyes of the Aztecs, which helped the outcome in favor of the Spanish. More than likely María wanted to assert her allegiance to the

Spanish Crown and all its institutions so she could continue the printing privileges her family garnered through the years."

As usual, Jen and I prefer to focus on different aspects of the same thing. "That family ran their printing business with impunity because they were kissing cousins with the Inquisitors in Mexico," says Jen. "Didn't the guide tell us that they printed the *Auto-da-Fé* that resulted in innocent people getting torched in the square? I don't care if you accuse me of revisionist sentiments, but inhumanity is heinous anytime anywhere. Two wrongs don't make a right!"

Annette remains silent as if Jen's rebuke had been directed at her. I notice Annette pinching herself in self-flagellation where the viper bit her repeatedly. I can't find the words to comfort her, but Jen lightens up the gloom in the air by suggesting, "Why don't we go to Antwerp, while we're at it. We'll remake our pilgrimage to the Plantin-Moretus museum, again. You two bookworms do your thing, and I'll drink some beers."

Annette peers closely at my painting of the *Vision of the Cross,* which shows the Christ Child turning away from the warmth of the Virgin Mary's breast while reaching with open arms towards an angel holding the Cross.

"Annette, you have an eye for the works of Maarten de Vos," I say. "The painting you're admiring is from 18th century Cusco. It's very probable that it was based on a composition by de Vos, who was so influential in the Spanish Colonial world, yet never traveled there. We must admire the genius of the native artists for solving problems of appropriate color, pigments, and enhanced compositions."

Jen throws another punch. "You rock, Maarten. It didn't matter if you personally didn't know people across the world; you left a huge universal legacy!"

Annette rolls her eyes in dismay, but delights in Jen's persistence. Could it be that Jen's hawkish temperament reminds

Annette of Fuzzy's pugnaciousness? "I understand the meaning of the painting," Annette says. "It's saying that the Christ Child accepted His future Passion. I know this is going to sound shallow on my part, but what is the royal blue of the Virgin Mary's mantle called?"

"Ah, you are a true art detective, Annette," I say. "It's called indigo blue, and you're correct because it was also known as royal blue. In the Middle Ages it was so valuable that if a non-royal wore this color he or she could be imprisoned."

Jen's New Age tendencies creep into the conversation. "I took a course in color therapy healing and it's believed that indigo is the color of divine knowledge and the higher mind." She clears her throat dramatically. "Indigo relates to the ability to view one's world from a lofty and responsible perspective, a long-lasting perspective, if you will."

"Jen, I promise that we will talk about the bigger issue here—the tragic victim. I know Annette would love to hear about how indigo pigments were made in the Andes."

"Go for it, girlfriend," Jen says. "Just don't leave out the part about how the young indigenous apprentices died of lead poisoning. Incidentally, impoverished Andean children continue to die in record numbers of lead poisoning."

"Okay, we'll start with the *poison*." I stress the word poison to indicate to Jen how in her zealousness she can often be insensitive. Thankfully, Annette is engrossed in the painting or overlooks her godmother's pesky passionate nature.

"In their quest to create halftones, the Andean artists mixed white with their pigments. The white lead was mined in Azángaro in southern Peru. Jen is correct, the young apprentices let the lead sit with a little vinegar in pots for a dozen weeks, or so. Then they scraped and powdered the white lead for ceruse known for its opaque white qualities. The lead dust blowing in the workshops changed to black sulfide which was absorbed into the body. They suffered from painter's colic, *colica pictorum*; the symptoms were severe abdominal pain and constipation. Some of the young girls showed the tell-tale blue line on the gums within one week of working with certain pigments. It was considered a slow death."

Jen stands up to point to the white lace on the robe of my *Archangel with Harquebus*. "So, in order to achieve the diaphanous qualities of the white lace so redolent of the Flemish artistic tradition, we can assume that many young indigenous kids died a slow and painful lead-poisoning death."

"Yes, Jen. A poignant illustration on your part; it took the wind out of my sails. All I can say about indigo blue is that since it is a natural dye it is the least toxic. However, as you point out, I'm certain that the young maidens who gathered the plants when they were in bloom and then soaked them in water to ferment, were also brutally mistreated."

"I know I am being a tyrant on this matter, Paloma. I am on a mission to save one victim of sex trafficking. Her mental health is declining fast, and in her agony she cries out your name. I know you don't know her, but I do know that if you choose to help her, your life will never be the same again. Once you decide to become involved, no team of lawyers can buffer you from the transformation of your life and hers." She walks over and holds my hand and stretches to hold Annette's hand, whose head is bowed in prayer.

Annette has been holding a Rosary. It now dangles from her clasped hand with Jen, and by extension, with me. Annette lifts up her Rosary and says, "It will cause good works to flourish. It will obtain for souls the abundant mercy of God."

Jen says, "Amen," but hammers away with ferocity. "We should all feel her pain, Paloma. The crime that was inflicted viciously upon her should hurt all of us. She had massive black and blue bruises on the outside, but what about the wound in her soul? We can't allow her to become another indigo-gathering maiden forgotten by time. Paloma, you have the heart and the resources to make her life better."

I have tried, in the past, to make other people's lives better—sometimes with minor success, sometimes with consequences I couldn't have imagined, and sometimes my efforts seem to do no good at all. Should I elect to help this girl, the road ahead for me is nothing but pitfalls. I instantly relive all the wrong paths I've taken in my adult years, from being a trophy wife to Charles, a greedy art collector, and an inattentive mentor to Ochanda. I don't want to regret making the wrong turn at this major fork in the road. This girl is too fragile for my mistakes. Jen has always been all heart, but I pride myself on logic. "Annette, are you up to informing me about sex-slaves here in Southern California?" I ask. "I was overwhelmed with all the online data on human trafficking when I researched the loathsome subject after the first phone call. I want to hear it from your police experience."

Annette walks around as if patrolling her beat. "L.A. and Southern California are a microcosm of the rest of the country. More and more people are being trafficked into our area to perform every despicable sex act. Minors, some as young as 12, from all over Mexico, Guatemala and other Latin American countries are smuggled illegally into California for sexual exploitation. These victims generally are taken as sex-slaves to work in residential brothels. On the average each victim is expected to have sex with forty men per day."

"With that many men going in to these brothels, why can't law enforcement stop it?"

I'm embarrassed to ask the naïve question.

"We made arrests all the time. But there's just so many of these residential brothels. Plus, the criminals keep moving the locations and the girls. They want to prevent the girls from establishing roots or escaping. It's tantamount to trying to stop the drug trade. The criminals set up the brothels in discreet houses or smaller apartment buildings. They advertise in code. We busted one network that advertised an all-night delivery of tacos, meaning sex-slaves, of course. Another network handed out business cards. The johns contacted the number on the card and exchanged money out on the street and they were given a token. The sex-slaves turned in their tokens at the end of the day."

Jen interjects, "Remember the antique shop in Paris that used to sell the old metal tokens from the legendary *Les Belles Poules* brothel? I thought it was hilarious back then. I didn't see it for the insidious form of slavery that it is. I read a credible report that said that 92% of women involved in prostitution want to leave prostitution."

Annette wants to finish her wretched presentation. "Aside from the residential brothels, there are the massage parlors, the truck stops, the escort services, hostesses and strip clubs, and the mac daddy of them all, pun intended, internet-based sex trafficking. It's overwhelming and it's tragic. 75% to 90% of all women in prostitution were sexually abused as children and 85% are addicted to drugs or alcohol."

All the abhorrent statistics Annette rattles off should move me to tears and action, yet they do not. Unlike children acting out aggressive behaviors after watching violent media, I wade in the muck and mire of abominable human trafficking statistics totally desensitized. I realize it's an abysmal existence for so many young women throughout the world, but I sit in my sunny and delusional universe twirling my opera-length South Sea pearl necklace in such a way that I don't hear the infant Chinese girls left to die or the screaming Indian brides immolated. I pretended not to hear or understand the odious words the victim cried out to me on the telephone on St. Joseph's Day. Now, in her muteness, I get an earful of her unspeakable truth.

Jen looks like a caged animal rattling its gates. "Annette, you're right," she roars. "We're connected to every single victim of sexual exploitation. We can collectively work to influence laws and policies. But right now, I propose that we focus on this one innocent girl who was kidnapped, drugged, repeatedly raped, and left in an unventilated cubby to die. She's our child, isn't she?"

"My books and my paintings are my children," I blurt. My superficial answer repels all of us. Annette even shields her Rosary to her chest. I can't believe that I uttered this statement and worse yet, I attempt to explain my position. "My books have a patina of their previous owners' misfortunes, they convey their discords and—"

Jen rests her hands on my shoulders and softly says, "You're just anxious about what you will say to the victim. We're not really sure what her real name is or what she'll say to you. She didn't have any identification on her and when she was briefly communicative she gave three different names. Would you like to hear how she was discovered?"

I nod yes and close my eyes.

"After Annette was doing better at the hospital, and the dogs were at the vet, Larry showed the police a house near the Sunset Strip. Evidently, the she-devil had taken Larry there once. At that time, he thought there was something sketchy about the rear guest house." She attempts to tug at my heart by adding, "Larry's grandmother told him to trust the angel on his shoulder, and this time it paid off. The police found both houses totally empty except for a camouflaged hidden space. That's where they discovered our victim, make that our daughter, dehydrated, but alive. It appears that there had been a second victim in that same suffocating space, but there isn't any of trace of her. They say it's a miracle our girl was spared. Since these traffickers are notoriously brutal, they suspect a woman trafficker, with a trace of humanity, might have spared her life. Larry shared his suspicions about the harpy's involvement with art forgery and art theft with the police, but the police turned their dubious eyes towards Larry instead."

"But aren't you glad that the police place a high priority on innocent victims of sexual slavery instead of chasing art forgers?" Annette says. "Art is art, but a human being is truly priceless."

"They inspected his apartment with a fine-tooth comb," Jen continues. "Apparently, the she-devil is a prime suspect in the killing of two men at a bar in Madrid a couple of years ago. They told Larry that an Ecuadorian woman and her Paraguayan cohort picked up men at bars and spiked their drinks so they could rob them. They were known as the women who give you the kiss of death. Larry is in a world of trouble for allowing the beast to move in with him while she prowled maliciously around Hollywood. Thankfully, Shelley, who's a member of Larry's bicycle club, is a defense attorney and she's helping him out. Larry's a noble spirit in every sense of the word. That he got mixed up with the she-devil just shows the power and cunning she held."

We're waiting for the phone call from the director of the center where the victim is housed. She'll speak with Jen first, then she'll talk to me, and if she deems me helpful, she'll allow me to speak with the victim. These ground rules grind against my excessive hubris. I'll decide who I'll speak with, and not the other way around, is my immediate thought.

Jen reads my mind. "Do you mind if I play your Andean music? The pan pipes should put us in a constructive and benevolent frame of mind, don't you think, my peaceful dove? That *is* the meaning of your name, Palomita."

Jen is trying too hard not to look anxious. "You know that music aids in the recall of information," she says. "It might even trigger memories of a language someone hasn't spoken in years."

"Gee, that's subtle," I say. "Now I'm supposed to remember Kichwa, a language I haven't spoken since I was a child. What do you know that you're not telling me, Jen?"

"Just what I said. Let me rephrase it: past memories, images, personal experiences can all be stimulated by certain songs. In your case, I hope that the Andean folk music can put you in a frame of mind that might help you recall things."

"Jen, what am I supposed to remember before I speak with the girl?"

"The director believes that you hold the key words that the victim wants to hear. She apparently can't trust anyone unless she hears certain words or a key phrase from you."

Always the cop, Annette demands, "If she's not talking or if she's mumbling in Kichwa, how can the director know what she's saying? They're not trying to entrap Paloma somehow, are they?"

"I should have mentioned that they brought in a Kichwa interpreter," Jen says. "She could only get a couple of sentences out of the victim. That's how they were able to cobble together the fact that she expects Paloma to tell her something she longs to hear."

"How about 'open sesame,'" I suggest.

Jen lets that snide comment glide like water off a duck's back. She's trying to prepare me to rescue a victim any way she can. "The director and the therapists are at their wits' end trying to help the girl. It's worth a shot, Paloma. You know you have the best memory of anyone. Just close your eyes and meditate on the music. You once told me the *zampoña* flute reminded you of a sloth hanging from a tree in your grandfather's plantation. And don't forget the time you gave my grandmother orchids and told her, in Kichwa, that you hope her life blossoms like flowers."

"Oh, fine, I'll try your memory game, but Annette has to play, too."

"I'm cool with that. I like this music."

After a few minutes of listening to the calming effects of the songs, I must admit that some Kichwa words began to effervesce in my mind. I pictured Esperanza telling me, *mikuylla warmi ñusta,* eat young princess, as she placed a slice of papaya in my mouth.

The tempo of the music accelerates to a snappy allegretto and Jen starts to dance in the manner of Andean folk dancers. It's either her instinctive musicality or her celestial guide leading her feet in the shuffle and stomp and arm pirouettes of the indigenous dancers. "How about adding elements of dance therapy?" she says.

"You're nuts, Jen, but we've come this far. Why not?"

I start to move a bit stiffly but at the moderately fast tempo of the San Juanito song. I get an arresting flashback of Esperanza chasing me at my cousin's wedding. One of the ranch hands chases her as she's chasing me. The sash at her waist is blood red and her long braid swings from side to side like the metronome sitting on my grand piano today. Esperanza lifts me up in the air and cries out, "*ñuka kurimi kanki,* you are my gold," but her eyes were looking lovingly at the young and virile man, and not at me.

I share my flashback with Annette and Jen. Jen insists that I repeat the Kichwa words several times. "One sentence might lead to another. Come on, say it again."

Annette doesn't know about my nanny's arranged marriage with the abusive old man. She innocently asks, "So, did they get married and live happily in paradise? Surely they don't have the awful divorce rate we do in California."

The caw of the black telephone on my desk rings its bad omen. It has never brought me good news, I suddenly realize, as I stand frozen on the marble floor. Its dark messages have always been about death, accidents, and an immaculate voice shrieking, "*Yanapaway vichaytukushkami kani!*" I repeat these words out loud several times.

The crow phone caws its morbid message again and we ignore it. "*Tukuylla patpatami llukchikun!*" I repeat these sentences over and over.

Jen understands that I'm trying to burnish these words in my memory. She opens all the drawers in my desk. She finds a mini recorder and looks elated when the battery still works. She holds it up to my lips as if she were interviewing me for a news program.

I recall the first phone call. The girl cried out to me in Kichwa, but my brain translated it to Spanish and English in one fell swoop. "Help me! I'm in a cage. They're plucking all my feathers," she cried on St. Joseph's Day.

Finally Annette can stand it no more and picks up the receiver. It's the director. "Please hold," Annette says. "We're hearing an answer to our prayers."

"*Mana kalluta charini,*" I cry into the recorder, "I don't have a tongue!"

Jen sighs, "It's time to help your goddaughter."

"Please talk to the director, I'll be right back," I tell her.

Annette detects my anxiety and follows me at a considerate distance, but I shut the door to my bedroom suite.

Once inside I approach my *prie-dieu* prayer desk with trepidation. I kneel on the soft velvet pew and I gaze at a painting of the *Dolorosa,* Our Lady of Sorrows, from the Quito School. The sorrowful eyes, willingly burdened with the cares of the world, penetrate to my core. I realize that even if I were to recall the Kichwa words the girl so craves to hear, they would be meaningless without Divine intervention. An overwhelming sense of peace surrounds me, and I recall the ancient nun in catechism class who told Jen and me that the Mater Dolorosa will defend us and protect us in our spiritual battles with the infernal enemy. It frightened us as children, but the day has arrived when her words ring so true.

I sense my anchor of arrogance loosen from its depths. The barnacles and chips of rusty iron float away. I no longer cling to the chain of hubris; I let it drift away forever. There is only one petition that I repeat over and over, "Mater Dolorosa, please heal my innocent goddaughter."

After speaking with the director, whose demanding tone revealed how concerned she was that this conversation could turn out to be a dead-end, she finally allows me to speak to the girl.

I hear a dulcet and faint voice, like a distant flute played across the ravines in Quito, asking me in broken English, "Missus Paloma Zubiondo, please, you to tell me sweet words babysitter call to you when you was little in Quito, please Missus."

My eyes dash from painting to painting searching for a clue. Instead of hearing the *zampoña* flute playing on the sound system, I feel the grip on my throat from the amber-eyed devil in my paintings as he laughs at my long self-deception. He sticks his tongue in my ear and whispers, "Sorry, *ñaña,* you ain't gonna remember jack-shit!"

I hear the poor girl whimpering at my prolonged silence. I wrack my brain but all I manage is a simple stall tactic. *"Un momentito, por favor."*

Annette prays fervently and Jen fans me with a book. "Tell her you'll help her," she suggests.

This offer does not satisfy the victim, and she sobs loudly. "Please, Misses Paloma Zubiondo, what do babysitter talk to you, please."

I take a chance and suggest, *"ñuka wawa urpikulla,* my little girl dove?"

This barely appeases her. "Yes, more, please."

I bat Jen's fanning hand away from me. I take another shot at the magic words. *"Ñuka pani killaku,* little sister moon?"

Her sobs subside. "Yes, good, please remember more, please."

My eyes rest on the emerald green earrings of the Immaculate Conception painting. I can see my nanny fastening my tiny emerald earrings for me. She would hug me tightly and say, *"Ñuka rumiku kanki,* you are my emeralds!"

I'm afraid the director will soon end my fishing expedition. Softly I enunciate these words because the girl's life depends on them. I repeat them again in question form while Jen records me. *"Ñuka rumiku kanki?"*

The dike walls crack and a torrent of words escape from the girl's mouth.

"I am Esperanza's granddaughter. *Me llamo Fé, a sus ordenes, Doña Palomita."*

I want to put her on speakerphone so we three can share in the charm of her Andean sing-song cadence. Her name is Faith and she's at my service. How could anyone not be enchanted with such a gallant and antiquated way of saying, nice to meet you?

Fé's old-fashioned graciousness overwhelms me. Despite the horrors she's endured she's compelled to honor her grandmother's request. I choke up as she tells me, "Doña Palomita, my teensy grandmother gave me your wee gold necklace to hand over to your hands. She's kept it in our little altar at home. We always prayed for your well being and for the itsy day she would see you again."

Between the tears, I hold back a nervous laughter at her exploding diminutives, those terms of endearment that ooze from the honeycomb of my ancestral land. I feel my nanny's arms as she hugged me endlessly and whispered sweet nothings in my ear.

As Fé's voice becomes stronger and stronger she tells me all about the last seven months of her life in Los Angeles. She lived in Echo Park with four other Ecuadorian girls in a one-bedroom apartment, and they all worked at the same garment factory downtown. She loved learning English at night school because her grandmother, my beloved nanny, had assured her that as soon as she mastered English, she was to call me and impress me with her intelligence.

I'm about to ask Fé more questions, but Jen jots down a quick note that says: Let her vent, just acknowledge what she says.

It works because innocent Fé wants to tell me more. She starts crying again, and then I hear a fusillade of Kichwa and Spanish and English. "*Wiwakuna ñuka shunkuta mikurka,* the animals ate my heart, I shouldn't have trusted Montserrat, but she to have university degree and *muy inteligente.* She love my stories about you and your nanny, *mi abuelita Esperanza.* You very rich and *muy elegante.* She want to meet you."

Thankfully I remember Esperanza's words to me, "*Ama wakaychu wawaku,* don't cry little girl."

She moans and continues. "The *gringos* in Hollywood sleep all day, so we clean their houses at night. I was scared. One night Montserrat tell me, 'Dress clean like school girl, the old *gringo* like clean maids.' He to pay two hundred dollars."

Fé is weeping uncontrollably. I hear the director and the therapist discussing whether to end the call or not.

Fé shouts into the receiver, "It's too hot, *araray!* I drink the mango juice that Montserrat gave me. Now *Mana patpa charinichu*, I don't have wings anymore. How can I fly home again?"

The language of my nanny is embedded in me like a tick and it took this young girl's anguish to extract it. I repeat my nanny's pious words to Fé. "Under thy protection, we seek refuge, Mother of God." Fé calms down. I tell her softly, "*Pakta wasiman rishunchi,*we will go home together." I correct myself and tell her that we will fly home together. "*Kalpashum nukanchik wasiman, Fé. Kalpashum nukanchik wasiman.*"

Gathering the Indigo Maidens is rooted in research on three historical women: Isabel Santiago, María de Rivera Calderón y Benavides, and Modesta Ávila, and in the time and societies in which each lived. I was entranced by the thin threads of facts that are known about each woman. Fortunately, the volumes of information on their respective eras kept me intrigued for over a dozen years of travel and research. Ultimately, I wove these filaments of facts into this work of imagination.

Some of the other players in the novel are also historical. The maxims quoted throughout this work were written in Spanish by Baltasar Gracían (circa 1601-1658). His perceptive observations ring as true today as they did in 1647. The engraved print designs and oil paintings by Flemish artist Maarten de Vos (circa 1550) contributed to the artistic development during the Spanish Colonial period in the jurisdictions of Nueva España and Perú. The Plantin Press, known as the *Officina Plantiniana*, existed in Antwerp from the 16th century until 1867, and printed the *Missale Romanum* that included the engraved print of the *Assumption of the Virgin* by Maarten de Vos. Fray Jodoco Rijcke and Fray Pedro Gocial, as their names were recorded in the Quito archives (circa 1550), established the San Andrés School of art and music in Quito. All literary works cited herein are also factual.

The Spanish royal crown granted special mercantile privileges to the indigenous women in Quito during the Colonial period. The woven indigo cloth known as *paño azul* was a highly desired textile throughout the region, and was produced in large quantities. The facts about the artist Miguel de Santiago, both his prodigious paintings and his legal troubles, are corroborated by many sources.

The state of Oaxaca, Mexico is an acclaimed center for textiles, wood carvings, and the festivities during the Day of the Dead. María de Rivera Calderón y Benavides and her ancestors were acknowledged publishers and booksellers in Mexico City from 1631 until 1755. The Mexican engraver, Baltasar Troncoso, is remembered for his masterpiece print, *La virgen de Guadalupe intercede ante la peste del Matlazahuatl de 1737.*

The cities and towns mentioned as locations where thefts of Spanish Colonial art have recently occurred are factual, as is the painting of the Quito Immaculate Conception that is listed on the FBI website on stolen art. The plight of the Ecuadorian victims of human trafficking for sexual exploitation is well documented.

Modesta Ávila's protest against the railroad in San Juan Capistrano, California, and her legal trials are factual, but the details of her death at San Quentin State Prison remain clouded. The Reverend August Drähms was chaplain at San Quentin State Prison, where he conducted social science investigations. Chola Martina and Polonia Montano were residents of San Juan Capistrano (circa 1850-1900). The Acjachemen are a Native American people in Southern California. Reverend Joseph Mut was the resident priest at the Mission San Capistrano from 1866 to 1886. Mission San Juan Capistrano continues to be known as the Jewel of the Missions.

The native Andean language known as Kichwa (formerly written as Quichua) in Ecuador has evolved since the 17th century. Therefore, the Kichwa words in Chapter Two are written as they would have been written in the Spanish Colonial era. The other chapters contain the contemporary spelling of Kichwa words. I'd like to express my gratitude to the Kichwa translator, Dra. Rosa Chuquín Pupiales, and the Quechua translator, Ing. Miguel A. Andía Guerrero.

I am very grateful to my editor Catherine Knepper. For their constant words of encouragement on this novel, I'd like to thank my friends: Domenika Lynch, Christina V. Vera, and Dr. Dan Duran.

With all my heart, I'd like to thank my family for their constant love. To my dad, Marcos Argudo, for enrolling me as a youngster in the book-of-the-month club, not only for books written in English, but for those written in Spanish and French. To my mother, the late Inesita Argudo, for her poetic use of the Spanish language, and for keeping the traditions of Ecuador alive in our home. To my sister, Carmita Buck, for always taking care of me and our extended family. To my brother, George Velástegui, for his wise counsel on any matter.

Lastly and most of all, to my sons and my husband for their everlasting love.

Monarch Beach, June 29, 2011

Gathering the *Indigo* Maidens

Cecilia Velástegui

About This Guide

We hope that these discussion questions will enhance your reading group's exploration of Cecilia Velástegui's novel, *Gathering the Indigo Maidens*. They are meant to stimulate discussion, offer new viewpoints and enrich your enjoyment of the book.

Questions for Discussion

1. In the first scene of the book, Paloma is alone in her hilltop sanctuary with her paintings and her books. She claims to enjoy her well-ordered and largely solitary life. By the end of the book, do you feel differently about this scene? Does Paloma have other motives for isolating herself besides a love for order? If you could ask Paloma at the end of the book what she thinks about herself in the opening scene, what do you think she would say?

2. Who owns a painting? Paloma describes various types of collectors, some with very little respect for art in general. Should important paintings serve as investments for the rich, or are they a collective legacy of the human race? What would Paloma say about the ethics of private art collections?

3. Paloma collects a specific kind of painting, Spanish Colonial devotional paintings, and most often images of the Virgin Mary. She has intellectual reasons for her interest in this particular genre of painting. What are her personal connections to these works? Why does she surround herself with these images?

4. Why is Paloma so resistant to believing there really is an Ecuadorian girl being held as a sex-slave? Why doesn't she call the police the minute she gets the phone call?

5. An interesting theme at play in this book is the complexity of charity. Paloma is bombarded by requests for help, but she knows she can't save everyone. And yet she helps where she can. She helped Luis's sister find a job. The best example of this conflict is Ochanda, Paloma's scholarship student. Paloma gave Ochanda an education, yet the girl clearly resents her. Is Paloma right to expect gratitude? Why is Ochanda so resentful? Did Paloma's generosity come with too many conditions or was it Ochanda who didn't assert herself?

6. What is the legacy of a childless woman? What is the legacy of an artist whose work is credited to men while her name is lost to history? What is the legacy of empire? How are these questions at play in the novel and especially in the mind and heart of Paloma? Why is the idea of legacy so important to her? Is legacy what she is really searching for when she collects her paintings or sponsors Ochanda?

7. Why does Paloma have only one photograph of Charles displayed in her home? Why do you think she chose that picture? What does it say about their marriage?

8. Were you surprised when Paloma ate the note she finds in the mission? Why do you think she did this? What was she saying with this slightly bizarre behavior? Can you imagine a situation where you would eat a letter?

9. Compare Esperanza's prospects for marriage with Paloma's marriage to Charles. Paloma feels she personally limited Esperanza's potential for marriage by clinging to her too tightly. Is this guilt misplaced? What does it have to do with Paloma's marriage?

10. How are Baltasar Gracián's quotes used in this novel? Do you think they add to the story?

11. Can you compare Paloma's relationship with Ochanda to Isabel Santiago's relationship with Cholita?

12. Why does Isabel seem to be such an angry person while her servant Cholita seems to love life in the time before she is attacked? What is different about the way these two women process the experience of colonization?

13. Why does Cholita add a brush stroke of red to the foot of the Virgin Mary in the painting before she kills herself?

14. The women from the market take it on themselves to punish Cholita's attacker, but they do this in secret. Are there any other examples you can find in this book of hidden resistance by conquered people?

15. What are your thoughts on how Larry exemplifies the adage that "love is blind?"

16. Once Montserrat's abuse as a child is described, is there sympathy for her later actions?

17. Jen and Paloma share a profound friendship. Why do you think that despite their obvious different lives and perspectives on life they continue to support one another? Other than a shared past, what keeps their friendship deepening?

18. María de Rivera Calderón y Benavides blamed the decline of her publishing business on aggressive competition, yet she and her ancestors had previously profited from their affiliations with the same ruling entities in Mexico City. Do you think that she ever realized that her sense of entitlement contributed to her neglect of the business?

19. Would you regard Modesta Ávila's actions to protect her livelihood as an act of impetuosity or activism?

20. Many languages, written, spoken, and symbolic are used in this novel. What is significant about a person's "mother tongue"?

21. The word indigo has many meanings in this narrative, from the literal sense to the figurative. Discuss the various meanings of indigo as they relate to the characters, their experiences, and their perspectives on life.

Bibliography

Austin Alchon, Suzanne. *Native Society and Disease in Colonial Ecuador.* Cambridge: Cambridge University Press, 1991.

Archivo Metropolitano de Historia. *Actas del Cabildo Colonial de San Francisco de Quito: 1676-1683.* Quito: Publicaciones del Archivo Metropolitano de Historia, 1998.

Baggerly Older, Cora Miranda. *Love Stories of Old California.* Bedford: Applewood Books, 1995.

Bauer, Arnold J. *Goods, Power, History: Latin America's Material Culture.* Cambridge: 2001.

Beebe, Rose Marie, and Robert M. Senkewicz, eds. *Chronicles of Early California, 1535-1846.* Berkeley: Heyday Books, 2001.

Beebe, Rose Marie, and Robert M. Senkewicz. *Testimonios: Early California through the Eyes Of Women, 1815-1848.* Berkeley: Heyday Books, 2006.

Bookspan, Shelley. *A Germ of Goodness:The California State Prison System, 1851-1944.* Lincoln: University of Nebraska Press, 1991.

Borchart de Moreno, Christiana. *La Audiencia de Quito: Aspectos Económicos y Sociales (Siglos XVI-XVIII).* Quito: Ediciones Abya-Yala, Ediciones del Banco Central del Ecuador, 1998.

Bowen, Karen L., and Dirk Imhof. *Christopher Plantin and Engraved Book Illustrations in Sixteen-Century Europe.* Cambridge: Cambridge University Press, 2008.

Carrera, Magali M. *Imagining Identity in New Spain: Race, Lineage, and the Colonial Body in Portraiture and Casta Paintings.* Austin: University of Texas Press, 2003.

Cobo, Bernabe. *Inca Religion & Customs,* trans. Roland Hamilton. Austin: University of Texas Press, 1990.

Colegio de Nuestra Señora de la Asumpción. *Constituciones de el Colegio de Nuestra Señora de La Asumpción.* Mexico City: La Imprenta Real del Superior Govierno, de D. María deRivera, 1734.

Cossio del Pomar, Felipe. *Arte del Perú Colonial.* Mexico City: Fondo de Cultura Economica, 1958.

Damian, Carol. *The Virgin of the Andes: Art and Ritual in Colonial Cuzco.* Miami Beach: Grassfield Press, 1994.

Dean, Carolyn. *Inka Bodies and the Body of Christ: Corpus Christi in Colonial Cuzco, Peru.* Durham: Duke University Press, 1999.

Descalzi, Ricardo. *La Real Audiencia de Quito Claustro en los Andes.* Quito-Barcelona: I.G. Seix y Barral Hnos., 1978.

De La Maza, Francisco. *El Pintor Martín De Vos En México.* Mexico City: Universidad Autónoma de México, 1971.

De la Torre Reyes, Carlos. *Treasures of Quito.* Quito: El Sello Editorial, 1990.

De Vos, Dirk. *The Flemish Primitives: The Masterpieces.* Princeton: Princeton University Press, 2002.

Donahue-Wallace, Kelly. *Art and Architecture of Viceregal Latin America, 1521-1821.* Albuquerque: University of New Mexico Press, 2008.

Estabridis Cárdenas, Ricardo. *El Grabado en Lima Virreinal. Document Histórico y Artístico (siglos XVI al XIX).* Lima: Fondo Editorial de la Universidad Nacional Mayor de San Marcos, 2002.

Frère, Jean-Claude. *Early Flemish Painting.* Paris: Terrail, 1997.

Garcilaso de la Vega, El Inca. *Commentarios [sic.] Reales, que Tratan, de el Origen de Los Incas, Reies [sic.], que fueron del Peru, de su Idolatria, Leies [sic.], y Govierno.* Madrid: Oficina Real de Nicolas Rodríguez Franco, 1722.

Giles, Mary E. *Women in the Inquisition: Spain and the New World.* Baltimore: Johns Hopkins University Press, 1999.

Gracían, Baltazar. *The Courtiers Manual Oracle, or, The Art of Prudence.* London: The Sign of the Unicorn, 1685.

Garcían, Baltasar. *Oráculo Manual y Arte de Prudencia,* Edición de Emilio Blanco. Madrid: Ediciones Cátedra, S.A., 1997.

Gauderman, Kimberly. *Women's Lives in Colonial Quito: Gender, Law, and Economy in Spanish America.* Austin: University of Texas Press, 2003.

Griffiths, Antony. *Prints and Printmaking: An Introduction to the history and techniques.* Berkeley: University of California Press, 1996.

Guaman Poma de Ayala, Felipe. Trans. David Frye. *The First New Chronicle and Good Government.* Indianapolis: Hackett Publishing, 2006.

Gutiérrez, Ramón A., and Richard J. Orsi. eds. *Contested Eden: California Before the Gold Rush.* Berkeley: University of California Press in Association with the California Historical Society, 1998.

Haas, Lisbeth. *Conquests and Historical Identities in California 1769-1936.* Berkeley: University of California Press, 1995.

Heckman, Andrea M. *Woven Stories: Andean Textiles & Rituals.* Albuquerque: University of New Mexico Press, 2003.

Katzew, Ilona. *Casta Painting.* New Haven: Yale University Press, 2004.

Kelly, Eric P., *At the Sign of the Golden Compass: A tale of the printing house of Christopher Plantin in Antwerp, 1576.* New York: The Macmillan Company, 1938.

Lamott, Kenneth. *1853-1972 Chronicles of San Quentin: California's Oldest and Most Famous Prison.* New York: Ballantine Books, 1961.

Lane, Kris. *Quito 1599: City and Colony in Transition.* Albuquerque: University of New Mexico Press, 2002.

Lavrin, Asunción. *Sexuality and Marriage in Colonial Latin America.* Lincoln: University of Nebraska Press, 1989.

Ledesma, Clemente de. *Dispertado [sic.] de noticias de las santos sacramentos. Primer Tomo.* Mexico City: Doña María de Benavides: Viuda de Juan de Ribera, 1695.

Kennedy, Alexandra, ed. *Arte de la Real Audiencia de Quito, siglos XVII-XIX.* Quito: Editorial Nerea S.A., 2002.

MacCormack, Sabine. *Religion in the Andes: Vision and Imagination in Early Colonial Peru.* Princeton: Princeton University Press, 1991.

Minchom, Martin. *The People of Quito, 1690-1810: Change and Unrest in the Underclass.* Boulder: Westview Press: 1994.

Mier y Terán Casanueva, ed. *Casa de la Primera Imprenta de América.* Mexico City: Universidad Autónoma Metropolitana, 2004.

Moreno, Agustín. *Fray Jodoco Rique y Fray Pedro Gocial: Apóstoles y Maestros Franciscanos De Quito.* Quito: Ediciones Abya-Yala, 1998.

Moreno Proaño, Agustín, y Hector Merino Valencia. *Quito Eterno: Iglesias y Conventos.* Quito: Ediciones Paralelo Cero, 1975.

Myers, Kathleen Ann. *Neither Saints Nor Sinners: Writing the Lives of Women in Spanish America.* Oxford: Oxford University Press, 2003.

Navarro, José Gabriel. *Religious Architecture in Quito.* New York: The Metropolitan Museum of Art, 1945.

Navarro, José Gabriel. *La Pintura en el Ecuador del XVI al XIX.* Quito: Dinediciones, 1991.

Pacheco, Francisco. *Arte de la Pintura: Su Antiguedades y Grandezas...V. 1.* Madrid: Imprenta de Manuel Galiano, 1866.

Paniagua Pérez, Jesús, y Gloria M. Garzón Montenegro. *Los Gremios de Plateros y Batihojas en La Ciudad de Quito (Siglo XVIII).* Mexico City: Universidad Nacional Autónoma de México Instituto de Investigaciones Estéticas, 2000.

Phipps, Elena. *Cochineal Red: The Art History of a Color.* New Haven: Yale University Press, 2010.

Pitt, Leonard. *The Decline of the Californios: A Social History of the Spanish-Speaking Californians, 1846-1890.* Berkeley: University of California Press, 1966.

Pollard Rowe, Ann., Laura M. Miller, and Lynn A. Meisch. *Weaving and Dyeing in Highland Ecuador.* Austin: University of Texas, 2007.

Rishel, Joseph J. and Suzanne Stratton-Pruitt, eds. *The Arts in Latin America 1492-1820.* Philadelphia: Philadelphia Museum of Art.

Salvat, Juan. *Arte Colonial de Ecuador: Siglos XVI-XVII.* Quito: Salvat Editores Ecuatoriana S.A., 1977.

Sánchez, Rosaura. *Telling Identities: The Californio Testimonios.* Minneapolis: University Of California Press, 1995.

Socolow, Susan. *The Women of Colonial Latin America.*
Cambridge: Cambridge University Press, 2000.

Stratton, Suzanne L. *The Immaculate Conception in Spanish Art.*
Cambridge: Cambridge University Press, 1994.

Thompson, Angela. *Textiles of Central and South America.*
Wiltshire: The Crowood Press, 2006.

Twinam, Ann. *Public Lives Private Secrets: Gender, Honor,
Sexuality, and Illegitimacy in Colonial Spanish America.*
Stanford: Stanford University Press, 1999.

Van Havre, Gustave. *Les Marques Typographiques de L'Imprimerie
Plantinienne,* Anvers: Bureau D'Édition, 1990.

Vargas, José María. *El Arte Quiteño en los Siglos XVI, XVII y
XVIII.* Quito: Litografía e Imprenta Romero, 1949.

Vargas, José María. *Los Maestros del Arte Ecuatoriano.* Quito:
Imprenta Municipal, 1955.

Vargas, José María. *Arte Quiteño Colonial.* Quito: Litografía e
Imprenta Romero, 1944.

Vargas, José María. *María en el Arte Ecuatoriano.* Quito:
Litografía e Imprenta Romero, 1954.

Woodbridge, Hensley, and Lawrence S. Thompson. *Printing in
Colonial Spanish America.* Albany: Whitston Publishing
Company, 1976.

About the Typeface

This book was set in Berkeley Book. The Berkeley typeface is formerly known as the University of California Old Style or simply as the "Californian." Since *Gathering the Indigo Maidens* is a quintessential California novel, revealing both the old Spanish California and the contemporary, diverse, California, the tribute to the former "Californian" typestyle is relevant and befitting.

Frederic W. Goudy created the first Berkeley typeface, between 1938 and 1940. Tony Stan of the International Typeface Corporation (ITC) redesigned the typeface in the early 1980's. The Berkeley typeface is elegant, classic, and inviting.